DEPTH

SOUL SEER CHRONICLES, BOOK 5

S.J. CAIRNS

Black Thumb
Publishing

Cover design by Getcovers
Logo created by S.J. Cairns
Logo image by CNuisin depositphotos.com ID 265803116
Tree vector by Nikhomtreevector depositphotos.com
ID 391682124

ISBN 978-1-7782611-2-1 (Ebook)
ISBN 978-1-7782611-3-8 (Paperback)
ISBN 978-1-7782611-4-5 (Hardcover)

Black Thumb Publishing
Ontario, Canada
www.sjcairns.com

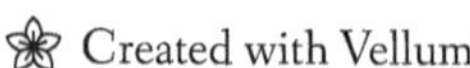 Created with Vellum

ACKNOWLEDGMENTS

My Quillies writing group will always be number one, but I would also like to acknowledge some others in my word-filled world. All my more recent acquaintances, writers struggling to find their publishing family, and those who make a point to help those trying to learn the craft. We all start somewhere. When we readers morph into writers and seek others to share our stories with, the world needs your fresh perspective as well as the lessons from experienced masters.

Be open enough to learn and be humble enough to teach.

Grandma,
Examples of your kindness towards others different than yourself will
survive beyond the years I have had the privilege to learn from you.
While our beliefs differ, my faith in your heart is unwavering.
Thank you for your understanding.
(Communicated in life, published posthumously)

1

OPEN-DOOR POLICY

Adjusting the twisty things of my binoculars made the crowd scurrying down the cold street blur and crossed my eyes.

"Cockflop!" I pressed my fingers into my eyelids until they burned. "There should be a class on how to use these stupid things."

Vincent snatched them from my hand, stuck his glasses on the top of his head, and peered through the binocular lenses out the windshield, using small movements to adjust them. "Your lack of patience is matched only by your faithful bastardization of the English language. Here."

I scoffed, snatched the binoculars back, and squinted through them. Still not quite right yet better than they were. "What demented worm-humper am I looking for this time?"

"I will be certain to point out any demented worm-humpers next we cross one."

I dropped the binoculars in my lap and glared at him. Freezing my ass off on countless surveillance runs left me no more enlightened of the evil within the Sovereignty then the day I found out Magics had an established form of law enforcement. Vincent was confident Tainted Magics were crawling all over the city courthouse where they existed in small pockets of Creations within the veil where the Sovereignty did their business alongside the Blind. Believing him was easy, but after months of him pointing out someone he guaranteed was proof of the need to dismantle them, the clean soul glows of our targets proved otherwise.

Winter reared its icicle-dripping beanbag and streaked bare-assed through the city. Cold seeped through my grey suede boots, the tights beneath my jeans, a wool sweater over a t-shirt, plus my black wool coat, gloves, and a scarf. Nothing soaked up the chill dampening my bones, leaving me snot-nosed and shivering in a twenty-five hundred plus pound freezer. A silver 1967 Plymouth Barracuda freezer which ran me a good chunk of my "trust fund" from Olive for my involvement in closing the Creation. A cheap buy since the guy sold it for his daughter's tuition money and assumed Donovan was the buyer.

Not that it mattered when dear ol' Vincent wouldn't let me keep my car running or use a spell to heat us up in case one of the non-Tainted evil people he had me stalking happened to catch a whiff of something witchy other than themselves. Tainted or a bunch of Blind assholes, right now, all I wanted was a space heater and a spiced hot toddy.

"If this one turns out a dud like the others, you're stuck helping me pick out a Christmas gift for Donovan."

Vincent glanced at me with the repulsion of a stranger off the street asking for a spare kidney.

"Hey, if I'm freezing my ass off for this cloak and dagger wannabe P.I. routine, I should at least get something out of it."

"Kim or Serena would be a better choice than I."

"Nope. You'd be a perfect present-picker-outer."

Vincent's nostrils flared enough to showcase some type of emotion I couldn't read, but I knew he would troll a mall for hours if I was serious about it. Which I was.

While Donovan and I weren't strapping on labels for the last few months as much as we were testing the efficacy of my birth control and wasting time together, I figured a present was within the realm of something you do for your husband from a different lifetime whether he buys something for you or not.

"Where does Donovan believe you are? Shopping for a holiday outside his beliefs?"

"*Pfft.* I like you less by the second. And why in the fried shit-pickles would it matter? I don't answer to him."

"You answer to him with deceptions, so in essence, yes, you do answer to him."

The Sovereignty surveillance excursions were Vincent's and my little secret. To look at it as lying bothered me when an omission was more accurate. No one was in-the-know. Not Kim, Olive, or Serena. When Vincent asked for discretion without explaining in full detail why, I agreed, thinking no one else would think it was newsworthy. He knew Donovan could detect my lies, so I assumed all would be revealed after the first outing. Could Donovan detect the omissions I gave him over the last few months? He wasn't a lie detector I could beat with a tack in my boot, but he never called me out.

"Whatever. I don't interrogate him on his whereabouts every second of the day."

"You wish to."

"Get bent, buddy."

I struggled with aspects of Donovan's and my relationship. Jealousy being a big one. Sex managed to cock-block my previous relationship's happiness and paved the way for Donovan and me to become whatever we were. Our—or at least my—suspicions and trust issues weren't the neon sign Vincent made them out to be.

The daunting list of conquests on Donovan's belt and my unfaithful and abusive ex-fiancé equalled a healthy amount of warranted caution as far as I was concerned.

Especially when Donovan's conquests were still booty-calling for a repeat to the point of having to change his number. I never told Vincent about them. If he dug into my thoughts hard enough, when I was too irritated to augment my defences, as I still did around Donovan, he would see me drowning in a sea of green, surrounded by Mr. Dimples and his faceless exes all shoving their tits and ass and whatever else into my face.

I let Vincent lead me into guilt-ridden duplicity as I pretended Donovan would be cool with what we were doing behind his back. He wouldn't be, but fuck it if I needed the reminder considering Vincent was sturdy as a statue without a hint of regret. He blamed the Sovereignty for us needing to investigate them in the first place and causing my needed omissions, but I had no one to blame but my chicken-shit self.

"Tailored suit."

"Wha—A suit? Donovan has suits. More than you'd think. All tailored."

Vincent blinked and chinned out the windshield, holding up the binoculars. "Refocus. Grey suit. Black wool coat."

I smirked. "We got a deal?"

A crease between his green eyes deepened.

"Come on, Santa. Wingman my holiday season. Mr. Grey-Suit is gettin' away."

His nostrils flared. "Deal."

I celebrated with a short-lived raise-the-roof and peered through the binoculars to see a middle-aged man with dark blond hair swing a briefcase and clutch his wool coat closed against the wind. His dress shoes weren't weather appropriate to scoot down the street and into a diner, coffee a higher priority than the expensive wingtips he probably had a closet full of. I lost sight of the target as the diner door closed behind him.

"What of their soul?"

"Huh. I thought we were tailing Magics?"

"We are."

"Well, Mr. Grey-Suit about to add to his mushy middle is Blind."

"Impossible." He conferred with the list in his lap comprised of the suspected Tainted. Many were scratched out as we whittled down targets without soul glows.

"You sure?"

He didn't answer, unblinking while lost in the war with my observation and his list.

"Who is he?"

He looked out the window as if he could see the target's soul himself. "Christopher Leisemeyer."

"Okay. Why don't we follow ol' Christopher, and you can buy me a cappuccino and a blueberry Danish and slip into his head?" Getting my icy hide out of this car and into the warmth and sweet smell of the diner was more attractive than figuring out who Christopher Leisemeyer was or wasn't.

Vincent jumped out of the car so fast I scrambled to shove the binoculars into the glove box. He opened my door for me as if I were already slowing us down, while casting a suspicious glare at passersby.

"Where's the natural stalker-gaze I've grown to love? Down-shift the tension. We're downtown. Everyone's suspicious."

He shoved his hands into his coat pockets and crossed the road. "I am not a stalker."

"Says the man stalking someone."

He opened the door and side-eyed me.

"Better."

Two customers behind our target were as much of a buffer as we were going to get. If Christopher turned and saw Vincent straight-backed and stone-faced, the buffer would count for nothing. Magic or not, you can feel when someone's staring at you, and Vincent stood out on the best of days.

I wrapped my arm around Vincent's, smiling when he looked down.

"You think that wholly necessary?" Telepathy didn't use enough power to tip anyone off, though removing my arm would strike a

diner patron as awkward and would make us memorable. He had known this and squeezed his arm tighter to his body instead of pulling away.

"It'll make sense to onlookers."

"You are unsuitable considering your age."

"Pfft. You're not ancient. Well, you're as old as swamp pus, but you're immortal and look maybe ten years older than me. Too young to be my dad, yet old enough to gain me a bit of wisdom and security since your fancy loafers are more expensive than Christopher's. Chances are he won't look my way since I appear unattainable, or he'll concentrate on me instead of you. Same for others. Now, get your head into his instead of mine."

Vincent shook his head in clear exhaustion with my tactics and got to work. Tricky business if the person you're listening in on is thinking more about his coffee order than his deviant behaviour, though Vincent was a master at mind reading. Once Christopher sat down with his order, he read a paper and checked out the door as if waiting for someone. I moved positions, providing Vincent a natural view of me and Christopher behind me.

Movement caught my eye. Blake raised a mug to his lips, staring at me over the rim at my arm still wrapped around Vincent's, and back at a young woman across from him.

"Oh, fuckgasm. We have a problem. Big, big problem." I had to force myself not to pull away from holding onto Vincent and controlling my facial expression.

Not only was it bad to have a Covener around when we were undercover on a self-imposed mission the Mother Coven had no clue about, but I looked all cuddly with Vincent, and Blake had no clue why. Instead, he sat there finishing his sandwich and glancing my way with a smug 'I caught you' grin.

"You order. I will deal with him." Vincent didn't approach Blake as this would draw more attention than we could afford. He kept the conversation telepathic as I stumbled through an order when I had no idea what Vincent wanted.

We took our food and drinks and sat on the opposite side of the diner in a two-person table, keeping our target in our peripheral. The diner was large enough for us not to be forced anywhere near Blake but not too large to lose sight of who may join Christopher. As we sat, Blake left with a suspicious eyebrow raised at me before scooting out the door, the female with him unaware of the exchange.

"What'd you say to Blake?"

Vincent took a sip of his steeped tea before pulling a face and reaching for the sugar. "I warned him against addressing us as we were in the middle of something and attempting to be discreet."

I gasped. "For real? You used the word 'discreet'?"

He nodded and took a deeper sip of his well-doctored drink.

"And you think that was helpful?"

"He refrained from approaching us."

I rubbed my hands over my face. "Are you damaged? Like, held under water as a baby damaged?"

"Why a—?"

The chair under me creaked as I leaned in closer. "I know you weren't born in this century, but how exactly do you think what you said would be interpreted by an asshat like Blake? Replay it in your head. I'll wait." I sat back and folded my arms.

He exhaled. "Sophie, I know what I stated as I was the one who stated it. Blake may feel jilted by my unwillingness to provide details, yet my concern for his emotional welfare is below that of my concern for the brand of polish used on the floor under my feet."

I leaned in again. "Doubt he'd be surprised by your assessment yet not what I meant. An asshat like Blake has a one-track mind, and it lands with precision on the tip of his dick." Vincent's blank expression meant I had to spell it out for him. "He thinks we're fucking."

His eyes widened, chancing a glance at other patrons nearby. "I— I would hardly think—"

I flopped back in my seat. "Ugh. This was so not worth a free cappuccino."

So much for my amazing ideas.

Part way through our drinks a woman joined Christopher. His wife. Vincent had nothing else to report if he got into Christopher's thoughts or found what he was looking for. I was too freaked out by Blake and what might come next. With the mission a bust, I chucked my stale Danish as Vincent downed half of his tea before we got back in my ice box of a vehicle.

A quack chirped with the arrival of a text from my new cell as I waited at a red light. I checked and saw a message from Whisky Hoarder, my saved name for Donovan. When I swiped open the message, I stared at a picture text of Vincent and me in the diner, arm-in-arm as I looked up at him, he smiling down at me. The message read: *Something u wanna tell me?*

"Fucking Blake!" I chucked my cell in the back seat, slamming my palm into the steering wheel. "I'm gonna hand that gossiping weasel over to the Raddies."

"How would you benefit from his death by an order of assassins?"

"Who cares about benefits? I'd let them have Blake for the sheer satisfaction of watching him burn."

A horn sounded behind me. I hit the accelerator with a jolt. "This is why most of the shit I did as a teen toed the outskirts of illegal. No matter what, I always get caught. Seriously! You'd think a simple overpriced cappuccino was too much to ask for."

"Then you buy next time."

I growled. "Why didn't I notice Blake's soul glow the moment we walked in? The one thing I can do without trying and I was hyper-focused on my freezing toes and fucked it up."

"Watch!"

I stomped on the brakes before barrelling into another car, the seatbelt digging into my collarbone.

I reached into the back seat for my phone as Vincent lectured me on road safety. Ugh, too far to grab. I added a jolt of power, and the cell flew into my grasp. "Look." I tossed it at Vincent who caught it and took a moment to open it. "If this wasn't a picture of us, what would you say about two people who look like this?"

He adjusted his glasses. "I would say this looks like a couple conversing while waiting in line. Your intended result."

"For our doughy target. Not for Blake and certainly not for Donovan. How am I supposed to explain that? Us being in the same place or even alone doesn't matter, but how we look and whatever Blake said to Donovan when he sent the pic does."

"Nothing salacious appears in the photo. As long as Donovan remains ignorant of our true activities, whatever explanation you give will suffice. Channel the acting skills you applied in the diner as your current emotional tirade may evoke questions."

He was right. While I freaked my shit, the connection Donovan and I shared was express shipping misery and panic right to him. If I were Donovan, I would be analyzing every hitch of emotion right from my shock to my scheming justifications. Lies stand out like a mustard-stained tie, unmistakable and unignorable. I can't have him thinking he has something to worry about with Vincent. Vincent's known me in many lifetimes but never like that. Not that I've double-checked this by reading my soul, but I was certain it was the case.

"You can drop me at my car and head off to Donovan's. We are done for the day."

Vincent parked in my spot at my apartment. His white SUV was too big to expect a good spot on a downtown roadside without causing a scene while trying to parallel park, so we took the Barracuda. Dropping him off and rushing to Donovan like some cheating wifey left me guilt-ridden for a different reason, but it's what I was doing once I ran inside to grab Bosco before heading out to Niagara-on-the-Lake. My accomplice's understanding smile and small wave as he left to head back to wherever he called home made no difference. I still felt like a dickhole.

On the way out of town, I scrambled for what to tell Donovan. Centuries of past lives together in no way meant I had to justify my daily movements, or he would be expected to do the same. After a few months of this hokey pokey, what I knew about Donovan outside of his bedroom and the prowess of his cooking and drink-pouring skills could fill a thimble. No dinner dates or hang out spots, nothing.

Years had passed since my ex totalled my perceptions of a healthy relationship. Now, somehow, it was only months since I trashed things with Caine. With him still trapped inside Diluculo, far out of reach on the other side of the veil, his release was priority number one, higher than this Sovereignty business. Being with Donovan without knowing if I should be mourning Caine felt wrong.

After parking in Donovan's driveway, I went to walk inside but couldn't. I put Bosco down and tried again. The door was locked. Never had I been stopped by a deadbolt when going to Aunt Lacey's. Donovan retained her open-door policy, one Coveners knew better than to use unless it was Coven meeting night or an emergency.

"Fuck a duck."

I rang the doorbell and waited.

Nothing.

Rang again and knocked.

No answer.

Instead of cooling my heels in the cold, I scooped up Bosco and got back into the Barracuda, fishing my cell out of my pocket to text Donovan.

Not what you think. I'm outside. Where are you?

Didn't feel like nuthin'

Let me in. I'm not fighting like this.

Sixteen-year-olds hide behind devices and bicker through miscommunicated texts. Adults fight face-to-face. Or they should. Being pissy over something I'll forget tomorrow was a few levels below the threat level of what the photo insinuated.

A few moments of Donovan's contemplation tickling the tether between us was torture before his face appeared at the front door. I went inside. Donovan headed towards the kitchen and disappeared around the corner. His contemplation shifted to controlled anticipation as I took off my jacket and boots at the entry, taking a moment to wipe down Bosco's wet paws.

I found Donovan in the kitchen and sat on an island stool. Now what? Even at the prospect of compromising our pre-relationship, I refused to break my promise to Vincent, and I hadn't thought of a solid reason behind what Blake got in the middle of. Instead, my thoughts were a mash of how quick things could go sideways.

I hesitated a few times.

"That hard to explain, huh?" He stood with the island between us, arms crossed, the connection burning with tension.

"Actually, yeah." I swiped at non-existent crumbs on the counter before stopping myself and folding my hands together. "I can't tell you why we were together."

"Excuse me?" He clenched his molars until the pressure in his jaw became mine.

"Yes, Vincent and I were in that diner together, obviously, but not together the way it looks in the picture Blake sent."

He kept my gaze for a long moment. "Are you fucking him?"

"What? Fuck you!"

"Fuck me? What do you expect me to think when you disappear for hours at a time and have been secretive, then I see you've been spending at least some of that time with Vincent? The guy hangs on your every word, has stalked us through time, and knows everything about you. Perfect next puddle to jump."

"No, you're right. I'm definitely hittin' it, and the diner was dessert, after the puddle jump of course, because before is just crazy talk."

"He must'a been good if you stuck around afterwards."

His reference to the fact I took off the first time we slept together while trapped in an emotional loop was a dirty hit under the kilt.

"Besides the fact you would get off every time I did, which was pretty clear while I was with Caine, if the photo is what you'd consider pornographic, you can keep it for your spank bank."

"The photo looks like more than sex."

"Wha—? Oh, I get it. You would be fine if it was just sex. You can wrap your head around the possibility I might fuck around, but the fact we looked like a functioning couple is a problem for you."

"Are you?"

I exhaled and leaned into the counter. "I'm not messing with anyone except you. It was innocent, and what you saw was all there was to see. And for good reason, I can't tell you why. You'll need to trust me, or I'm happy to leave."

A few moments of silence ticked by. The tension lessened yet still resonated. "If he has you lying to me, then it's about something dangerous, which is bullshit."

"It's not dangerous."

He nodded. "I can feel you're telling the truth, but that means you don't know what you're into either which scares me more." He leaned forward, the island still between us, he unable to hold my hands without a vision hitting, but his fingers twitched as if he wanted to. "In the past, if something like this came to my door, it would've stayed locked."

"If it came to mine, it would've stayed locked, too. I get it. But it's not what it looked like. It's just not."

A few repeat booty-calls were the closest thing to long-term Donovan ever had, and I was pushing his tolerance knowing our situation was different, and chances were he would forgive whatever I threw at him. Which made me an asshole. I took a mental note to talk to Vincent about bringing Donovan in, again. It didn't make sense to keep him out of the loop, and I hated the subterfuge. It was exhausting more than anything, and I didn't have the extra energy these days.

The flash of softness in his eyes said the fight was over for today. The core of the problem lingered to be argued about another time.

He rounded the island meeting me on my side and took the seat next to me, running his fingers along my clothed arm, his wordless tenderness testament of dodging a bullet.

I straightened, trying not to let his fingers distract me. "What about Blake? The Coven meeting's tomorrow, and he's a blabbermouth. I know you don't care what they think, but I don't want everyone looking at one of their Sect Leaders like they're being played, and I don't want them looking at me like I'm playing you."

He smirked. "Already taken care of."

"By the power of positive thinking? Or did the Raddies shank his ass like I hoped they would?"

"The Raddies, eh?"

I shrugged. "He might have a fighting chance but come out with a missing foot or finger. Well-earned."

"Yeah, he did." He shifted to the end of his chair and ran his hands up my thighs until he reached my hips. "When he sent the message asking if I knew where my girlfriend was and who she was with, I told him I did, and it was Coven business he should forget he ever saw."

"See, if Vincent had told the meddling bastard that in the first place, we could have avoided this." A tingle of a vision hit as I wrapped my arms around his shoulders and got close enough for our noses to graze, resisting the urge to kiss him as well as address the casual use of Blake's view of our relationship.

He pulled back. "So, it was Coven business?"

I laughed. "Good try, Slick. Like I said, I'll do my best." I stopped him from moving farther away. "Why do you think I was so pissed when I got the picture? Screwing Vincent is the last thing I want to be fighting about."

Any reservation about my potential cheating drained from the connection or accelerated the urgency as he closed the distance between us. A dash of anticipation shivered through me. An eagerness to feel nothing but pleasure and to forget the previous hour was a craving beyond the need for understanding.

He rushed forward and hiked me up onto the counter as he fought against his Psychometry. Whatever vision he saw evoked nothing but a devious smile, making me giggle and yearn for more of his warm hands on my skin as the heat within us grew.

I tightened my legs around him, erasing the space between us, and relished the tug on the back of my hair and his teeth on my bottom lip.

Control was a fine line I tried to rein in for the both of us, my failure rate higher than my shirt as it whipped over my head.

In an attempt to savour the moment, I pushed him away to break his visions and popped off the counter, walking backwards away from him as he returned to the present and looked around to find the present version of me.

I reversed to the stairs. He took a slow walk in predatory mode with a hint of power humming below the surface as raring to be released as he was.

Peeling off clothing as we went chipped away at our restraint. Patience thinned yet amped up the fun. The bed was too far. The bedroom wall hit my back with a chilled wash of exhilaration and welcomed reprieve from my spiking body temperature.

Up on my tiptoes, body entangled within his arms, nails biting sweat-slicked skin, lips bruising, hips grinding, I lifted and tightened a leg around him as he braced my arms against the wall and drove into me. My gasp echoed on his lips, the shock of pleasure was intense, making my head swim as we lost all control to the loop of emotions and his visions.

A rush of sensation had us clutching for the other, overwhelmed, breathless, encased in a greedy force taking everything without forgiveness and promising to remain.

Weightlessness ended with jarring disappointment as my ass hit the ground, pulling Donovan away from me, and stripping us both of our euphoric pause in time. I lost myself to waves of light-headedness from the after-bliss of pleasure, unable to stop moving yet incapable of doing anything more than writhe in place, including open my eyes or attempt anything close to words.

Light pressure grazed my trembling inner thigh after an innumerable amount of time, it accompanied with a dash of healing magic unable to erase my heightened arousal.

Donovan stalked over me, a predatory crawl I refused to scurry from, instead, taking control by rolling us over until the scrape of the carpet on my knees was observed and forgotten. The addiction to every thrust, every pinch, and every caress took over until we were hit with irresistible ruin all over again.

I collapsed on top of him, remaining a few moments before rolling off and onto my back. A shiver ran through me as the heat of our adventure subsided.

A grunt and whoosh was Donovan pulling the duvet on top of us, creating enough of a barrier between us to give him a break from his visions.

The cocoon of drowsiness followed as I tried to grasp the reality of time all but lost, as was the sense of how we got here. It took a few moments for me to grasp the events leading to staring up at his ceiling with rug-burned knees and aching hips.

Being an open book to him, no matter if choice was a factor, was as freeing as it was terrifying. Jealousy was good fuel for us both. As toxic as it could be, I lived every day for years guarding my heart. While still guarded, it was more a chain-link fence then the seven-foot reinforced steel it used to be.

A head nod of exhaustion jolted me awake. Still early night, the sun slanted through the blinds not yet so sleepy. If I slept now, I risked messing up my sleep schedule, making staying awake until The Lush closed a chore.

"Get your ass up." I whipped off the blankets and searched for my underwear, finding them near the wall where they fell.

Donovan groaned and rolled to his side, taking his time sitting up, and pouting when I put my bra on.

He sprang to his knees coming after me.

I yelped and planted my foot on his shoulder before he could stand. "I've had enough, Donny-boy."

"Donny-boy? Sounds like a challenge." He pounced again.

This time I was ready and erected a shield with a single thought and a pinch of power. I didn't put my all into it. My shield disappeared in a cloud. He stepped through, coming after me.

I ran down the hall, hitting him with a few more shields to slow him down, always making them crystal clear so he wouldn't miss my goading expression as I turned and fast-walked backwards. He amped up the challenge by ghosting, disappearing and reappearing, extra steps ahead, as I had seen him do in battle.

I anticipated his advances as we bounded down the stairs, sprinting through the first sitting area in a fit of laughter and empty threats as he caught me up in a telekinetic hold to pull me off my feet. I landed in his grasp with a squeal as we reached the kitchen. The vision hit him so strong I thought I smelled wildflowers before I broke contact.

"Spike his drink next time, sweetheart, or you'll never get him off your tail."

I gasped and spun at the sound of a stranger's voice. Power rushed to my skin.

Donovan thrust himself between me and a man standing in his kitchen.

The man raised his hands in defence. "Holy shit, Donny-boy! With power like hers, I see why you get so worked up."

The light brown-haired man with piercing blue eyes was like a sunrise in front of a stormfront. His dark, billowy soul glow clouded the kitchen. He raised an eyebrow and looked me over in my underwear.

"Why are you here, Brandon?"

"Funny thing, brother, I saw Joelly not too long ago." I fought against cringing at the name as he stuck his hand into a bag of popcorn I recognized from the cupboard. "She tells me she's got herself into some shit. Which, let's face it, is what Joelly does. Then she tells me to come looking for you if she goes missing." He popped a kernel into his mouth and chomped a few times. "Why do you think she would tell me that?"

"You expect me to decipher that psycho twat?" Donovan stood in nothing but his birthday suit, neither he nor Brandon put off by the nudity.

Brandon's eyes narrowed as if searching Donovan for facial clues. "You see," he paused to drop a kernel on the floor. I tensed, realizing he was feeding Bosco, "Joelly may be a crazy bitch, paranoid even, but she's one smart cookie and made sure to pass over some info." He tilted his head and looked at me. "Including stuff about you, sweetheart. I'm assuming you're Sophie. Or am I getting you in trouble, Donny-boy?"

"Yes, this is Sophie. I'll save you the trouble of torturing us and tell you Joelly's dead. I snapped her neck after the fight outside Diluculo and buried her skank-ass in a shallow hole for making one last try for me before being carted off to the Sovereignty cells. Now run back to Tobias and let him know what an obedient son you are."

Donovan was lying. Joelly went after me, not him, making me wonder what kind of danger I was in if Brandon knew the truth.

"Father doesn't know I'm here, though he will when I return." Brandon pitched another kernel down for Bosco who chomped it up.

The occasions I saw Donovan's father in a dream or when he mentioned him, it was all torture and manipulation. Actual torture as Donovan refused to lead his father's Tainted coven like his father wanted him to. Whether this brother was a blood relative or a kidnapped settler like Joelly, it was clear Brandon still followed Tobias's teachings.

"How'd you get in here?"

Brandon laughed. "I saw the wards protecting the house and figured I'd walk through the door and give you a scare. Someone named Gwen called to check in about the alarm. I assured her you two were safe but going at it too vigorously to care. Guess you missed the warning. Certainly didn't hear the phone or the microwave." He rattled the popcorn bag and looked into it in search of one he wanted.

Anger seethed within me.

"Careful, sweet cheeks." He splayed his fingers as sparks of power encased them. "Not my fault you find Donny-boy here so irresistible."

"Enough!" Donovan's silent caution to me across the connection matched his outward fury. A subtle warning for me to back down and let him lead. "If you're here about Joelly, consider yourself informed. Now leave."

Brandon crunched on a mouthful of popcorn and sauntered towards the exit. Relief he was far from Bosco brought my power down a notch, even if it meant he was closer to us. I resisted the urge to step back as he approached. Brandon was shorter than Donovan, though not by much, and Donovan never flinched as Brandon came closer.

"We know about Elsa." His voice was low, Donovan's emotions high at the mention of Aunt Lacey's previous name. "We know about Diluculo. We know about Evaristus and Loring. We know about the premonition. Consider *yourself* informed."

Brandon swaggered off and out the door, triggering the wards, creating an urgency we couldn't ignore. If only we felt it when he came in.

I ran for Bosco and knelt to him. He was fine, no blood or injury, still licking his buttery chops.

Once Vincent suggested it, I was able to give Bosco mental commands. He had been in the living room snoozing when Brandon came in. I could have told him to back away from Brandon but didn't want to do anything to tip the guy off and put Bosco in danger. A bit of popcorn wouldn't hurt him, and Brandon was eating from the same bag, so it wasn't poisoned.

After checking the front windows when Brandon left, Donovan sat on the couch. He was too quiet. His contemplation took me over so much I had to fight to focus beyond the connection.

I sat next to him. "Is it that bad?"

He shrugged, a hint of dimpled mischievousness on his face as he ran his finger over the edge of my navy-blue lace bra. "A tragedy he saw you like this. He's liable to sneak a hidden camera into my room."

"You're deflecting."

"Yes, I am." He snapped his fingers, and my bra strap unclasped.

"Hey!"

Before I could complain further, he swooped me up into his arms, which meant Brandon coming here was worse than he was willing to delve into. He was lost to his visions while the emotional and physical loop took us both over and had us forgetting about Brandon, his father, and how screwed we were.

2

MORE THAN SKIN DEEP

Healing abilities came in handy after another romp, my power taking care of any lingering discomfort so I could enjoy the after-sex bliss.

Tucked into Donovan's chest, surrounded in the earthy green glow of his soul and sense of consuming contentment, I didn't want to move ever again. I wanted the day to stand still to enjoy as we saw fit without having to deal with whatever crisis was on deck or whatever ones were joining us before the original crisis was solved.

Once I was being honest with myself, loving Donovan didn't require thought or extensive deliberation. Even if some days I drowned its obviousness in indecision, right now, not even my head overrode the ache of comfort I longed for since Brock's disappearing act.

The person who last evoked the emotion was a drifting memory. One who caused an ache far different than what injected the sensation of jelly into my muscles.

The men in, and missing from, my life couldn't find equal elbow room in my brain without causing me to either shut down or spill into overdrive. Balance was not a possibility, and either extreme turned ugly.

Urgency shot through me. The house's wards were tripped. Donovan took off like in old Road Runner cartoons, moving so fast I was surprised a zoom cloud didn't wisp behind him with accompanying wacky noise effects.

I tore on my underwear only to find them little more than a piece of fabric as if ripped off my body. A man's muffled complaints of nakedness and Donovan's boisterous laugh filtered up the stairs and bubbled within my chest through the connection. Again, running footsteps, these ones making it back to the bedroom.

Donovan burst through the door ripe with excitement and tossed me my bra that I left on the couch and a few items of clothing discarded in the hallway from round number one. I caught them and gawked at Donovan's huge grin I didn't see often.

I struggled to get my bra situated. "What's going on?"

"It's Fox." He telekinetically snatched his clothing from the floor and ran back downstairs.

"Who the hell is Fox?"

He was long gone, and I was left to piece back together my wardrobe, happy knowing Brandon hadn't made a second trip but equally confused at another unexpected visitor.

Descending the stairs, I heard him and another man's voice arguing over the symbolism of something I didn't catch. Donovan's stubbornness was in full tilt, testing the man, as evident in the man's impatient tone.

"Kid, you're lucky I'm doing it at all."

"Don't be a whiney old fogey. It's not like I'm not paying you."

Neither saw me when I entered the kitchen, too drawn into their conversation. Donovan stood toe-to-toe with a short-statured, heavyset Magic in his early fifties with thick curly hair past his shoulders and pulled back into a ponytail. If there wasn't a Harley parked out front, I would be shocked.

I opened the fridge for a bottle of water, and Donovan's attention snapped up.

"Babe, this is Fox. He's doing my tat."

Fox grunted. "Redoing your tat."

"Please. It's not even the same design."

Donovan and Fox bickered about the semantics of it not being Donovan's fault the last tattoo was obliterated by him and I dying as Fox was setting up his tattooing gear on the kitchen table. When our bodies disintegrated and reformed, any life-earned scars or tattoos didn't make the return. Same with my ears and belly-button piercings.

Donovan won. He was a paying customer and argued Fox would have more clients if he employed himself or I to do quick erase jobs for crappy artist's work or the Winnie-the-Pooh tat someone thought looked adorable at sixteen and over the years morphed into a mustard blob. More painful than a laser but a one-time treatment with guaranteed success.

"I don't need a thousand chicken-heads rolling through every time they change their boyfriend's tag on their tramp stamp. No thank you."

Donovan sucked his teeth. "Untapped potential."

Fox grumbled to himself like he had a mouthful to say and no energy to bother saying it.

The man himself was covered with different tattoos of varying ages on his arms, hands, and neck and probably the rest of him under the layers of denim and leather.

Fox cleared his throat and raised his gloved hands, already prepped for the work. "Nice to finally meet you." The glint in his dark-blue eyes was genuine and friendly.

"You too." I didn't mention I had never heard of him before and wondered what Donovan told him about me and why.

Also interesting was his soul colour. No Taint to his essence existed nor was he in any stage of immortality, though it was bright. The colour itself had me scratching my brain for the meaning behind it, thinking back to the Ballard Family Tome. Not the blue of a Persuader like Caine but a blue as dark and drawing as Fox's eyes.

"He's a Druid." Donovan was looking at me. I hadn't noticed as I was contemplating Fox's soul colour. He must have sensed my assessment.

Being a Druid was confusing since it meant his soul colour differentiated him by race and not by the power he could wield. Maybe it did. The Ballard Family Tome compiled a list, but it was incomplete.

Fox looked up from his equipment at Donovan, to me, then back to Donovan. "What's the matter with you, kid?"

"What?"

"What if I didn't want her to know?"

"As if I wouldn't tell her when you left? Better outed to your face."

"I'm gonna tattoo a butterfly on your forehead next time you advertise my lineage. Come here." Donovan's dimples flashed as he ducked from Fox's vibrating tattoo gun while Fox's face contorted in a ghastly yet comedic snarl.

Their relationship seemed to waver from supplier-consumer and ill-fitted friends. Granted, his biker boots were probably older than Donovan, but they interacted as if they faced Hell together and were closer for it.

Once the teasing subsided, Fox turned his dark blues on me. "Yes, my people were Druids, as am I." He squeezed a clear solution onto a paper towel and rubbed it on Donovan's shoulder, prepping the area. "Though it's customary to let people tell others themselves." He cuffed Donovan in the back of the head causing both of us to wince and Donovan's hair to stick up funny.

Fox didn't see my reaction as he donned a pair of glasses, turned on the tattoo gun, and grabbed hold of Donovan's bicep to steady his grip.

"Wait!"

Fox and Donovan jumped.

"Babe—"

"It's unwise to scream when I've got this thing in my hand, little lady." Fox looked above his bifocals with annoyance akin to glaring at a child screaming through the grocery store.

"The connection wasn't a thing when you did the last one. I don't exactly want the pain of a tattoo without the pretty conclusion. And definitely without a buzz going."

They laughed, and my blood pressure rose.

"He's not using ordinary tattoo ink, babe."

Fox crossed his arms with his specs back in hand. "When this little gremlin came to me, spitting a story about his sister offing you using your own magic, I reckoned even if you were the colour and metal type, what Van had in mind wouldn't settle right on the skin of a lady."

I didn't know what Donovan had in mind but refrained from arguing about what should or shouldn't be considered the right kind of tattoo for a woman. "I'm not opposed to tattoos, just never settled on a design worth carrying around. Plus, I couldn't afford to get it done by someone with more than a broken pen and a *Bic*-disinfected straight pin."

Fox gave a deep-chested chuckle.

"I knew with a few months you'd figure it out." Donovan drank something amber-coloured in a short, crystal glass, then looked my way, sensing my confusion. "He's made a special ink that'll create separation from the connection on an epidermal level."

"Potentially deeper. I give no guarantees." Fox readorned his glasses, pushing them in place with a gloved knuckle, and started up his gun.

Without time to disbelieve or approve the thought of something as such existing, pressure on my shoulder moved around where Fox was working on Donovan. I pulled down my swag necked sweater to expose my left shoulder. The skin depressed, but no design was left behind, nor did I feel any pain.

Fox paused mid-stroke, and the pressure on my shoulder disappeared. "We good to go?"

I nodded, and Donovan's nervousness morphed into scurried excitement across our bond. I couldn't speak, too focused on watching my skin as Fox worked.

After countless minutes immersed in the awe of the process, I realized how much planning this would have taken. Donovan knew there was something out there to lessen our connection in the most basic form and neglected to confide in me. I shouldn't have been surprised, but I was.

Bosco yawned at my feet as I perched atop an island chair. "Can this work on a larger scale?"

Donovan's dimpled cheek and trained gaze on Fox's work told me he refused to look at me. The connection bloomed with something close to dread at me asking.

Fox didn't miss a stroke of his gun. "This falls in guinea pig territory. I don't get a lot of clients with such specific needs. Since it's your souls that are connected, this only affects Van and leaves you untouched. Almost untouched. It's a surface spell, turning something as permanent as a tattoo into a superficial adjustment. No different than you dying your hair, with the addition of the numbing effect."

I got it. Since Fox wasn't tattooing Donovan's, or Van's, soul—I didn't miss the nickname—the additional spice of magic would leave me untouched with only the odd undulation of my skin as evidence of his needle work.

"Could it work at soul depth?"

Donovan's inward cringe was a pressure of a different kind as I felt his chest clench at my question.

"Do you want a soul separation?" Fox's intonation made it sound as dirty as a 1930's divorce.

To Donovan's credit, he didn't overreact at Fox's question in place of an answer.

No one looked at each other. Donovan focused on Fox's art, Fox focused on his job, and I focused on Bosco at my feet, leaning down to scratch the top of his head.

How could I answer Fox without hurting Donovan's feelings? "A separation would come in handy sometimes." Nothing definite or damning, though I wondered what Donovan was sensing through the connection.

"I bet it would." Fox readjusted his position and carried on his work. "Soul Magic like yours isn't some pussy new-age Wiccan love spell like cupid pissed in your Corn Flakes." Clearly Fox had some hang-ups with Wiccans, though didn't get into why, straying from the prejudicial rant. "Soul Magic is a branding. And like any other brand, no matter the amount of covering up, scrubbing down, or dressing up, it exists somewhere deeper than we can reach unless you cut it out. Dowsing the damaging physical effects is one thing. Obliterating the bond you tied years ago all together?" He shook his head, bushy brows raised, eyes still on Donovan's skin. "Not happenin'."

I figured as much and attempted to suppress any disappointment. I doubted I could follow through with eliminating our connection if a viable solution existed. Knowing it was an option if one day I grew to detest the sight of him would have made me feel less tied down and free to be myself with one-hundred percent knowledge that what I felt belonged to me without his influence.

I had never met a Druid before. Didn't know they existed outside of video games, so once we got over the awkwardness of the 'Am I stuck like this forever' question, I had more.

Fox answered my every inquiry without a hint of annoyance, even explaining his real name was actually Louarn, taken from a supposed famous warrior Alan-al-Louarn or Alan-the-Fox. Fox was better than Lou, as far as he was concerned, so he stuck with it and made sure others followed or didn't address him at all.

I laughed. Donovan looked up at Fox as if he had never heard the story before.

After a bit of history regarding the elusive evidence the Blind compiled regarding Druid existence, I found being a Druid faired little different than any other Magic I crossed. They all had a few things in common. One being the almost limitless possibilities their powers could produce, as well as the fact not every Druid could do the same thing, as every Witch or Sorcerer didn't always share abilities. Also, they were as likely to be good or evil depending on their moral compass.

The variation that stood out in my mind was how a Druid's power stemmed from spiritual connections. Fox explained he believed his art was a gift from the 'higher-ups' allowing him to guide others through their trials, celebrate their achievements, and mourn their dead through the ink in a spiritual healing of their inner essence by documenting their journey through their skin and body modification.

A lot to proclaim from a tattoo, but nothing in his expression led me to believe he felt this an overstatement, his purpose in life ironclad.

Another hour passed when Fox sat up to straighten his back. His belly jutted out from the bottom of his well-worn shirt as he did. His glasses left an imprint across his nose. He pinched the bridge before finishing his work by wiping off the excess ink from Donovan's arm. "Ready for the bitchin' part?"

"Is anyone? Ever?"

Fox exhaled hard. "Don't make me cuff you again." He looked at me. "I have to charge it."

Before I could ask what he meant, he grabbed Donovan's hand in a tight grip as if saving him from a fatal fall and laid a square palm over the tattoo.

Donovan squeezed his eyes shut and averted his face.

Power simmered in the room as Fox's lips moved in a murmur of words, then Donovan's power rose to meet Fox's. A scurry beneath my skin like terrified beetles gathered at the site of the tattoo, pinching the skin into the muscle, followed by the sensation of water spilt over me and then sucked back as Fox rose his hand a couple inches away from Donovan's shoulder. Fox pressed back down on the site of the tattoo injecting a boiling heat so hot I gripped onto the island granite to keep from falling, hoping it wouldn't snap off like a wafer cookie.

The burning grew to volcanic levels. When the tang of blood from biting into my tongue choked me, Donovan bellowed an "Okay!" and in one last shot of Fox's magic, the heat and pressure became unbearable before the molten heat cooled.

Fox smacked his hands together with a loud crack. "Now heal and seal it in."

Donovan rolled his healing magic through him, with equal impact on myself. The shock of so much pain to the salve of his healing was as much trauma as it was ecstasy.

I braced my cheek on the cool island counter. "I don't think you have to worry about chicken-heads traipsing into your shop for that. Holy fuckballs."

He chuckled. "You took it like a champ."

"Thanks. Not a clueless chicken-head. Though a warning would've been nice."

Fox hit Donovan in the site of his new work. "Probably would've lasted longer had this guy not wimped out."

They chided each other back and forth a few times giving me the impression they were used to griping at each other. I had never seen Donovan interact with someone on this level before. Almost like Fox was family, but family he didn't want to see ripped apart by starving hyenas.

"So, do I get to see what I felt like I sacrificed a limb for?"

Donovan's dimples caved before he dipped his shoulder towards me to show off the tattoo.

Fox's work was pure talent. Freehand, no less. The design was a hand. Its fingers splayed on the meat of his shoulder, palm up yet somehow still grabbing him like Fox's hand during the "charging," depicting aspects of Palmistry. Each line was represented, the life line, heart line, fate line, and on and on. Donovan had gifted me a book on Palmistry at my initiation into the Coven. Took me a while to read it, but I did and now had vague knowledge of what I was looking at. Enough I was willing to bet the tattoo matched Donovan's true hand.

"The rest is a sigil." Donovan traced the lines with his finger. The symbol comprised of circle upon circle with small symbols surrounded by Theban lettering. He pointed at the symbols as he read them. "This is my will: Evil will fear all I protect." I nodded without true understanding. Sensing as such, he went on. "A widely used method of sigil creation consists of writing out a concise want, need, or will for something to happen and then removing any duplicated letters and, in this case, changing the leftover letters to the Theban alphabet to create a representation of protection and art. Charging the sigil and then healing it absorbed the magic and the will outlined in the sigil into me, which is why you felt that part. More than skin deep, the sigil runs to the core. For you, too."

"Hmm. You'd think you might have let me in on the process first."

Fox chuckled again. He was hidden behind Donovan, so I didn't see his expression.

Donovan shrugged. "Wasn't sure it would happen at all. His are always surprise visits."

"As if you didn't miss my pretty mug, kid."

Donovan smirked at Fox. "Mhmm."

"A preferable surprise visitor than your brother. Even considering the whole searing magic thing." We were healed, but Fox's magic was unforgettable, much like Donovan's brother.

Fox straightened and groaned, side-eyeing Donovan. "Brandon?"

Donovan nodded. "None other. He got an update on Joelly's new address and stayed just long enough to inform me of Tobias's persistent memory regarding my place as well as knows all about Aunt Lacey, Loring, and Evaristus trapped in the Creation...all of it."

Fox ran a hand down his bearded face. "Guess it's not a stretch Tobias would come knocking at some point or send someone to do it for him. Brandon's still his lackey of choice, I see. You and your lady here have been in the spotlight lately. No offense as I know it wasn't all by choice. Regardless of how it happened, someone like Tobias wouldn't miss a chance to verify the rumours. You ready for him if he comes calling in person next time?"

I looked at Donovan, careful to detect any hitch in confidence or lack of.

"You know my father."

"You making my point or arguing it, kid?"

Donovan's dimple caved. "Fucked if I know. I'm as ready as I've always been."

"Which is?" I needed to know considering I might be standing next to him when Tobias showed up.

Donovan scratched a non-itchy spot on his neck. "He will either stroll through the door like Brandon did and talk shit, letting me know all the things he thinks I don't know in an attempt to intimidate me with open-ended threats, or he'll strike like a snake, and we won't know it until our next life if you can still read it in our souls."

I made a throaty noise. "Wonderful. And if you were to bet on his method of choice?" Donovan was a gambling man, and I was willing make a bet myself that he already knew.

Donovan glimpsed at Fox, who smirked in response. "Strike like a snake." Donovan was certain. "He's an all or nothing kind of Tainted Magic who won't make a move until he's constructed a plan he knows I can't wriggle out of. He's had enough failed attempts against me to know what I might try."

Fox didn't answer to verify Donovan's assessment but nodded in a slow deliberate way. He, too, knew Donovan's father in some capacity. And whatever that was, he understood if Tobias wanted to make a move, he would, and he would make it count.

Fox leaned onto his elbows. "Not much you can do unless you want to take him out first. I reckon you've got enough on your plate right now."

Check. I certainly didn't need to add more to mine. "Reopening the Creation, for starters."

Fox side-eyed Donovan. They exchanged a discreet look saying something to each other and leaving me out. No matter Fox's opinion, mine was non-negotiable.

"Right. All in due time." Fox didn't elaborate as if he thought it best to keep his comments to himself. He sanded his hands together as if ridding himself of the impulse. "Success for the day was small yet worth the aggravation of gathering the ingredients to create the temporary soul block. Now cover those titties, boy."

Donovan caught his shirt Fox threw at him. "*Pfft*. Like you can talk, old man."

"What?" He grabbed his chest. "My titties are modestly covered."

Donovan turned with a smirk I couldn't see and then took off towards the bathroom with subdued excitement, probably amped to check out the art himself and escape the conversation.

Bosco pawed at my foot, wagging his curly tail. I grabbed a liver treat from the container on the kitchen island and handed it down to him.

Fox patted the seat Donovan vacated and gave a heavy dark-blue stare leaving me uneasy.

I lifted a brow. "I don't wag my tail for treats."

He chuckled. "What'll it be? I'd love to de-cherry your too perfect skin."

"De-cherry?"

"You don't have any. Even if you hadn't said as much, I could've guessed."

"Riiight. Hmmm. Would your soul bond numbing concoction work for piercings?"

"Good question." He thought a moment, fingers playing with his beard. "If I tattooed the spot of the piercing first it would. Even a dot would do. And if not, Donovan could heal any holes closed while yours merely healed around the piercing."

Before I knew it, I was cringing, and Donovan was running out of the bathroom complaining about pain in his stomach. Since I missed my belly button ring and wanted a couple more in my ears, Fox pulled out some sample ring options and got to it, not without me walking away from a tattoo. After ten minutes of searching my brain for something special enough to tattoo, I thought of something I could not only live with but cherish.

It may not have been a masterpiece like Donovan's amalgamation of Palmistry and sigil protection, but for a novice like myself, scratching and buzzing vision was enough. After holding my ear forward so Fox could work, and keeping my eyes closed since it vibrated my skull, I had a Triquetra snuggled behind my left ear. A subtle replacement for my lost necklace Aunt Lacey gifted me the first night we met.

Never would the replacement suffice, yet it made me feel marginally better regarding the fact I would never see my beautiful necklace again. May never even see inside of Diluculo where I lost it and where—

Nope. I refused to bring him into this moment. He had his time and place, and it wasn't now. This moment was for Aunt Lacey and for Fox who was still staring at me with disappointment in my small choice, though agreed the symbol was special and suited me.

Fox took his gloves, off and rubbed his hands together. "Now to charge it."

I leaned away from him. "Ummm—"

"Included in every piece I do. For Magics, that is."

I sighed and shut my eyes. With what felt like a pointed finger, the searing heat drilled into my skull. The scratch-like buzzing of the tattooing which made my vision blur was a mosquito bite in comparison.

"Kinda fucked people pay you to torture them. Though easier than donning a gimp mask." I added a dose of healing power to the spot and took Bosco from Donovan. It took everything in me not to rub at the area.

Donovan slapped a large wad of cash in Fox's hand. "What's fucked is how much you charge for it."

"Shitbubbles. How much do I owe you?" I should have discussed price first since it looked steep enough to ski down.

Fox chuckled and took Donovan's money. "Right. Like your readings were free?" Fox grumbled, and Donovan smiled as Fox ignored me and took his case with him towards to the door.

"Wait." I stopped him. "How much?"

"The piercings were paid for in this kid's screams. And the first ink is on the house, little lady."

Donovan didn't actually scream, but he couldn't hide it when Fox punched through the skin of my belly button, twice in each earlobe, helix, and daith of my ears. I almost went for a small septum piercing but lost my nerve.

Fox smiled and put down his case, then grabbed my hands and squeezed them. "Take care of this pathetic shlub,"—he looked at Donovan over my shoulder—"and so will the next piercing, tat, brand or whatever you gain the stones to sit for."

I smirked. "No promises."

He chuckled, picked up the case, and went through the door, getting into a pickup truck, not a bike as I assumed.

Donovan closed the door behind him.

"So, Fox went to you for readings?"

Donovan sniffed. "I'm awesome, and he knows it."

We sat on the living room couch. I leaned on my hand and rested my elbow on the back of the couch, a sprig of surprise making me readjust and finger my new piercings I already forgot were there.

"I only did one palm reading for you in the beginning when I was doing my best to ignore your sweet ass since you were off limits, so bad example."

"And before I knew you could see my past through touch. Cheater."

"I'm accurate as hell, and you know it."

"Mhmm. Was he a friend of Aunt Lacey's?"

He rubbed his hands down his jeans. "Nah. I've known Fox longer than Aunt Lacey."

"Really?"

He nodded. "Soon after I left my father's compound, I was caught breaking into Fox's tattoo shop looking for money and food and trying to get off the street for a bit. Back then Fox had a dog named Hound." He rolled his eyes. "Yes, *Fox and the Hound*. He thinks he's freakin' hilarious."

"It is pretty clever."

"I'll let him know you think so. Well, Hound was a beast, and the bugger attacked me two feet in the door. When Fox found us, the pup was suspended in the air stuck in a silence spell. Obviously, since Hound was barking his ass off in a drooling mess without a sound, not to mention seven feet off the ground, Fox knew what I was, and I was in big trouble.

"Before I could bolt, Fox had the screaming of a thousand eagles in my head and the gnawing of invisible fleas in every pore of my skin."

I gasped.

"Yeah. Druids are symbiotic with nature, and in this case, nature spanked my ass."

I laughed and brought my feet up onto his lap. He caressed my knee and continued. "Once Fox had me puckered in the fetal position crying like a little bitch, I copped to what I came for. Instead of killing me, he got me something to eat and let me stay the night. He might look like a brute, but he's more teddy than bear.

"When I didn't take off in the morning, he let me stick around and work the register since his normal chick quit weeks before, and he detested paperwork and ringing phones. Even let me sleep in the back of the shop for free if I pulled my weight and shut it with any complaints." Donovan's smile disappeared. "Men my father sent tracked me down. I hadn't told Fox my last name for a reason. I figured if he knew I was a Sorrel, he would've run me off. Once he learned who was after me and who I was, he and another artist, another Magic, took care of them."

A fair assumption was that 'took care of them' didn't include free ink. "He still let you stay?"

Donovan nodded. "Wasn't too happy with me but kept me around. Gave me the cash for my first apartment and let me keep the job to pay for it. Plus, I did readings for him and willing clients."

"Why'd you stop working at the shop?" I never saw him work or speak of employment in any capacity except for the readings.

He toyed with the seam of my jeans. "I was being me. A fuck-up like usual."

"Self-sabotaging?"

"Guess that's what professionals might call it. Once Fox found out about my pickpocketing, though I never stole from him, I did from one too many of his clients, and it fell back on him. I left so he didn't have to throw me out and did readings at my place instead."

"And that's how you met Aunt Lacey."

"Yup." He held my hands and gave a dimpled smile with an excitement I didn't understand. "I've kept in touch with Fox, occasionally helped him out at the shop if he was desperate, but not much since I left."

"Sounds like you owe him a lot."

He nodded.

"Funny how I haven't heard of him before."

"Couldn't help yourself, huh?" He was still smiling. "Funny, I don't know what you and Vincent are up to." His smile remained casually accusatory. Neither of us elaborated, sitting semi-comfortable with our omissions.

He looked down at our clasped hands and rubbed them together along my fingers.

I gasped. "You're not getting visions." I would have felt them if he had.

He shook his head and pressed his lips to the back of my hand. "Lasting effects of Fox's magic."

I couldn't believe it. I felt the warmth of his touch, could sense his stir of emotions as he shared the sensitivity behind meeting Fox, all with no punch the visions injected.

"Why don't you figure out a way to use it all the time? With how much the visions blind you, I'd figure you'd keg stand a gallon of whatever it was Fox made on the daily."

He looked at me with his intense dark stare. "Would you take something to remove your Soul Seeing? Something more than dark sunglasses?"

He had a point. I wouldn't. Now that I was somewhat used to seeing souls, it only became too much when a large number of Magics were together. Remembering back to when Loring bound my powers and how naked it felt without my sight, I knew I would never get rid of it.

"I get it. But at least I can get around my Soul Seeing with sunglasses. Your visions get in your way of living in the present. Causes a barrier between you and the world around you."

"Yeah, but it would also leave me blind in a way I've never been. Interacting with you would be divine." His dimples caved in a softer way with an ache of yearning that washed through me. "I've never been able to touch you like this and stay connected to the 'you' in front of me." He looked down again as he ran his fingers along the inside of my arm and wrist, goosebumps rising in its wake.

A low moan rumbled in the back of his throat as I giggled.

"What would happen if I couldn't use my Psychometry and missed something I should've picked up and something bad happened? This was an experiment. A successful one, but we don't know how long it'll last."

"You don't have to do it, obviously. I just thought you'd be raring for some space."

"Space from you? Never. Not a chance."

No reservation waded within the connection. He didn't want our bond to end in any way. Having him say it reinforced my assumption. I didn't respond to him or let him know I wanted the same thing because I didn't know if it was true and any hesitance in doing so would be an awkward mess I was unwilling to face right now. His ability to touch without his visions was a big deal, and I wanted him to enjoy it.

We lounged on the couch in the living room Donovan redesigned for practical usage. Large pieces of furniture sat amongst Aunt Lacey's catalogue creation of expensive decor, historical artifacts like carved masks, and sentimental pieces including the framed faces of present and past Coveners.

The surprising part of chilling out together was it never led to sex. I figured he would be jacked to get me naked, but he wasn't. We cuddled up under a wool blanket surrounded by snacks and a snoring Bosco, always touching, squeezing every moment without the inconvenience of the visions in a contentment I never pictured him.

Running his fingers with a feathered touch along the skin of my forearm, lips to my shoulder where my tank top didn't cover. I pulled him closer and casually ran my fingers along his skin, then saw him watching me in my peripherals in the illumination of the TV in the dark room. A sad sensation crossed our connection. Maybe sad was too strong, but something sorrowful was on his mind. He didn't say anything, but it was there.

Mid-way through an action flick I felt the first spark of his visions. I kissed him deeply and kept our fingers entangled until he could no longer ignore whatever the visions were imposing on him. He still held me close, but I kept the blanket between us. It wasn't the same, and the sense of his loss was a heartbreak I fought to soothe.

3

SMELLS LIKE BURNT CHEESE

Breath quickened within the man's chest beneath my hand, my attention busy in a Soul Reading, sifting through present-day memories of Blake warning the man whose soul I read of a multitude of "Don't you dare" disclaimers before walking through Donovan's door.

Elbowing by the present to sift through boring-as-nails family outings, getting into minor legal trouble with friends, sidestepping embarrassing moments I never wanted flitting across my brain for more than the flash of skin I was subjected to, searching for—

"He checkout?" Blake's impatient voice floated around me as I was too enveloped by his friend Tyler's memories as a test since Blake wanted him to join the Sect.

Mr. Impatient groaned when Jared shushed him, ever ready to keep his best friend in line.

Like my first Coven meeting experience, Tyler's began with a harmless invitation to a tea leaf reading party. Tyler was ignorant to the full scope of the operation running in Donovan's basement and was creeped out by the *"chick gettin' handsy with me."* His thoughts said as much, even if he didn't tell me outright.

Digging into Tyler's past came with a reason. I needed to gauge his ability to keep the secret, which was a crapshoot and could change depending on circumstance. His soul didn't glow, but I wanted to see if there were latent abilities and discover potential barriers keeping him from engaging in the power.

At least that's what Kim decided I should be looking for in Sect recruits, which I think was her way of keeping me distracted from focusing on the fact Caine was missing meeting after meeting as we failed to figure out a way to get back in the Creation to save him. Kim's plan sounded solid but gave me top-level skeeze vibes and was more like being a seedy voyeur than a soul detective seeking out nuggets of treachery. And, so far, I hadn't given a flat out "no" to anyone.

This one was easy.

Some souls are more cryptic than others. Tyler's was wide open, no scuttling from my intrusion, intrigued yet with a passive go-with-the-flow attitude.

Deep within Tyler, I caught a glimpse of what I needed. An overall feeling rather than a visual of the obstacle he would face. With the knowledge I needed, I let go of Tyler's essence, the way Vincent taught me, and removed my hand from his chest.

"So?" Blake egged.

Thumping Blake's shoulder with a weighty hand, Jared attempted to thwart his buddy's enthusiasm, always playing peace-keeper and caretaker of his friends and Coveners. Blake was beyond containment and shrugged Jared off, looking to me for answers.

I focused on Tyler since I was reading him. "You check out."

Blake gave a triumphant cheer until I asked to speak with Tyler in private. His smile dusted into an offended glare before Jared dragged him away.

"Sorry." Tyler rubbed his hand over the stubble of his shaved head, his dark eyes searching back to his friends before moving back to the "weird girl" in front of him.

I smiled as his thoughts were as open to me as his soul. "It's all good. I just figured you could use some distance."

Tyler gave a breathy laugh.

"I know you've got no idea what's going on and think Blake and Jared either roped you into some weird role-play shit—sorry, no random orgy's going to break out tonight or any night." He looked down as his cheeks reddened, so I hurried my assessment. "And no one's playing a well-devised prank. You won't end up embarrassed on social media, and everyone here are good people. Well, Denise is a wretched bitch, but she's dating my brother, so we tolerate each other."

Tyler laughed more casually this time, as did I, happy to see him relax. "So, what exactly are you doing?"

"I was searching your soul for a few things. Yeah, I know, strangest thing you've ever heard. Understand, this group needs to be sure their secrets are kept secret when you leave." Tyler's forehead creased, not understanding my vagueness. "My main objective is searching for what may become an issue. To see if you're up to being more open-minded like the rest of them."

This was no better. He nodded, slowly, agreeable yet clueless.

Fuck it. "You don't believe for a second there's anything special going on here."

Tyler tensed.

I smiled. "It's okay. You think we're all cat-lady crazy but are intrigued because your friends must've brought you here for a reason. A reason you don't get and wish they kept their freaky Saturday night adventures to themselves."

"Um—I—"

"You won't believe me or them until you experience it. Was the same for me, so I get it."

I rose my power a bit, enough to open a window into Tyler's mind. *"Almost anyone can do this with some practice."* I watched as Tyler's split right eyebrow raised, he searching from my eyes to my unmoving lips. *"Jared and Blake can't, at least I don't think so, though they can do some freaky shit. Everyone here is special in some way."*

I waited for him to breathe and gather what he was going to say in his head before it escaped his lips.

"Everyone?" He scanned the room again with different eyes.

I smiled, trying to look half-way friendly. "Pretty well. All very different from each other."

"And you run the show?"

"Nah, son. Kim, redhead on the left," I pointed in her direction talking to Gwen near the stairs, "she's co-Sect Leader with Donovan. He owns this house." I heard Tyler's mental assessment of Kim as an emphasized *"cute"*, then his great surprise as he looked to Donovan sitting at the back table focused on papers strewn atop of it comprising of the dreaded premonition we were trying to interpret, Tyler thinking Donovan was a hell of a lot more than cute. Regret floated around the thought.

"I get the feeling you haven't told people you're gay, or bi, or however you identify judging by how guarded your assessments of our Sect Leaders were."

Tyler spun back to me, shock plain on his expression.

"It's fine. I would never tell anyone whether you joined us or not. Your story to share or to hide under your pillow. And in case that's your worry, no one's allowed here with that brand of hate, but since others can read your thoughts, it may not stay secret from Jared and Blake for long if they don't know already. Joining us could mean taking a leap. Selfishly, it's a comfort you're good at keeping secrets, though I'm sorry you've needed to keep yours."

A clear war battled across his face—one he wasn't ready to fight. If I never saw him again, I was willing to bet this was why. Joining would be more than a fun weekend group. It would potentially mean a lifestyle change.

"I did your initial assessment because of my Soul Reading ability, but Kim and Donovan take point in the meetings. If you don't come back, you can't tell anyone what you've learned here. We have ways to make it so you can't, but we'd rather not mess with your memory unless pushed to. It's a waste of essential ingredients and can get messy when your memories are full of holes.

"No one's forced to be here, so don't let Jared or Blake drag you back if you'd rather be anywhere else but in some basement, practicing what we do. Also, if you can't wrap your head around the idea of what's going on here, that mindset will be to your detriment and would negate the reason for coming back, so don't bother.

"And sidenote, there's a nasty side to all of this. All the good versus evil you see in the movies is real, or a version of it at least, and a few months ago we lost people. No, I'm not saying how, but if Blake and Jared were upset and not talking about why, it's because we lost our original Coven Leader." I heard the question in his head before he said it and refused to go over the deaths the Coven recently endured. I hoped I said enough so he could ask Jared and Blake questions before deciding.

Quiet with his thoughts, once I had said everything I was supposed to, plus a bunch Kim would have probably wished I kept to myself, Tyler rejoined his friends, blank stared. I had seen the look before, probably wore it the first day I walked into the basement and felt sympathy for Tyler's future sleepless nights.

There had been a few additions to the Coven members in the last few months with our highest attendance record yet. Not because of those numbers diminishment in the fight to trap Evaristus but because everyone was in full magic mode since then. Almost everyone present for the fight had gone through a remarkable transformation in outlook for the direction of the Coven. If you were going to be in it, they believed you should be actively working your craft, whatever it happened to be, or you were wasting everyone's time.

This was a huge change from Aunt Lacey's reign, the blame laying solely on Donovan's shoulders as he was guilty for engraving the idea into their minds. In the beginning he felt the opposite until he realized their progression, or lack of, could also bring their end since their cockiness grew exponentially with their talents. The

Coveners were adults and responsible for their evolution. As long as no one looked down their noses at any others who didn't feel the pressure of advancing their powers before every meeting, it didn't matter.

Done with the new guy, Kim approached me and squinted, grabbing my chin, and turning my head to the side and poking behind my ear. "What is that?"

I swatted her away. "What does it look like?" It wasn't a secret, hence my uncharacteristic ponytail.

"I thought all the new metal was a mood. But a tattoo? Ink doesn't disappear when you get tired of it. When'd you do it?" Her question came with crossed arms and a glare as if I left her out of the experience.

"Last night." I explained the hours spent with Fox, the charging required for our tattoos, and the result it had on Donovan's visions.

"Are you really surprised he wouldn't want the connection removed?"

"I know he wants it, I just figured he'd like to have a break where he can drink and get in bar fights or whatever the hell he does when we're not together."

"Please, he's too terrified."

"You sound sure of yourself."

Her brow arched. "If he doesn't have the connection, it's one less thing to keep you interested, and he knows the relationship is hanging by its fingernails. He needs it like some need an anchor baby."

This was disconcerting. I didn't like the way Kim made Donovan's and my relationship sound so tenuous, even if it was true. Outside appearances were one thing, but I wondered where Kim's evaluation had derived.

Kim was on the grouchy side today, so her optimism was nonexistent while cynicism reigned in its absence. I didn't argue. It was tense with Kim and Frog lately, so I figured she was projecting some frustration onto me.

"Well, whatever. Donovan and I are fine, though it'd be nice to see each other outside of this house."

"That's your fault, too."

I thought I might reach out and slap her. "I love you like the cool sister with the kickass wardrobe, Kim, but you're being a bitch."

"Ugh." Her shoulders slumped. "I know. I'm wearing it like a second skin I can't shed."

"Leave it to Denise to fill the Coven quota. She's enough bitch for us all."

"I'm still right." She earned herself the same look. "Donovan acts like he has all the right moves, but he's following yours."

"I'm all for righteous eighties Tom Cruise references, but if it turns into a football analogy, I'm sending you home to watch serial killer documentaries like a normal, well-rounded human being."

She took an impatient inhale and squared her shoulders to me. "Unless you tell him you want to see him outside of this house it'll never happen. Probably because he thinks you're ashamed to parade him around with this whole Caine thing happening. Everyone here knows you went from some great rescue and whirlwind love with Caine and then the next day you were with Donovan. They don't know all of what happened, but they know enough, including the connection stuff. He has no shame and refuses to let others' opinions on his life mean a damn thing to him, but he knows you care enough for the both of you, so he won't force it to be a public thing."

"What?" Shit, she was right. "Fuckweasal."

"Mhmm. You've got to take control of this one. If moving forward is what you want to do."

Donovan was a mind reader, an actual one, but we kept our thoughts guarded from everyone including from each other since I started working with Vincent, which happened to be immediately after returning from closing the Creation Caine was now stuck in. Of course Donovan would think it was because of Caine.

"Salix?" Blake's tentative voice broke my thoughts. "Sorry, Sophie." He forgot not to use Coven names around newbies, and Tyler wasn't far away.

"Yeah?"

He looked at Kim and then me. "Sorry about the picture. It's not my business if you're doing Vincent, I was just looking out for Donovan."

Kim crooked her head at me. "What's that now?"

"Oh. No. It's fine. Thanks."

"I mean—"

"Really, Blake. It's fine."

Disbelief it was all forgotten still clouded his eyes, but he nodded and rejoined Jared and Tyler.

Kim poked my shoulder. "Doing Vincent?"

"Dude! Shut your face. Like I need more rumours flying around. Bad enough Blake thinks it."

Kim leaned against the wall. "Slutty McSlutterson. No wonder Donovan hides you away like a kept mistress he also calls cousin."

"'Kay. You're being a bitch again."

Kim crossed her arms and exhaled heavily as I tried not to parrot her attitude.

"I'm not doing Vincent. Blake's a moron who jumped to conclusions like a tabloid journalist getting bored of hairless clam-shots."

"He took a picture of you with Vincent? Did you have your hairless clam out?"

"Well, if all the hottest celebs can do it, why can't I?"

She gave me another eyebrow raise, refusing to engage until I told her something.

"It's not like I was stroking him off under the table with my toes. We were at a diner together. Fully clothed. Blake saw us, snapped a paparazzo pic, and sent it to Donovan."

Kim laughed.

"Not funny. Look, I'll tell you what I told Donovan because I can't stand lying anymore. For the past few months, Vincent and I have been working on something." Kim pulled a face. "I can't say what because he doesn't trust anyone at this point. Believe me, I'm wearing him down and will tell you as soon as I can."

"Hmm. I'd rather you be screwing him. I'd imagine it'd be boring compared to Donovan, but he's had centuries to perfect—"

"Stop it. I'm not doing him."

Her gaze narrowed to a slit, staring at me. "This smells like burnt cheese."

I rolled my eyes. "I'm not skinning unicorns or pulling the wings off fairies, but I can't confirm or deny anything further."

"Fine."

Fine was never fine when coming from Kim's mouth. At least she knew something was going on. Not that it helped her attitude.

Not wanting to say anything more as Kim was too negative right now to dig herself out, I called for everyone to take a break for food. It wasn't my job, but the Coveners listened regardless.

As usual the delectable eats were put together by Louise. Once she returned to the meetings, her food didn't hold the love it had before, and it took a while of leftovers before her heart was back in it. No one outside her immediate family and friends attended Henry's funeral, and Louise didn't attend the first few meetings after her husband's passing until Kim and I went to her home to speak with her about returning.

Same with Deidra. Losing her girlfriend Rachel was too much, but she eventually returned after travelling out of the country for a bit. It was a dreadful prospect to go to anyone's house after their loved one died to convince them to return to a Coven responsible for the death of their one true love.

In a way, it wasn't the first time Kim and I had done it. Not in exact terms, yet same idea when we, plus Vincent, entered Eli and Bernadine's cozy living room and turned it into a place to bear bad news. While Bernie broke down hearing of their daughter Jet and Caine's entrapment within Diluculo, Eli was fierce. We hadn't thought bringing Vincent would come in handy the way it did until Eli's power almost decimated everyone in the room including himself. Able to grasp Eli's essence and hold it firmly within his fist, as only as Soul Extractor can, Vincent talked Eli down while Kim and I pleaded with Bernie to allow Vincent the room to set Eli's head straight.

Thankfully, Jet's son Andy was on a playdate with a neighbour kid or learning the day his mother may never come back would have been a nightmare he would replay in his sleep.

Once tempers cooled and Vincent put Eli's soul back, his anger turned and, without needing their permission, was set to join in any way possible to reopen Diluculo and retrieve his family. At first, Vincent protested, claiming Eli's vengeance could only fuel evil and may rocket him down the same path as the rest of the Tainted Berisford family. Even if it saved his daughter and nephew, neither Caine nor Jet could live with themselves for being Eli's downfall. That path was constructed with the greedy and ignorant souls of Berisfords for centuries. It didn't need Eli's too.

I promised to get them back. The memory of Bernie's sad eyes was what drove me to seek progress when leads stalled out. Unfortunately, even with contacts—reputable or other—not even Vincent could promise such a thing. Now, he was focused on taking down the Sovereignty, and I was left with requests for daily progress reports from Eli, and I never had much to offer. Not even Olive could find anything in the Ballard attic.

Sometimes focusing on what was right in front of you was easier.

Since everyone was heading upstairs for food and Donovan's concentration was allocated to the papers in front of him, I walked to the back of the room as the basement emptied and sat across from him. No doubt he knew I was there, though he didn't acknowledge my presence.

"Have we never had, like, a date-date 'cuz you think I'm ashamed of you?"

"Yes." He responded without lifting his gaze, eyes still reading over a sentence of the premonition on the pages in front of him like a rigid typewriter.

I felt my lips open in a silent gasp. "Fucknuggets. I can't believe Kim was right. I'm totally your kept mistress you call cousin."

He didn't comment, but the connection was twisted with his confusion.

"I'm not ashamed of you."

Taking a breath, eyes still preoccupied, Donovan shifted the papers in his hands. "Maybe not, but you're ashamed of yourself for being with me. Basically the same thing."

Was it? Either way, it equalled us holing up in this house and pretending like it was normal that I essentially treated it like my second home. Even if it began as a mode of safety from our mounting enemies, we now spent the days having sex and straying from conversations like these.

I knew how he felt about me, how could I not? Did he know how I felt about him? Wait. How did I feel about him? If I didn't know, he sure as fuck didn't. And I never attempted to tell him because I didn't want to complicate things while in a whirlwind of survival mode.

Damn. I felt like an asshole. Deserved to feel like one for leaving him hanging and expecting his satisfaction with whatever feels I threw his way. Chances are I didn't chuck any at him. This made me a raging hypocrite. I knew exactly what it was like to ride the roller-coaster of another's unwillingness to be present or aware of their action's emotional repercussions. It left the one on the ride from hell in a state of hypervigilance, questioning what they did wrong.

How could I let this happen?

The tips of my ears burned with my cheeks, the heat of my racing pulse climbing up my chest into my throat and visibly darkening Donovan's skin. He shifted in his seat and narrowed his eyes at the page as if fighting to concentrate and ignore my heightening agitation. And still, he wouldn't say anything. I made him feel as if he couldn't, as if he didn't have a voice in this, because he didn't. At times he tried, and it was either untimely, as when I was still with Caine, or it was too soon after Caine and I broke up or when he was trapped in the Creation, as was my current excuse for not facing this.

The emotions scurrying between us were an amalgamation of a

tattered mess neither could unravel right now, not in the middle of a Coven meeting.

At odds with how I believed my life was going and how everyone else so clearly saw differently, I took off upstairs, blinking through the sting in my eyes and ignoring the shake of my chin. I didn't remember slipping on my boots before walking into the street, but the crunch of snow under them told me I had. The plan was to jump in my car for a few moments of escape, but I was blocked in by Conveners' vehicles. Needing fresh air, I wasn't going back in, and not even the chilled backyard could dampen my self-deprecation, so I took off on foot.

Cold wind blew through me, doing nothing to cool my overheated skin. Eyes down and thoughts inward, I kept trying to remember a conversation with Donovan that may have given him a sense at where I was in this whole relationship mess and came up with ones where I ended up walking away or focusing on myself and my fears instead of listening for two seconds about what he thought.

He was formidable and persistent and much more patient with me than most others, and I shit all over his efforts. Vincent even pointed this out a couple of times, and those times, again, I brushed him off and avoided the topic, happy to leave the conversation to another day when it was more convenient to deal with. Now, I was doing it again.

I stopped and looked up from the snow-packed sidewalk intent on going back and facing Donovan, finding none of the houses around me familiar.

I started back the way I came. I was directionally challenged, but didn't I walk in a straight line? Did I turn any corners?

An icy wind blew up and battered me, throwing my hair around my face, making me stop and brace myself in only my sweater until it stopped. When it died down, I continued on, confused, quickening my pace to a fast walk as I retraced the steps I took.

I stopped again when I saw the sidewalk ahead of me had a layer of fresh snow covering it. If I was just here, my boot prints would be visible.

"What the fuck is happening?" No one was there to answer, and I sure as hell didn't know.

Everywhere I looked I was dipped in confusion, unable to distinguish one house from another, assuming I was stuck in side-street hell in an unfamiliar town, truly a lost cause. Yet, I saw no street signs in the distance. How could the blocks be that long? They couldn't be.

Donovan's worry began as a subtle niggling and then doubled, hitting me as if he registered my panic. How could he only notice it now? Maybe he realized I was gone off-property and not in the backyard. In flight mode, too locked in my thoughts to pay attention, I forgot my phone back at the house, still in the basement where I left it while doing Tyler's reading.

My toes were freezing, a sign Donovan was outside, the snow soaking through his shoes. The freezer-burnt sensation of my ears, my numb cheeks, and nose tip doubled. He was frustrated, and I didn't blame him. This was fucked up and having him out here searching for me made me feel like a moronic damsel in distress and more of an asshole considering how I had treated him lately.

"Sophie." I spun to the voice calling my name and saw a woman standing in the middle of the empty street.

How did I not notice her sooner? She was the only thing out here with me and far too beautiful to bypass without a second glance. Her dark hair flowed in the wind instead of being thrown around, her complexion Photoshop's nightmare, and her dark soul a blotch against the white snow around us.

Shit. She was Tainted and somehow knew my name.

Donovan's frustration turned to fear. Or was that what I was feeling? I didn't mean to be scared, but I was lost and freezing. If I had to escape, I wouldn't know where to head for safety.

My lungs burned as if Donovan was running while I tried to slow down my heart rate and convey confidence I was empty of.

The woman glanced down the street. I followed her line of sight and saw Donovan running towards us, the street around us familiar again, complete with cars driving down a side-street in the distance. Did the woman alter what I saw to get me lost?

Donovan's attentions were glued to the woman, the crease between his eyes one of surprised denial gaining my attention.

She nodded her head once. "Donovan."

The woman knew him as well.

He slowed as he reached me and stared at her, a little shake to his head as a heavy cloud of breath hung in front of him.

"I know this is strange for you, to see me after so many years. And my apologies for taking advantage of you, Sophie. Your being lost and freezing was not my intent, though resulted in what I had hoped for." She looked back at Donovan. "When I imagined seeing you again, this was not what I envisioned."

I knew I wasn't that hopeless. I would get lost during trick or treating as a kid, but I could walk a straight line and know where I came from.

The woman smiled, a flash of dimples deepened, and I heard Donovan's breath catch.

Holy shit. It couldn't be.

"Why are you here?" My question broke the silence as my lips quivered, teeth chattering against Donovan's numb bewilderment so strong it made concentrating difficult. I could make a good guess at the woman's identity, but her dark soul added another layer to how messed up this impromptu meeting was.

Gaze swaying in my direction, the woman spoke confidently above the wind. "I've come bearing information and a bit of advice. Reopening Diluculo will start a chain reaction and you have no idea how far the falling dominoes will reach or what they will knock down in your pursuit to release the Berisfords."

Geez, does everyone know about it? "Why do you care? By the looks of your soul, releasing Evaristus would be like resurrecting Jesus."

I felt an inward cringe from Donovan at this and wished I had revealed the state of her soul glow with a little more tact.

"Evaristus is an imbecile. I do not follow his doctrine anymore than I follow Tobias's."

Donovan's dread shifted to conflicted relief.

Her eyes swept to him. "I left your father's faction long before you. Regardless of my loyalties, my suggestions should be considered. Trapping Evaristus and Loring was the best thing for our side. They are reckless in their flamboyant pursuit to enlighten the Blind. I would rather the Blind be extinguished than to be aware of our kind's existence, but I do need my coffee poured like everyone else, and the Blind are the closest you get to useful slaves of convenience. Reopening Diluculo will unleash Evaristus, and you will never trap him again. In doing so, he will rejoin the human world instead of hiding in his Creations. We will all suffer."

"Why not deal with it yourself?" It was the first time Donovan spoke, his voice low and hesitant.

She tilted her head. "I know you're beyond the naïveté you speak with, Donovan. Your father alone will be ready for the moment of Evaristus's escape. Not only will the Sovereignty never allow it,"—she turned to me—"and you won't infiltrate them no matter the surveillance runs you post. They're far more skilled than average Magics." She looked back at Donovan as my cheeks heated against the brisk frost. "Some covens will gather against your attempt."

"What's it to you?" The guarded challenge in Donovan's voice was shaky.

"Like I said, we don't need a Magic like Evaristus on our side. He exposes us and makes life more difficult to muddle through. You can't exactly use someone if they know they're being manipulated, now can you? Of course, I have my own motives that hold no bearing over this. Botching Tobias's plan would sure give it a shiny Yule bonus."

"What does he plan to do?" I wanted to know.

"Have you been listening?"

I felt like a scorned child, but it was Donovan talking next. "There has to be more, Rosemary." He knew her name. This surprised me. "You wouldn't seek us out to let us in on something we could have guessed on our own. What do you want?"

"A truce."

"What?" I shivered through the word.

"You need more help while your people are split between getting into Diluculo, since you have no idea how, plus your ridiculous fantasy of breaking down the largest establishment of our kind on either side."

"Why wouldn't you bring this to the Elders? We have no authority."

"Oh, you do." Rosemary smirked and showed off those dimples again. "Others within your flock will follow your lead. The foretelling makes that clear. I fully expect you will bring my proposition to the counsel as a whole, and its democratic process will result in its swift dismissal. But believe me when I say they will come around so quickly you won't have time to wallow in failure."

How did Rosemary know so much? Maybe she had the powers of clairvoyance. She wasn't the only one, and there were going to be some trying times coming our way whether they led to the events she stated or not.

"Consider my proposal. Seek out your Elders. Expect resistance, and I will contact you soon."

"We're reopening the Creation. If you're not on board with that, then we have no truce to consider." I needed this to be clear.

Rosemary took a moment. "Compromises can be made. We have to start somewhere."

She turned and walked away from us without speaking further about it or talking more to Donovan who so clearly had so much to say to her.

"We need to get back." He took hold of my arm and was guiding me away, looking back for Rosemary who had disappeared.

"That was your mother, wasn't it?"

"Could be." The dissociation in his voice spurred a bushel of questions I couldn't make myself ask him.

We made our way back to the house. I was right. I hadn't gotten far, and whatever she did orchestrated the meeting.

When we got inside, the rush of warmth had me shaking out my body as if I could rid myself of the cold. Instead of rejoining the others in the basement, Donovan waved me upstairs. As we reached the cocoon of his room, I jumped onto his bed and pulled the blankets up around my shoulders as he ripped his sweater off and replaced it with a warm one from his dresser and tore off his wet socks before sitting on the edge of the bed.

"Your dimples. They're hereditary." Rosemary had them, not to mention how familiar her eyes were. Everything spoke of her being Donovan's mother. Though she showed no motherly proclivity, it didn't mean she hadn't created him.

"I haven't seen her since I was," he paused, "maybe five or six." He struggled with a fresh sock since his feet were damp. "I told you before I didn't know who my mother was, but none of the other women had dimples, and neither does Tobias, so it was an easy guess. It's not like she was my actual mother, like *your* mother is a mother. She was a womb, chosen with purpose."

Ouch. While true, how horrible a practice it was for his father's coven to engage in. Tobias pegged himself the ultimate father, while mothers had no influence on their child's lives. Typical narcissistic asshole. Being unable to know who birthed you, but knowing it was someone you saw on a regular basis, would be maddening. My fists clenched at the thought. How could Donovan live surrounded by lies and hidden truths as a daily routine meant to be accepted? Heartbreaking for an innocent child. No wonder he had attachment issues.

He finished getting his socks on and leaned his elbows into his knees, running his fingers through his dishevelled hair. "She left my father's coven for another. Headline news back then, but I was a kid and didn't care to understand."

I crawled to him and wrapped my arms and the blanket around the both of us, hoping to surround him in a brand of caring and support he lacked as a child. I laid my head against his back, staying there as he rubbed my sleeved-covered arm and sank into my embrace.

"I'm sorry your family is popping out of the woodwork like a macabre and traumatic version of *Whack-A-Mole* when you don't have a mallet or a way to end the game. What do you want to do about them? Or, what can we do?"

Fox verified his brother and father were enough to fear. I didn't like the thought of any of Donovan's Tainted family weaving their way into our lives, even if it gave Donovan a chance to face them and what they did to him. This wasn't family therapy. His brother and father wanted to control him in a way they never could when he was younger, and his mother wanted him but not in a loving, motherly way. They all had an agenda resulting in Donovan having to give up aspects of his current life.

He turned to face me, fussing with the blanket to keep it around us and rubbing his hands over my cold jean-clad thighs. "I'm not fully unprepared. I knew they would try, eventually. Well, at least I knew my father and brother couldn't stay away forever. Rosemary is a surprise I doubt even my father anticipated."

I mirrored his cockeyed, guarded smile. Nothing about this was foreseeable, as far as I was concerned. Sure, his family sounded certifiable, but they have had years to come after him. Anticipating their involvement wouldn't change my fear of what this addition of danger meant for us.

In our closeness, I found myself holding my breath too long, trying to regulate the shake of my body, happy for Donovan to interpret this as a reaction to the lingering cold. "Rosemary was confident in her intel. She trusted whoever told her or is putting a lot of faith in a premonition we haven't totally figured out yet."

"Which is another thing. How she knows about it at all is questionable."

A good point I could only shrug at. Regardless of how Rosemary found out or if the Elders agreed to her truce, this did nothing to sway me from my mission to release the survivors from the Creation. With the possibility of letting out Evaristus or even Loring—if they survived being entrapped—Donovan knew I would risk my life and a civil war. No amount of arguing would change my mind.

"I didn't mean to send you running."

He surprised me out of thoughts of Vincent or Ranlyn locking me in a basement somewhere to keep me from cracking open the Creation. "Oh. Umm, you didn't. I didn't realize how bad I've been treating you. Kim knew. Maybe others did, too. If so, that makes it worse. To hear you felt as you did, and hadn't put me in my place, made me realize what a mangy douche I've been. I know what it's like to have my feelings dismissed or unrecognized as something remotely important enough to register. I wasn't doing it on purpose and was more so ignoring my own feelings at your expense, intentional or otherwise."

He nodded but didn't comment.

I shrugged the blanket tighter around my shoulders. "I needed free-thinking air, and there were too many people here. You don't deserve the mop bucket treatment, but at the same time, this isn't easy for me. Well, the parts with talking and clothing on, anyway."

He smiled then raised a brow. "Mop bucket treatment?"

"Taking you out when I need you and then sticking you back in the closet without a second thought. Like a mop bucket."

"Right. I'd like to think I have more purpose than a mop."

I giggled. "Yeah, you do. To more than just me, even if I've rejected any attempts to label whatever we might be to each other."

"There's no label for what this is." Cocky or blank-faced was Donovan's default. The seriousness with which he delivered this stripped me down without touching my clothes, the heat in my face an elevation in blood pressure that also shone through his dark eyes.

I managed to nod and stare across at him but not much else. He was right and left me without argument. No modern labels could be slapped on our old souls and stick with any amount of validity. And the term "soulmates" also didn't fit. We weren't a perfect match. If anything, our souls were mated, and we discovered ways we fit beyond the normal definitions of perfect. Complementary and contrasting ways equalling something with a big dash of sense.

This didn't mean it settled well in my gut, which slithered like a bag full of snakes, unfamiliar with this level of intimacy.

He straightened and gave a breathy sigh as if registering the sensation within me. "You've been through a lot. I didn't wanna push. When you asked if I thought you were ashamed of me, it was the asswipe in me answering."

"The ass-wipe in you is honest."

"Still. You deserved a half-decent explanation." His tongue ran across his lips in a quick swipe. "I know you love me. You don't say it, but I know it. And I know what's between us is real and that I'm only slightly terrified you'll get back with Caine if he's still alive and we manage to free him." A hint of a smile lightened the tension. "You can't find it in you to be open to accepting us as we are. Not until this Caine stuff is taken care of. I wish our relationship wasn't dependent on his rescue, though I'm willing to lay low 'til then or until whenever you're comfortable doing more than messing up my sheets."

"Hmm." Seemed like a better answer than crying, which I didn't want to do.

"You could read all about my willingness to take it slow if you dropped the mental barricades."

"Technically, you would just need to drop yours."

"Goes both ways, babe. As long as yours are up, so's mine."

Fair. In his place, I would do the same, though probably wouldn't handle it as well.

He sat back and smirked at me. "Soooo, surveillance, huh?"

I felt my mouth open, forgetting Rosemary had ratted me out.

4

———

TAINTED REUNIONS

O kay, fine. Donovan knew about the surveillance runs on the Sovereignty. Whatever. Vincent would get over it. Maybe. Probably. All Donovan knew about was the surveillance of the Sovereignty members and trying to figure out which had Tainted souls and were deemed untrustworthy, something Vincent couldn't figure out on his own since he wasn't a Soul Seer. Figuring out which members were on which side was important to Vincent's plan, which I didn't elaborate on because it was the extent of what I knew. Donovan didn't push it as the instantaneous wave of shame rolled off of me, but his curiosity nudged the connection. In his position, I would want to know everything, but surveillance details would come secondary to being fixated on why he couldn't tell me and why Vincent gained precedence over remaining honest with each other. His restraint was impressive and made me feel worse for keeping him in the dark.

As we rejoined the Coveners, it was clear they all thought we had snuck off for some one-on-one time. In a non-sexual way that was what happened, though sex was the only perceived reason for our absence.

Kim came towards me holding Bosco.

"We weren't having sex."

She covered his floppy ears with a ghastly look on her face. "His young mind shouldn't be subjected to your nonsense."

"In dog years he's probably older than you."

"But he's still a virgin."

"I just met Donovan's mother."

Kim's blinked at the 180-degree shift in topic as Donovan's stare fell heavy on me.

"What?" I rolled my eyes at him. "Kim's your co-Sect Leader. We can't bring this sketchy deal to the Elders without her knowing first."

Donovan surveyed the area around us. Others hovered in the living room, so we took a seat at the table in the near empty kitchen. The title of "mother" may not have fit as snuggly as a baby in a bassinette, even if it's what Rosemary was whether she rose to the role or not. We went over the conversation and proposed truce.

Kim dipped a chip into some kid of orange-coloured dip. "No way the Elders would agree to a truce. Maybe Vincent. Never Veata or Ranlyn."

"And the bit about forgoing the reopening of the Creation was a deal-breaker." I felt it necessary to repeat this again and again if needed.

Donovan leaned back in his chair and crossed his arms. "Even if it's Caine's own damn fault." Kim stared at me as I stared at Donovan. "What? He jumped back in. I'm merely stating a fact. And since no one saw Jet before getting our asses out through the pass-way across the veil, we don't know what condition she's in. She could have also been kidnapped from the field. We have no way of knowing either way."

"He's alive." They looked at me, and Kim's eyes narrowed. "Like, when Caine was in the park, I wasn't one hundred percent, but now I am. I can't say the same for Jet, where she is or her condition, but Caine's alive."

I left out that I didn't know Caine's condition either. I wished I did. While he was stuck in his sleeping curse, I saw him every time I fell asleep, knew exactly how miserable he was, and I tried my best to lessen the dread of his never-ending nightmare. Now, I got to lie awake and imagine the horrors he was likely facing and chase away rebounding guilt for not rescuing him already. Or at least finding a way to connect with him beyond a gut feeling that he was still breathing. If Evaristus and Loring were still alive, it may mean he was enslaved as a Puppet. The thought of him in zombie-mode at my ancestor's whim was heartbreaking and caused a cramp in my chest every time I let myself think of it.

"Mmm." Kim was excited and took a moment to swallow the food in her mouth. "I wonder if Nya can connect with Gareth like they did when Caine was in the park. That's how you two were drawn to each other before, right?" This was debateable. "He's on a different plane, but so what? He was then, too."

I looked at Donovan, a slow burning anger was present, but this look was one of question. Did he think it was possible?

Donovan shrugged as he read me well without getting in my head. "New direction is a start." He got up and paced a step. "Let's assume we brain meld this, find a way to make contact. It'd come in handy when it came time to get survivors out. A strategy from the inside-out works far better than scrounging around in the dark. Even if we find a way inside, we still need to track down Caine or at least someone we know in there to make a quick and safe extraction. We made it out once. I'm not up for dying giving it a second try."

"Apparently you've given it some thought." Kim got a look of boredom from Donovan.

I shifted to bring a foot up onto my chair. "If it can be done, I'm game."

"No kidding, babe, but we still need a plan, and we won't get one from playing stalk the jock with Vincent."

"Stalk the jock?" Kim looked at me. "Is that like hittin' up the gay bar? Wait, is that where Blake really saw you and Vincent? Because that I could see."

"Kim."

"What? The guy wears loafers and presses his khakis."

"Stop it."

"Fine. Then what jock are you stalking?"

As with Donovan, Kim was jilted to hear about the secret surveillance runs. "Who knows if you can trust this guy. And don't tell me you can because you've known him for a thousand years. You haven't known him long in this life, so the others don't count. And now you're re-enacting some buried aspiration to be a modern Sherlock Holmes with tits? And keeping it from us at his insistence? You haven't died enough times in the last year? Because that's probably where you'll end up, and then he'll disappear for another hundred years or whatever."

"Wow." He drew out the word. "You really were bitten by a bitch bug tonight. You and Denise should team up."

Kim shot Donovan the finger.

"Hey, Denise!" Donovan yelled across the kitchen as Denise was out in the living room with some others. She came into the kitchen with suspicion. "Kim caught your bitch virus. Wash your hands better after using the washroom."

Denise's expression pinched, and she shot him the finger before disappearing back into the living room.

"Hey, you even speak the same language."

Shooting him a look capable of drilling holes through a body if she dosed it with a little power, neither Kim nor Donovan backed down.

"All right, children." I kicked the stool Donovan was sitting on to get his attention away from Kim's scowl. "Have you found out anything more about the premonition?"

Donovan straightened and rolled a shoulder as if shaking off irritation. "It's spirals of conjecture. Yes, we're supposed to reopen the Creation and split the Covens because we're awesome like that. I've been reading over a section that today's reappearance of Rosemary could shed light onto. I believe I can interpret a part of it as explaining a truce between us and Rosemary."

"What did it say about your evil mommy, exactly?"

Sharply spinning to Kim, Donovan recited by heart, "The unioned lead an adverse syndicate conceiving a renegade band which cracks foundations of the faithful in halves of seething snakes."

"What the fuck? That's what we're working with?" Donovan nodded at Kim. "In what dolphin to black bear language does that mean we're throwing in with mommy-dearest?"

Throughout the hours of staring at the creased and worn pages of the premonition he copied from Ranlyn, Donovan knew it forwards and backwards. I couldn't make sense of it, so when pieces like this popped up and fit snugly with the picture the obscure words painted, he knew there was no other likelihood.

"Rosemary approached me and Sophie, us being 'the unioned.' The Elders stated this when they first crossed the premonition due to our lives lived together through our connection. And if we were to join Rosemary, it would definitely be a 'syndicate of antitheticals'."

"Hmm." I side-eyed him. "You had to look that word up, didn't you?"

He popped a dimple my way. "It means opposites or contrasting."

"Oh, of course. I knew that." Kim raised her hand.

I raised my hand as well. "Yup. I totally knew that."

"Sure you did." He exhaled. "Working with Rosemary is definitely enough to break the Coven and make people turn on each other. Snakes, bears, wolves, tutu wearing mongoose, whatever animal you choose, they'll slaughter each other over this."

Cue the freakout.

Look at what I was sacrificing to get Caine out. The others too, but admittedly, I wouldn't be so gung-ho if I didn't know people on the inside. Vincent was champing at the bit for his chance to dismantle the Sovereignty, not that he would open his pretentious mouth and tell me why, and nothing he had shown me so far made me think the Sovereignty's downfall would benefit Magics' existence. I followed the lead of others I trusted, but how could I be sure they didn't either have their own agendas or were working off inaccurate information?

With a stink-pile of non-answers, I didn't know what to do and figured getting my hands on the premonition pages again and trying to decipher them myself would leave me with nothing but a brain-pounder of a headache. Besides, it wasn't Donovan's ability to decipher them I questioned, it was everyone's judgement, including my own, since I didn't know enough of anything to make an informed decision.

———

The fact the Barracuda was a summer vehicle had no impact on my decision to let it ride through winter squalls. No way was I locking her up in some garage for the season. It deserved to be showcased year-round. Especially since Canada had limited warm months and I could fix any rust or other damage with a push of healing power.

Car issues would be a welcome distraction if it meant not dealing with every other problem in my life.

Driving the Barracuda through the back roads to the Ballard Family Estate was beautiful. The snow-capped trees and icicles hung from their branches like a fantasy landscape. All completely unappreciated by my preoccupied mind.

I parked outside of the estate. Donovan and I waited for Kim who took more care on the roads. Olive didn't have a car, so we couldn't tell if she was home, though I hoped she was since the point of us being here was to pick her brain and search the attic for anything to help Nya within me connect with Gareth in Caine. Not that I needed an excuse to go through the attic shelves.

Leaving the car running to keep the heat on, I tightened an elastic around the end of my braided hair, amazed at how long it was getting, distracted by my thoughts. "Do you think we'd give a shit about bringing down the Sovereignty if we never found out the premonition said we would?"

Donovan shifted in the passenger seat to bring Bosco onto his lap. "Chicken and the egg head-fuck?"

"Made to order. I'd heard of the Sovereignty for all of five seconds before I was partly responsible for pulling its legs off."

Donovan smoothed back a long strand of hair I missed, a vision threatening to blind him.

I resisted the giddiness his almost-vision caused. "Exposing examples of evil within it, sure, why not? Bringing injustices to the public to cripple it? Peachy, I guess. Turning it into grave dust? How will actual injustices be handled without the lawmakers in place to hold them accountable?"

"Shove them into dog crates and stick oatmeal through the bars?" He joked but disappointment dripped like honey from my chest into my gut. "The Sovereignty isn't falling tomorrow, babe. We may not have the answers yet, but it doesn't mean there aren't others who've thought this through and have a master list of ideas on how to establish a solution."

He was right. If the premonition spoke of others following our charge for change, it meant someone had the foresight of what adjustments needed to be made, or at least an inkling and a roster of some rebellious, take-down-the-system type mofos who could breathe life into those changes.

Maybe that person was Vincent. I needed more from him. Next time I saw Vincent he would be schooled in my priorities. If he wanted my continued focus on all things Mission Sovereignty, then he was going to help everyone escape Diluculo.

Kim drove up behind us, and we climbed out of the Barracuda into the crisp day to meet up with her. Bosco ran to the nearest bush. As he lifted a leg, I noticed my cousin Serena's car was parked on the side of the estate, out of the way of potential blowing snow. The rest of the driveway was cleared, though no way Olive did it herself unless she had a spell to do the heavy lifting.

Heading under the arched entryway of the old mansion to stay out of the wind while waiting for Bosco to finish, I fished out the front door key. Unlike Donovan's, and Aunt Lacey's before him, Olive's door was always locked. Having the key was handy, even if we could unlock the door without a lock-pick kit. Donovan claimed to own one. Why? I decided against asking and would use a spell if it came down to it.

A few steps into the place and the bloom of magic from the estate —or whatever spirit resided within it—spread within my chest, welcoming and identifying me as the next heir when the time came.

Through the time warp that was the estate, be it the oval chandelier igniting the formal sitting room or the thick plank wood flooring, I loved every room as we headed up a grand staircase.

Pulling out and turning the decorative corner squares of the doorframe of one door amongst many on the second floor, the clicking within the walls told us we got things right. Even more when the door slid into the wall pocket to expose the rather small sewing room.

Boring to someone who assumed the sewing room served no other purpose. If the green-washed walls caught your eye, you weren't in-the-know.

I sat behind the antique sewing machine and used the wooden crank like a safe's combination lock. Four spins forward, two back, twelve forward, eight back, six forward and listened as the metal shelving unit popped from the wall like the house itself gasped at the intrusion.

Behind the shelving unit was a winding, metal staircase to the attic hiding all the family's magic essentials. I expected to find Olive when I pushed up into the attic access door, instead, Serena and Jared were together on the meditation area pillows.

"Oh, shizznizz!" I backed away, fleeing from what I saw going down, and knocked into Donovan. His damp-soled shoes slipped on the stair below him, the domino effect hitting Kim next. She flailed, clutching Bosco and the railing. Both their complaints echoed through the attic. I waited for the sound of rustling clothing to be done before yelling up an apology to my cousin and waiting another moment before popping my head up.

Jared was now a few feet away from Serena, his expression one of shock like they were caught fooling around by her parents. Odd to see such a large man look so small.

I stepped all the way into the huge space to let Donovan and Kim up behind me. "Sorry, guys. Guess we need a sock-on-the-doorknob system."

"I-I should go." Jared straightened the neck of his shirt as Serena laughed.

"Nopesies." I threw my jacket on Olive's desk chair. "You're staying. I might be a cock-blocking clam-closer, but I'm not rushing you out the door. There's plenty of rooms and privacy spells to go around. It's not my house, so don't fuck up the sheets unless you plan on laundry ruining your afterglow."

Serena pet Bosco before getting up and doing up the button of her jeans. "We're good, cuz. You and Van can have all the privacy and laundry fun you'd like."

"Van?" Jared and Kim questioned with extreme amusement as Donovan glared at me.

"It's Donovan. Always and only Donovan." No one would think to question his seriousness, and judging by their expressions, they were noting it for the future.

"You know," he said, grabbing hold of my belt loops, spinning me to face him before I could turn away, and pulled me close until his hips hit mine, "you don't have to tell your cousin everything."

Giggling, I wrapped my hands around his shoulders. "Firefly isn't for everyone either, but they do what they want."

"None of that!" Kim shouted across the vast space. "If they can't get naked," she pointed at Serena and Jared, "neither can you two, Firefly. Or you and Van can choose a room, let them get back to where they were, and I'll just leave."

Jared looked like he was going to pass out from embarrassment, distracting himself by focusing on my pug buddy looking tiny in the guy's hands.

Donovan made an irritated growl then pecked me on the lips

quick enough a lick of desire jolted through me before he made space between us.

"Where's Olive?" My voice carried across the attic to Serena.

"At some lunch thing, helping Uncle Lewis try and trigger Aunt Priscilla's memory."

Since the Apish Coffer was used to remove a protection webbing from around the Creation and stole every one of Aunt Priscilla's memories consisting of our Uncle Lewis, it was a hard road for everyone to watch. We made it our mission to make Priscilla comfortable, and slowly the memories of her husband and their life together started filtering back. Photo albums featuring the two proved they were married, as did their children. Her struggle was tragic, but struggle she did, finding her way back to Lewis a little more every day.

Having Olive gone was a snag. We could have made a precursory phone call to ensure she was home, but I needed a trip to the attic anyway. I loved the house in its entirety since the moment I set eyes on it as a dust-filled abandoned property, the memory of it stamped out of the minds of my family by my God-fearing and ego-shattered grandmother. The attic was a special place for us Magics. Not the whole family knew about it, but those who did couldn't deny the attraction to the hundreds of magical treasures it held. I needed a bit of time with the old-world charm of the estate before returning to work at The Lush the next morning—something connecting me to my roots, providing sufficient distraction while somehow still working towards the goal of reopening the Creation.

Drew took me back as a bartender, and Donovan loathed the fact I insisted on working at all after receiving the money I had from Olive, but those dollars wouldn't last forever, and I took a part-time post. According to Donovan's kidnapped-sister-slash-almost bride, Joelly, Drew and my co-worker Eddie were nearly killed by those after either her or me. Drew didn't make mention of it over the phone, so my guess was his memory was erased.

Another worry for tomorrow.

Since Nya's power within me fed off of surrounding energy, organic or otherwise, whatever entity of magic that was a part of the house became a constant supply of ammunition, which made using my power easier when adding in the powerful hum of the attic itself. The welcoming flood of energy in my chest was like a tight hug every time I entered the estate and may have been my true motivation for coming.

These days my trials consisted of the cohesion within aspects of power within me. Aunt Lacey and Vincent were certain if I could weave my vessel with the powers inside it, then using them would be more effective. It also benefitted Donovan since it caused him such pain. Nya's power was consuming, and when it took over, Donovan was an ant under my boot, unnoticed and unimportant, leaving him in a twisted heap.

Everyone found something to do. Donovan and Kim sifted through literature for anything that might unlock the Creation, even though Olive was certain from the beginning she didn't possess what was needed or even knew what it was that would do the job. I worked on being one with Nya's power, apologizing when it overwhelmed Donovan and caused him pain, which happened often. Jared and Serena were busy with each other. Practice was involved but couldn't have been too much considering the laughing happening. I wasn't sure how serious they were. Outward appearances showed them comfortable in the "having fun" stage, but if not somewhat serious, I hoped she didn't bring every one of her flings into the attic.

Cross-legged in the meditation spot Serena and Jared used to get better in touch, I filled myself with Nya's essence. Donovan was protected, acquainted with the buzz of power without the negative effects as I read the energies of those around me, settling on their soul glows as the hum resonated through me, making me heady and some-what disconnected from myself while Nya's power pressed its influence.

Pushing it further added something new to my sight. The objects around me held an energy I hadn't seen before. Kim examined something I saw as a ball of light. When I pushed it a bit more, most of the objects from the shelf shone until my eyes watered and shock vibrated within me. I didn't think the objects had souls like people, and the kaleidoscope of colours confused me more. No mention of this was in the Ballard Family Tome.

I was beginning to think the tome left out all the important stuff on purpose.

Reaching out the energized fingers Nya's essence provided, I tried envisioning Caine to find him in Diluculo. His short dark hair, thick brows, and grey eyes were fresh in my mind, yet nothing happened.

Remembering what it felt like during the fight with Evaristus when Caine evoked Gareth's power, I strived to connect with that instead.

I couldn't find him, but I found something else I worked to zero in on.

I heard Donovan call my name and felt the energy of his body as I kept my eyes closed.

"Did it work?" He spoke as if afraid to scare me.

"No. Nothing I've felt before. Not in Diluculo. Closer."

I worked harder to decipher the confusing sensation, worry evaporating as the curiosity of Nya's power ventured through the estate. "Are there people here?"

"You tell me." The hardness of Donovan's tone was an indicator of readiness if I confirmed there was.

With the thickness of the floor beneath us and the solid construction of the home, unless you booted the entry door as Adam once had, we had no way of knowing if anyone else was in the estate.

"I think someone's here. Nya's power is reading the energy of people on the main floor."

"People or Magics?"

I explored their energies, too loud to be Blind. "Magics."

"Maybe Olive's back." Kim's voice was now as close as Donovan's.

"No. They're men. They—" I gasped, eyes wide. "They're searching the house."

"How'd they get inside? Aren't there property wards?" Kim was right. The estate's wards should have kept any Tainted Magics away.

"Who's here?" Serena and Jared were now alarmed.

Donovan shushed everyone from bombarding me with questions. Serena tilted her head, looking at him as if questioning who he thought he was trying to shut her up. A look he ignored.

I stood, still focusing on my power picking up on the targets downstairs. "Tainted are searching the house looking for something to open the Creation. Olive closed it. They're assuming she can crack it back open." Even we thought the attic's shelves held the golden ticket inside the Creation.

We ran for the attic entrance, fighting to keep Bosco inside instead of following us. His scratching at the door and howling was loud enough to hear through the dense material. Donovan cracked the door to the sewing room entrance enough to see out in the second-floor hall. Footsteps raced up the stairs.

He shut the door without letting it click closed and looked at me. "Care to lower your mental defences, babe? Might be easier to coordinate a telepathic offensive attack."

Even if he was right, I was positive he was opportunistically getting inside my head. Since the others didn't have the power to shield their thoughts, they were already good to go. I gave in and took a moment to relax myself enough to open up the barricades around my thoughts.

With the pathways open, Donovan gave a command, and we spilled out into the empty hallway. Sounds found us first, the intruders ransacking the estate. Breaking glass infuriated me. These sheep-humpers were destroying items without care for their worth. Who knew how long they were here or who they were important to? It didn't matter if they could be fixed, the disregard for the inanimate objects lashed my power out like a whip as I was still partially fueled by Nya's power.

A dark-souled man barrelled up the stairs, turning to the left, his back to us. He forgot to check his corners and didn't see our small group. Donovan twitched in my periphery, ready to take the guy out, but I was faster. I reached out and swept the man off of his feet with a telekinetic hand up, keeping him from hitting the floor. A snap of my fingers silenced his potential screams and another quick yank had him at our feet.

"Cesso." Kim's quiet spell made the man slump, unconscious. I didn't know where she picked that one up, but it was effective and easy to remember. I made a mental note to use it in the future.

Donovan looked on in minute shock of how quick Kim and I worked. The moment passed, and he pointed to a room. *"In there."*

Jared gathered the one-hundred and ninety pounds of dead weight and laid him out on the floor of the bedroom Donovan suggested. When he came out, Donovan telekinetically shut the door and used a locking spell to keep the man contained. The man may have been out of commission, but that wouldn't stop his buddies from finding him. This would.

Donovan lifted his hand to stop Jared from closing the door to the sewing room, then motioned with his fingers to leave it open a crack, I assumed in case we needed a quick retreat into the attic. Jared followed orders by closing the door enough it appeared closed by anyone doing a quick search.

"Fan out," Donovan's voice echoed in everyone's head.

He cleared rooms on his way towards Olive's bedroom. Jared and Serena checked the other rooms as Kim and I went downstairs.

We heard movement skittering everywhere. Whoever the people were, they weren't afraid to make their presence known. Our cars outside indicated expected disruptions for our house invaders, maybe seen as a challenge since they knew their search would be interrupted. Probably yearned for the excuse to kill anyone brave enough to forge a counterattack.

I gave a wordless instruction for Kim to holdup as I wanted to search the minds of our intruders from a safe distance. A peek into one without their mental guard up told me they were Puppeteer devotees desperate to release their Master. Unlike so many others around Evaristus, these were not Puppets. They contained full control over their free will.

Deeper, I read that someone told the devotees about the attic and the treasures held inside yet were instructed to search downstairs for a secret passage to the basement where they may find what they searched for.

An image of a man flitted like a translucent picture in front of my eyes, picked up from a devotee's mind. The man was giving out the group's directives. Average, light hair, lighter eyes, a mustache covering obvious scarring of a hair-lip, and long scruffy beard. Wherever this man got his information, it was flawed, and only now did it make sense why the basement entrance was in the attic. No one would think to start at the top of the estate to work their way down, and the attic was safeguarded. Whoever built the house was a tricky SOB.

I knew where the basement was and that at one time it was used for torture, but I never ventured down there before. In a big old house, belonging to a family of Magics no less, I assumed secrets were hidden in every floorboard and light fixture and wondered if Olive was aware of all of them.

Everything looked important or potentially handy to unlock a pocket of existence within the veil. It could be anything.

Regardless of what they wanted, we needed to get them out of here without alerting their coven to send more devotees.

Murder wasn't a reflex and hopefully avoidable considering it was mid-winter and digging a grave would be difficult. And, of course, for the assumed reasons, I reminded myself, happy Kim couldn't listen in to my dark inner ramblings. Donovan wouldn't hesitate if the need arose, but I didn't want to shed blood in my ancestral home for any reason.

Squeaking at my side were Kim's bare feet on the hardwood. She rounded the corner into the front parlour and whispered the same spell as on the man upstairs. The young man, lanky with broad shoulders hidden beneath dark clothing, contrasting with his dyed blond hair hanging in his face, gasped, eyes wide and wheeled towards Kim.

Nothing happened. No passing out or freezing up. A self-satisfied laugh rumbled in his chest as his dark soul poisoned the space around him.

I bared down as a flare of his magic was aimed for Kim. Nya's magic lashed out, taking him over, his shirt lifting and covering his face, wrenching his head back. The fabric tightened and trapped his arms behind his back like a straitjacket, and he toppled to the side. I hit him again before he went down, throwing him onto an antique love seat, sealing his pant legs together at the seams, and twisting them up and back a foot away from reaching the top of his head.

He couldn't run, couldn't move. If he did, he had a better chance of suffocating himself. Unless he chewed his way through his shirt and could straighten his throat, he would calm his ass down or die in his panic.

I didn't know if the spell would hold up, but I had no intention of babysitting duty when more crashing spilled from another room.

I checked back once more and saw the man's open mouth against the fabric of his shirt. He was screaming, but no one could hear him. Would be a good indication he got loose once we could hear him freaking out.

"Nice touch, babe."

I gasped and turned with my hands up before realizing it was Donovan. A devotee wouldn't call me 'babe'."

He admired my work on the love seat. "Silenced as good as Hound was. Happy I could add to your repertoire."

"Who's Hound?" Kim kept her voice low, but they both were too loud considering more devotees were still skulking around.

We didn't explain who Hound was, and I skipped over that part when retelling her who Fox was. No time for it now.

Donovan kneeled at the bottom of the staircase, murmuring something. Serena and Jared interrupted him as they came down. He paused before continuing, then pressed his palm into the open area between the banisters. A shield stopped him from pushing further. "Now they can't double back, and it traps the other two up there."

"Two?"

He nodded. "Another's out and locked in Olive's bathroom. You didn't feel it?"

Donovan's version of someone being "out" was hands-on compared to Kim's method. I looked down at my knuckles. Nothing. The low hum of Nya's power must have blocked the pain and healed us, somehow leaving Donovan upright.

A deep voice from another room called for someone named Jeremy. Following the voice through the long room used for the estate's restoration celebration, working our way to the kitchen, the impatient person called for Jeremy again.

Out in the open of the long room, no banquet tables and chairs to use as cover, we were exposed. I proceeded in a fog of Nya's power and Donovan's cocky lust for confrontation. He took a lingering moment to look at me from eye to eye before proceeding. Something about my eyes tripped him up. They must look different with Nya's power activated.

We stopped as the deep voice calling for his friend became clearer with his heavy, booted footsteps. The owner of the frustrated tone came around the corner and skidded to a stop when he saw the five of us.

Nya's power drained and reared up, unstable, difficult to hang onto. "The dick-swab Tainted Photographer." His was the first Tainted soul I had ever seen. He showed up at our family reunion, snapped paparazzi pictures, and then baited me into a trap where Caine's father tried to end me electrocution-style in a storm drain. I couldn't forget his face or his cur soul glow. He was weak. His soul no darker now than when he colluded with Caine's father, Daniel, and Loring in the failed kidnapping attempt. I was lucky Ranlyn saved my ass.

"Marco!" The Tainted Photographer's eyes bugged before he

took off.

The Tainted Photographer sprinted towards the kitchen. The doorway out of the banquet room filled with a set of deep eyes belonging to a man I assumed was Marco. The snivelling Tainted Photographer cowered behind the guy as Marco lifted his hands with a twitch of power that enveloped the room.

I slipped and tumbled forward into the wall, bouncing off, but spun-out without hitting the floor. I was upside-down, the ground two feet below me and getting further away. I flailed to try and right myself like a drunken astronaut and saw the others were in the air as well.

I thought he was telekinetically playing with us, but a serving table against the wall, decorative plants, and paintings were floating as well. We were buoyant, not being pulled around as if on the end of a leash.

The Tainted Photographer pointed at us heading towards the ceiling with knee-slapping hilarity so hard he activated his smoker's cough.

"How do we reopen Diluculo?" The gravity controller, Marco, spoke above the obnoxious Tainted Photographer's laughter.

None of us answered. I didn't know what to expect of Serena and Jared, though knew hoisting Donovan and Kim into the air wasn't enough to start them talking. I twisted to try and find my cousin, eventually seeing her. She was too busy flailing and trying to gain her footing twelve feet or more above the banquet room's floor.

A shock of free-falling sent my gut into my throat before I crashed into the floor with a jarring thud, echoed by the others' bodies. Glass shattered and wood splintered around the room. Sharp twinges of pain shot through me in waves of nausea as I fought to breathe. The expensive carpet did nothing to buffer the landing. I searched for the others and saw Serena rolling on her back, grabbing at her hip. Her cries and curses sailed above the moans and aggravation of everyone else being toyed with.

A scuffle and urge to fight had me turning in time to see Donovan sprinting for Marco. The Tainted Photographer ducked and braced for the attack. Marco lifted his hands, and we were raised off the ground again, floating before Donovan could reach him. A surge of his power was released into the wall, missing its target.

"Where is the entrance to the attic?" Marco's tone suggested he was a seasoned interrogator. A mix of boredom and necessity, attempting not to appear desperate for answers while commanding we view him as a serious threat.

Again, no one answered.

Anger tensed the thread of connection. Mine? Donovan's? Probably both. This asshat was in my ancestral home, breaking things, and now trying to break my friends and family. And here I was floundering around like a clumsy bird knocking into things.

Marco injected gravity back into the room. We plummeted. My breath caught in my throat as Donovan sprang the moment his feet touched the ground, ghosting, disappearing and reappearing, driving his foot into Marco's chest, and launching him back into the Tainted Photographer.

Donovan was fast, but Marco snapped away the gravity anyway, sending us back into the air. Marco used our discombobulated state to stand up and then drop us when we were five feet off the ground before stealing gravity again.

I landed on my fingers, folding them backwards with a sickening crunch under the full weight of my body. The pain pissed me off more and worsened as I shook while muscling each finger back into place before healing.

Serena and Jared both had streaks of blood down their faces and cradled an injury or two. I couldn't get to them to help. A tingle in my chest caused panic and confusion until I realized it was the power of the estate. It was there, caring for me as it could, urging me to fight against the sick game of *Yo-Yo*.

Spinning around in zero gravity wasn't the safest way to start shooting off hits of power, but we couldn't let Marco win.

As if he heard me, Donovan braced himself against the wall

Spiderman-like and reached out towards Marco, telekinetically dragging him into the room by his foot. The guy grabbed onto the door frame, losing the tug-of-war, and was pulled into the room without gravity.

He, too, was quick and grabbed the Tainted Photographer's leg, whipping him into the no-gravity room at Donovan like a shot-put champ. Donovan wrestled himself back into the doorway like he was swimming from a shark and into the hallway behind him where he found his footing in the gravity-soaked doorway.

Donovan grabbed the Tainted Photographer. Power heated within my hands, disintegration power. The Tainted Photographer screamed. He and Donovan whirled in a tumble as Donovan was bucked off the guy as he flailed in pain. Donovan shot a hit of power at the guy, but he lifted his hands and redirected the hit at me. I ducked out of the way and ended up headbutting the ceiling, my nose ringing and tears blurring my vision. When I could see, droplets of red streamed into the air around me.

Laughter came from down below. I blinked through tears and saw two other devotees caught up to their leader, losing it when they saw us all in different degrees of getting our asses kicked.

A deep growl resonated as a pain dug into my shoulder and tingled across my chest. The Tainted Photographer started screaming. A terrified, squealing shriek as if he glimpsed into his worst nightmare. He continued to wail, staring at Donovan until his eyes rolled back and his whole body went limp. He bounced off the ceiling and bobbed there like a lost balloon.

Was he dead? Couldn't be as his soul glow was still intact. What did Donovan do to him?

"We need to take these guys down, babe. We're sedated fish in a barrel, and you and I are the only ones useful enough to do anything about it."

"Distract them, and I'll get Kim in working order."

"What? How will that help?"

Steadying himself and sending a barrage of hits at Marco and the devotees to cover me let me spin around so I could crawl across the ceiling to Kim. She was curled into herself, cradling her hand, her instincts like the rest of us, to put her hands down to catch her body knowing they wouldn't be able to take her weight, but reflexes told her to do it anyway.

Her wrist bones weren't right, jagged edges pressing into the skin in odd angles threatening to punch through. "Heal me."

Healing her meant getting the bones in place first, so they didn't heal in their awkward position.

I sucked in through my teeth. "Shysty. This is gonna hurt."

"Quick, quick, quick. Come on."

I pushed my healing ability through her at the same time as pressing everything into place. Or what I hoped was the right place, wishing on a lucky star the simultaneous effort would lessen the overall pain and get Kim back in the fight.

Kim's shrill scream was a shock of a high-pitched squeal in my ears at close range, matching the din of battle behind us.

She sagged in relief and cradled her arm, flexing her fingers. "Get us off this fucking ceiling."

"Treat it like any other surface. Use it as your new floor and work with it instead of against it. We need you, too."

A hit in the shoulder had me colliding into Kim and spinning off into the wall. I twisted and fought my hair out of my face to see Donovan bouncing from wall to ceiling, evading hits like a dodge ball pro.

"Slimy prick. I got this." Kim closed her eyes and spoke in what I thought might be Hebrew. The moment her spell was done, Marco and the devotees hit the ceiling so fast they dented the plaster, cracking it with body-sized indents. White specks floated around them like snowflakes.

Kim laughed. "See how they like fighting on an even playing field."

"Badass." I lifted my hand for a long-range high-five she countered.

If Marco could have reintroduced gravity, he would have done so to make his life easier. Instead, he swore and fought off his cohorts who tried grabbing onto him to keep themselves steady. He couldn't undo whatever Kim did.

Donovan sent a dimpled half-smile her way, impressed.

When I got to Serena, Jared was with her. "Your hip?"

Serena nodded but couldn't speak.

I tried to position Serena the way I needed her. "Hold your man's hand."

Whether he was or wasn't my cousin's man, Jared let Serena take a strangling hold of his wide palm as she pulled him close. Grabbing my cousin's ass to steady her, I used the pressure of power as I had with Kim. A cry out in pain, Serena kicking her leg out below her into the space where the floor should have been, and then a dull pop, meant it worked.

Serena breathed heavy and rubbed her reddened face. "Dude, this sucks donkey balls."

Jared muttered something, massaging his sore fingers.

"Soph—" Serena regained my attention as I had looked around for Donovan and Kim exchanging blows with the devotees. "Can you get us down?"

"Nope. Maybe if we hurt Marco enough the magic will drop. Attack from here if you can or stay out of the way."

"I don't think I can add much."

Serena was right, so I raised my power, wrapped my arms around her like a hug, and pulled away to create a bubble of a shield that grew around her the farther I went. She stared wide-eyed at the transparent film around her, poking it to test its durability. With a few feet of buffer, it would do the trick for now, but I didn't know how bad a hit it could take, so I warned her to keep to the corner.

I gorilla-crawled my way back to Donovan and Kim. He was bouncing off the walls, using them as leverage to escape or launch himself at the devotees that had grown in numbers since I left him.

A shot of power winged Donovan in the side, flinging us off the wall like a ping-pong ball and into the middle of the room.

Jared sent his own shots at the enemy and moved with surprising agility.

"We could really use Nya's power right now, babe." Donovan healed burned and ragged looking skin on our left side.

Going hog-wild on them might get our asses beat considering our limited back-up. Nya's power was an easy fall-back, but it couldn't solve everything. We needed to get them out of the estate before they blew a hole through ceilings and took a more direct route into the attic.

If I could blow the ceiling off so Jared could use his elemental ability, I would rather—wait. I didn't need the roof peeled off when a window would do.

I figured out a plan and let Donovan know.

"Genius." He grabbed hold of the gravity-free serving table scratching up to the ceiling near him and flung it across the room. It spun like a frisbee and crashed through the large bay window. The chill of the snowy outdoors blew into the room as step one of the plan entailed.

I shot a net of power at Marco, it catching his arm and gumming up his quick rebound as Donovan shot himself off of the wall to head to Jared. I scuttled across the ceiling like a crab as Marco struggled to free himself of my webbing, throwing out walls of shields which broke into jagged shards and impaled Marco's band of misfit thieves.

Donovan made it back to me quicker than I thought he could move. "We need to corral them into one corner."

The enemy was jumping around like cats on catnip trying to shake off my attack, too spread out to maximize our next strike.

Snapping energy at my back added to the thrum of power in the room. Jared was gathering strength around him, stirring the room with cool air flowing in through the broken window. Floating debris soared to the end of the room, bounced off the walls, and gained speed as they spiralled.

Jared overshot, injecting too much power into the room, and sent himself skidding along the ceiling before snagging on a chandelier. Holding on, eyes closed, he kept up the torrent of cold wind. His elemental powers were controlling him as if he let go an inch they would cut out and life-ending consequences would follow.

The frigid blast went through me and stole my breath as if I had jumped in a frozen lake. White puffs of air billowed from Donovan's lips as he looked on at his inexperienced Covener and braced for attacks from the devotees now scrambling to protect themselves with ineffective or failing shields.

The ceiling slicked over with a sheet of ice, sticking my shoes to the surface. I peeled them away but couldn't keep them unstuck when I had to steady myself. The chill bled through my shoes and clothing as I tried to tuck my hands into my sleeves and curl my face into my arms. I wanted Jared to dial it down a notch, but he was hurting the enemy in a way none of the rest of us could.

A devotee got a foothold and scrambled away from the worst part of the icy wind. I gave a power-fueled shove and flung him back into the line of damage, he careening into a fellow devotee and breaking their shield.

We couldn't run away from the wind in the long room. I peeled my shoes off of the ceiling again and tried but bailed hard and slid on my side. The sting of ice burned my bare skin, slicing up my ribs.

The wind Jared drew into the room from outside increased. I inhaled at the frigid onslaught and choked on my hair whipping around my face.

Kim's shrill scream echoed as she tumbled past me in splayed limps and red hair out into the hallway. Getting enough of my hair out of the way to focus on her showed she escaped Jared's wild wind-storm, yet still stuck in float-mode. Her spell must have locked us in Marco's anti-gravity. Kim shook herself off and peeked into the room, windblown but safe.

"Roll!" Kim's tiny voice didn't reach me, but I could read her lips enough and understood her pantomiming instructions.

I peeled my sleeved-covered hand off the ice under me, and I forced my body to straighten against my muscle's protest, then sprung forward into the worst of the wind, allowing it to barrel roll me.

A jarring halt stopped me. I wriggled around and got a face full of biting wind and icy shards. I fought to find my bearings but couldn't see where I landed. My nostrils burned with every inhale as I tried and failed to find my way to safety.

A hefty tug on my leg had me scratching at the floor to stop myself from getting captured by a devotee. A gulp of iciness didn't help, my coughing echoing in my ears, the pop of my eardrums a treat until I noticed the wind stopped.

I blinked and squinted to the crunch of icy eyelashes, relieved when I saw Kim's red hair before seeing her face. She was the one who grabbed me.

Shivering didn't quit, neither did the sting of my wind-thrashed skin. Donovan and the others were still out there, and he was getting the brunt of it.

I pulled myself to the doorway beside Kim, my dexterity a total wash, so I used my hands like clubs. Debris blew around like a tornado stuck in a freezer, the wind itself mostly snow it was so thick and frigid. I squinted through the run-off of the wind hitting me in the threshold and couldn't see anyone.

I turned to Kim. "Think of Marco."

She was confused and then understood I wanted her to use her locating power and complied, pointing off to the right corner closest to us. "He's that way."

"And Donovan?"

She took a moment and pointed to the left where I had been, but deeper into the room.

Jared was where I saw him holding onto the chandelier, and Serena was off in the far-right corner, the best place to be as the wind would be coming through the window at her left and missing her. She wasn't clear of it all, but it would hurt worse to drag her into the room through Jared's line of power to have her to join us.

I opened a channel into Jared's thoughts and saw him struggling to control himself. He was fueling the torrent against his need, wanting to stop it yet compelled to dig deeper and find strength to continue and take out the enemy.

"Stop! Jared, you can stop now!"

I didn't hear anything back as he was too consumed by the intoxicating elemental energy.

"Donovan, you're closer to him. Make Jared shut it down before he kills us, too."

"Cah-hant...Can't. B-bind...Bind them." Donovan's thoughts were a driving panic of his inability to find me. His efforts to erect a shield failed under the thick frigidness of the wind. He waited too long and was now handcuffed by helplessness.

A deep burning clenched the meat of my shoulder. Pinching heat spread over my limbs, livening them in a rush, chasing the cold away enough to think clearly.

I realized Donovan wasn't telling me to bind Jared. He was thinking of Marco and the devotees. If Jared dropped his power now, the enemy would be frosty but still a potential risk. We banked on Jared pulling off a hail Mary for us. He overdelivered. I should have used Nya's power from the beginning like Donovan suggested. We went with the Jared tactic because I suggested it, insinuating I didn't want to dig up Nya's abilities.

I didn't enjoy the feeling of the ancient power taking me over since I haven't mastered controlling it yet, but now Jared was in the same boat. When shit hit the fan, I needed to learn to taco-hoof my fear and use the arsenal I had. I was a vessel. I was gifted this power and was letting it chill in my back pocket like a trump card for a rainy day instead of whipping it out like an overconfident internet creeper for all to see.

A physical inhale and metaphysical sense of letting go had my power at the ready, it ever present and needy, waiting for permission to stretch out and have fun. Nya's power was close behind, hypervigilant, roaring to act, to punish what was hurting us. The difference between the two was all too real. Familiarity came with the pair as well, but not as much as I would have liked, my power and Nya's were still new to me in many ways.

Protection of Donovan and the connection was first and foremost, though I doubt he would care about the pain if it meant getting this over with.

Nya's greedy power took the wheel too much, creating a foreign scene before my eyes. I found strength to push out in front and retake a sense of self while siphoning the ancient essence inside me. A frigid wind roared, as did the voices of the others. Not their true voices but their inner ones. Donovan was still far into the room and off to the left. He wondered what I was doing and wished he could fold into a tighter position to stave off the cold or to access his power properly to stop Jared on his own. Failure saturated his mind, one that marred him as it always did, planted deep by the hands of another.

The Tainted Photographer was awake and wished for death. I wanted to grant him his end. Wanted him to breathe his last breath and end his wretched existence, but something in me said it wasn't right. No. It wasn't me who wanted to end him, it was Nya's power. With her influence cutting me off from what felt like myself, it would be easy to end him...too easy. He never respected the life of others including myself, so why not?

Donovan would say it would change me, and the man's life wasn't worth altering my existence, that's why not.

Jared was consumed, so much so I wanted to allow him the freedom to continue. To feel relieved, to purge himself of the desire we Magics repressed. The draw of his energy and of his cathartic release was a fresh dose of spirit I needed.

Why did I need this? I didn't. This wasn't me.

I shouldered Nya's power to the side a little more where its influence was less overwhelming. A solution was what I needed. Something to break Jared's purge of power or something to counteract him.

A tingle of heat grew within my chest. I pressed my hand into my breastbone, unable to extinguish it as it worsened. Not Nya's power, yet not my own. The estate's?

It lessened to its usual degree of presence whenever I was in the house, but I understood what I needed.

Like a bubbling volcano, a warmth spiked and flowed out of me, targeting Jared through the torrent of the wind. A prickling sizzle ran down my arms without the pain the smell would suggest.

Jared's thoughts changed from an unknown bliss to confusion, anger, and then fear. He didn't want to stop, and then he wanted whatever was happening to him to end. Wind still roared through the room but was now heated. Relief swooned in the minds of those in the room, but I didn't want this for anyone except for Donovan. I needed the devotees incapacitated and shielded them from the warmth they craved, directing the heat with one hand, and blocking the devotees from it with the other.

The ice box of a room was now a sauna. Water rained down from the ice-covered ceiling as it melted and then floated to the ceiling, pooling in the swirling wind, as zero-gravity took it over.

Jared still refused to stop. His power was voracious and tried to overthrow mine in a desperate need to thrive uninhibited.

I increased the heat I was putting out, concentrating it on Jared and leaving Donovan to gather his strength and shake off the rest of his chill.

"End this now before I am forced to harm you." With my warning made plain, and Jared insisting on bowing to his power's will, I elevated the temperature further in hopes he would understand my threat was not empty.

Pulses of energy still surged through Jared in desperate attempts to find purchase on his slipping power. Each one I smacked down and pressed him with more heat.

The superheated wind snapped from the air, disappearing in one last pulse of defeated energy. Jared's deep-chested howl bounced off the walls and hit my ears with a dull sound as I left his thrashing thoughts. He was panicked with no understanding of what happened or how he went from pure love to stark agony.

"What the fuck was that?" Kim flinched and backed away when I looked at her, grabbing onto the wall to steady herself as we floated.

Nya's power drained from me. I had forgotten Kim was beside me. "What?"

She blinked and shook her head, pursing her lips closed.

Another roar echoed from the room. Jared's.

I grabbed the door trim and pulled myself into the open space to get to him, floating up to the ceiling.

"Bind them!" Donovan pointed back near me into the right corner of the room and then shoved off the wall and shot himself towards Jared.

I had forgotten this was what he wanted me to do before I delved into Nya's power and lost focus. The devotees were curled into themselves, skin tombstone grey, they shivering and moaning in hypothermic failure.

Finding my power to bind the devotees was easy with Donovan's frenetic energy across the connection. I used the spell Kim had, saying "Cesso," and left them to stick to the ceiling.

"What'd you do to him?" Serena was steadying herself, looking over Jared. I couldn't see what she meant from where I was, but she was accusing Donovan of something.

My shoe slipped on wet plaster, and I slid on my stomach across the ceiling. A burning scrape singed my palms and my stomach. I looked around to try and see the small crowd and what they were doing, only able to see Donovan shoulder Serena out of the way and anchor to the chandelier. Serena was pissed, and Kim took it on to remind her Donovan could heal. What he needed to heal was still a mystery to me.

When I finally ceiling-crawled my ass to the rest of them, I saw the pink flesh of Jared's arms, tugging and floating around him like tiny, mangled wings. His clawed hands trembled, too painful to clench into fists.

I did this to him. "Jesus fucking Christ. I'm so sorry."

"That was you?" I didn't have to look at my cousin's glare to see her fury—it was alive in her voice. I earned it, but I could fix this.

Donovan knew I needed to make this right and was able to stall until I got there.

"Do I put the skin back in place?" I didn't want him to scar and wasn't sure it would make a difference.

Donovan didn't answer my mental question. Not a good sign.

"Why do I always lose skin when you're around?" Jared's voice trembled as he spoke through clenched teeth reminding me of the first time I channelled Nya's power in Ranlyn's backyard and supercharged the atmosphere. Blake hit Jared with a bolt of lightning. I hadn't seen his chest since but gathered he was left with the reminder. I didn't forget what happened and it was another reason why Nya's power wasn't unholstered without good reason.

"Oh, you know, sweet guys make good guinea pigs."

"Hey!" Serena backhanded me in the arm. "You could've killed him."

Jared made a weak chuckle. "Lesson learned. Now heal me."

I awakened my power again, ignoring Kim when she asked what lesson Jared was talking about. There wasn't time to explain. Jared needed to be whole again and letting him think it was all his fault wasn't right. I didn't know what happened. His power overwhelmed him as much as Nya's power overwhelmed me. We were both as lucky as two teenagers with a broken condom between them to escape unscathed.

I started to guide his peeled and floating skin in the direction I needed. "Jared, ever have your balls waxed?"

"What?" He panted.

I raised my brow at him.

He rolled his eyes. "Once."

I tsked. "Chicks and their high demands. This is gonna hurt worse."

"Awesome."

"Actually, Donovan's gonna take an arm, and I'm gonna take the other. More pain, quicker result."

Jared cringed when Donovan and I revved our power to the

surface in unison. We started at Jared's shoulder and smoothed the skin down, healing as we moved the skin into place. Zero-gravity worked with us as the skin floated instead of sticking to itself like cheap cellophane.

Jared sucked in a hiss and held his breath as we worked. His mouth opened in a silent scream when the healing hit its peak, a vein in his temple and neck muscles straining, before punching out an exhale when we finished. He leaned back, his torso floating in reclined relief as his legs kept him attached to the chandelier.

Serena grappled him with a cheek kiss and a tight hug as Donovan, Kim, and I rested upside-down.

"Binding them didn't give us our gravity back." Kim peered down the room at the devotees still bound and floating like dust bunnies. If they were cold, you couldn't tell.

Why didn't I direct all of Jared's power at the devotees and then sneak up on him and bind him instead of battling his power with Nya's? He's a Seedling. He's no match for an ancient power like Nya's while also fuelled by my own. When I was using her power, it numbed all those thoughts, cut my creativity. Her power sliced through my conscious with swift decision making on a mission to get the job done regardless of collateral damage. And best way to force Jared to stop what he was doing was to make him.

"Sophie?"

I blinked and looked to Kim in question, her red hair splayed out and floating around her making her look fierce as I figured mine did as well, both a tangle of knots.

"What's wrong, babe?" The detachment in Donovan's voice reflected how quickly I shut down what had me distracted.

What would have been a deflected answer was interrupted when a high-pitched scream trilled down the hall.

5

HOUSE GUESTS

Olive was home and must have stumbled across Jeremy still bound and contorted on the loveseat. Nice to know my spell still held up, though he was going to need a chiropractor.

"Leave the bound tainthole and get in here!"

Gasps echoed when Olive, Lewis, Priscilla, Gloria, and Iris entered the banquet room. They yelped as they saw us on the roof, Lewis unable to stop himself from crumbling in laughter.

"Hi." I waved at them. "The world's worst home makeover show hosts are here to ruin your day."

"What in Hilda's hat are you doing up there?" Olive pressed a hand to her chest.

As ever impressive as Gloria and Iris's hats were, their expressions were aghast as both rolled their eyes at us useless Seedlings.

"We'll clean up when you get us down." Donovan overstepped my impulse to apologize, going unnoticed as my family looked at each other as if they didn't know how.

In a huff of unintelligible insults and a hearty "Good gravy", Iris awakened a flare of magic, lifted her hands, and recited an incantation. The moment the last word was spoken, we plummeted towards the ground in a myriad of choked screams before we were stopped feet above the ground like our bungy cord hit its end. Water fell with us, splashing to the floor with a room full of debris.

"I suggest you right your feet beneath you." I supposed this was what passed for generous as far as Iris went since she could have let us bounce off the carpet.

We scrambled to get situated, which wasn't easy since there wasn't anything to grab hold of. I felt like a flailing turtle stuck on its shell.

Gravity took over. My stomach lurched for my throat again, and I landed in a squat and rolled onto my side onto the soggy carpet. The devotees landed with a loud thud since they weren't given the freedom to use their feet.

Everyone was up and stretching their legs. My equilibrium was off, my knees jelly-like as I retrieved Bosco, thankful he was too preoccupied with trying to escape the attic instead of investigating what he might eat or destroy.

Whatever Iris did to reverse the anti-gravity magic, it didn't touch the binding spell on the devotees. I didn't know why and was impressed at how much the aunts could do and how they were so nonchalant about it.

After running the late party crashers through what led to us playing astronauts, we now had an issue. What do we do with the devotees?

Lewis fixed his glasses. "What about the Sovereignty?"

"Nope. Not an option." I refused to work with them. I didn't need them seeing my face and then figuring out I was working with Vincent to spy on them.

Priscilla squinted at me. "This is what they were created for."

"Please." Gloria poked Jeremy, still stuck in pose worthy of Cirque du Soleil in the front sitting room where we sat. "These ruffians wouldn't hold a moldy match of importance to those Sovereignty shysters."

"Gloria, don't touch the captives. Even we have better manners than that." Olive and Gloria exchanged a look before Gloria huffed and sat in a chair.

I had yet to ask any of them of their opinions regarding the Sovereignty, but I would put money on at least Gloria and Iris being on my side. Whether or not they would engage in a coup to take the Sovereignty down was another question, one I wasn't confident enough to wager on.

"She's right." Donovan meant what Gloria said and not about our manners since I probably was as curious as Gloria to see what would happen if you poked them.

"I wouldn't hand the Sovereignty a tissue let alone a case." Creased expressions turned my way. They didn't know why I was anti-Sovereignty and really, neither did I. "What about screwing with their memories?"

Mischievous grins crossed my wild-hatted aunts, a glint in their eyes telling me they were game. Some debate arose but in the end was our best option.

Memory tampering was tricky business. Erasing it was cruel, even if deserved, so we needed to create a concentration of magic that would distort their memories instead of erasing them, so they wouldn't recall a single freeze frame of where they were headed or why. All while mixing in an additive that would repel them from ever returning if they so happened to break through the memory scramble.

"How do you get them to suck it back?" Serena sat and watched while Gloria and Iris mixed ingredients in the kitchen as casually as baking a cake from scratch.

"Force it down like medicating a dog."

Serena's face twisted. "Have fun with that. No way I'm sticking my fingers anywhere near their mouths."

"There's always the cellar." Donovan's suggestion earned more than my glare.

"Nice thinking, boy." Gloria didn't stop mixing as Lewis and

Olive refused to entertain the thought. Not that I would let it go that far, though I still wanted to see the basement.

"And why not?" Iris handed her sister something that looked like dried dung beetles. "It was those devotees who tried to kill these Seedlings. Justice is earned."

"The Seedlings?" Gloria huffed as she added ingredients. "These invaders disturbed the sanctity of the estate and damaged estate property. That alone earns them an organ removal or two."

Serena raised her hand. "I'll help with the clean up."

"Please, child." Iris scoffed as Gloria finished. "This house needs no caretaker. She takes care of herself."

"I meant after the organ removal, but sure, I'll clean up the banquet room, too."

I smiled at my cousin and popped up to sit on the butcher block. She would probably do better with the organ removal cleanup.

"The estate is a 'she'?" Donovan's question was better than what Iris and Gloria planned to do with the organs once they were removed, and I wondered if there was a spell or two they could be useful for.

"And if she takes care of herself, you'd think the house might've thought to clean a little while Olive was gone." Serena poured on the sarcasm. "Clear the dusty shelves. Maybe run off the hordes of rats and spiders settin' up shop?"

Gloria kept her attention on the steaming pot in front of her.

Olive exhaled. "I suppose she was as depressed as I was. Earth's creatures would be better company than none at all."

I wasn't sure if Olive thought of the estate as female or why Gloria was so certain it was, but a power from the estate was clear within me as it was within Olive.

"Your presence has reawakened her zest, my dear." Gloria managed to exude sympathy while her tone remained stiff. "I imagine her wits have normalized since your return, though clearly she needs work on her wards." She sucked her teeth. "Those fools should not have breached the property line let alone had their way around, defiling its corridors with their evil—"

Lewis cleared his throat. "All right, Gloria."

"Hmm. All right is not the words I would use, brother."

As fascinating as the walls around us possessing a human set of fluctuating emotions and the ability to heal itself was, we came here for a reason. The devotees distracted me from finding Gareth's magic in Caine as I had in the park. Maybe I needed to be closer to the Creation to pull it off. I wasn't about to miss the makings of Gloria and Iris's memory altering skills Kim diligently typed into the note section of her phone, so instead of heading up to the attic, I picked their brains on the plausibility of connecting with Caine using Aunt Lacey's vessel-jumping relatives as the bridge.

"Cannot be done." Iris's adamant dismissal was disappointing.

Anger in Donovan flared across our connection. "It's already been done. Gareth and Nya's powers connected when Caine was in the sleeping curse. It's how they met."

"*Pfft.*" Gloria scoffed as Iris claimed, "Apples and oranges."

"Why?" Iris rolled her eyes at me. "No, really, why? I need to understand before I can strike it off the list of things to drive myself insane with staring at the ceiling all night instead of sleeping since I know he and whoever else are stuck in a place full of rotting bodies, psychopaths, and zombie Puppets controlled by a sociopath aren't sleeping like puppies in there."

Gloria turned to me and wiped her hands on a hand towel. "You wish to tap into an ancient nexus through, not only a separate plane of consciousness as with a dream state, but through the veil into a locked Creation. This isn't leapfrog, girl."

Iris gasped. "Nexus."

Gloria turned to her sister. They stared at each other a moment, Iris nodding, her oversized and bright-coloured hat bobbing.

Gloria pointed at her sister. "Nexus Transference."

Iris splayed her hands. "Precisely."

"Hmmm. The ingredients—"

"Small sacrifice."

"Containment?"

"Ownership?" Iris clasped her hands together and looked to her sister as if asking for permission.

Gloria smacked her lips. "Fine." She turned back and stirred the cooking mixture.

Iris clapped and smiled so big I saw a bit of a snaggle tooth I never noticed before and started breaking apart some type of herb Kim knew as she added something to her notes.

I looked at Donovan with frustrated awe. He shifted his weight from foot to foot and looked down at the floor.

"Okay. Love you both, but I'm going to set fire to your hat collection unless one of you explains what the fizz you're talking about." The two turned to me with hardened glares. "Yup. Including the ones on your head." Gloria opened her mouth. "Unless you're giving me an explanation about what Nexus Transference is and why containment or ownership matters, I don't want to hear it, and I don't have time to be nice. We've been floating around and kicking each other's asses. My patience has taken a beatin', so if whatever you're talking about will connect Nya's power to Gareth's, please, out with it."

Gloria turned back to the stove leaving her sister to deal with me. "A Nexus Transference spell cannot be completed by you, Firefly."

"Then why are you excited?"

"A Nexus Transference spell can only be performed by two beings of shared bloodlines. A shame for any potential children if yourself and Caine were related. We may have loved them anyway, dear, but people would stare."

Donovan's heartrate rose a tick or maybe it was mine as it took everything in me not to follow through with my hat burning threat until she went on.

"Besides, the blood of the body within the veil is not the key to access the Nexus Transference. Only that of the soul within the vessel can accomplish what we need."

"So...." Kim looked up at the ceiling, thinking, "we need the blood of a relative of Gareth's?"

"Not just the blood." Gloria tapped the large wooden spoon she was using on the side of the pot. "The genetic solution calls for the body and the blood."

"Any other ideas?" Serena chomped on a sprig of mint. "'Cuz I'm pretty sure the family of the dead dude squatting inside of Caine were maggot meal before our people invented toilet paper."

However old toilet paper was, she was probably right.

"How close does the relation need to be?" Olive tapped the counter with her nails in thought.

Gloria was stirring again. "Presumably the closer the relation the stronger the connection, though we have strong covens to make up the difference if required."

Olive turned to Donovan. "Are you not by some degree of relation to Elsa and therefore of relation to Gareth?"

We side-eyed each other in a mirrored "Duh! Holy shit!"

I never thought about he and Caine having such a tight connection between them, but the cosmic joke was a real side-stitcher. Or would be for someone like Loring. Whatever this Nexus Transference spell was, it meant Donovan taking the brunt of it instead of me. He was careful with the emotions crossing our tether once he got over the initial shock, but he refrained from commenting on if full participation in the spell was on the menu.

My cell rang—Vincent—stopping Donovan from needing to express his eagerness for the plan.

I answered, ignoring Donovan's relief at the distraction. "Hel—"

"Eli has joined the Tainted to open the Creation."

"What? Fuck. Hello to you, too. And no, he didn't. He wouldn't."

Kim arched a brow at me in question, hearing only half the conversation.

"My sources are credible."

"Eli wouldn't do that. Fighting the Berisford path is number one to him. Jeopardizing that would—"

"Destroy his family? Who do you think begged him to assuage the association? Bernadine lost her daughter. Nothing can prevent a mother from rescuing her child, including reconciliation with old friends who bathe in darkness."

I couldn't wrap my head around it. Reaching out to dark contacts for information was one thing. What Vincent was talking about was not an info mission, it was a desperate shift in values, ones Eli and Bernadine held to and created a life around. If what Vincent said was true, then they were hedging their bets against their daughter having no one to return to if she was still alive and they managed to break her loose.

"If the information travelled my way, it stands to reason they have either been following this plan since they learned of their daughter's entrapment or have delved too deep within a dark path for us to dig them out."

"I have to go." I hung up.

"What do you wanna do?" Donovan must have overheard Vincent. His genuine question was a tad surprising, especially since he was offering to help Caine's people.

"We have to go."

Donovan nodded and was on my heels as I raced back up to the attic to grab my purse and our coats. Olive was at the front door when I got back.

"Firefly, what's happened?"

"Watch Bosco for me? We're going to Caine's Uncle Eli's." I laid a peck on her cheek and threw Kim her jacket. "You comin'?"

She made a brief glance back towards the kitchen as if she could see Gloria and Iris cooking up the memory concoction through the walls between them. Kim had a partial process of memory tampering now written in her phone, thrilling the Kitchen Witch in her. I didn't wait for her answer, but she raced after Donovan and me as we were getting into the Barracuda.

The ride was quiet as I was stuck in my head, thinking over what

Vincent told me and what we could be walking into. How could they do this?

A slow-moving pick-up truck had me twitchy until the road was wide enough for me to pass it.

A push of Donovan's irritation crossed the connection. My mental walls had snapped back up, and he wasn't happy about it. I couldn't relax enough to worry about offending him or not, and I didn't want to have a telepathic conversation with Kim six inches away.

Kim pulled herself to the edge of the backseat, gripping the front ones. "What did Eli do?"

A red light stopped me, the road too busy to go through it. Eli. That idiot. He was going to get himself killed. Maybe Vincent got a hold of some bad intel. He had to.

"Why am I here if you're not talking to me?"

Donovan huffed. "Vincent conveniently discovered Caine's aunt and uncle's ties to some evil sons'a'bitches in hopes of saving their stupid kid."

I sped around another slow fucker too scared to drive through a half-inch of snow. Donovan may not have been able to hear me, but he couldn't mistake the "shove it up your ass" across the connection if he tried.

"Why would they do that?" Kim was confused. "They know we're still trying."

"He's exploring a route we wouldn't." I glared at Donovan then back at the road before getting stopped by a stop light in the middle of nowhere. With no other cars in view, I ran it, ignoring Kim's protest. "Eli sacrificing his soul for his family is nothing. He and Bernie probably think they can use their Tainted buddies and walk away without lasting damage. As long as Jet and Caine are safe, they think it's worth it. Plus, we've got zilch done for months. Why would they trust us to get the job done?"

Rhetorical question, and they were smart enough not to answer.

Fuck. Caine and Jet were paying for my laziness. Nights spent fucking around with Donovan—literally, since it was easier than facing my inner bullshit—instead of digging up contacts like the ones Eli was messing with or ones on the fringe who might know something more than nothing. Running surveillance jobs with Vincent, looking for Sovereignty corruption when we already knew the kind of sick fucks inside the Creation, anything, everything than what I should have been focused on.

Making sense of why Eli and Bernadine were doing whatever they were doing wasn't the problem. Understanding the consequences they were willing to incur to save them was.

My heart broke for Jet. If she was alive, there was a nightmare waiting for her.

I parked and turned off the engine, looking through the windshield and counting the cars in the long driveway stretched outside of Eli and Bernie's farmhouse. When Vincent said Eli was working with the Tainted, I didn't think he meant this moment.

Neighbours would think there was a party, but you couldn't hear anyone out front.

"Sophie—" My name on Donovan's lips was a testament to his fear of what we might be walking into.

"No."

"No what? I hate it when you two do that. Spell it out for me. What's happening?"

I shook my head. "They wouldn't let anything happen to me."

"This is your fault."

I spun to Donovan as shock and anger railed through me.

"That's what they think, not me. None of this would've happened without you. Caine's father tried to take Caine out. In saving him, you brought him into their daughter's life, and both have suffered for it. It's a twisted truth, but it's what their grief-stricken minds are thinking to better justify this gathering." I wanted to argue and couldn't. "Don't go in there wearing the protection of their love before Jet and Caine were swallowed by the Creation. Unless you join them, you're an obstacle in the way of getting their family back, and you'll pay for it. And do you remember what I told you I'd do if you fell in with the wrong side?"

I thought back a moment, remembering our conversation a few months ago in his basement when we spoke about if we should fear being turned by the Tainted. He said he would follow me and find a way to bring me back because he knew how the Tainted world worked firsthand.

I nodded at him.

"Good. Let's go."

We got out of the Barracuda and shut the doors with a push instead of a shove to keep quiet. Birds sat in a tree out front, chirping and bopping from branch to branch. Chances were the enemy wasn't belly crawling between the cars. Sneaking up on a herd of unsuspecting evildoers wasn't a tea party I was into crashing, though it was one I wanted to get a sense of before announcing our presence.

A chirp a bit louder than the birds came from my right. Donovan, signalling me to hold up as he walked on the right side of the cars while Kim and I were on the left. He reached down to touch the silver Acura between us, and I felt the grip of his vision run through me. When he let go, he paused and tapped his temple.

I dropped my mental walls, knowing this was what he wanted, before he reached out and touched the car again.

The rush of Donovan's vision hit as it always does, but this time I saw it, he sending it to me telepathically to watch with him, stealing away the snow-covered grounds around us and replacing my sight with the inside of a car, the road rushing by through a windshield in front of me.

"It's pretty sweet. Working with a Berisford, I mean."

I looked in the rear-view mirror and glared at the soul patch who thought he knew everything, stopping myself from calling the guy a fucking tool. Didn't stop me from laughing. "Eli's not the breed of Berisford to be proud of. Once his daughter's free he'll flip on us like overdone pancakes."

"Come on, Darren." Soul Patch pulled himself forward to talk at

the man next to me, whose goatee was about as pathetic as the guy's excuse for chin pubes, especially now with all the grey he was sprouting. The look Darren gave the guy had me howling as he slunk back into his seat. "Eli can flip to our side at any time, and with his hot-ass daughter rotting in the Creation, I'm willing to bet it's soon."

"Bernie swears Jet's not dead, and Michael won't allow Eli to take us down." The teen sharing the back seat with Soul Patch was a blond cherub in a constant flush from chin to his hairline.

"Please, kid." Darren turned in his seat. "Will, are you sure Pampers here is one of us? Far too optimistic." The fact Darren was questioning Soul Patch proved he was a shit judge of character. The kid looked down at his hands, no guts whatsoever.

"Nah, Graham here is all about the cause." Will punched Graham's shoulder, making him jolt with the hit as he shrank with his balls. "Once we get our Master free, he'll bow with the rest us, and the Master will enjoy an Architect on his crew, right?" Graham nodded but looked unprepared for the day. "If we ever get it right, that is."

Darren groaned and turned back in his seat. "Weak faith."

"Weak?" Will's laugh had enough snip I gripped the steering wheel to stop from reaching back and teaching him a lesson in respect. "Born and raised with faith—remember that Judas."

"I'd rather a mid-life Judas than a nascent child raised in faith." Message delivered. No one had anything to add, and I was able to drive in fucking peace.

The road in front of me disappeared, the rigidness of the vision bleeding away. My breath hung in the cold air on the driveway we stood in.

I cleared my throat to stop from shaking off the uneasiness the vision caused. "Recognize any of them?"

Donovan shoved his hands in his jacket pockets. "Front passenger. I can't remember his name. I'm pretty sure he had dealings with my father. Probably nothing."

Kim scoffed. "Anyone working with your Tainted daddy isn't nothing."

Donovan glared without answering. She was right, and he knew it. As did I.

Donovan headed towards the house. We followed.

They let me take the lead. I was confident until it came time to knock on the door. Was a knock the way to go? Or should we boot the door in with a war cry? The others were waiting for my move, so I did what was natural and knocked.

Only after I did, it hit me that Donovan was next to me. I wanted him to be at my side the moment Vincent told me what Eli and Bernie were up to, but now he was on the porch of Caine's family home, and it felt disrespectful. The only other time he had met them was the day Caine and I broke up as the direct result of me sleeping with Donovan. This could make things worse.

I reminded myself there was a driveway of cars of the Tainted and three of us to stand up to them. Donovan's presence may complicate negotiations, but if I sent him back to the car, I was left with Kim and a houseful of the Tainted. Perfect. Another example of an ill-conceived plan.

The shake in my hands was as much from fear of anticipating what we might find in the house as from my own failing to figure out what dangers I was walking into before the moment of impact. I rushed off to confront Eli and Bernie knowing they wouldn't be alone. I was a moron for thinking Vincent was mistaken, and my naïveté now put the others in danger.

When no one answered after I knocked again, I got the hint no one would. "Maybe we should try out back?"

"Or maybe we should break in and see what we find?" Kim had her face huddled behind the turned-up collar of her green wool coat, hiding from the grating wind of the openness surrounding the house, yet no less willing to pull a B&E.

I looked to Donovan who scanned the area with a measured calm I wished to master. When it came to B&Es I knew nothing except the time Serena and the rest of our childhood friends used a butter knife to pry open a window of an empty unit in the complex a few of us lived in as kids. We stayed five minutes and booked it back out the window with our hearts drumming with adrenaline.

His smile dimpled his cheeks. "I should be insulted." He grabbed the door handle, his lips fluttering in a spell. Nothing.

"Performance anxiety?"

"Never." The purr in his voice brought a heat to my chilled cheeks before I berated myself for the ill-timed hitch in libido.

"Ugh. You two can stain the sheets later. Open the door before I lose my nose to frostbite."

"They're warded against spells. Let's see if they were smart enough to spell against routine solutions." He reached into his jacket and pulled out a small leather case.

I leaned over and saw him unzip a lockpick set. "You carry that around wherever you go in case of what, a cozy joint to ransack?"

He sneered up at me. "I'm nothing if not prepared."

"Mhmm."

He used a couple of tools on the lock, the pull of concentration creasing in my forehead as he focused on the task until he turned the handle and straightened with a cocky smile.

"I need a set of those." Not that I had broken into many places before, but they looked handy.

"Here." He zipped up the case and handed it to me. "I have others. Lessons included if we leave here alive." He stopped me from opening the door. "I mean it. No Hail Marys. They have an agenda and a mission to get their daughter back. Don't test them if you don't need to and trust they'll follow through with any threats they make."

I nodded, not wanting to believe him.

I pressed the door open a crack, listening for a hint of movement. I didn't hear anyone, so I poked my head through. Donovan braced his forearm on the door, and I realized it was in case someone smashed it into my head and tried to crush my skull. I opened it farther, and Donovan followed next to me, his keen concentration sweeping the entrance and living room off to our right.

Couch pillows were crumpled and on the living room floor. Dust bleached away the colour of the furniture drowning beneath it. The coffee table was littered with soiled dishes and used glasses. We didn't need to worry about our dirty boot prints on the floor as no one else was. The carpet was filthy, saturated with mud and dirty snow. The smell alone was a cry for help from Mr. Clean and a gaggle of rubber gloved minions. The family I met not so long ago would be embarrassed by the condition of their home.

Donovan stepped to the edge of the wall to look down the hall to our left. He shook his head, not seeing anyone.

"Andy's here." Kim pointed towards the hall Donovan checked that led to the bedrooms. I remembered her guiding light. She had met Andy before, so she could recall him and send her feelers out to find him.

I bolted for Andy's bedroom, ignoring Donovan's protest to slow down. I twisted the handle on his door, finding it locked. "Andy?"

No answer.

"Probably spell-locked and sound-proofed so he can't hear what they're doing out here." Donovan tapped my arm. "Lockpicks?"

I handed him back the lockpick set, and he changed spots with me as I contemplated how he came to that conclusion so quick, knowing it was probably done to himself or children of his father's coven and why. I didn't want this for Andy, and while Donovan worked on the lock, I hoped Kim's guiding light steered her wrong and we would find an empty room.

Antsy to get inside, I looked up and down the hallway, checking and rechecking for interruptions.

This one took Donovan longer to crack. The caster's way of ensuring whoever tried to break through had a rough go at it. When the lock gave, Donovan swore under his breath, his triumph running through me as he pushed the door open.

A tiny gasp had me pushing Donovan aside to find Andy on the floor, shocked and looking up at a stranger before then focusing on me. Tears sprung to his eyes. He jumped up, abandoned his Legos, and ran at me. I wrapped him up in my arms and swallowed back tightness in my throat.

Kim scooted in and closed the door behind her.

"Is Mama with you?" Andy's choked question threatened to unravel me.

I wiped a tear from his cheek. "No, buddy, she's not. Are you okay? Why are you locked in here?"

He nodded. "I wander too much."

Ugh. My gut clenched at the impact at what an adult must have told him. Poor kid. "Where's your grandma and grandpa?"

He gave me a one-shouldered shrug.

I faked a smile and stood. Andy held onto my hand. I looked up at Donovan with a lingering question silent between us.

"Of course he can."

If he had said no, I would have brought Andy to my place or the estate, but I wanted some place safe to bring him.

I knelt back down to Andy. "I don't know what's going on here, but I don't think your mama would have wanted you kept behind a locked door. Do you want to leave with us?"

His eyes widened as he nodded.

Thank fuck. I didn't know what I would do if he pitched a fit. Kidnapping him was a bit much, and he would scream, which meant I would have to subdue him. The kid's been through enough without his say so. I couldn't imagine putting him through yet another trauma. I had his trust right now—I wasn't about to break it.

"Okay. Get some toys together." I found his backpack and a small tote, and we started shoving things he might need into them.

Kim bent to shove some socks into the backpack I was holding. "What about the barn?"

The barn was big enough to hold a sizeable group. With Andy in the mix, confronting Eli and Bernie was a dangerous prospect. We could sneak out and squirrel Andy away from here, but then I still had the issue of Eli and Bernie and potentially a barn full of people after me once they realized Andy was gone. I came here for a reason. I needed to try.

According to Donovan's vision, Eli and Bernie were over their heads and setting them straight or knocking them down a couple pegs was what got me out here. Finding the house a mess and Andy locked up put a fire under my ass.

"Kim, can you take him to the car and be ready to take off if we have to? We need to verify what brand of shit Eli and Bernie have stepped in and who they've stepped into it with. Maybe we can convince them to back off from their crazy plan before Jet has nothing to return to." Kim stared at me. I knew what she was thinking. Why go out there at all? We could take off, but they would track Andy down. Plus, I wanted to help Eli and Bernie before their desperation buried them. "We need the backup, but Andy needs you more. If something happens and we don't get out of the barn, take him back to the estate."

"You can't!" Andy's outburst made me flinch. I didn't know if the room was still soundproofed after we opened it.

"It's okay."

"No. There's bad people in the barn."

"I know. We'll be—"

"They're mean!"

"Okay, okay." I was down at his level again, but he wouldn't settle.

"Your grandma and grandpa are in there, right?" Donovan spoke over me and Andy. The kid stopped and looked up at him. "Right?" Andy nodded. "We have to see if they're okay. If they want, they can come too, if you're okay with that."

Who would have thought Donovan had the key to getting the kid to stay calm? Not me.

A backpack and a tote full of odds and ends, Andy with a stuffed chicken tucked safety beneath his arm, and he was as calm as he was going to get. We headed down the hall to the closet and flinched when it squealed as I opened it to pull out his jacket. No one crashed in and stopped us, so we ran out with all we had and strapped Andy into the back seat of the Barracuda as quickly as we could. The faster this was over with, the better.

"We'll be right back, okay?"

Andy grabbed my sleeve before I could escape. "Pinky promise?"

He let go of me to curl his pinky, making sure I didn't leave without making it official. I forced a smile and shook his little finger with mine before he could see my whole hand shaking from adrenaline and anxiousness.

I threw Kim my keys, closed the car door as lightly as possible, and followed Donovan back into the house. He was rock-solid while I was ignoring the tremble over my whole body. The theory of facing a barn of Tainted was easy when I focused on the goal of saving Eli and Bernie from making a mistake they couldn't come back from. But what if they didn't want to be saved? They would be an extra two people against us instead of protecting us from their new friends.

Was I insane to think we could make a difference? Probably, but I needed to try. Jet and Caine were gone, and no one else was around to remind them who they were and why they turned their backs on the Berisford family Tainted way of life.

Kim knew what to do if we didn't make it back from the barn, but how she would explain it to Andy was all on her.

Passing the living room and kitchen, standing by the back door to the barn, nothing was out of place besides matted snow leading to and from its entrance.

"You got a plan?" Donovan peered outside and then back at me.

"Don't die. Don't kill anyone. Tap dance my ass out of there with Eli and Bernadine remembering who they are so Jet and Caine have family to return to."

His lips twisted. "Sounds good to me, though I can only guarantee one of those things will happen. Before I make you guess which, let's get out there."

We headed towards the barn, tentative in case we hit a boundary spell. Instead of any warding, we were hit with an energy so potent it froze us mid-stride. No individual usage of power could create that or even a few individuals together.

This was bigger. Untamed. Darker.

I pushed forward, drowning in anticipation and rise of power as Donovan readied to meet whatever we encountered within the barn. If only to protect ourselves, I followed suit and felt the hum of energy through my body. The concentration of force pouring out of the barn left me no sense of hope for success.

Without giving myself the time to retreat, I grabbed the metal barn door handle, surprised when it turned. Something caught the door and whipped it open all the way. Reflex took over, and I gripped the handle before I was slurped into the room like a soup noodle. My feet lifted off the ground up into the air by a sucking vacuum. Donovan grabbed my jacket-covered wrist tight enough to feel my bones grind. A slice of pain across my right palm loosened my grip.

My scream was lost to shock and the whirlwind of the barn. My hair twisted in my face, blinding my view of the inside. Donovan was still in the doorway, holding onto me and onto the metal threshold, his feet wedged into the toe stop. His focus went from me to the room behind me, the horror in his dark eyes enough for me to pray he didn't let go.

My body twisted in the sucking wind behind me. I looked back to see whatever Donovan did and couldn't make sense of the scene in front of me.

In the middle of the barn, a vacuous hole inhaled everything that wasn't tied down from tools to work benches and even a bike. Darkness spewed into the room around it as flashes of light struck within. Standing around the room like telephone poles in a hurricane were the bodies of at least twenty others.

Bernie strained to see who was at the door, saw us, and turned back to the sucking hole in the room. The lack of concern in Caine's aunt's features was as shocking as whatever she was looking at.

"It's a portal. They're trying to portal across the fucking veil!"

Donovan was appalled. My mental defenses were last on my mind, all thoughts squarely on the atrocity threatening us all.

Those in the barn weren't getting swallowed up by the portal, which meant they knew this would happen and planned for it with a spell to root themselves in place.

"Don't let me go!" The echo of my internal scream was another pain in his and my skull. I knew he would never let go on purpose and would jump in after me and anything not bolted to the barn walls. Now we had to hope the portal didn't suck in the barn with it.

His grip tightened as I felt myself slip enough to pucker at. My coat created a barrier from his visions but was causing his grip to fail.

I slipped another half-inch and flailed, trying to hang on to the inside handle with my other hand but not able to grab a hold on it.

Whistling through the barn walls pierced my ears as the portal grew unstable, warbling like it struggled to hold its form.

A deep scream had me craning to see who it was. A man close to the portal in a yellow polo shirt twisted backwards to reach for the man behind him. I recognized both men. Polo shirt guy was Grey Suit I tailed with Vincent in the diner, the other was the one Donovan remembered in the vision from the car. This man didn't feign a hand in assistance before the terrified polo shirt man screamed, was ripped from his hold, and devoured by the portal.

The portal thrashed in place with greater instability, yet with expanding power as if it got an energy boost from its polo shirt guy snack.

My hand stung. I looked up, frantic to see Donovan. He adjusted his grip on the door frame, blood dripping down his arm and flying into the room. The only thing keeping me from being the portal's next meal was Donovan, and he was losing it.

Another bellowing scream. Another Magic gulped down by the gluttonous portal. It would eat them all without making a dent in its infinite stomach.

Weightlessness hit me, and I screeched and thrashed around.

"Pieceofshitmotherfuckingchrist!" Donovan had me by my jacket-covered arm, and I had nothing but a broken off handle in my hand.

"Don't let her go! Can't lose her! Don't fucking lose her!" His panicked thoughts mirrored my own as his muscles were strained to the limit, veins in his forehead bulging.

While power was all around us, getting purchase on my own was too far away. I guessed his was too, but I couldn't tell if it was what kept his hold on me. He leaned back, trying to counteract my flailing weight and vacuum of the portal as his grip slipped closer to my wrist.

I stared back into the emptiness of the hole as if I could will it to give up.

The cries of others pitched above the torrent of the wind before they were lost to the hungry gulp of the portal.

Something inside the portal moved. A haze of grey blocked out the black emptiness behind it, steady amongst the thrashing gust as I watched it seep out of the portal and hover in front as if it were surveying the room with unseen eyes.

"No!" Graham, the young guy in Donovan's vision was terrified of it.

A few Magics were between him and the haze. He shook his head. Not in fear but as if it was speaking to him. He screamed something into the wind I couldn't hear and then was free of his rooting spell. He was raised into the air before being guided instead of sucked towards the haze, kicking and screaming the whole way.

Weightlessness was a horrifying fleeting sensation before I smacked into the barn floor. Pain was a heavy blanket over my whole body, skull pounding with my adrenalized heartbeat and throbbing in my hip and shoulders.

I gasped, raised my head, and saw Donovan's legs and then his shocked face as he scrambled up and reached for me. He squeezed me tightly and pressed his lips to the top of my head. Relief soared through him as his chest heaved with exhaustion. I squeezed him back in unsaid appreciation, thankful he was not another of the portal's meals.

The portal was gone. Everyone stared at the ground. Through their legs I saw Graham, the teen from Donovan's vision, laying on the barn floor curled onto his side.

"Graham?" Soul Patch, Will, called out for him. His was the first voice we heard, muffled in my ringing ears.

Graham opened his blue eyes and stood with smooth movements looking down at himself. Will called his name again. Again, he went unanswered.

When Graham looked around at those within the room, I saw nothing of the shy Magic in his glare. Graham was no longer Graham.

Eli and Bernie were responsible for what happened here. They were my reason for coming, but I wasn't about to stand still and let Graham tear me apart to give them a chance to apologize. Especially not with Andy and Kim waiting for us.

"You. My Summoners." Graham's voice mixed with that of whoever was inside of him, his light eyes, still his own yet possessed an animal-like sheen as they gleamed in the failing light of the barn. "Unworthy blood called me out." Those animal eyes peered up. I half-expected something to be on the ceiling. "No. You prove useful."

Fuck. Was he talking to Graham? Was Graham still in there like when Nya's power took me over too much? No soul glow told me otherwise, and I missed what it looked like before he was possessed, too bent on not getting sucked into the nothingness to notice.

Graham lifted his hand. An energy from him caused my own to react, rushing to the surface in fear without an escape. A dark spot in the barn opened up in front of him, another portal.

I scrambled to my feet, feeling Donovan grab my arm as if ready to run.

No magnetism drew into the portal this time, no vacuum effect. The portal opened, Graham walked into it, and it closed behind him.

6

———

A GREAT CHANGE

"'**K**ay, evil-doer expert, should we skedaddle or what?" Of the two of us, Donovan's experience with the Tainted was paramount. The fact his green soul was left clean was a miracle. Looking on at the Magics now standing in Eli and Bernie's backyard, we were outnumbered.

"No." His tension while looking at the Tainted around us was enough to make my back ache. "We'll look like a threat, and they'll come after us. We stay. Say what you need to."

"Yeeaahh, I'm thinkin' we should skedaddle our asses back to the Bat Cave." The lust for confrontation was lost after what I saw in the barn.

"Too late, Robin."

I looked at him and followed his line of sight. Bernie and Eli were headed in our direction.

"I'm no sidekick."

Donovan gave a gruff retort as our purpose for party-crashing reached us.

"Sophie." Eli dipped his head as Bernie came around him as if her husband dragged her along, neither addressing Donovan.

"Eli. Networking?" Okay. Maybe a tad confrontation lingered within me.

"Why are you here?"

"Got a call about your new friends."

He looked at his wife and then back to me. "I'd do anything to get Jet back."

"The fact you side-eyed Bernie,"—I paused until she looked at me—"means my intel about who organized this reunion was true. When Jet returns, will you let her know what it took to break her out? Fill her in on the names of the people who died in there or everyone who dies now that you've let that thing out? Not to mention the pimple-popper it possessed."

Eli's gaze fell on me like a bag of heavy bricks, and I clenched my teeth to refrain from cowering.

"My daughter is imprisoned, probably doing everything in her power to stay alive. I will not allow anyone to stand in my way of doing everything I can on the outside to ensure her struggle is worth it."

Donovan made a throaty noise. "Having an inexperienced Architect summon a demon is a far cry from what I'm sure she expected her doting parents to do to ensure 'her struggle is worth it'."

Architect? Demon? I wasn't following.

Eli turned to Donovan and stepped closer to him. Donovan's smirk grew with the challenge, nothing in the thread of connection telling me he considered Eli a viable threat.

Bernadine surged forward, her eyes cold, detached. "We didn't know that would happen. The portal was the experiment, not the thing that came out of it. We wanted to create one that would skip the veil."

Donovan chuckled without humour. "Your new BFFs knew exactly what would happen. It doesn't take that many Magics and super-Velcroing yourselves to the floor to make a portal. Play the ignorant bystander all you want, I sure as hell don't give a shit, but others like your daughter and Caine would. You're a Berisford. You know what those kinds of Magics are capable of, and you've been out of the game too long."

"That so?"

"It is." A slight pitch in power and a few moments of a trance-like state was Donovan filtering the vision we saw into Eli and Bernie from when Donovan touched the car. If their mental defences were so weak or non-existent, then the Tainted glaring at us from twenty feet away could see it too, though they didn't step in to take action.

Eli and Bernie blinked back into themselves. Before they could react, I bookended the vision. "Whether Jet would approve of doing your psychopath ancestors proud to save her or not, there's no way you're convincing me she'd want Andy locked up while you test it out, hoping you would survive so he didn't starve to death with no hope of getting out of the room to save himself."

Eli looked to the ground and shifted on his feet as Bernadine glared at me.

"We've taken Andy somewhere safe." Exaggerated, but my car was safer than this house.

"You did what?" Bernie's holler ate up the space between us, her breath a blast of stale coffee.

My turn to hold my ground. "Locked in his bedroom while his grandparents are creating portals and summoning demons with the Tainted is no place for a kid. We took him somewhere where he'll be safe until his mother can take care of him herself."

"You have no right!"

The Magics in the yard took a few steps towards us, curious and ready to defend their new friends.

I clenched my fists to stop myself from wailing on her. "How dare you cry the victim after what you put him through. We didn't need to steal him, he jumped at the chance to get away from the 'mean people' you have running around here. Sink in your shame for what you've become or relish in the fact you think you found a solution, but don't make him watch this go down, and don't fight us to get him back. Let us care for him while you run your experiments before you ruin his memories of you."

Bernadine and Eli stood stiff, condemning me in their minds of whatever they thought I deserved, but they didn't move against me.

"Funny thing," I shifted my weight onto my back foot and crossed my arms, hoping Bernie wouldn't take the moment to strike. "We may have figured out a way to communicate with Caine inside the Creation. To confirm if he and Jet are still alive, if there are others, if Evar or Loring are after them."

"Coordinate an escape," Donovan added, earning their fleeting attention before I regained it.

"Other avenues existed before running to Evar's devotees in some harebrained scheme. Jet wouldn't want to live knowing she was responsible for her parents' death."

"You know nothing." Bernadine's nostrils flared with restrained hate. "If you were a parent, you would understand the lengths of utter depravity you would travel to ensure your child's safety. I refuse to let my baby rot in some hellhole."

"So, you create one in your barn instead?"

Bernadine took a step back, I thought in exhaustion for the topic, but saw the dead calm of her expression for what it was. Resolve. "Your plan will fail as everything else has. Now's the time we do what's needed."

From one blink to the next, it happened. Dread washed over me as the light of Bernadine's soul dimmed when a punch of darkness spilled into her soul glow. "Lord love a duck. I guess it's that easy."

Bernie crossed her arms. "What?"

I let out a breath in defeat. "You may as well join your friends. Your soul already has."

Confusion creased the expressions of Jet's parent's faces. Until Eli got it. "She's Tainted?"

I found myself looking over the soul glow of the woman who helped shape Caine's future, seeing the whips of darkness curling her soul glow. Nothing akin to Loring but a seeping evil nonetheless. This is how it starts.

Maybe if we worked faster....

I found it in me to nod and look away. "I hope for Jet and Andy's sake it's reversible." Bernie glared at me, meeting my eyes with zero regret. "We'll let you know if contacting Caine works." I turned my back on them figuring they had enough to mull over, half-confident they wouldn't attack when my back was turned.

We headed to the car to return to Olive's for Kim's car and hopefully some babysitting tips. I jumped in the driver's seat with a running reel of Caine and Jet's expressions of confusion and pain at what had happened today and what Andy went through. I really did hope Bernie's Tainted soul was reversible, her family needed it to be, but the ache in my chest told me nothing would get better until Jet and Caine were home, alive and well. Such pressure of the future of a whole family, and we only held a thread of hope we could do anything about it.

"You sure about this?" Donovan's tone was hard.

Andy and Kim now sat in the back seat laughing over some word game Kim made up associated with the farm animals we passed to keep him entertained. He seemed distracted, and I didn't want to risk it.

I gave Donovan a quick side-eye and looked back at the long country road out the windshield. "I'd rather wait and talk privately."

"Let the draw-bridge fall, princess, and we can."

This mental barrier thing was getting to him. I huffed and dropped it. *I have no clue if this is a good idea. I hate that it came down to him needing to be taken away from there, but no child should go through this on top of having no idea where his mother is. I can't even imagine what this is doing to him. Would you have left him there?"*

"Are you kidding? They're walking billboards for good people gone bad. No way Andy should have to watch that."

"*They really are good people. Scared and not thinking long-term, but still good people.*"

"*Yeah, well, fear is at the hearts of all dark fuckers. That and greed, and it don't matter if children are in the way. They suffer all the same.*" I knew he was thinking of his own childhood, but that was as far as he was going to go with the comparison.

"*We could be them.*"

"*No, we couldn't.*"

"*We were given the chance to join forces with your mother yesterday. And we're still considering the deal.*"

"*Babe, I'd never say yes to that woman.*"

"*Never? Even if it was me stuck in the Creation?*"

"*Do I have to worry about Caine being stuck in there with you?*"

Words were unneeded to express the anger this evoked in me and rattled the connection.

"*Fine. Yes, I'd think about it. But at the same time, I'd figure out exactly what help she could provide and find a way to do the same without her involvement.*"

"*Then why aren't we doing that?*"

"*We haven't exactly had much time to think about it, have we? I don't know what Rosemary's into, who she works with or for. Nothing. I want to figure this out, and I'm not stupid enough to keep my eyes on one problem when we have this whole thing with the Sovereignty going on, too. And now, we have some teenage Architect with a goddamn demon in him. Who knows where the fuck he could be?*"

Right. I almost forgot about Graham and confirmed with Donovan what I gathered, that an Architect is a portal maker. Which means there's no way we could track him because he could go anywhere at any time. No wonder the demon thought he was the only worthy Magic in the barn.

"*Maybe Olive will have some ideas.*" I doubted it, but who knew. Vincent would be my next call, but I wasn't sure about what Ranlyn or Veata would say.

"*They won't say anything because Vincent won't tell them.*"

Donovan answered my unprojected thoughts, showing again, that he was much better at mind reading than I was. *"Vincent's smart as hell, probably has connections in every city, but I'm willing to bet he said shit-all to Ranlyn or Veata about Eli and Bernadine's friends."*

"Why would he? They're not in his Coven. He was giving me a heads up because he knew I'd give a shit."

"Granted, but how'd he know in the first place?"

"Like you said, he probably has connections in every city." I didn't want to admit I knew yellow polo shirt guy was a Sovereignty member or my suspicion he was Vincent's inside man at the Sovereignty and probably the one who tipped him off about the barn activities.

"So, you're basically willing to believe everything Vincent says?"

"No." I strained to keep my mental voice controlled, negotiating a slick turn, and revving back up to speed. *"What's your beef with him? I don't get it."*

"To be blunt, I think he's fucking you. Not properly fucking you, though how would I know since you shield me from whatever's in your head?"

"Fuck you."

He shifted sideways to face me. *"I never rummaged through your brain before you knew I was Telepathic. I could do it right now. You wouldn't even know how deep I'd gone, but I don't because I want absolute transparency between us, and I don't want to push you away by being overbearing when your attention is already so captivated by Caine and getting into Diluculo, plus the Sovereignty business on top this bullshit with Eli and Bernadine. You've got about ten plates spinning right now. I just wish we weren't one of them."*

I wrenched the wheel and skidded to a stop on the unpaved shoulder of the road, leaving Kim's question of if everything was okay behind as I slammed the door shut and walked to the back of the car.

Donovan followed. "Why do I always have to chase you?"

"I told you I didn't want to talk about this now, and you insisted we did anyway but turned it into an opportunity to drudge up shit that has nothing to do with the situation. I can't concentrate on the road with a kid in the back seat and deal with your accusations without putting us all in the ditch."

"I never said you have to tell me everything. My point was that I could pluck everything from your head if I wanted, and I never have, even when you admitted you were withholding important info from me."

"The guy in the yellow shirt."

Donovan blinked, confusion crossing the connection.

"In the barn, the yellow polo shirt hoovered into the portal."

"What about him?"

"His name was Christopher Leisemeyer. He worked for the Sovereignty. I know this because he was one of the marks me and Vincent were tailing. He's Blind. Not good or evil, or maybe both, but his soul doesn't glow to me, so I can't tell." The icy air ached in my chest, causing me to clear my throat. "When Blake sent you that stupid picture it was because Christopher went inside that diner, so we followed to read his mind and see if he knew anything or if he was meeting someone of interest. We pretended we were together so we would look like two normal people out for lunch, but Blake happened to be there because I have a pissy leprechaun shoved up my ass who likes to shit out bad luck like a Play-Doh stamp whenever I sit the wrong way."

A moment passed in quiet. "You think you're a believable couple?"

"Donovan!"

"Shit! Sorry for trying to bring some levity to your pissy leprechaun."

I huffed and paced a step.

"Thanks for telling me." His tone was soft, the edge of his temper smoothed. "I wish I didn't have to tear it out of you."

I nudged a block of ice with my boot and worked to regulate myself.

"What if what Vincent's doing puts you in danger?"

"Come on. Vincent's stronger than you."

"Probably smarter too, but you don't hold the same importance to him as you do to me, meaning he wouldn't automatically pit himself in front of you. You're an adult and can make your own decisions—his accountability ends there."

"He's saved my ass in Diluculo and literally buried it in one of our past lives. I seriously doubt he'd let me die that easily."

"He did?"

I nodded. We never did speak about the happenings in Diluculo, though Kim had told me about the burying thing as I was too out of it at the time to hear him. I gave a quick explanation, attempting to alleviate any doubt from Donovan's mind.

"With all this talk of Vincent knowing us for so many lives, doesn't it seem weird that it's more like he knew *you* more than he knew me?"

"No. We're not the same people every time we come back. I know we're always us, but circumstance plays a role. Apparently, we were never this way with each other before either. Always either fighting or scrambling to be with each other, we just were." I shrugged and ran my cold hands over my wind-knotted hair.

The thought of it all still baffled me. Tragic lives spent with Donovan I didn't remember but the fragmented visions that haunted Donovan since the beginning ensnared between wanting to know everything and wishing I could tear loose what had already burrowed itself within my memory. A giant excavator probably couldn't manage the job they clung so close to me these days. A skin I couldn't escape but poisoned me a little more every day.

If only Caine and Jet could be released. Jet could reclaim her son, and we could concentrate on other things. The battles that wage within us on a rotating cycle had one or the other in a state of depression so often true happiness was more than a fingertip away. It was floating somewhere in a deep dark place like the portal, a wasteland not a hand would be stupid enough to reach for.

"What the fuck are we going to do with a kid?" I gave a half-laugh half-sob as I leaned into my hands on my knees.

"Oh, it's we now?" Craning my neck to look up at him, I was relieved of panic to see his dimples flash. "Be grateful he's not in diapers."

"That's okay." I straightened and started back to the Barracuda. "You'd be on full diaper duty if he was."

He snort-laughed. "Doubts, babe."

Before we reached the car, I projected a question to him. *"Are you sure about turning Rosemary down?"*

"I'm sure Rosemary's screwing with us, but I intend to look further into what she said."

I nodded, and we got back into the car. Watching Bernadine Taint with the vengeful intent of saving her daughter scared me. It happened in a snap. I didn't want working with Rosemary to cause the same in anyone, but I also didn't want to be Tainted by whatever measures we were forced to make because we turned down Rosemary's offer in the first place.

We plunked into the warmth of the car, and my tires found the slick road back to Olive's.

"Uncle Van, can we hit the Mickey D's drive-thru?"

When we turned back to the kid, his little face was all serious, but Kim was losing it next to him, hiding behind a hand clasped to her mouth as her gaze hit the floor.

"Sure thing, kid." Donovan's poker face was flawless. Mine, not so much as I glared at Kim in the rear-view mirror.

"What?" Her blue-green eyes widened in feigned innocence. "He's practically related."

A dimple creased both of Donovan's cheeks. *"Worth it to see you smile."*

Andy was shy as we went through the estate locking mechanisms into the attic where Olive, the aunts, Lewis, Priscilla, Serena, and Jared all stood smiling down at him while I introduced them. He came alive once meeting Bosco. They saw Andy in the attic when Donovan was accused by the Elders of colluding against them, but his face was a new one to Jared. He and the Coveners had heard of the kid who saw spots on you before you died. Jared's suspicious expression was too obvious, as if he were watching to see if Andy saw spots on him. I prayed Andy's initial shyness wasn't an indication of him seeing spots on anyone and was happy he was too busy with Bosco to notice.

I peeked at Andy across the room where I had set him up with a Happy Meal, he sneaking Bosco some fries and laughing as my pug companion chomped them down. "She went all murky and Tainted right in front of me. I've never seen anything like it. Is it reversible?"

Lewis fixed his glasses. "I've heard of a reversal, yet never encountered one myself."

"Neither have I, Firefly. Not that that says much since I haven't been in the company of Magics for thirty years."

"It's possible." Gloria's grumbled optimism was surprising.

"A great change in perspective is required." Iris fiddled with her skirts while seated at Olive's desk. "As great a change as the one that precipitated the Tainting."

Getting Jet back, with the added bonus of Caine, may be enough to do that. What would happen if it wasn't and her daughter's return created a foundation for the justification of Bernadine and Eli's actions?

Donovan's inquiry of the devotees who broke into the estate, and were now nowhere in sight, broke my worried thoughts.

Marco, Jeremy, the Tainted Photographer, and other nameless followers of the Puppeteer had their minds successfully altered, filled with useless information, and sent on their way since all they had in way of information was their motives for breaking in, which we knew was to find what they hoped would reopen the Creation.

Olive fluttered her hand as if the devotees were old news. "What about this demon that came out of the portal? You said the teen didn't know what was happening?"

"Clueless as fattening up a pig for bacon." I ignored Serena's "Ewww" and looked at Donovan. "Though I was flying backwards in the air most the time."

"No. He was clueless and petrified. I think they brought the kid in because of his Architect ability. The demon sure knew this."

"So, the kid's like the Apporter?" Jared had a good question.

"Olson wishes." I wondered if Donovan knew this as fact. "No. Apporters can travel from one point to another. Architects can move through space, time, realm, plane, whatever. There's no way the kid understood the magnitude of his gift, and the people around him, including Eli and Bernadine, exploited this, hoping he could jump across the veil even with it locked down. Though, I don't think they realized something would come out of the portal and take Graham over. Plus, you can't control a demon."

I doubted they knew as well, though Eli and Bernadine fostering the circumstances in which this occurred still left them accountable in my book.

"Are you going to your Elders with the Architect issue? Or are they already informed?" Gloria brought up a good question, though an uncomfortable one.

"I'll call Ranlyn." Donovan's response was flat. I suspected for my benefit, showing he wasn't allowing the information to be passed to Vincent alone, fearing it would stop there, and the consequences of being involved with that, would weigh too heavily on him.

Even though we fell on different ends of opinions regarding Vincent, I prayed Donovan would keep his mouth shut about yellow polo shirted Christopher and the possible connection to the Sovereignty. He did in front of everyone else, but with Ranlyn I couldn't be so certain.

"What about this Nexus Transference spell?" Kim looked around her. "Do we have what we need here?"

"Do I believe it can be done?" Gloria raised her brows. "Of course."

"But you don't know how." I guessed, annoyed by Gloria's unwillingness to say so.

Gloria swiped invisible dust from her shirt sleeve. "I myself, nor the attic, possess the accessories to do so. For a price, I can procure them."

I gave a hollow single laugh. "Fine. I'll pay."

Olive clucked her tongue. "No, you will not."

Gloria glared at Olive. "This is not a Ballard Coven expense."

Olive met her sister's challenging stare with equal attitude. "You're not the one in charge of such things. Caine is among those who fought to have me released from The Royal, then housed me until the estate was habitable. A charitable deed far beyond anything the rest of the family made." Shame flooded the features of the older members present as none of them questioned Olive's thirty-year committal. "As far as I'm concerned, Caine is an unofficial member of our Coven and an otherwise decent person of whom does not deserve his fate."

Kim lifted her hand. "And there's more than just him trapped in there."

"Precisely my point. Our Coven should not be alone in paying the bill for the rescue mission, but if we are, then I'm proud to do so."

"We spoke of contact, not release." Iris squinted. "Are we now contributing to the path the premonition portended and bringing the wrath of the Sovereignty down upon this family?"

I couldn't help but feel embarrassment for my part in that premonition and my silence involving the Sovereignty, but this wasn't the time to lay it out.

Olive waved her hands. "This has nothing to do with that damn premonition, Iris. I care for the people trapped with those monsters. One of our own. If the Sovereignty wants to make it their business, then let them wring their dish towels over it."

With a resentful promise to do what was necessary to create the connection between Caine and Donovan with help from the Nexus Transference spell, we gathered up Andy and piled into my car, Kim following in her own.

After the quiet ride as Andy napped with his head tilted back and his mouth wide open, Bosco half on his lap, we showed him to his temporary room, unsurprised when he chose the western themed room on the main floor. Andy ran his hands over the rope in the wooden horse's mouth in the corner, which was probably more for show than for play, though it wouldn't surprise me if he used it anyway.

We stuck the small amount of Andy's stuff in the distressed dresser while he was busy setting up action figures in a battle scene on the rough-wood bench at the end of the bed. Once Bosco came inside from a pee break, they scuttled around on the floor before we snuck out to the kitchen.

Kim bit into a pear and wiped her mouth with the back of her hand before grabbing a paper towel. "What school does Andy go to?"

Donovan looked to me, and I registered the "Oh shit!" moment. "Is it Winter break yet?" Donovan and Kim shrugged. None of us had kids. Donovan didn't even have proper schooling, so no one knew what kind of timeline we were looking at.

A genius, Kim was. Once we asked Andy the school's name and his grade, we found the school's website. We sat at the desk in an upstairs office Donovan had set up looking at their December calendar stating Winter Break didn't start until the twenty-third. It was only the sixth, so we had many days to go.

Driving him in was an option, but I didn't want to give Bernadine or Eli the opportunity to get to Andy, and we couldn't sit there and watch him all day. They were ashamed when we confronted them, but it was after that when Bernadine went all dark. I have no idea what they're thinking and wasn't willing to risk it.

If Winter Break came and went, then we would have no choice but to look into alternatives since I knew from my studies that kids couldn't miss more than two weeks of school without authorities becoming involved. And we didn't need the extra complication. For now, he wasn't venturing out farther than the front door without strict supervision.

Kim devised a witchy idea she thought couldn't miss.

"Is that really necessary?" I followed her to the kitchen where we found Donovan frying something on the stove while simultaneously looking over papers strewn over the kitchen table.

I followed Kim to the basement, pausing to check in on Andy in his temporary digs. He had set up a battle scene with Bosco as the enemy. His pug jaw snapped to try and catch the little cannon balls Andy shot in his direction.

"Make sure he doesn't eat those, okay buddy? It'll hurt his belly." I envisioned sifting through his backyard minefield to make sure all of the little black balls were accounted for and took a moment to send a vision to Bosco of the plastic cannon balls making him sick and another of him catching and spitting them out, hoping he would listen to the directives without spoiling Andy's fun.

"'Kay." Andy's flicker of attention brushed me off as he continued his siege.

In the basement, Kim was talking, but I found it hard to connect one sentence to another as she scrambled through the closet for Aunt Lacey's grimoire.

She plopped down on the couch next to me making me bounce. "You'll definitely have to wait until after hours. Leave a message for the principal to give to Andy's teachers. And go with family emergency. Oh! In the east coast, so it doesn't sound like he's skipping out west on a ski trip to have fun instead of missing 'critical days of learning'."

Her air quotes had me chuckling.

"Laugh now, but this is foolproof, my willowy friend."

As I continued to be amused at Kim's candour, she shuffled through the frail translucent pages for what she was looking for.

I took an unsettling breath after reading the title Kim pointed at. Phonetic Conversion Spell. I looked over the long list of ingredients and instructions in Aunt Lacey's wispy script, wishing I had Donovan's gift to touch and see her when she wrote it.

"There's no way we have all of this here."

"Don't underestimate our stock, girl." Kim plopped the open grimoire on my lap, it so heavy I was sure Donovan felt the impact. "Aunt Lacey didn't need a wide range of goodies because she was born super awesome, but the rest of us still need a boost. Most of the time ingredients can be supplemented if you don't have the exact ones. Assuming they have the same properties, they will have the same desired result. Somewhat dangerous, but we are working with ones I'm familiar with."

"Screwed up a spell real bad, didn't you?"

"Soooooo bad. Thankfully, Aunt Lacey was supervising and restored Gwen before she suffocated, but you won't see her volunteering to be my guinea pig too often."

"You stopped her breathing?"

"Removed her lungs."

"Kim!"

"She got them back. Plus, she's a smoker, so they were probably restored clearer than before I took them."

I had no clue what the desired result was supposed to be, but it sounded like a small room for error was present when dealing with supplementing ingredients. Note to self—always have a Magic with greater powers to supervise your experiments.

"This is going to take a while. Go play with your boyfriend." She pointed at me. "Nothing cheeky. There's a child under this roof now. Everything in the libido department should come to a crashing halt."

"Thankfully you're the sweetest, offering to take Andy whenever we need some nookie time. You're such a doll, Kim. Thanks in bunches."

"Don't you dare."

"No really, bestie. Awesomest chick ever." I made quick for the stairs with two thumbs up, disappearing upstairs before she could yell at me.

Checking on Andy again, Bosco was panting and knocking over Andy's carefully set up army, so I let them be, finding Donovan still in the kitchen. Alternative to taking the seat across from him, I swept his arm aside and landed on his lap, planting a deep kiss on his lips that filled the both of us with lustful surprise. Before it grew legs and carried us to more naked endeavours, I pulled away, breaking the vision he was inundated with. The pressure of his large hands cradling my back made it damn near impossible to resist, so talking was my greatest distraction.

"Apparently, the fun ends there now that we have little eyes and ears around."

Donovan's brow crooked. "Why be powerful enough to bring down ancient Magics and an empire of self-righteous bastards if I can't get some play when I want it? It's called magic, babe. You even know how to do it when you feel like it." He pecked me on the lips, earning a glimmer of a vision that sprung then ebbed in a flash.

I took the seat across from him. "Sorry I don't think to use it for everything and anything I do."

"According to this hot mess of a premonition, you possess a great power that with the 'fated at your side will double in ferocity and quell those who seek vengeance'."

"Yeah? Well, since you know it's going to happen, I'm sure you can quell enough for the both of us."

"That doesn't make sense."

"That entire bible of bullshit in front of you doesn't make sense. Everything that comes out of your mouth when you're talking about that crap finds its way to my brain and is just as quickly purged out its nearest escape hole."

His dimples caved. "This crap will happen whether we prepare for it or not."

"True story, but how are we supposed to prepare to not only take down the Sovereignty but find a way to open the Creation to save Caine, Jet, and whoever else is stuck in there? Also, kill the unkillable Evaristus who according to everyone is still alive and kicking with

Loring possibly licking the tip until he gets out? Plus, deal with the Architect, Eli, Bernadine, and their flock of evil assholes. Oh, and your truce-wielding mommy who pops out of the woodwork like a dimpled whack-a-mole much the same as your brother did, minus the dimples. I'm assuming I'll meet Daddy in no time, though I might be busy with the rest of all that. Or I'll be babysitting a six-year-old when I have less experience parenting that I do cooking. If those pages can answer how to take care of all that, then you can call Fox back here to tattoo every word of it across my ass."

"Language." Kim came into the room and fished around in the cupboard, pulling out a box of salt. "Andy will regurgitate every word you say. When Jet gets back, she'll be looking at you two to re-educate him."

Donovan leaned the chair back onto two legs. "What the fuck's the salt for?"

I had to laugh.

Heavily sighing in the exhaustive effort of trying to turn Donovan into anyone but his bastardly self, Kim explained the salt was for the spell, then swiped another small jar off the spice rack and sauntered back to the basement shooting him the finger as she went.

Almost as soon as she disappeared down the hallway, we heard a gasp and Kim's apology to Andy who saw her flipping us off. We howled in echoes that rounded the kitchen.

7

PANTS ON FIRE

The first night with Andy in the Western themed room was rough in the sleeping department. Not for Andy, he was conked-out and snoring, exhausted by the day's events. Not that Bosco minded as he added to the snoring. I kept expecting Bernadine and Eli to lead a pack of devotees through the wards, slaughter us, and retrieve Andy like in a Liam Neeson movie.

It never happened.

Monopolizing the time I should have been sleeping before an early afternoon shift at The Lush was the train-wreck of Kim's bright idea to use the Phonetic Conversion spell.

Inhaling the disgusting concoction while concentrating on the memory of Jet's voice smelled no better than huffing paint thinner fumes from a paper bag and looked the same. The instant headrush subsided enough for me to call Andy's school principal and leave the planned message on their voicemail. I added an email for Andy's teachers to send important lessons so he wouldn't fall behind.

Pure genius.

Until Andy came running into the room with panicked excitement looking for his mother, only to find me. Nothing could erase the expression of heartbreak as Andy burst into tears and ran to his room. Kim talked to him and wiped his red eyes until he eventually fell asleep, but I couldn't find it in me to speak to him again in case I messed up and the sound of his mother's voice came out to add to his trauma. It would take hours for the effect to wear off.

No matter the amount of reassurance, I couldn't switch off the visual of Andy's tortured expression.

Donovan's exhaustion eventually won out and took me under with him into a restless sleep of painful dreams full of memories I wished to forget. Whether it was the younger face of Donovan's mother, Aunt Lacey, or Andy, both of us battled each other for equal opportunity to mess with our heads before the early morning alarm turned them all to dust.

"You need to quit. For good." Donovan groaned with a husky grogginess, stretching his back muscles with his arm over his head. Even the sight of him wrapped in the comfort of his blankets, somehow still looking sexy with crazy bed head and red creases across his face from sleeping on his belly, I sat on the side of the mattress wishing I didn't have to move. Nothing could make me rejoin the sandman and his taunting nightmares.

Donovan trying to talk me into quitting the bar job was a regular occurrence. Every time I responded with, "Bills don't pay themselves". His go-to answer involved him taking care of me or reminding me about the money I got from Olive and how I was next in line as heir to the Ballard family fortune. Never did I think he was joking. The bar wasn't important to me. No emotional investment kept me working there, but after my leave of absence, Drew took me back. I knew I couldn't do it again so soon without expecting to never return, and The Lush was a palatable backup plan. The money from Olive would run out quicker than he thought. I preferred to let it simmer in the bank as it was the first time in my life I had a nest egg, and right now wasn't the time to use my safety net.

I padded into the en-suite bathroom, wincing at the shock of cold tiles against my bare feet. After I was done, I found the bed empty and made my way to the kitchen. Sitting perched on a stool of the island was Andy donned in his race car pyjamas as Donovan poured pancake mix into a frying pan. Ducking out the door would have been ideal, but I braved the possible scrutiny of a six-year-old and pulled out a singles bottle of Sunny-D from the fridge, offering one to Andy who accepted it with a sleepy nod.

Sleep crusted in the creases of Andy's eyes reminded me of Jet. Something like that would have been handled by a mom, and I was no substitute.

"What are you doing today?" I asked Donovan, pushing Jet from my mind as I opened my drink.

"Hmm. What would you like to do today, kid?" Donovan flipped a pancake to reveal its lightly toasted belly.

"We can build a snowman."

Donovan gave a small laugh. "Sure we can. I bet even Bosco will help." He looked down at Bosco who had parked himself at Donovan's feet in hopes of delicious cast-offs.

I felt bad for leaving Andy with Donovan. Not because Donovan was irresponsible, which of course with most things he was unless it included protecting others, but because to Andy, Donovan was a stranger.

After last night and breaking his little heart, I thought maybe the day of us being away from each other would settle the tension. He seemed fine, too strong for a six-year-old, the issue more so my guilt.

Promising to see him later, I made quick for the door and began dressing in layers to brave the cold awaiting me outside.

Before I could slip my boots on, Donovan caught up to me with nervousness swirling in his gut. "I'm contacting Ranlyn today."

Tucking my jeans into my boots, I looked up at him. "Okay."

"Just giving you a heads up. I won't say anything about Vincent and the surveillance or the yellow shirt guy, but you should probably call Vincent and let him know. I'm sure you'd rather I don't lose my shit on Vincent, but I was going to."

No doubt he was. I was surprised he hadn't already. Did this constitute as progress? This bitterness towards Vincent wouldn't lessen easily. The moment he could, Donovan would confront Vincent, but I hoped it would be through the safety of a cell line.

"I'll call him." I donned my black pea coat and reached for the door handle.

"Hey, speed racer." He pressed a firm palm against the door, stopping me from a clean exit. He wrapped me up in a strong hug that melted the chill between us as I found myself clinging to him. "Andy will be fine with me."

"I know."

As we parted, he pressed his lips to mine. Tidal waves of adoration spilled over before he pulled away. When I turned over the ignition of the Barracuda, the feeling lingered and settled into my bones as I waited for the beast to warm up. Gliding on the high Donovan's kiss etched onto my sleepy heart, I made it into work without the stress of the last twenty-four hours weighing me down.

———

The afternoon was slow. A couple regulars had some food and drinks in front of them but were otherwise low-maintenance, so I checked my school dashboard site for my forgotten assignments and worked on them on an app on my phone. Never used to having a cell on me twenty-four-seven, Donovan gave me the idea to try working electronically to make my life easier since I still refused to give up on my Psychology degree.

Mrs. Valone took interest in me after I reached out and pleaded to take lower marks to hand in assignments late. She encouraged me to push through and commit, having enjoyed a few papers I handed in. The work became a way to avoid dealing with failing to crack open the Creation. A selfish one, but one which worked and ensured I didn't waste the tuition dollars.

A cleared throat had me looking up from my phone. A lean man with short auburn hair, ten years my senior, and wearing a cashmere navy-blue sweater wore a smile and held his coat slung over one arm. Whatever his day entailed, I doubted he planned for it to include a dive bar. He looked like one-hundred-dollar bills shoved into a pleather purse.

"Sorry 'bout that. What can I get you?"

"Whisky. Neat." He took a seat on the stool at the bar while I grabbed a glass and a bottle. "Looked like schoolwork. What are you studying?"

I put the glass on the bartop. He extended his thanks and waited for me to answer. "Psychology."

He took a sip of his drink and nodded.

"I know. A bartender-slash-psychology student. I'm clichéd like that."

He chuckled. "Nah. A cliché would be if you were a psychology student and an exotic dancer."

"No offence to exotic dancers, right?"

"Of course. Consenting adults have a right to their choice of money-making endeavours."

"You sound like a man of experience."

He straightened. "Do I?"

"You're an expensive sweater comfortable in a swanky joint like this? Maybe you're a chaps-wearing cowboy after whatever pencil pushing management position gets you through the day."

"Right. Because exotic dancing is an equal opportunity profession."

"Sure is."

He laughed and reached out his hand to shake mine. "Chase Llewellyn. Not an exotic dancer."

I shook his hand back, noticing the smooth surface of someone who didn't work with his hands. "Nice to meet you, Chase."

His flashed a full set of perfect teeth. "Can I call you Sophie? Or do you prefer Soul Seer?"

I pulled my hand from his grasp.

"Maybe Salix?"

Fuck. Fuck, fuck, fuck.

"Or Firefly? I do enjoy that one. So whimsical."

Chase was as nonchalant as if he revealed himself as one in the loop of the Magics of his city everyday.

"Sophie's fine."

All my quick assessments of this man changed. His easy confidence was now arrogant, his casualness more condescension than comfort as he took another sip from his glass as if to show his hand wasn't shaking, he unaffected by outing himself and confronting me. Not his first time.

"You surround yourself faultlessly with those who lay their life at your feet." He surveyed The Lush with new disgust. "To my dismay, this was my only option of monopolizing a fraction of your time without the white knights drawing their swords." He gave a smug laugh as I stood, muscles clenched in anticipation, suddenly missing Ranlyn as my constant bodyguard. "Though this is a quaint organization I wouldn't pour a dime more than needed into its cash register." He looked down at his glass. "Not for an establishment that fills expensive bottles with cheap swill. Not that anyone attending this place could clock the difference."

He was right. No one ordered whisky neat. It was always mixed or shot so Drew refilled good bottles with the cheap stuff and was never called out. College kids couldn't tell, and the regulars were too pickled to care.

Chase was beyond the need for two people in this conversation and was content with proceeding with his purpose. "My soul, you see..." He tilted his head back. "...or rather the soul you do not see..." I noticed that off the bat, which was my fault for thinking a lack of soul meant they were safe. "...is hidden from you for a purpose. Regular practice for those of us in the Sovereignty to avoid detection from you and the Soul Seers of your family since they have recently come to light. While you were casing my employees hoping to discover clues in their souls, you would have seen nothing but the working lawman and women of the Blind."

Ranlyn once claimed only he and the Elders knew a spell that could douse a soul glow and hide it from a Soul Seer. Apparently, the only secret was that Ranlyn was an idiot.

"I know about the premonition." He downed the remainder of his drink, his face screwing up at the taste. "I know what you plan to do with my company, and I'm here to let you know we are aware of your rebellion. I'm extending the warning in hopes to deter you from this coup my brother has codified before blood is spilt in the name of a false enemy."

My expression or my thoughts must have betrayed me as Chase paused and then clucked his tongue. "Guess Vincent has yet to reveal his true motives." Chase had me by the metaphorical short and curlies and knew it. "It's as simple as that, Firefly. Vicious sibling rivalry and nothing more. Vincent wasn't our father's favourite, did not possess the ability to take over the company, and fell into disuse. Until now when he seeks out a Seedling in attempt to prove his weakness is otherwise what it appears. Believe when I say my brother is using you to settle a grudge that's brewed for centuries and has absolutely nothing to do with injustice and everything to do with the temper of a spoiled child."

Chase stood to his feet, a victor moving towards the door before stopping and turning back to me. "I'm sure the moment I leave your next move will be to bring my visit to Vincent's attention." He slipped his coat on. "Do extend my greetings and be sure to let him know the deal is still on the table."

With his point made, Chase headed towards the exit, disappearing before he reached the door.

I did nothing but stand there like a muted pawn, a messenger in the midst of some battle who always ends up returned-to-sender with a spear in their back or an axe or a bullet depending on what movie era you were talking about.

My power rushed to the surface as I fought to calm myself. Chase said it was his company. His. The head of the Sovereignty showed up to personally feed me a cease-and-desist order against further action.

No, to educate me on what he knew I had no clue about. I was a chump. Vincent made me one. All I could think about was how gullible I was. Donovan was always suspicious, but not me. Not really. I was all about Team Vincent.

My cell vibrated in the pocket of my teal sweater. I wanted to throw it against the wall. I felt like such a moron. Even if the Sovereignty deserved to be torn apart like a Barbie doll, Vincent played me. No excuse existed for not mentioning the company he talked me into taking down happened to be his family's company.

Why hadn't anyone else said anything? Why didn't Donovan know?

The text message was from a worried Donovan wondering if my anger was a run-of-the-mill work incident or if something else was up. Texting him back would take too long. I needed to talk to him in person.

First, I had to think. Did I want Vincent to know I knew about Chase and his link to the Sovereignty? Did I want to try to keep it from him and see how long it took him to reveal it himself? Did I want to ask Donovan and risk him flying off the handle and give him another reason to deal with Vincent himself while I was stuck at work?

With hours left in my shift, I was trapped. I could walk out, of course I could, but I made a promise to work. Taking off would fuck up Eddie's day or whomever Drew hired while I was gone.

Calling Kim was a safer outlet. She wouldn't run to Donovan or anyone else and might be a good sounding board in trying to figure out what I should do next. I hid in the back pretending to be pulling a case from storage as I called her.

"That piece of shit!" She hissed into the receiver after I blurted every detail the second Kim picked up the phone.

"I don't know where to go from here."

"Kick his lying ass."

"Vincent's like a thousand years old, and he taught me most of what I know in more than one lifetime. He could end me cleanly."

"Maybe he'd let you win."

I laughed. "Doubt he'd be so guilt-ridden."

"I know you. There's no way in hell you'll be able to sit there and talk to Vincent without spilling your guts and expecting answers. Call him up and bitch him out."

"But what if that's what Chase wants?"

"Who cares what Chase wants?"

"I do. Well, no. I don't give a troll's belly-button lint about what Chase wants, but he's the head of the Sovereignty, something I never even thought to ask. How could I never ask who led the organization I was putting my life on the line to take down? You know why? Because I'm a sheep. The stupid kind of sheep who walks into the electric fence over and over until it pisses itself and dies."

Kim giggled. "Vincent's blinding that way."

"Meaning?"

"Like you said, he's really old, has went through a barrel more than any of us, and since you shared some past friendship, you were complacent to believe everything he said."

I sighed into the receiver. "If by complacent you mean a dill-hole, then I'm right there with you."

"Then call me dill-hole number two because I never saw this coming."

"That bastard. He's gonna love this."

"Why would Vincent love this?"

"Not Vincent. Donovan. Of course, he called it. Said he thought something was fishy with Vincent and not to trust him. But like a shady lawyer, I defended the wanker, and now I have to admit Donovan was right."

"Good luck living this one down." Kim laughed as I groaned into the phone. "Don't tell Donovan until you get home."

"Not my home. His home."

"*Pfft*. Semantics. At least then if he takes off on a tirade of ass-kicking you can stop him before Vincent grinds him into Donovan-soup."

"True. Ugh." I rubbed my face. "Damn, this sucks."

"Yes. Yes, it does."

We ended the call. Drew hadn't come looking for me yet, so I dialled Vincent.

"Hello?"

"Hey liar, what's up?" Not the subtlest.

"I beg your pardon?"

"Why would I call you a liar? Hmm, let's see. Maybe because I was just bombarded, at work, by a visitor who had an interesting tale to tell about you."

"Who would that be?"

"He told me to tell you, 'Hi,' and, 'The offer's still on the table'." If Chase was as clever as he claimed, I figured this would be a dead giveaway. Silence on the line confirmed I was right.

"Charles." He said the name like it was a dirty word.

"Charles? How many brothers do you have?"

"What name did he give?"

"Chase Llewellyn."

"Llewellyn is accurate. As with Elsa and most Magics in high profile positions where the Blind may take notice, Charles found it necessary to create a new moniker every century or so. Though the Blind are so self-absorbed, they tend not to notice the man has been in office for four hundred and fifty years and has yet to sprout a grey hair."

"Hey, ass-juggler. My reason for calling was to point out the fact that I'm done being a sucker. I'm not sticking my nose out believing everything you say anymore. You've lost that right."

"Do you mind if I sp—"

"I've had a million-in-one things happen in the last twenty-four hours or so because of this inane pursuit of injustice when I don't even know of the injustices that have apparently happened. I almost got eaten by some crazy portal demon that crawled into a vessel in the midst of puberty, and now I have to care for a six-year-old when I have a dog. No kids, Vincent! For a reason!"

"Where are you?"

"I already told you, I'm at work. And no way you're swinging by for a chat. I will personally castrate you with a julep strainer if you do."

"Understandable. I would not jeopardize your employment for a mere conversation, Sophie."

"Don't patronize me, Vincent. I still have hours until I'm free from serving duty, and I'm full-up with enough of your bullshit for one day."

"We will convene at Donovan's then."

"Fine!" I hung up the phone hating the fact he assumed correctly where to find me.

Screaming at Vincent clear into the night wasn't what I had in mind when I dialled his number, though if I had been thinking proactively, it should have been expected. Hopefully he'd wait for me to show up first, so I could avoid walking into the midst of fists flying, but you could only hope for so much when you had luck like mine.

When the vibration of a follow-up text from Donovan shook my pocket and my waning patience, I tore off my sweater instead of putting the phone in my purse.

My neck itched with the overheated aftermath of my anger.

Managing to avoid responding to Donovan the rest of the shift, I fought a tug-of-war with what I should do and what I wanted to do. Many times I had been resolved in texting him when the opportunity was present and I wasn't busy with demanding customers.

What started out a rather routine shift, morphed into a steady and inescapable mash of random events including an ambulance call for a pool ball to the nose, a livid overreaction for a mix-up in burger condiments, and a brawl outside not involving the bar but spilled over to a customer's car's side mirror getting ripped off when the fight landed in our parking lot. A chat with the cops and struggling with The Lush's ancient security cameras was a treat. All seemingly engineered to keep me from making that responsive measure.

No matter what I did, I couldn't find a moment to text Donovan, and then Eddie showed up for the late-night shift, and I could breathe.

Due to the overwhelming shenanigans during my shift and the supernatural inconveniences woven within, shift change with Eddie ran long.

The drive to Niagara-on-the-Lake would give me time to process how to broach the subject with Vincent in front of Donovan. Scenarios of how each would react played like movie clips in my head.

A chilled wind followed me into the front foyer of Donovan's home. With the configuration of the house allowing me to see a straight shot into the kitchen, viewing only half of it, it was enough to see that not only had Vincent already arrived, but so had Ranlyn.

As I grumbled at my luck, kicked off my boots, and hung up my coat, I drew closer to the mystics in the kitchen to find it was far fuller than it first appeared. Seated at the kitchen table, out of view of the front door, was Veata and the Apporter, Olson.

It took me a moment to register the fact Olson had no soul glow. He must have taken something to temporarily extinguish his Tainted essence as he sat comfortably amongst the nuclear glows of the others, besides Donovan's whose soothing green glow was smothered in their intenseness.

The group stared at me as I approached. "Where's Andy and Bosco?"

Donovan leaned back against the counter in front of the sink with his arms crossed. He didn't make eye contact when he mumbled, "Andy's room," loud enough for me to catch.

Nodding, grateful they thought of the innocents first and foremost, I still had to ask, "Is he locked in?"

This caught Donovan's attention. "Nope."

I nodded again. "Someone wanna play news anchor and catch me up? I wouldn't want to start and learn you've already heard the highlights." The derision in my voice was unmistakable, yet this painfully fell short of motivating a stir in conversation. "If we're not talking, I'm showering and going to bed because I worked all—"

"Are you considering Rosemary's truce?" Ranlyn stymied my protest.

Sucker punched by the impromptu question, I never thought Donovan would truly confer with the Elders. I was trapped in a lingering slack-jawed second where my sight peripherally caught Donovan's minute shake of his head. A tiny movement, desperate to portray the proper warning.

Seeing this action set me in panic mode. I didn't want to lie to an Elder, especially Ranlyn, but we technically had yet to make the decision regarding Rosemary.

With a half-second passing since the question had been asked, stretching beyond comfortable, I managed an answer. "We could have accepted Rosemary's proposal on the spot, and we didn't."

"I would hope not." Ranlyn's inscrutable dark blues weighed down on me in a way I never felt from him; he was clearly unsatisfied with my answer. "Maybe the Berisford's weakness will be proof enough of how easily intentions lead to darkened souls."

So, Donovan told them about our visit to Caine's family's. Surprise, surprise.

Erasing the steps between us, Ranlyn approached me and grasped my forearms with the tilt of pleading in his expression. Donovan straightened in my periphery, tension blooming within him as if primed to intervene.

Ranlyn squeezed my arms and took a moment. Whatever I expected this conversation to entail, I didn't expect tears in his eyes. "I know what the premonition states you are to do. Please, Sophie, do not lead them to this. Maybe things are set in stone, maybe not. I know you're good at heart and motivated by love, but proceeding with this path will not just end lives." His strong grip tightened enough Donovan felt it, his anger rising. "It will sentence their souls to a fate worse than any death, and the guilt that follows will erase the rebellion to a pack with their hearts halved by grief for the consequences of their impulsive actions."

I spun my arms in his grasp and held onto to him as he did with me. "Don't you think I've struggled with this every moment since the premonition was revealed? I never want to find myself lost in that darkness or even simply Tainted by it, but I can't justify leaving Coveners in Diluculo with Evar and Loring and whoever else might kill them. Nothing can make me change my mind about that. But I won't act as Eli and Bernadine have and seek out evil to work it out for me. I don't know if using them as they use us is worth it in the end or will or won't change me in anyway, but something needs to be done.

"You're the Elder of a great Coven, Ranlyn. Standing passively while this happens will be what divides this Coven, not me." I allowed our arms to drop while he still stood close. "Releasing those in the Creation, killing Evaristus and Loring, finding injustices within the Sovereignty—I didn't give a shit about it until someone told me I should. Now, there's too much happening to ignore without feeling like an irresponsible bystander. I can't watch what Aunt Lacey and the other Elders built burn down around me. I can't."

Mentioning Aunt Lacey would either weaken or strengthen Ranlyn's resolve. I had to try. "I knew her the least of everyone in this room, but I know she wouldn't sit back and allow any of it. Not only that, she'd get the job done, save a butt-load of lives, and keep clear of becoming the fuckers she's fighting, so don't be a hypocrite."

Ranlyn's face twisted with confusion.

"Olson is Tainted because of the work he's done for this Coven, and yet you trust him enough to cart you around and sit in on important conversations like this one. I'm not saying I want to be him, but I am saying you can't fear for your life and use the people you're fighting against then look down your nose at me doing the same thing."

He settled back a step. "So, you've made your decision."

"Nope. Still head-fucked on the issue. I'm leap-frogging from one moment to the next, but I'm still moving. The separation of the Coven doesn't need to happen. If you worked with me, guided me in figuring this out like Aunt Lacey would, then at least I'd have someone I trusted to look to when I run out of places to jump."

Ranlyn wandered a few steps away from me, his unfocused stare portraying a bleary indecision growing by the second.

"This should not be a 'fight with me or against me' ultimatum." Veata's small commanding voice stunned me as it was the first time she spoke since I arrived.

I looked at Ranlyn. "I don't want it to be, Jeeves. I will be one-hundred percent honest with you at every turn whether that means being ousted from the Coven all together, but I will do what I believe is right with or without your permission. That might make me an insubordinate dickhole, but it's happening."

Ranlyn crossed his arms. "Yes, you've made that clear."

I had and was happy he understood I wasn't budging regardless of his opinion. Getting a resolved Elder, even one as young-looking as Ranlyn, to budge on anything was like pushing down the CN Tower with chopsticks. In the beginning of the conversation, he was immovable. While I rambled on about purpose and a sense of urgency regarding reopening the Creation, not forgetting to add how my brain wasn't too grief-drunk to trust someone like Rosemary, Ranlyn started asking questions instead of sticking to judging me.

Intrigue did not constitute agreement on the subject, but it was a start.

While I would accept the price of being booted from the Coven, it would break my heart. Aunt Lacey brought me in. The Coveners saved my life before I knew anything about the magic world or show-cased any powers of my own, for no other reason than helping because they could. I owed this life of mine to them and didn't plan on spitting their efforts back in their faces by disappointing them and myself.

I wouldn't know what to do without Ranlyn and the Mother Coven in my corner and didn't want to find out what that looked like.

8

ILL-FASHIONED PLANS

Cracking open Diluculo was never a notion Ranlyn opposed. Doing so to potentially release the monsters within to play havoc with Magics and Blind alike was unjustifiable to him when considering the consequences outlined in the premonition. The Sovereignty became the biggest bone of contention, especially for me now that I knew all I did.

"Like I told you on the phone,"—I looked at Vincent as I now stood by Donovan at the kitchen island—"I refuse to be a chump while you play me."

"I was not playing you."

"You lied."

"I omitted."

"And I'm the idiot in either equation, so you're just as fucked."

Donovan stood and looked between us. "What did you omit?"

Since I came to the party late, I assumed Vincent already told them of Chase's visit to The Lush. He hadn't, so I did.

"Motherfucker!"

Ranlyn and I jumped at Donovan's outburst.

Vincent took it as he took everything. Unflinching. "If I revealed my connection to the Sovereignty, you would have never believed my motives were anything but personal."

"Isolating me took care of keeping your secret, didn't it? You knew I was some little witchling too green to know what questions to ask, so you leaned into me the importance of lying to Donovan and everyone else. All so you could, what? We accomplished shitfuckall. You don't think I would have found out eventually?"

"Why didn't you say anything?" Donovan directed his own question at Ranlyn who looked stunned. "There's no way you didn't know about Vincent's family being the ones behind the Sovereignty the day you mentioned the premonition."

"I didn't think Vincent would bury it. Your ignorance isn't my fault, though highlights how unknowledgeable and desperate you were and still willing to run headlong into danger." He shook his head and ran his fingertips across a few days' beard on his cheek.

Ranlyn was right. I should have known before it came to this, but I never thought to ask Vincent's last name, and worse, I never thought to question Vincent at all.

Leaning his large hands on the counter as his weight poured over it, Vincent fixed his green eyes behind his glasses straight into mine. "I have not always steered you clear of harm in the past, and the consequence of that left me broken beyond my understanding, but with your mind fully open this time around, failure would risk more than I ever dared. I was trying to save you from the burden of too much. I should have known better. Regardless of this new truth, my crusade remains. The premonition places you and Donovan at the forefront with me."

"Things can change."

"Not this!"

Few times had I heard Vincent raise his voice. In the beginning with my training was the first. Now, frustration gushed from somewhere deeper, crashing down his tight-laced composure.

I matched his aggravation with calming contrast. "Fighting a war I know nothing about is one thing already checked off my bucket list.

Leading this with you, considering everything I could lose when I know more about digging for gold in the Bering Sea than I do of the Sovereignty, is a suicide mission I didn't elect for. I trust you and our extensive history enough to believe your family is as messed up as you say, especially after meeting your brother, so I've been doing what I can to help, but the Sovereignty, as a whole legal system for Magics, could be doing nothing wrong for all I know."

"Nothing wrong? Do you know what it feels like to have your eye sockets branded?"

I scoffed. "Actually, yes. In high school it was all the rage. Like drugs but better."

Donovan sucked his teeth. "Knew I should'a went to high school."

"Trivial example." Vincent counted off on his fingers. "Vein constriction, psychic organ removal, appendage dislocation and alterations, fear practices, soul suspension...Any magic you can dream up, including your own, is taken and twisted—" He rang his hands in emphasis, "—into something wretched and perverse. A product of a loss of humanity in its lowest form."

"If it was Evar in there having all that done to him—"

"It's not!" Normally the epitome of composition in times of stress, crisis, and even battle, the disgust and desperation leaked from the cracks of Vincent's button-down façade like breaks in a dam as his fair cheeks reddened with anger. "*If* it was, my fight would be unfounded. If only the Sovereignty cells were empty of Seedlings like yourself who are fresh to the power and made unfortunate mistakes. First offenders or offences with low victim impact or exposure to the Blind are tried and sentenced to outlandish consequences. Magically inclined who know nothing of their lineage and an inadvertent discharge sends them in that place where a monster holds the keys, without consideration of basic human rights."

"How are you so certain of these injustices?" Ranlyn questioned.

Vincent wheeled on his co-Elder standing behind him against the wall. In Vincent's new position his face was hidden to me, but

Ranlyn fought and failed to remain straight-faced against whatever Vincent's harsh features portrayed.

"My family raised me to become a lawman of their world. The Llewellyns are notorious for their underhanded righteousness, as if letting off those in high-ranking positions of Coven politics or others with the funds to make it disappear is a true show of justice." He turned back to me. "Please, do not walk away from this because of one bad decision. I would rather excuse myself from all involvement than see it left for another century or more to lay at waste by my family. They do not age in there."

"Your family?"

"The prisoners." He took off his glasses and pressed his finger into his closed eyelids before placing the glasses back on his face. "In the cages of the Sovereignty, you live as long as they decide. No such thing as a precedent. They dole out sentences case by case and forget those who have been found guilty until someone brings them to their attention. Before you ask, no one does except the grieving families of the convicted. The Llewellyns have no sympathy for what they believe are the nepotistic ramblings of people who think their loved one is beyond the reach of the law."

"I've lost kin to the Sovereignty." Olson's husky voice spoke from the corner of the kitchen still seated at the table, surprising me simply for speaking at all. "They disappear and are never again seen."

Veata nodded, her cloudy stare as if lost in thoughts of her own nightmares akin to Olson's.

Ranlyn leaned onto the back of a kitchen chair across from Veata. "If you agreed, why haven't you taken Vincent's side from the beginning?"

Her frown creased her features. "Nothing new comes from blotting them out. Can't be done."

"I assure you it can." The resolve in Vincent's tone was cinderblock solid.

She shook her head at Vincent. "This is not your first attempt, Extractor. Spare my distrust in your ability to succeed where you

have failed. I refuse to be among those whose ability consists of repro-
ducing negative results and ending the lives of the dedicated who
follow your ill-fashioned plans."

"The premonition proves this time is in no way comparable."

"The premonition doesn't mention success." Donovan knew the
premonition well, so this didn't make me feel better.

"The mention of failure is missing from the premonition as well.
You know this."

Donovan dipped his head to the side, conceding the point.

"Nothing in the pages speaks on conclusion for either side, only
the events that lead to an unmentioned ending. The deaths of those
who believed in the cause are tragic, but they knew what they were
getting into before it came to the attempt. Not that this eases my
guilt."

What first was a mission of impossible odds now grew as the
failed attempts were spoken of as if there were a great number of
them. Although I was totally pissed this meeting needed to happen, it
shone a light on the ugly mole he was hiding.

"Still. When we were on surveillance and even before, you kept
talking about taking down the whole system. Do you have an alternative to what the Sovereignty does? 'Cuz no way could we leave
Magics without lawful consequence, or as soon as the Sovereignty
goes Jenga, rampant chaos will spread like a zombie plague, and the
Blind would pay the most."

Vincent crossed his arms. "A solution has been in the works for
centuries."

"Really? What do you plan to do?" The scrutiny in Ranlyn's eyes
was near invasive.

"No."

"I'm sorry?"

"No." Vincent shook his head. "Knowledge of the solution is too
precious to be revealed when the project has been in the works for so
long. When I have your full backing of the dispersal of the Sover-

eignty in its entirety, then you can be trusted with this information. Not until then."

I actually giggled. I couldn't help myself. Vincent was holding all the cards leaving no choice but for Ranlyn to stop straddling the fence. Curiosity may win out, but Ranlyn was more the weighed decision type.

When the furious gaze of everyone hit me, except Donovan who was trapped in the euphoria of my giggle, I stopped after great effort. "Okay, fine. I'm somewhat half-sorry. Knowing the exact details of the contingency plan doesn't make my decision final—I'm just happy to hear there is one. If you say you have an alternative, one which means fairness for Magics not out to fuck over everyone else, but actually a fair system of governing, then I'm all for being a part of the muscle bringing down the current assholes to make way for what you have in store. What I'm not up for is blind obedience, not to you or anyone else, so I need details when I ask for them and to be brought in on important information more than a hot second before needing it. Other than that, I'm golden."

Vincent didn't hide his sigh of relief.

"Me too." Donovan clapped his hands together. "And not because of Sophie but for the same reason that brought her to the same conclusion. Unlike her, I don't trust you." I tensed as he focused on Vincent. "I wish to fuck I could, considering our history. Lucky for you, I trust the Sovereignty less and have heard of some of their tactics. Most as rumours, as with most shady politics, but I know my father works with them, and no one associated with him is innocent."

Vincent hid his reaction well enough no one commented. Nonetheless, I saw how what Donovan said impacted him. He didn't like how things were, but he had another ally, and that was a start.

"I'm in." Olson made a slight head bow. "I'm sure I can be useful."

Vincent returned the bow. "Another willing Magic on our side is valuable, and you certainly will be."

"Funny." Veata wasn't laughing. "Hinapouri and Miklos were the ones itching for battle where there wasn't one, and here we are, the Elders against them to take down the largest collective force of Magics known to our kind." Her thin lips cracked a wry smile.

"I haven't cast my vote." Ranlyn was scratching at his short beard again.

Veata rolled her unseeing eyes and wrung her hands on her cane handle. "Don't be a yellow-bellied fool, Ranlyn. You'll join. Have the stones to declare it."

She had me giggling again. This time I wasn't the only one.

"Fine, I'm in. Only if Rosemary's deal is refused."

No one complained, not even Donovan, though it meant his mother's coven would attack us on the field outside the Creation when we opened it to get out the survivors.

Ranlyn leaned into the kitchen island. "If this goes bad, even if we're not killed, you all understand we'll need to go into hiding, right? Not just us within this room but all who opposed the Sovereignty, and all associated with the Mother Coven."

I hadn't thought of that before.

"Maybe we can fashion ourselves a little Creation of our own and repopulate an army." Now Veata was smiling. "Though, of course, before agelessness, I'm certain my eggs had dried up long ago, so it'll be up to you, Salix, to re-establish the flock. Don't start until after we're out of the fray. A pregnant soldier will only weigh us down."

I erupted with laughter. The visual was grim but with the crusade—as Vincent called it—that we were embarking on began that night with the six of us in understanding we may not make it to the other end alive.

I sipped my drink and turned to Vincent. "Did Donovan tell you Christopher Leisemeyer is dead?"

"Didn't get that far." Donovan placed a steaming cup of tea in front of Veata.

Vincent's brows cinched. "You are positive?"

I nodded, seeing this was a great loss. "Yellow polo shirt, swallowed up by the portal in Eli's barn before some fog demon thing shoved itself into a teenage Architect before disappearing God knows where? Yup. Definitely him."

Vincent nodded and took a moment in thought.

"I'm assuming Christopher was how you knew to direct me to the Berisford's in the first place?"

Vincent tilted his head to the side and back. "Not all within the fold of the Sovereignty deserves the same fate as my family. Most truly do."

"Your lovely brother let me in on the fact that they know of the premonition." Vincent's expression went blank. He didn't know this. "They've taken precautions, including dosing their employees with whatever it takes to hide their soul glows from me. I guess Christopher wasn't Blind after all." I looked to Ranlyn on the stool next to Vincent across the kitchen island from me. "I thought you said the other side didn't possess the formula to do that?"

"I believe that one would be my bad, as they say." Veata lifted her teacup in mock salutation and then took a sip.

One of the Coven secrets Evaristus or Loring pilfered from her mind when she was a Puppet must have been the recipe.

I wasn't about to rub it in.

"Do we have a timeline for this potential takedown of the 'largest collective force of Magics known to our kind?'" The holidays weren't far off, and I wanted time with my family in case going into hiding, or dying all together, became a reality. I wasn't ready for goodbye, temporary or other. It wasn't the first time I had to contemplate never seeing them again and leaving them clueless as to why, but it never failed to inject a heavy guilt into my gut.

"Such an endeavour takes times to percolate, to manage, so to speak." Vincent shifted in his seat in thought. "Without access to the Sovereignty members' soul glows to distinguish core values and therefore potential allies, another mode of contriving true intentions will need to be assessed."

"Good." Mental note made: Contact the fam with holiday plans. "While the Sovereignty is on the back burner, my focus is on opening the Creation. And before anyone argues with me about how else this will negatively impact the Mother Coven,"—I looked at Vincent—"or potentially fuck up your plans to dethrone your evil fam-jam if I die before we face them,"—Vincent didn't comment, and I looked to the rest of them—"my aunts are figuring out what Donovan needs to contact Caine on the inside."

I told them about the Nexus Transference spell, not that I knew exactly what it was. After mentioning the bit of the Ballards footing the whole bill, Veata laughed, and Ranlyn offered to put in his fair share of the Mother Coven's funds. A small victory the aunts will be happy about.

Hashing out the logistics would wait for another night, including side-stepping the fact Hinapouri and Miklos were somewhere in the mid-stages of their own plan, though no one had heard a moan from them since Diluculo was shut down.

It was late. They may have been our Coven Elders, but it was still Donovan's house, and we had nothing more to add tonight, so they left.

After sneaking Bosco out for a late-night pee and tucking him back in with a snoring little boy, we meant to go to bed but were too wired.

Donovan held out the premonition pages. "Can you read these to me?"

"Do you want your socks ironed, too?"

He recoiled, leaning back in the kitchen chair. "What?"

"Forget how to do things yourself?"

"No. Nor would I treat you like a nineteen-fifties housewife without expecting you to kidnap Fox and force him to create the cure for the connection."

"Good." I sat across from him and took the small stack of paper.

"I've read these pages a million times. I need to hear them in someone else's voice." He rubbed his hands across his face as if prepping himself to listen, the pressure in my face equally satisfying.

As I went over them, I was happy to see most of the predicted events had already happened and was easy to decipher or at least to assume that's what it was talking about, but not all.

"—imbuing of the green feeble magic of an evil womb with the essence of the ancient wife." I stopped. A spark sizzled somewhere in my memory bank as I finished the line.

"I know." Donovan put his arms over his head and leaned his chair back on two legs again. "I don't get that either. Move on to the next part."

"No." I don't know if the word actually left my lips, too concentrated on what it meant.

"Sophie?" He must have called me more than once to resort to my real name. "You know what it means."

I nodded and laid the pages down. "I'm supposed to give you more power."

He let his chair drop back onto four legs. "What?"

"Aunt Lacey. She said—" I pictured her in the Creation when Caine and I fought Evaristus.

"Sophie. Please." Donovan was beside me now.

"Come on." I left the kitchen, he following me to his room. I sat on the bed with my legs crossed, he hesitant to do the same. "Telling you this way will be easier."

He settled in and waited.

"When Aunt Lacey let me live—"

"Let you?"

"Yes. When Evaristus shoved my soul from my body, before you were freed from the canopy contraption, she was there. She's our Soul Shepherd, meant to guide us into our afterlife, but she refused to do it. Instead, she clued me in on how to put Evar temporarily down and said that one day I might be stronger than her. Something or someone kept her from telling me everything she wanted to, but I couldn't see anyone else. She saved our lives."

Donovan's adrenalized grief and anticipation of what I might say next made my stomach feel like worms were slithering around in the acid.

"Before she was torn away, literally torn into the nothing as if on a leash, she said you couldn't help with Evar, but one day, you would have to match my strength. Her last words were to make you stronger."

He shifted in place. Antsy. "If she said it, it's possible."

I shrugged. "Evar did it with my ancestor Alorha by giving her our Soul Seeing power and made the Ballard Family of Magics, but I don't know how he did it."

"Something to find out on Ballard Coven night. You're descended from Evar's power, meaning you can conceivably do everything he can."

"Except I can't. Probably because of years of diluted blood and power. Besides, I don't want to be a Puppeteer."

"You're a Sorcerer. Who knows what you can do?"

"So are you."

"Exactly. You have the capability to be a vessel because you're a Sorcerer, which means I have the power to hold more power than I was born with. Maybe not as much as you but still more."

"Maybe." I didn't want to get our hopes up. If Aunt Lacey hadn't mentioned it, I wouldn't have thought it possible. Now? It could be.

"Um. Did—did she look okay?"

The emotion across the connection lifted with my smile. I raised some power and nudged his mental walls, feeling nothing in my way, and funnelled the memory of my time with Aunt Lacey through to him. When his breath hitched and shock ran through me, I knew it worked, and I watched the changes in Donovan's expression as quiet tears fell from the dark pools of his eyes.

When the memory ended, Donovan blinked, and I wiped away my tears as he sat in awe, struggling to compose himself.

He kept his head bowed for a solid two minutes before wiping his tears away and looking up at me. "We have to find a way."

9

MUNDANE ENDEAVOURS

Thursday was the only day everyone in the Ballard Coven could partially agree upon to meet. My expectations for a good turnout were low as I drove the Barracuda through blowing snow down thin backroads to Dunnville, white-knuckling it to stay out of the ditch. Donovan stayed at his house with Andy and Bosco instead of them being on the roads when they didn't have to be.

Looking around the expanse of the large attic space, my nostrils still stung from the abrasive cold wind outside. I did a rough headcount and judging by the cars in the driveway already being covered in snow, about ten members made it out. Serena and my brother never skipped a meeting, so their presence didn't surprise me. Same with Ronnie. Chelsea and Shannon were among the missing, as was Kassie, though I didn't find going without Kassie's attitude a negative. The aunts didn't make it, neither did Leon or Tapi, not surprising since they came from further out, though Kevin and Lewis were busy setting up the tech for those using video or teleconference options, so no one missed out if they didn't want to.

Once we warmed up and settled into what everyone wanted to work on, I focused on reading the souls of my fellow members to discover what stopped their powers from being released. Like my other Sect, their barriers were much the same.

Fear was rampant, locking away their potential as they struggled with the existence of Magics in the world and in their blood. I blamed our grandmother for this and anyone like her who spouted lies and hatred about our kind. Their fear was fuelled with "what ifs." What if the power is evil? What if the gift I have is dangerous? What if this alienates me from my family? My life? On and on. Convincing them they would be fine was a blatant lie. They may not be, but they would still be a target for being in the Ballard Coven either way.

I pinned Olive down to ask her about giving another person power as Evaristus had to our ancestor Alorha. She knew as much as I did. "And there's no book here besides the Ballard Family Tome that mentions Alorha?"

"I'm sorry, Firefly. Our library is extensive but delves primarily into incantations or the tools in which to drive our gifts. Personal histories are not within them except for the Ballard Family Tome. We only know Alorha's name through you, which is why I'd love for you to add your experience to the pages."

"Ah, yeah. I'll get on that."

"I can only imagine how hard writing it all down would be, considering how you learned of it, but your knowledge could one day serve another one of our family or someone you love as they should have for you."

"I know. I promised I would."

Olive nodded and pursed her lips.

"I will."

"I know you will."

I hoped I would as I knew how important it was to the family's history, but I understood her disbelief in me doing so anytime soon.

I switched topics to mentioning I wanted to let the members in on reopening the Creation and the potential takedown of the Sovereignty.

Olive's lips twisted a bit, and she closed her sweater as she crossed her arms. "Why do think they need to know?"

I sat on the side of her desk. "Why not? They're just getting into the depths of the Magic world, and all of that could change. They could be in danger just for being affiliated with the Mother Coven. Whether that's from Evaristus, who is also their family and wants them dead, or devotees or any number of other Tainted enemies. And if we make it past all that, then there's the Sovereignty to consider."

"And you're certain dismantling the Sovereignty is within Magics' best interests? The ones with soul glows on the lighter side of living?"

I nodded. Getting into the nitty-gritty of the situation would reveal Vincent's plans. Ones I didn't want rolling around in anyone else's mind if I could help it. Who knew who might try and pry it out of her if they caught a glimpse of her having the tiniest bit of useful information besides the fact I told her it would be happening at some point. Less was safer.

Strewn amongst the large pillows in the meditation area, Olive and I stood in front of the members as I let them in on everything I could. By the time I finished, I fought to catch my breath, everyone looking at each other as if they wished they had written it all down.

Olive touched my arm. "Let's not mistake this as campaigning to join the cause." Her tight smile made me realize this was her fear all along.

"Oh no. This isn't like the last battle at Diluculo. When we reopen the Creation, and if Evaristus escapes back into the world, he will be a thousand times more dangerous because he'll treat the Blind like he does within his Creations."

"Wasn't that what he was doing anyway?" Adam adjusted his dark sunglasses as he still fought with his Soul Seeing ability.

"Not exactly. Evar locked himself away from the rest of the world for a long time. He chose to live within these Creations, playing King Fish in his little mouldable pond. The Blind are easier to make his Puppets, so he was snatching them up off the street or had his devotees do it. Now that he knows his bloodline is still active, and after what we did to him, he's probably got a mission in mind. He won't care if he exposes Magics to the Blind. He'll take over and slaughter anyone he wants until he's taken down. And we don't even know how to do that yet."

"And these Sovereignty jerks are stronger than him?" Kevin narrowed his eyes at me as if trying to work the specifics.

"The Sovereignty is the law makers of our kind. Their power is the actual power of a Magic, yes, but also of intimidation and fear since they can imprison you when they want without much recourse. Think corporate corruption without identifiable badges."

"So, like dirty cops with old power as strong as their cojones." Kevin stood and adjusted his shoulders, uncomfortable on the floor.

"Since they're made primarily of men, that might be accurate. Think bigger. Like a crooked government instead of a hick town sheriff."

They all were looking at each other now, their worry plain on their faces.

"I'm sure some are good,"—I was quick to amend—"but Vincent's convinced they're mostly like his father and brother, and I trust him with that." The catch in my throat was a surprise. I should trust him. I wanted to, even told him I did, but the hint of distrust for my oldest friend was larger than I expected. Thankfully, they were all too busy trying to work it out themselves to notice.

Some were amped to join the cause, especially Adam, Serena, and Kevin, but as was said from the beginning, this wasn't a recruitment speech. They needed to know what was happening in their world, and no newsletter was circulating to keep them in the know.

Once I was satisfied they weren't going to put on some stretchy pants to better fight in, they went back to their magical education with a little more vigor than before my announcement.

Adam and Serena knew I was holding back when speaking to the others, so when they got their chance, they caught me alone near the reference books, but I was tapped out and held back on mentioning the truce Ranlyn refused to make. Instead, I grabbed the Ballard Family Tome and flipped through aimlessly as I walked back to Olive's desk.

Adam followed. "How's Denise?"

I looked up from the tome to see my brother fiddling with a vial of dragonfly wings. I took it from him and put it back on Olive's desk before he shook them into dust. "How would I know? She's your girlfriend."

He made a small nod, his usual tells were covered by his dark specs. I snatched them off his face.

"Dude! Give 'em back." He groped around for them with his eyes closed as I dodged his lanky arms.

"You'll never get used to it if you wear these all the time. Now what's this about Denise?"

He kept his hand across his eyes. "I haven't talked to her in a couple of days. I figured you had."

"Adam!" I gave him a not-so-light cuff to the side of the head.

"Hey!"

"I told you not to screw around on her. She's a pain in the ass as it is. You don't need her pissed off at you. I'm not getting in between your drama."

"I didn't do anything."

"Like I believe that, you little worm."

"I didn't. She's being all weird cuz of the band stuff, and I don't see her enough. Same shit, different bitch."

"Adam...."

"We're not broken up. She's just refusing to talk to me."

"Good." Serena popped in hearing the end of the conversation and picked up the vial of dragonfly wings and shook them as Adam had. I grabbed them from her and pocketed it. "Whatever." She poked Adam's hand over his eyes. He pulled away as if she were trying to pry it off. She laughed. "If anyone can whip you into shape, I bet it's Denise."

He scoffed. "Doubts."

I slipped into Serena's mind—her mental fortitudes non-existent —with instructions. She smiled. We lunged at Adam, forcing him to the ground, and holding his hands at his sides, laughing. I was telekinetically strong enough to take him on myself, but this was more fun.

"Open your eyes, rockstar." Serena grabbed his forearm with both hands, he unable to shake her off.

The bright orange Koi fish tattoo on Adam's arm didn't look right. The colour started bleeding away beneath and around Serena's hands. Adam's squirming became urgent.

"Oohfuckshit! Hands off!" I gave Serena a telekinetic shove off my brother. She slid to a stop and glared at me in shock.

Adam grunted and grabbed his arm. "What the fuck—"

I slapped his hand away from gripping his bicep. "Don't! Don't touch your skin."

He squeezed his hands into fists, fighting the pain as his skin greyed.

I thought it was a latent disintegration magic like my own, but instead of the greyish-black I expected, this was dust-coloured. Adam's skin hardened instead of falling apart.

"Stone." The word on my lips a mere whisper.

"Stone?" Adam tried to scramble to his feet, but the limb was too heavy and kept him down on his knees, struggling against the weight.

I ran to Serena still on the ground and dragged her towards Adam. "Reverse it!"

Serena pushed me off. "I didn't do anything!"

Whatever she did, the discolouration kept moving, growing up his arm.

I grabbed Serena again. "You did this, accidently, but you still did it. You need to reverse it. Close your eyes and find your power."

She blinked at me, mouth open, saying nothing, red-cheeked, and frantic.

"Now! Do it!"

The others were gathering around us, their voices adding to the panic. If Serena couldn't fix this, we were all going to stand around and watch my brother turn into a statue. Of all the times for Serena to lose it, now was not the time. If I could beat her into concentrating and finding her power, I would turn her black and blue, but she would probably kick my ass, and Adam would still look like Medusa's lawn ornament.

Looking to Olive was useless. Her advice-giving attempts were drowned out by the other's clashing voices.

What do I do?

I slipped into Serena's brain to block the others out. *"Don't think about power or any of that technical shit, just grab his arm and imagine it as it is normally."*

Adam was sweating and yanking on his arm. He couldn't stand up but was flailing the limbs he could in effort to take off or something. I don't think he knew. He just kept panicking. Either way, it wasn't helping Serena focus.

"Think of the tattoo, Serena. The bright colours. Think of Adam's skin like the feeling of mine on your hands." I moved my hands to hers and squeezed. *"Soft and pliable."*

"I don't feel anything." I knew she meant she didn't feel her power. She shook me off and smoothed her hair behind her ears, her thoughts bathed in fear of touching him at all.

This was Serena's magic, she needed to be the one to expel it, not that having been told this helped. Adam's whole arm was now stone, it creeping across his chest, forcing him to writhe on his back like an overturned turtle.

Things were out of control. I couldn't think myself, unable to keep my power stable enough to reach into Serena's head anymore. Donovan's panic thrummed in the connection at not knowing why I was freaking my shit, distracting me further when he wouldn't give up when I tried to nudge aside his oppressing emotions.

"Fuckthisshit." I stood and spun to the group. A shield bloomed from my open arms as it had outside Diluculo. The warning to go away and stay away, clear in the snapping of a cooled electricity caused them to jump away, an extra layer of soundproofing buffering the three of us from the rest of the coven.

"Jesus fuck!" Serena popped up to her feet, looking around us.

"What's happening? What are you doing?"

I ignored Adam and reached over him to my cousin, now able to speak at a normal level. "I need you to concentrate on me, cuz. You got this."

I sat on one side of Adam, pulling Serena down on the other side of him, and placed her hands on the arm where the creeping stone started.

She pulled away from me. "Dude! I could hurt you, too."

I telekinetically pulled her hand back to me and forced her to grab him again, not removing my own hold. "You won't."

I put my other hand up towards her and pressed a warm power through to her chest where I always felt my own. The tingle on my skin and deep breath my cousin took in told me I awakened her powers instinctual need to protect itself.

"Feel my skin on yours. Pretend it's Adam's. Imagine you hit the rewind button and his skin is clearing and shedding off the weight of the stone."

Serena closed her eyes, fighting to let go and settle into her vibrating power. Her shaking exhale coming too quickly as her power grew and thrummed under my hand. I added a layer of protection to myself but couldn't be sure it would stop her untrained power from infecting me.

I added images to her mind of Adam's skin as he was moments before he started to turn. He squirmed under our hold, his shoes scrapping on the plank woods floors.

After a moment, Adam inhaled with a gasp. "I think it's—"

I shoved my hand over his mouth to keep him from distracting her.

Serena couldn't see her progress, her eyes still closed. Adam stuck his tongue out onto my palm like when we were kids. I pulled it away and shushed him before wiping my wet hand on his shirt. It all forgotten as we watched the pallor of Adam's chest began to return to normal, then work its way backwards, spreading in a creeping pace as it had overtaken him.

Adam twitched his fingers as if too scared to fully flex yet. He stared down at his body, straining to see through the soul glows and bright shield around us.

The vibrancy of Adam's Koi fish restored. He was lucky it didn't disappear all together. He jumped up, surprising Serena who still had her eyes closed, as he moved away from her as far as he could while within the shield. He rolled his shoulder and rubbed his arm and chest as if needing to feel it for himself that everything was as it should be.

"You did it!" Serena blinked from Adam to me as I got up and pulled her to her feet, wrapping her up in a hug. "You even look brighter."

She opened her mouth like she wanted to say something to Adam but was staring at his arm instead.

Adam's eyes welled over with tears when he looked up at me, then he pressed his fingers into his eyelids to block out my soul glow. "God, this sucks."

"I told you it gets better." I looked at Serena. "For you too. You have no idea how many times I accidently used my power."

"Doesn't make me feel better considering I nearly turned him into a statement piece, but damn." She took a step towards Adam and punched him in the shoulder. His eyes popped open enough for a wayward tear to escape. "You're lucky I'm awesome."

He wiped his eyes. "Real awesome."

I dropped my power, and with it, the shield. The Coveners were happy to see us standing again, asking questions about what happened and about the shield. I pulled Adam away from Ronny grinding him about Serena getting the upper hand.

"Is that why you're not around Denise? You can't handle her soul colour?"

"The colour's fine." He wiped his eyes of more tears and squinted at me. "It's the searing pain that's a mood killer."

I laughed, thinking back to all the headaches my Soul Seeing caused.

Once the rubbernecking and questions stopped, everyone fell back into their own use of the attic, which meant I was back in research mode at Olive's desk.

Adam interrupted my reading again. "I didn't realize that was you outside Diluculo with the whole shield-thingy."

I shrugged then realized when I had done it before I thought it was from Nya's power. Apparently, that wasn't the case.

He looked me over. "Your soul is weird."

"No, it's not," I shot back self-consciously looking at Olive, Lewis, Priscilla, and Serena who also stood around Olive's desk. "It's different 'cuz I'm a vessel. There's two sources of power instead of one."

"Oh, that's all?"

I gave him the finger and was reminded of something, looking at my uncle. "I already asked Olive, but I'm asking everyone I can. Do you know how to gift someone else power?"

"Gift it? Like a box of chocolates? Can't be done."

I sighed and closed the tome. "Yes, it can. Evar did it to create the family we spawned from, so it means we can, too."

"You sure about that?"

A duck started quacking, my cell ringing, showing Vincent's name on the screen. "Never mind." I answered the call. "Do you have good news for me?"

"Only if you happen to be the demon who has been terrorizing the Blind as reports of a young man appearing and disappearing scales social media outlets."

"Your great news makes me tingle with delight."

The others gave me a suspicious side-eye as I stepped away, anticipating a more detailed explanation.

Vincent cleared his throat. "Definitely a demon. One feared in

Chili and Argentina for possessing locals and being the harbinger of all evil and disease."

I took a few more steps away from the others and lowered my voice. "A Chilean or Argentinian demon that was, at some point, dumped into some dark wasteland or different dimension or wherever he crawled out of, and is now in the body of a portal maker?"

"It would appear so."

"Wonderful." I pressed my fingers into my eyes. "Any hint of how to take down a Chilean or Argentinian demon who can go anywhere it wants at any time and doesn't give a hangnail's thought about exposing magic to the Blind?"

"Some ideas are being explored."

His tight tone told me they had nothing and were trying anything and everything they could think of.

"Right. So, any leads on where Graham is now?"

"Try not to think of Graham. This demon is known as Gualichu. Believe when I say no aspect of Graham remains within that vessel. If the demon were to leave the Architect's body as we speak, it would be an empty shell."

"Comforting." I didn't know anything about Graham besides the two minutes of Donovan's vision and his possession within the barn, but he didn't deserve to be chewed up and digested by some demon. His innocent features will be the face of terror for many. "And this Pikachu could already have killed Graham and kept walking around?"

"Gualichu. And yes. The demon expels the host's essence to replace it with his own upon possession. The body dies when untethered from the original host, unable to withstand the initial intrusion, however, reanimation is but a function of survival for the duration of the demon's time within the vessel." Vincent's scholarly tone, while speaking of something so devastating, was off-putting.

I sighed at the thought of how innocent and gullible Graham was. It wasn't his fault he was raised by devotees, used for his gifts, and then taken too early in a failed and useless experiment. What a waste of life. And now we had to worry about what he might do to people. The Blind, Magics, Vincent didn't say, but I figured a demon wouldn't care about whom it was tormenting. Especially when it could do whatever horrible thing it does and zip off.

"Is this something your brother and the Sovereignty will be involved with?"

"My brother would not lift a finger to deal with something as such when it benefits him so greatly."

"Benefits? What does he get out of a demon set loose on the population?"

"Such a mystery preoccupies the Blind and keeps the attentions of Magics elsewhere than the inner workings of his corrupt system, as it has with the closing of Diluculo and any other crisis among our kind since the Sovereignty was created. Letting Chase think this tactic works also plays to our advantage. The revolt against the Sovereignty is stronger than ever regardless of the addition of Gualichu. Those working to ensure the takeover happens are eager to begin when preparations are complete."

"Listen to you. A demon is running amok and you're practically giddy."

"I am simply expressing—"

"It's fine." I laughed at his knee-jerk excuse. "You've been at this for a long time. I get it. Just wish we could do more about all these immediate threats, your family included. Either way, getting the Creation open is still my main objective. The Sovereignty and the demon will have to wait their turn. Clearly, you and whoever else are working on the demon issue, so if Chase and his power-hungry Sovereignty jerk-offs want to hang back, I'm fine with that. The quicker we crack open the Creation, the faster we can deal with the rest."

He sighed into the phone. "Yes. Your focus is plain. And my wishes to assist you in achieving them have not altered. I have also neglected to properly thank you for making my personal mission one of your own, even if it falls second to retrieving those from the Creation."

"Hmm. You're right. I'll take your thanks in gift certificates for a spa. A nice one. Will probably need it to clean all the blood out from under my fingernails when this is over."

He chuckled. "You have my utmost thanks, Sophie Saterlee."

"Okay, fine. That works, too."

I ended my call with Vincent and returned to my family still at Olive's desk arguing over the likelihood of a Magic gifting someone else power. They didn't know what Aunt Lacey told me, so I understood their confusion, but our family having any power at all should prove it was possible. I dropped back into reading the tome again, grasping for a shred of information I could use to make it happen.

———

Morning came all too soon. I jumped in the shower, knowing if my lids slid shut they would never creak open in time for my shift at the bar. A spark of mischievousness hit me a second before a sudden chill up my back, billowing into the shower as a naked Donovan followed it in.

"So, we're on shower terms now, huh?" I looked over my shoulder, my back to him.

His large frame had ample space in the luxurious stand-up. His teeth shone white, dark eyes cautious yet optimistic in his closeness as water rolled over my shoulders.

"It's not like I've never seen every part of you." He slid by me beneath the hot water steaming the glass doors.

I stepped back and crossed my arms over my bare breasts.

"Never showered with a guy before?" He raked his hands through his hair and tilted his head back into the water, which ran down his sculpted body.

"No, actually." I fought not to cover myself, drinking in the glorious sight of him.

"Hmm." He grabbed a black bottle and squeezed a blue liquid into his hand, lathering his hair and then his body.

I breathed in the bold familiar scent, surprised as I always thought it was from a spray-on cologne. Donovan was a simple creature. A hair and body duo lasting all day made total sense for a low maintenance guy, especially since it hit me below the belt, giving an everyday chore the biggest impact with minimal effort. Washing away the suds strengthened the aroma in the steamy space.

"You were with Brock before Caine and whomever else before that."

"And?"

His lips downturned at my curt response. He took a step back conversationally, fighting his curiosity.

Was it something most couples did? He made it seem like he had experience in a couple's shower situation, though he had never been in a relationship before. Is showering with a booty call a thing? Shower sex came to mind as an easy way to gain or cause a concussion, but he was sturdy and had the strength to hold someone up. I doubted he had sex in this particular shower since it was Aunt Lacey's house until recently, but you never know.

Maybe thinking about him having shower sex with someone else wasn't the best idea. The direction my overanalyzing took me had me feeling jealous and defensive, not to mention stupid for feeling either. Also, mentioning him alluding to my exes was a reminder I didn't need while I was naked and vulnerable.

In the span of a moment, I mulled over the impact of him mentioning Caine and Brock and the newness of this showering together step which left me with a raw sense of instability. We were pushing forward relationship-wise every day. Some days the intimacy became too much, and I had to dig in my heels and push through or take a step back. Wanting things to stay unchanged until I could wrap my head around the life-altering events that have already occurred was beyond my grasp and kept spiralling into further chaos.

Even now, I warred against booting his tight ass out of the shower to reclaim my space and getting him to pirouette so I could watch the soapy water flow down the same tight ass and let him claim me in an untested environment. The crooked smirk he flashed questioned which I was going to settle on, nothing within it telling me he would be pissed either way. Freedom of choice without consequence alone earned him brownie points.

He made it clear he was following my lead, but he wouldn't be him without pushing boundaries a hair past the line, knowing I held myself back often enough to regret it. Self-sabotaging measures? Shoving people away didn't mean you didn't want them. A learned behaviour for both of us. By remaining a deep-rooted tree in a storm, you earned trust. This shower stunt was his way of communicating his trust, and he was happy to stand under the water and wait as I decided if and when I was ready to reciprocate.

———

I rode the elevator to my apartment on a mission to trade out some clothing, surprised when the metal doors slid open on the sixth floor as I was lost in thoughts of my morning shower. Deciding I was ready for the next relationship step with Donovan or compartmentalizing so I could enjoy myself, I didn't know which I decided, but I could still feel the pressure from the top of the glass shower door digging into my palm and the rasp of the tile wall scraping against my shoulder blades.

"Dude!"

I tensed in a whole-body cringe and fell against my apartment door.

Kim stood at my side with a laundry basket in her hands. "Hello, headcase. I was calling your name. Like, where are you to?"

I pressed my hand into my racing heart. "Holy fucknuggets. I didn't hear you."

"Clearly. Sure you didn't piss yourself on that one?"

"Fresh as a daisy. Might have sent Donovan for a new pair of drawers."

"Speaking of—" She stepped closer. "Did the ball and chain freak out when you told him about the V-man's lies?"

"Please. Do tell."

It was Kim's turn to wheel around and screech. Rosemary stood a few feet away and motioned for us to follow her into the laundry room across the hall from Kim's and my apartments, not waiting for us to protest.

"Who the—?"

I grabbed her arm. "Do not leave me alone with her."

"Who is she?"

I was already headed to the laundry room, the door left open, though it never did that on its own. When Kim and I were in the same room with four machines stuffed into it, the scent of dryer sheets and over-dried wool irritated my nose. The door closed behind us, irritating me more.

"Why won't you take the deal?"

Answering wasn't easy, so I looked to my ally. "Kim, meet Rosemary, Donovan's mother. Rosemary, Kim, your son's co-Sect Leader."

Kim's eyes cut to me and then back to the woman now showcasing her dimples in a tight grin. "How nice of you to drop by your future daughter-in-law's for a chat. In the laundry room."

My turn to side-eye her.

"Why won't you take the deal?" Rosemary was all dark-haired beauty and restrained fury.

"Because we don't need your deal. With our Elders on our side and a cause worth fighting for, we'll pull the numbers we need without the addition of your kind."

Kim shifted in my peripheral. She understood Rosemary was Tainted. Even though we were closest to the exit, it didn't mean we could arrive before Rosemary attacked when all we had was Kim's basket of dirty clothing as a weapon.

"You speak with confidence of numbers you cannot fathom. The Sovereignty is not merely a Sect within this retched town—its spines shape the Magics of the world, a system as old as the oldest of us and more ruthless and cunning then Evaristus can imagine. And what of Evaristus himself? Breaking through the Creation will eventually bring down the spear of the Sovereignty, but it will also release Evaristus from his bonds. You think your numbers are fruitful enough to cover both factions?"

"This isn't a high school party you need an invite from the cool kids to get into. You wanna help? Prove it by showing up and take your ass home when it's done."

Rosemary shook her head. "Expect our presence, however, the defining point of this proposal is to prevent the aftermath that will ensue as the Sovereignty and Evaristus fall. The slaughter will not end there. We have no reason to allow it to. When we face our enemies there will be three factions ripe for the picking, all distracted by a more important kill. Our deal will prevent needless death."

"Why do you care?"

Rosemary's gaze fell heavy on Kim. "It only matters I do."

Power nipped at my skin, maybe Kim's as well, as Rosemary's frustration was boiling over.

"Why didn't you bring this straight to Donovan? I'm sure it would warm your son's heart to think his mother actually gave a shit about him since you abandoned him." Her attention swung back to me, distracting her from Kim but didn't help the bloating power in the room.

Rosemary didn't answer as quickly as I thought she might, composing herself or fighting for the words. "Donovan shares my blood, yet genetics create no sympathy in my son's heart. Not for me. Because I am a smart woman, I know wherever you lead, Donovan will follow."

"Then you've failed on both fronts." False confidence had my hands shaking while I fought to keep the tremble from my voice. "Things change, of course. You can check in and see how your son is doing since you care so much to extend the olive branch in hopes of saving his life. I'm assuming Donovan is why you're wanting this deal so bad, no?"

Her gaze narrowed. "He protects himself quite thoroughly and, as I found the other night, is beyond my reach. Ripping down the wards saving his ancestors' home is not worth the fight or exposure it would take to get a word in. With the child in his care, Donovan would be far less likely to converse if I did."

Updated surveillance intel made it to her, making me wonder if she was sitting outside of Donovan's place under a cover spell or if she had flunkies do it for her.

"At least the wards work. After today, if you or any of your flock venture through these doors, those wards and more will be added to ensure the Blind here are protected. I don't care if it's of the upmost importance. Next time, call."

Rosemary gave a slight head bow in agreeance. "Your precious Blind are safe from me. With your kind comes my kind, and one day those worlds will clash at these doors or at the doors of the dingy bar you call worthwhile employment, again, and it will be no fault but yours for insisting on continuing your mundane endeavours."

Ugh. Another person telling me how I'm putting everyone in danger for living my life.

"The offer of a truce remains. Justify its purpose if needed with the understanding it will save lives. As I found you, I'm certain you're resourceful enough to seek me out."

I nodded, both of us knowing I wouldn't try.

We moved aside, squeezing to the walls to allow Rosemary through as if her Taint was contagious. The laundry room door opened and closed behind Rosemary at her will, and she left me with a harsh glare I had seen from her son and liked it about as much as I did when I received it from him.

Kim plunked her basket on the top of a machine with a clang. "Wow. You can really see where Donovan gets it all."

I craned my head to the side to relieve the tension trailing my neck and between my shoulder blades. "His looks, yeah. Though, I can't see how he got away with a clean soul with parents like his. Not that his mother raised him, he had his sadistic father to contend with."

"Was it really that bad?" The interest in her tone was serious, but it wasn't my life to spill.

"It's worse than you're thinking. Much worse than Caine's dad."

Since Caine's father tried to kill him multiple times, I wasn't sure how she viewed the comparison as she nodded without pushing, dumping her basket of clothes into the top loader, and turning on the water.

Since she got part of the news, I filled Kim on the full conversation. "Sorry you weren't there. You should've been."

"Who cares. We have Ranlyn, Veata, and the Apporter on board. But Vincent's own family? If he can't throw in with them, how much loyalty is he going to show us?"

I shrugged. "If you heard his speech and the way he talked about them, you would've cried." She raised a brow at me and poured what looked like homemade detergent from an old pickle jar over the wet clothing and shut the lid. "He unravelled in a way I've never seen him. Not in this lifetime, anyway."

"I don't know about all that. Can you imagine though?" She grabbed my arms. "We're actually doing this. I still don't know how it's happening, exactly, but it's happening. Like, it's the fucking Sovereignty, Sophie."

"I don't know exactly how either, but believe me, it's as messed up as it seems." I pulled away from her to rub my hands over my face.

"And it's not just the Sovereignty, we're pissing off Covens on both sides." She gasped. "What if we have to fight our own Coveners? We can't assume they'll fight with us once they know everything. Could you put down someone like Gwen or Louise?"

"*Pfft.* No. Maybe Denise, but I doubt we'd have to." Though it was the first time I thought of it. They were our Coveners. Hopefully they would join us or stay out of it.

"When do we tell them?"

"You're asking me? It's not my Sect. They should probably know about the premonition and who the Sovereignty is first if they don't know already. The Ballards know."

"Really? Damn. I'll have to talk to Donovan."

She went for the exit, and I grabbed her arm to stop her. "Do you think I should quit or move? Or both?"

"Why? Because Mommy Dearest said so? Don't get in the habit of listening to your in-laws."

"She's not the first Tainted thing to meet me in places where they could've posed a danger to the Blind around me. Whether we fight and win, fight and lose, or make our claim and are hunted by parties on both sides, it gets messier from here. Us living here puts people in danger."

"So does driving the beast of a car of yours, but you're not going to cut up your license."

"Shitty comparison and insulting to the 'Cuda."

She smirked at me. "Honestly, Soph, ever since you joined the Coven it's been nothing but chaos, but it's been awesome in every way. Besides the deaths, obviously. If quitting your job and moving into Donovan's—because we both know that's where you'd go—is something you feel you have to do, then do it. They may come looking for you at The Lush or here anyway. They're evil pieces of rotting shit. They'll do whatever the hell they want no matter what, so I say fuck 'em, and we'll meet them outside Diluculo."

Classic Kim to pull off a pep talk.

We went out into the hallway, escaping the squeal of the washer. "Now all we need is to figure out what's needed to contact Caine, and we're set."

Kim's door flew open, giving us our third scare of the hour. Frog stood gripping her door. "You know where Caine is?"

10

HARBOURING GRUDGES

Frog's six-foot-five frame loomed over me in the hallway of our apartment. "You know something about Caine."

"I don't—"

Kim grabbed her boyfriend's arm. He turned to her, making her drop her hand. "We have no clue. That's what we're trying to figure out."

His damning glare shifted back to me. His finger in my face. "I don't believe you for a second."

I looked at Kim, seeing she had no idea how to get him to back off. Laying out Caine's best friend when the guy had a right to be pissed off was not on my to-do list this morning.

He lowered his voice. "If I find out you—"

He was cut off by my apartment door opening. Ranlyn rushed out and pressed me to the side as he gripped Frog's shoulder. Frog hissed as a spike of power tingled the air of the cramped hallway, he struggling until Ranlyn let him go and stood back.

Frog inhaled, eyes narrowed.

Ranlyn smiled and reached out to shake Frog's hand. "Nice to meet you, Wesley."

"Ah, a-and you, too." Frog shook his hand in return and then smiled at Kim and me.

Ranlyn reached for my open apartment door. "Sophie and I need to go over something real quick. You have yourselves a good day."

Frog smiled. "You, too. See ya, Sophie."

"Righto. Later Froganator."

Frog turned to return to Kim's apartment as Ranlyn went inside my place, waiting for me to follow.

Kim mouthed, "What the fuck?" to me.

All I could do was shrug.

I closed my door behind me and locked it, unsure why since Rosemary was gone and Frog was, whatever he was. "Could've used your Jedi skills at the estate, Jeeves. What the fizz did you do to—?" I gasped as something caught my peripheral. The Apporter was in my kitchen. "Jes-fuck! Okay. I've jumped out my skin enough for one day. Though it explains how you got into my apartment. How can I help you, stalker? Or are you here to yell at me as well?"

Ranlyn's light eyes panned to the Apporter who nodded and disappeared.

"Oh great. I'm in trouble."

He stepped towards me.

I stepped back.

He stopped. "I wouldn't do to you what had to be done to Frog."

"Which was?"

"A spell to distract him. He will forget meeting me, but he may eventually remember the exchange among the three of you. I bought you time, not a solution."

I crossed my arms. "Good to know the clock on another future fuck-up is running. What has you breaking and entering today?"

His hands were at his sides, he rubbing his fingers together instead of talking.

"Hmm. You look like you're about to tell me my nose job isn't as good as I think it is. You wanna spill before you—"

Ranlyn rushed forward and pulled me into a hug. He held me tight for a lingering moment before letting go.

"Are you dying?"

He cracked a smile. "Probably."

With his pink sparkly soul glow returned to the first stages of immortality instead of the white and silver of most Elders, he was probably exaggerating, but you never know.

He sat on my sectional and sanded his hands together. "Please tell me I can trust him."

The aching plea in his voice was a slice to the heart. I sat on other part of the sectional facing him. "Not talking about Frog, I assume. Though once the spell wears off, he'll be a pain in the taint again."

He looked up at me, his gaze as desperate as his tone. "Vincent. Tell me this rebellion is just. Tell me he will bring us to a resolution that doesn't destroy the Coven and anyone who follows us."

My turn to sit and stare.

"Fuck." He dropped his face into his hands and then popped up to his feet and paced. "You've known him for centuries."

"Wha—? I met him the day you called him in to save Kim and Miklos."

"But you did. Versions of you knew him."

"Apparently."

He stopped and glared at me.

"I don't remember those lives. I just know what he's told me."

"You...." He stopped, then paced a step, stopped again, and put his hands on his hips. "You haven't read your soul and confirmed it yourself?"

"Well, no."

"Sophie!"

"What? Looking at other lives won't prove if all this is worth it in this life. Plus, he knows things he shouldn't otherwise." My thoughts slipped to Millicent and Isaac and the way they died. He knew without me saying. Though I didn't have any control over shielding my thoughts at that time. "Shit."

Prickles of power wafted off Ranlyn as if he couldn't contain himself, his pacing gathering steam.

"Did you overhear Rosemary?" Getting attention off Vincent seemed like a good idea.

He paced another moment before stopping, crossing his arms, his tongue grazing his lips. "Yes. I followed her here and ducked into your apartment."

"She's not happy."

"Rosemary has never been happy."

"Ouch."

"Truth."

"Still. She's pissed. Turning down her deal might mean more deaths on the field when we open the Creation. More than our own Coveners pissed off at us for opening it in the first place."

Ranlyn surprised me by sitting, though he couldn't relax, perched on the edge of the cushion, and leaned into his elbows on his knees. "I didn't want my time as Elder to be spent in bloodshed. Now I'll be known as the Elder who led his people into a civil war to rival that of the Witch Wars."

"Don't shoulder all the blame. I don't make things easy for you."

He chuckled as if I were understating the obvious. "We need a segue."

"Damn. Quick subject change. I must be a pain in the ass."

He smirked at me. "Vincent has a cell of Magics itching to take up the cause against the Sovereignty. Ones within and outside the Sovereignty ranks who harbour a grudge and manage to hide it until it's time to activate the plan, doing so now with the premonition as their proof it's time to come out of hiding." He looked down at his hands. "And will also showcase the details to other allies."

"Isn't telling others letting everyone and their poodle know what we're doing? Why are we warning people who may end up trying to stop us?"

"Most won't fight against us with something like this. Neither would their poodles. They'll choose to be a part of it, or they won't."

"Too simple."

He shrugged. "Too late now. Soon we'll either have an army of allies or an army of enemies joining the ones we already have."

"Shit. Guess we're outed."

He nodded a slow cautious nod as if unsure of this being a good thing.

"Hmm. Suppose I should call-in sick to work."

His attention snapped up. "You returned to working at that bar?"

"Don't look at me like I've switched to dragon speech. You're hanging by your fingernails to make your life normal and like other Elders. Well, the last Elders were in the Witch Wars themselves. Seems like your reign is running its course as normal as it gets for an Elder. I was trying to resume my life as it was before Cai—" I couldn't continue. I huffed instead. Pissed off at myself for bothering to try and put thoughts of him aside and carry on as if I had everything under control.

Ranlyn reached forward and grabbed my hands, cradling them in his. "We'll figure this out. Just promise me you'll hold on until the end. Keep faith in me and in the Coven in hopes to bring us back together. We might be the reason it's all falling a part right now, but we can also be the solution."

I squeezed his warm hands. "Maybe if I knew who saw the premonition, I could glimpse it myself and maybe see something not in the pages." He let my hands go. "Not gonna happen, huh? So much for doing this together."

"The person the premonition came from wants to remain anonymous for that very reason. They don't want to choose sides, but they will, and they're in more danger for being the one to see what would happen. In the hands of the wrong Magic—"

"They're a guinea pig with a host of weaknesses to exploit. Gotcha."

"Sorry."

"Don't be. Keeps things organized enough for us to come out on top."

"Especially with the young Architect popping up."

"Ugh. Any chance we can bring the demon onto our side?"

His brows raised. "You want a demon on our side?"

"I sure as fuck don't want one against me. If it can be done, recruit that sucker with the promises of CEO to his mistress without the anchor baby. Unless the anchor baby is the equivalent of saving Graham. If so, slide it into negotiations. Graham was born to a Tainted family, but I bet he could be flipped."

He tilted his head a moment. "Sure you don't want my spot at the Elders table?"

"Nope." I slapped his knee. "Your butt groove is permanent. Find another with your strength to take up the fourth spot."

We stood, and he hugged me again. Tight.

"I'm not dying today, Jeeves. Unless you're planning to take me out and save yourself a heap of trouble."

He pulled away. "Nah. I still need you to spy on Vincent for me."

"Right. You're smiling, but I know you're not joking."

He kept smiling and didn't comment further.

I grabbed the extra clothing I needed, he insisting on waiting, following me out, and riding along back to Donovan's. I called in sick on our way, elated the new-hire was itching for hours. I would deal with a permanent resignation later.

When I pulled the Barracuda into Donovan's driveway, Ranlyn held my hand again with an unknown sense of thanks and security enough to be on his side in this shitstorm.

Something popped into my back seat.

"Fuck!"

The Apporter.

Ranlyn laughed.

"Fuck all of you today. Get out of my car."

Ranlyn was still laughing as the two of them disappeared.

Inside, I stripped off my winter gear and plopped down into a kitchen chair across from Donovan reading the premonition pages.

"Did you finally get fired?"

"No, but I called in sick."

"For anything important or to hug and handhold with whomever you met instead?"

"Hmmm. Jealous, are we?"

He looked up at me for the first time, the sense of "no kidding" crossing the connection. Always jealous. I knew the feeling.

"It was Ranlyn."

He put the page in his hand down, his jealousy worsening.

I went over what happened with running into Rosemary, making the mistake of calling her his mother and gaining a glare and a reminder of how he doesn't have a mother. Calling her his "rent-a-fetus" garnered the same look. Moving on to the conversation with Ranlyn loosened the tightness in his shoulders.

"Good to know I'm not the only one who doesn't trust Vincent. And good call on verifying our relationship with him in the past. Reading your soul for answers should have been done already."

"Why? Our past doesn't make us the perfect couple today and seeing him in suspenders wielding a pocket watch won't make him more trustworthy now than it did back then. Everyone changes."

He disagreed, though refrained from commenting.

"I'll be quitting the bar, too. I know you've been lobbying me to for forever, but now that other Magics know what we're up to, I pose a greater danger to the staff and patrons with all this Sovereignty bull-cocky on the line."

"Bull-cocky?"

"Do you prefer cow shit?"

"Why?"

"Because not everyone's into horns. Utters may be more your style."

"Babe, I'm all about a good set of utters."

"Mhmm. Well, instead of utters, you get to take us shopping with Vincent."

"Right. So, working is dangerous, but shopping is perfectly safe?"

I shrugged. "Gotta do it now before the Covens can make their minds up about us and I'm housebound like a sheltered debutant. Plus, Andy's been begging for it."

Andy and Bosco came in from outside, both panting from playing, Andy's nose running from the cold. I grabbed a hand towel as Bosco shook snow from his short coat, stopping him from running through the house.

Donovan stopped Andy from taking off his coat and boots. "Gross. Go take care of that in the washroom, snot face."

I looked up and near gagged at the sight of Andy swiping stringy snot off his face with his glove and then ran to the bathroom giggling.

11

THE GLITTER OF SALE SIGNS

"This is a bad idea." Donovan pulled me aside as Andy was struggling with his boots.

I tucked my scarf into my jacket. "You just hate the mall."

"Any sane person would, especially around Christmas. It's gonna be a madhouse."

I laughed. He didn't.

"Do you realize how easily Andy could be taken with that many people around him?"

I gave him a withering look. "All caregivers fear kidnappers. And since you're a powerful man of Magic, you can keep him safe while he waits to see Santa."

"Right." He rolled his eyes at my half-assed attempt to flatter him. "Do the Berisfords even celebrate the Christian holiday?"

I took a step closer to Donovan so Andy couldn't hear us. "Does it matter? He's insisting on seeing Santa. Friends at his school will have done it, and I figure he's got lots to ask for. I already talked to him about what not to say so child services aren't pounding down the door, but this is important to him. He may spend the holidays without any family. I may not be able to give him his mother back or knock his grandma around enough to shake her Tainted soul out of her like a creepy snow globe, but I *can* do this. You're more than welcome to stay in the car."

Groaning, Donovan grabbed the keys to the 'Cuda before I snatched them back. We climbed in leaving Bosco behind to guard the house since he wasn't a fit-in-your-purse kind of pup.

We were meeting Vincent at the main entrance, and it took me a few circles to find parking as Donovan cursed under his breath the entire time while I suppressed the giggles. Finding a spot meant we had to walk a bit. I held Andy's hand and reiterated the warnings we had him repeat on the ride over. Rule one, never leave either one or both of our sides. Rule two, always be holding one of our hands. Rule three, tell us if he sees someone he knows. Rule four, tell us if he sees someone or something that makes him feel weird. "Weird" was a better word than "scared." I wanted him to have fun but needed to know if at any point things were off in case I didn't see whatever he saw.

Rules or not, it was a nightmare for Donovan. His dark eyes scanned the parking lot, the cars, the crowd, everything and everyone. I reminded him this was our last chance at normalcy, having as much success convincing him as I would encouraging him to attend family counselling with his mother. Christmas wasn't a Coven tradition, but I was raised with twinkling lights and manic trips with other sweat-covered mall goers obsessed with finding the perfect gift no one remembered in a month's time. Or likely to regift it and spend the next year praying the gift-giver didn't notice.

"What do you want?" I let Andy go through the door first as Donovan held it open.

"I want to be at home where we're safe and survive all the evil—"

"Can it, Wendy Whiner." I smiled down at Andy who was too busy to overhear Donovan, scanning his surrounding with wonder instead of suspicion, giving me the impression he'd never been to the mall before. I looked back at Donovan who was searching our surroundings for a different reason. "For you, I meant. What in the h-e-double hockey sticks do you want?"

"I don't need anything."

"Thankfully Christmas is about *want* and not need. Something you'd rather not have to buy for yourself."

"And here I thought it was about stealing our ancestral traditions and commercializing the sanctity of our festivities to make up for year-round failing commerce."

I sighed. No way was I going to mess with that.

Vincent stood inside the main entrance, looking like he had dropped out of another time. He clutched a wool coat draped over his arm, posture broom-handle straight, wearing a stiff-looking sweater and tweed trousers. He peered down at his cell through thin framed glasses, or looked to be, though I saw him gaze at the feet of those passing him with suspicion, peering up at some and dismissing others.

He spotted us and closed the gap, pulling me into a tight hug. "After this, we are square and then some."

Ignoring the nudge of jealousy from Donovan, I hugged Vincent back and laughed.

With the pretence of an embrace, one not as tight as with Vincent since I had to avoid touching Donovan's skin, I lowered my voice. "Let me know what toys Andy plays with, and I'll buy him that." He nodded when I pulled away. "Are you sure there's nothing specific you want? You may end up with an ugly moose sweater."

He shrugged. "I need more sweaters."

As if I would buy him a moose sweater. Though might be a good gag gift.

I gave him a quick peck before leaving with Vincent, ignoring the air of suspicion from Donovan, which I guessed was directed at Vincent.

"Any helpful ideas so I don't end up buying socks?"

"Maybe the socks can match the moose sweater."

"If only I was so lucky."

Vincent didn't comment.

The tingle of magic had me looking up at him. A mask hiding mild terror had him preoccupied. He cringed when others came near, the twitch of his hand tipping me off to what was actually happening. Vincent was using his power to make other mallgoers stay a comfortable distance away from us. The almighty Vincent wasn't worried about being out in the dangers of the Blind world or out of the safety of Donovan's home. He had social anxiety and was doing his best to create an open pathway to avoid contact. I had been around big groups with him before, but they were with other Magics and in times of crisis. This must be beyond his coping skills.

"Might wanna dial back the comfort zone. No one can see it from here, but the speedy race track you've cleared for us might look suspect on camera." No one was ahead of us now for fifteen to twenty feet, they moving aside without knowing why.

"The Blind are too enamoured by glittering sale signs to notice if I leapt twenty feet in the air. Probably tell themselves it was a seasonal gimmick meant for their entertainment."

He was right. Everyone was in their heads or busy window shopping, elbowing through the crowd to get inside for the deal of the season or were teens with their friends blocking the walkway and going nowhere quickly. There was an easier way to do this, and if I made it to next Christmas, I was buying everything online.

Vincent pointed out a music store which sold more than CDs—smart, since they faded out years ago. T-shirts, older Blu-Ray sets, mugs, action figures, and anything else needed and unneeded were on the shelves. Since I knew Donovan could find something in here to like but didn't know what, I stopped in for a gift card and met Vincent outside the store where he could better control the crowd.

I needed more and not just for Donovan. Gifts for all the

Coveners seemed a bit much. If anything, we should have done a secret Santa thing. I started randomly buying things figuring the gift, no matter how small, would fit someone.

Vincent was more useful to help carry bags than for gift ideas.

Finding a game store, I checked off a few more and grabbed the latest console for Donovan since it was something flashy I knew he didn't have. While he wasn't a typical gamer, he did have older systems, and this one could be used for other things as well. Plus, it was an easy return or sell if he didn't use it.

"Hey there, stranger."

I jumped at the voice in my ear, turned, and saw my father. "What are you doing here?"

His brow raised and he looked around as if to say, "Duh!"

"Right." I laughed. "Is Ben here, too?"

"And Adam. Somewhere. Thought I would find them drooling over *Final Fantasy* or some Pokémon thing or whatever the hell they're into these days. Didn't expect to see you."

We stepped outside as a kid about Ben's age pushed by to point out something to his mom already nagging at him for running off again.

When Dad's eyes flitted over my shoulder, I turned to see Vincent standing close with a blank expression I knew as cautious patience, waiting for me to tip him off to the potential danger if needed since my mind was blocked against his telepathy.

Shit. "This is Donovan's—umm, uncle. Vincent, this is my dad, Thomas Saterlee."

"Pleasure to meet your acquaintance, sir." Vincent held up his full hands as an obstacle for a formal handshake.

"You too." Dad looked at me. "Who's Donovan?"

Double shit! When it came to dating Caine, Serena spilled the news to my dad. With the craziness of life, and since Donovan and I hadn't settled with a relationship label, I forgot to tell my dad about the split with Caine and about Donovan's existence. I had less of an explanation of how I met Donovan than I did Caine.

"New guy?" Dad filled in the blanks as I stood gaping. "What happened to Caine?" It didn't matter Vincent happened to be there and was introduced as Donovan's uncle, Dad had no qualms about possibly pissing a stranger off when he wanted answers.

"It's kinda complicated." My cheeks burned so much no way my dad didn't notice.

"Always is."

"I assure you, sir, Donovan is of reputable character and cares deeply for your daughter."

"Is that right?" Dad turned to Vincent and used the flattest tone I had ever heard from the man who gave me life.

I wanted to fall on the cheap Samurai sword in the shop window next to us. Then all over again when Andy ran up to me and grabbed hold of my leg and went on about all the stuff he wanted.

Trying to listen to Andy while aware of my dad's acute curiosity of who the random kid was seemed more difficult when my dad turned to Donovan with an extended hand. I felt the twinge through me as a vision hit, nothing with extreme emotions attached to it, but enough to make the mental note to ask Donovan about it later.

"Your uncle here assures me you are of reputable character." How Dad managed to say this straight-faced, I didn't know.

"Thanks for the good word, Uncle Vince." Donovan stuck his hands into his pockets as Vincent gave a small dip to his head in recognition, though I bet it was the first and last time Donovan would get away with calling him Vince.

"This your kid?"

Andy was still hanging onto me. "I'm Andy. Uncle Caine's nephew." The pride in his voice for remembering the connection was adorable.

Dad looked at me. "Caine...your ex?"

"Yuppers."

The edges of his lips down-turned. "You did say it was complicated."

"Very. So, what are you getting Ben for Christmas?"

Andy pulled on my jacket sleeve and called my name as Dad prattled on about some game Ben wanted, but they were already out of stock at this mall location. I glanced down to see Andy pointing off somewhere I hadn't looked yet. Dread from Donovan crossed the connection. Something was wrong. I peeked, and with my height advantage overlooking my dad and the food court, I saw Graham possessed by the demon Gualichu standing amongst the crowd of indulging shoppers.

No way a demon was at the mall to visit Santa. What the hell could it want?

I smoothed Andy's arm down to stop him pointing and dropped my mental fortitudes, hoping the others did the same, while I etched my smile in place to cover my panic as my dad kept talking.

"What the fuck do we do?" I wasn't sure Vincent heard me, but he and Donovan were glancing at each other and over at Graham, so they knew of the danger.

"What do you want, Soph?"

"Oh, umm...." I used my father's question to look away as if thinking.

The soul glows of other Magics moved through the crowds, working their way to converge on Gualichu. One of the Magics looked our way, at Vincent, who I saw nod in my peripheral as if he was instructing them.

Gualichu surveyed the Blind in the food court, not reacting as if he saw the Magics, so I assumed he didn't. My father certainly hadn't seen him. Not that he would know anything different since he couldn't see souls, which meant he wouldn't know why I was dragging him out of the mall if I tried.

What in the shit was Vincent doing? And who were those Magics he was directing? Did he know the demon would be here?

I realized I still needed to answer my dad. "A hair straightener would be good. Adam could help there." My dad laughed, but it was true. My brother's primping skills were greater than mine, as was his hair straightener. "And, ah, books or a bookstore gift card is always a winner."

"As if I would forget about books. It's a given each year."

"Yeah, well, can never have too many books." I laughed, maybe too much, maybe not enough, my attention was divided. "Are you meeting Adam and Ben in the food court?" I couldn't see my brothers, but thankfully Ben was with another Magic.

"Eventually—"

His answer was cut off by a hum of power so strong it caused us to take an involuntary breath in, my father included. At first, I thought Dad could feel the power, but it became clear everyone could, Magic and Blind alike. Not the energy of a magic the Blind could use but of power around us so potent no one could ignore it. Gualichu's power.

When Dad swayed on his feet, I grabbed his arm, awkward as I shifted my weight, and Andy was still holding onto to me. "Shit. You okay?"

Dad mumbled something about hating shopping before he stumbled and collapsed into one of the leather chairs set up for tired shoppers and early morning mall walkers.

I tried calling him, using his name, but he was unconscious.

"Sophie?"

I looked back to see Andy standing, wide-eyed, arms up and clasped in front of him. Other mall goers fell as my father had, all but ones with soul glows. Shopping bags were strewn all over the ground, trays of food spilled as they hadn't made it to their tables, the Blind no longer screens for the Magics tracking the demon to hide behind. After the thud of the initial fall, the mall took on an eerie silence besides the buzzing of power throbbing through the area and classic holiday music.

Eyes closed, chin to chest, my dad was still breathing, so I assumed the rest were.

I reached out for Andy and he came to me, looking around him as I fished out my phone and called Adam.

"Soph—"

"Shut up. It's the demon I told you about. We're at the mall, too."

"I'm with Ben, but he's—"

"I know. I'm with Dad. Everyone's unconscious. Other Magics are on it. Keep Ben safe and help anyone around you if you can."

"How?"

"Put them in a comfortable position on their sides in case they bashed their heads and go into seizures. Don't leave Ben alone and be sure you know where your exit is in case you gotta run or hide. Can you see any Magics around you?"

"No. How long will this last?"

"No idea."

He was swearing as I hung up.

Vincent had dropped my bags, took off, and was crouched behind a section of plants separating the food court from the rest of the mall, Donovan doing the same.

"Sophie—"

"Shhh." I had Andy squat down next to the chair my dad was in, hiding him from the demon's line of sight if he headed our way. "It's okay. Other Magics are here to help."

"What about all the people?"

"Like my dad, they're just sleeping."

I sent a telepathic, *"What's happening?"* to Donovan, but he didn't answer, and I couldn't see Graham or the other Magics while knelt down.

I stood, still holding onto Andy's hand, and noticed Vincent's attention was on a woman leading a group of Magics sneaking up behind Gualichu who was now standing with his arms out, eyes closed, without notice of his surroundings.

Moving with the oiled, stealthy grace of a jungle cat, the woman with a soul glow akin to Vincent's, fit with strong lean limbs and cropped hair, fixed her glare on her target and cross-stepped her way behind a pillar of a jewellery store less than thirty feet away. Lincoln was with her, now following her as he did Anne-Claire before she was killed in the fight outside Diluculo, soft-footed with long-strides as he crept.

"What are they doing?" I sent Donovan's way.

"No clue."

Vincent had to know, but his brain was on lockdown. I didn't want to screw up his communications with the other Magics and put everyone else in more danger.

Others I recognized with glowing souls moved into view including Jessabelle and Arden whom I had met at Ranlyn's, but the others were strangers, some coming out of doorways and popping up in places I didn't see until they made themselves visible. Gualichu was too self-involved to see the Magics gathering against him.

A blast of energy shot out of each of the Magics. I caught a yelp in my throat and ducked down over my dad and Andy as their collective powers sparked my own. When I opened my eyes, a shield was exactly what lashed out and around me, Andy, and Dad. I looked down at my sleeping father, thankful he didn't open his eyes. Andy was looking up and around him, hands over his ears.

Crashing and yelling filled the echoing space. I stood within my shield, smoothed out its ragged edges, and peered out to see garbage cans had been thrown aside, signage blown off the walls, and a creeping electrical spark crawling along every surface between the Magics and Gualichu, surrounding the demon.

The force interrupted Gualichu from whatever he was doing. His borrowed eyes surveyed the power encapsulating him within it like an electric cocoon. Did he see the Magics doing it to him? Did he know what they intended to do? I couldn't tell.

He lifted his hand. A portal appeared in the small space in front of him. He stepped through it and left the Magics targetless.

All power in the room dropped, including my shield.

Arden booted a food tray. It pinged off a table and whatever unconscious Blind in its way. He turned on his short-haired leader. "I thought you knew what you were doing!"

The woman yelled back at the man in a language I didn't know as Arden switched tongues and yelled back in kind as others joined in.

"Stop!" Vincent's enraged voice rose above the others, making me jump. "The Blind will stir in moments. You have your orders."

Vincent spun on his heel and headed towards me. I met him halfway, but he didn't stop, grabbing my arm and ignoring me when I tried to pull away. He stopped when we reached my still unconscious dad and Andy. The kid's gaze was wide as we barrelled towards him until Donovan went to his side and glared Vincent down. Donovan's anger fuelled me as I twisted out of Vincent's grasp.

"Your father will wake with questions."

"And he'd kick your ass if you tried that in front of him." A middle-aged, five-foot-five Blind man was no match for an immortal like Vincent, but the rest of the mallgoers would be awake soon, too, and Dad would have no problem making a scene.

I stepped to Andy, who hadn't moved from the spot I left him. He reached for me, and I picked him up, only then realizing how heavy a six-year-old was as he strangled my neck. He nodded into my hair when I asked him if he was okay, then we noticed the mewling of those around us as people started waking up.

I shifted Andy's weight onto my hip and warned him my dad was Blind like most of the rest and couldn't know what happened, promising him to get him out of here soon.

Prompting a kid to lie to adults wasn't my best moment, but I figured Jet and his grandparents had started that train wreck as soon as he could talk about seeing the spots that pre-empted a person's death. Not being the first to curb his honesty didn't make me feel any less guilty.

Dad's eyes fluttered open, and he looked around a moment before sitting up straight.

"Slow down. You okay?"

Vincent walked away, on his phone with someone, while people around us started to rise to their feet. I noticed Donovan didn't help any of them struggling to stand, not that I was surprised since he would get visions from them if he tried, though chances were he didn't care to either way, too focused on wanting to bring us to safety.

Dad pulled off his glasses and rubbed his eyes and face. "I think I turned thirty again."

I would have laughed if people weren't crying and voices were starting to rise. The charity bell ringer had a good gash on their head as I'm sure many others did as well.

Dad stood, testing his feet but looked steady. "You guys okay?"

"We're good." I knew he included Andy in the mix and even spared a glance in Donovan's direction.

"The Sovereignty's on their way, as is their Blind cops. We need to go." Vincent's warning overlaid my father's questioning about what happened.

I put Andy down and grabbed some bags as Donovan grabbed the bulk of them so I could hold Andy's hand. I looked to my father and the crease of confusion between his eyes. "I'm getting Andy out of here. Call Adam and tell him and Ben to meet you in the parking lot, yeah?" I wanted to be sure they got out of dodge. Adam was a Magic. Last thing I needed was him to be taken if the Sovereignty knew who or what he was.

Dad touched my arm and turned us away from Vincent. "We should wait. The police might have questions."

"What if it's a carbon monoxide leak or something?"

"I think we'd still be out of it if it was carbon monoxide, though that's good thinking."

"Call me later?" I said as Vincent already started walking away.

"Yeah, yeah. Go to the hospital if you feel wonky."

"You too." I had to raise my voice and wasn't sure if he heard me above stores pulling their metal accordion doors shut and locking them against potential looters and the cries of everyone else panicking, but I couldn't wait any longer. I knew Dad would be fine. If the Sovereignty showed up and found us, we wouldn't be.

Passing an As Seen On TV store, a Sport Chek, and an Old Navy brought us to an escalator where the crowd bottlenecked, frantic to escape to the main floor street exit. I thought it was overkill seeing as how none of these people even know what happened but had to admit I would be hauling tail outside as well. Not frantic enough to knock over children or old ladies, but I had to remind myself some people had issues this situation would throw into overdrive.

A shove pushed me off-balance. I stumbled and struggled to keep upright and my hold on Andy before we hit the ground. Donovan was there and booted a shaggy-haired man, throwing him against a wall. He then slid down and slumped to the floor. Donovan's lips moved in a spell, the energy alive in my chest, though I didn't know what he was doing to the man who looked to struggle to stand as if being held in place.

"Keep up!" Donovan pushed a channel through the crowd for us, passing a Winners and a Dollarama before escaping into the sun-bleached winter day.

Everyone outside was in a state of "what-the-hell-was-that?" most re-telling their experience to the closest stranger, readying themselves for a story they'll re-tell every trip to the mall.

"Where's Vincent?" He said the Sovereignty was on their way. You would think he would have waited for us.

Donovan was taller than most and was looking around without seeing anything but the Blind. No soul glows were in the mix, though if they were following the new Sovereignty rules, their soul glows would be hidden to me anyway.

Donovan grabbed Andy's other hand. "We need to get to the car."

"It'll be a madhouse trying to get out." Those who weren't standing around were honking their horns and revving engines at those not moving fast enough from whatever horrors they imagined. Carbon monoxide, like I told my dad, some kind of silent terrorist attack, which in essence it was, or some future conspiracy theory that would hit social media if it hadn't already.

Andy's clunky winter boots slowed him down as we ran to the

side of the building to where I parked the 'Cuda. So much so, Donovan handed me some bags and hoisted Andy up into his arms so we could move at more than a shuffle.

Too many people were distracted to see Donovan telekinetically open the trunk as we ran up on it to throw the items inside, shutting it with the same technique, and opening all our doors as I jumped into the driver's seat. Sirens were blaring as we slammed them shut and yelled for Andy to buckle up, not bothering with my own in case we needed to escape quickly.

A police barricade blocked us from the closest exit. Maybe they were trying to hold in who they may think was the criminal who started all this, but they could have been with the Sovereignty, too. If they weren't, Blind cops couldn't save us from the Sovereignty. They couldn't hold everyone, and we didn't have time to argue or wait for the officer to search the car. We needed out now.

I managed to squeeze out of the line and headed for a different exit.

Donovan dialled Vincent as I was swearing and honking at the people trying to cut me off.

"Sophie?" Vincent was on speaker phone.

"Deserter! Where the hell—"

"Where are you?"

"Ahh...." I looked around. "Near the back. Trying to exit onto Tremont—"

"Stop now!"

I slammed on the breaks. Horns blasted behind us. The exit we were headed towards was also barricaded by cops. No, not cops. They were armed and clad in body armour but nothing like the local police wear. Had to be the Sovereignty masquerading as some type of SWAT team.

Vincent confirmed what we were seeing and told us to steer away from them.

"There's only so many exits, Vincent!" Donovan continued with a slew of profanity under his breath as I looked around trying to find a hole within the cars nudging in around us. "Where the fuck do we go that won't send us to a Sovereignty prison?"

"Drive to the loading bay beneath the mall. When you reach the long tunnel, stop at the fourth docking station on the left entering from the standard exit of the bay."

"You know where that is?" Donovan's brow was deeply creased, dark eyes focused out the windshield.

"Yup." Vincent hung up and I craned my neck to check around us for a way out of the line of cars we were crammed into.

Trapping us underground in a loading bay might be safe-adjacent, but I had to trust Vincent knew what he was doing and would be there himself to do a monster cover spell strong enough to sneak out under. Even if it meant ditching the car and walking passed the Sovereignty.

Trust wasn't easy when Vincent had directed a team of Magics against Gualichu as if he expected the demon to be there and let me bring a child to the mall anyway.

Turning into the loading bay and then finding the docking station he mentioned, the large garage door, at least six feet off the ground, began to rise. Half-expecting Vincent to meet us and a slew of Sovereignty officials to be on his tail in the perfect "We gotcha!" moment, we were met by no faces at all.

I took my hands off the wheel, holding them out awkwardly. The car lurched forward a moment and then crawled, unguided, up an invisible ramp towards the yawning mouth of the docking station.

Was this supposed to happen? Where is it taking us? I grabbed the door handle in case I had to jump out, then remembered Andy in the back seat. I couldn't leave him.

Once the car had progressed enough for us to see into the garage, we saw nothing but concrete walls. No dollies, no random bits of equipment. Concrete walls and nothing more.

Something wasn't right.

An unseen energy buzzed around us, evoking our own to swell and trigger our connection, taking incredible restraint not to let the loop of power take us over. Funnelling the power into an offensive focus, we were ready to strike if a trap meant certain death. Andy needed to make it out no matter what happened to us.

The car rolled to a stop as the garage door started to close behind us. I reached back for Andy. He took off his belt and scrambled into the front seat onto my lap, keeping silent as he grabbed a hold around my neck. The heavy metal door touched down with a resounding clunk, closing us in, and the scene out the windshield blinked into view.

The car filled with a gasp from all three of us, then louder when a scruffy-bearded man tapped on the driver's window. He waved us forward. I knew from the connection Donovan had no clue where we were or what was hiding beneath the mall and took another moment to gather himself enough to take Andy from me so I could retake control of the wheel.

A knee-high concrete barrier provided a window overlooking a place none of us knew existed. Levels. So many levels held people and places so full of magic and soul glows, they blurred under the strain to take them all in. Not Magics escaping the chaos topside. They went about their business as if they didn't know anything about the young Architect possessed by a demon, standing or walking around in what looked like an enormous, converted parking garage.

The scruffy Magic with a musty soul glow directed us to park off to the side. A few other vehicles were empty and waiting for their owners, but not many considering all the people I saw.

Looking over the barrier showed the place delved floors below us, at least thirty or more. No wonder a constant energy buzzed with every breath. People used their powers without fear like the Blind doing mundane things without thinking. Sellers of all kinds, Magics of all kinds, people of all kinds, living their lives in a place a thousand times bigger than Diluculo.

Donovan and I looked to each other. His suspicion clouded my awe. How could he not know of this place? I was a Seedling to this world, but he grew up in it. Could it be that guarded of a secret?

Where was Vincent? No one was there to direct us further. The soul glows I saw were all on the good side of things, but this didn't mean it was safe for Andy or us for that matter. His little arms were no longer clutching to me. He looked around in his own amazement, and I held tight to his hand in case he decided to explore on his own.

I took out my phone and dialled Vincent, noticing one thing I hadn't through the bright of their soul glows. Everyone I saw move around be it adult, child, or animal was dirty.

When he picked up, he didn't say "Hi" or give any greeting, skipping right to directing us through crowds of stares from people who knew we were outsiders and either skittered off as if scared of us or stared us down as if we were wearing skinned puppy coats.

A man stepped in front of us, blocking us from going farther. He exuded a sense of enhanced strength, whether it be his soul glow or his biceps as he wiped something greasy onto an already greasy sorry scrap of fabric. Not car grease but food grease judging by the cubby behind him with steaming pots floating over questionable fire sources. Though he only stood to Donovan's chin, the air of "man in charge" was lathered all over him.

"You checked in?" The man's stance was wide, and too many others were around to push by without jostling them and making ourselves bigger targets.

"Why? You head dick?"

Laughing off Donovan's superficial dig, the man flicked dirty, blond bangs out of his face and crossed his flannel-covered arms.

"Head dick doesn't have a dick." Another younger man closer to our age with matching hair colour and blue eyes of who I guessed was his father, stepped up, happy to educate us.

"Quiet." Daddy warned and son sniffed and shook his head, taking a step back without moving. "What're your names?"

"Why?"

The man's stare shifted to me. "Much can be said with a name, honey."

Rage sprung through me like my blood caught fire, Nya's power igniting enough for a stifled groan through pressed lips to escape Donovan.

The man rocked back on his heels, looking half-intimidated, half-impressed. "Now that says more than a name."

"Sophie!"

Vincent's sharp tone doused my anger. His strong grip on the shoulder of the man further sealed Nya's power back in place.

"They are welcome."

The blond man squared his shoulders to Vincent. "Says who?"

"I do." An accented voice came from behind the men. Vincent and the man parted enough to reveal a short, slender woman. "Let them through, Rodney." With a nod she motioned with her brunette head at us to follow her. Vincent led the way as Donovan was in back with Rodney and his son tailing us.

The connection between Donovan and me buzzed with a mix of uncomfortable emotions as we made our way to wherever the woman led us. Bypassing aisle after aisle of cubbies so stuffed with people or belongings or both, not to mention with things I had no names for. Knowing we could still be in danger had no impact on my curiosity, making efforts not to stare a chore.

What was also curious was how comfortable Vincent strode through the sea of Magics. This calm manner may have been because he had travelled beneath the mall before or because he was an immortal and didn't often find himself uncomfortable in new surroundings, but I couldn't get a read on him.

Cool fluorescent lighting lit the place poorly, while others used spelled lanterns or fire creating a cave that smelt of a mixture of cheap incense, boiling meat, and wet basement. Eyeing every corner I could, while trying to keep the other eye on people tripping over themselves to protect their cubbies from us seeing inside, I realized this place was an underground market and home all in one. The impression of home made evident by laundry hanging over chicken wire fencing walls of a cubby floored with sleeping bags instead of goods.

The conditions were deplorable. Those living in the cubbies were used to their environment, but I couldn't help wondering why people with such obvious power would settle for lower than basic standards. Why here in a hive of Magics? Were they hiding? I had so many questions.

12

SCREENING PROCESS

Our walk took us to a walled-off section with actual walls, not the chicken wire or dividers of the cubbies. The roof couldn't match the loftiness of the underground ceiling double the height of the building, but it was adequate. Inside was a large office with everything you would expect to find, including file cabinets, a couple of desks, and computers. Nothing out of the ordinary for such an extraordinary place, except for the fact it was clean. Obsessively so.

Before Andy heard anything more damaging, he was set up at the other side of the office with a colouring book I was surprised they had. I strategically placed myself between Andy and everyone else, untrusting of our new friends regardless of how kid-friendly they appeared.

"You're lucky you're allowed admittance here." The woman pointed at Donovan and spoke with what I figured for a Russian accent watered down from years in Canada.

Nodding in response, Donovan stood without complaining as if he was a good ol' boy.

"I assured her you are not that brand of Sorrel." Vincent's

comment explained why the blond man questioned what our names were. They wanted to know our heritages since they couldn't see souls to verify a lack of Taint.

A humourless laugh escaped the woman, and still Donovan said nothing, leaving me confused at why he was so quiet.

"Jesus Christ, Nora!" Rodney's booming voice made me jump. "We're letting Sorrels in now?"

Nora leaned back onto a large desk, her light blue eyes hardening in Rodney's direction. "Take that tone with me again and I'll remove you from your position, strip your mind, and hand you over to Michael. Hear me?"

Whoever Michael was, the threat worked as Rodney settled back into rank.

Donovan chuckled. "No need for dick around here."

Rodney glared at Donovan.

Nora straightened. "Not yours."

Donovan's reaction towards her as compared to Rodney's further confused me. Maybe he knew she was in charge and wasn't challenging her?

Nora stood and focused on me. "You're the Soul Seer Vincent speaks of. You think you got brains enough to tear down an establishment held in place for longer than your people have had power?"

I exhaled, resisting the defensive arm-crossing everyone was doing. "I know nothing about you but a first name—one you didn't offer but said by your goon." My turn for Rodney's glare. "I don't know why we needed an escort into this secret magical dungeon, but a name doesn't earn you girl talk. Before anything else, I wanna know what the hell this place is."

Nora smiled revealing a wide mouth of near-perfect teeth.

"And why I didn't know about it." Donovan's addition was less important to me.

"Your people aren't allowed here." Rodney's mini-me found his confidence.

Donovan took a step towards him. "What the fuck do you know about my people?"

"I know you torture innocents for sport, you evil piece of shit!"

A zing of pain rang through my fist as Donovan lashed out and punched Rodney's mini-me, bringing Rodney senior into the fray in an attempt at breaking it up.

Andy was rattled, standing scared in place, crayon in hand. I cringed at the hits Donovan took and told Andy it was okay, knowing how empty it sounded.

A push of energy I felt through me had Rodney up against the wall. Donovan held him there, intent on going after Rodney's son who grabbed Donovan's throat in a grapple that had me gargling.

A flash of red string-like tendrils hit both men in the heads. I was thrown backwards by a shock that laid me out. My head pulsed with my heartbeat. I squeezed my skull like a vice, rolling into the fetal position with my knees under me.

"I told you!" I heard Vincent scream above the watered-down sensation in my ears.

Nora's concentrated form of discipline to put them down like scrappy dogs was overkill. If the point was to test Vincent's warning of me and Donovan's connection, she got her proof.

"Sophie?" Andy knelt over me.

I looked up at him. Red filled my vision of a teary-eyed Andy. I told him I was okay, but the sound of my own voice hurt my brain, and his soul glow was punishing.

How Nora managed to give me the worst instantaneous migraine in my life, I didn't know. As bright as her soul was, she held no specialized soul colour, which apparently said nothing about her strengths.

A piercing jolt of Donovan's healing magic had me throwing my head back, his groan in pain joining mine before I could open my eyes enough to enjoy the relief.

"Apologies, Vincent." I heard no true regret in Nora's voice. "Violence like that is why his kind are not permitted within The Chiff."

Vincent helped me to my feet. "Violence coerced by instigation is not the violence you fear."

Andy hugged me, and I smoothed his hair back. So much for protecting him. "The Chiff?" I repeated as Nora said it like "Shiff." "That's what you call this place?" I waved off the chair Vincent offered, not wanting to be seated if something else happened but motioned for Andy to sit down.

Nora re-established her position, leaning against her desk, and looked over at Rodney and his son gathering themselves, not as quick to heal as Donovan and me. While Nora waffled on answering me, Donovan came over to me and Andy, knowing we were okay but asking anyway. With some coaxing, Andy went back to colouring or at least pretending to.

"Does she have an issue with straight answers?" I mumbled to Donovan though figured Vincent could hear since he was close by.

Donovan checked over his shoulder at Nora then turned back to me. "No. She has an issue with me."

"Who cares if you're a Sorrel? Bigotry's an excuse." If she didn't trust me or Vincent with all the Magics walking around and bunking in those cubbies, there had to be a few who could reveal Donovan's true intentions and eliminate him as one with the Sorrels his father led.

"Much more than familial bloodlines concern her." Vincent was focused on Donovan, and I felt something close to shame roll through the connection.

Vincent turned to address Nora. "Their need for immediate safety will be my debt. For the good of the insurgence against the Sovereignty, you need to lay waste to your personal history with Donovan."

Donovan's dark stare flickered my way as I absorbed what Vincent revealed. "Sorry."

Oh. "Geez Louise. Are there any bomb-ass female Magics you haven't been inside? I'm conflicted with slapping you and giving you a high-five."

His right dimple caved with his half-smile. "The region's not that big."

Nora and Vincent had continued speaking as Donovan and I whispered amongst ourselves. Her thin arms were lost in the wool of her sweater until she stepped next to Vincent.

"My name is Nora Slavkin." She extended a hand to shake, which I returned. "I inherited this mess from a lazy father and brother who thought of nothing but containing the secret of our existence, only to lose their lives to evil such as the Sovereignty who are no better than the Sorrels." It was clear Nora was a businesswoman with a burden. She looked back at Vincent. "Their presence in this very room proves I can reach past my personal dramas. Trusting either of them will take more."

"Why? I didn't break your heart." The quip earned me an unforgiving glare.

She took a step towards me. Donovan flexed with expectation of an attack, but Nora wasn't looking to get physical. "Evil seeps in and destroys as children. You are a fool to believe he can be anything more."

"Can you see souls?" The question had Nora staring back at me in restrained fury. "I can see that Donovan's soul is pure and bright and a wonderful shade of Seer green. In this life and in others, I have trusted him with my life and will every day from here on out. I don't need you to believe me because I don't know you or give a shit if you care. If you're on board to take down the Sovereignty, return a kid to his mother,"—I thumbed in Andy's direction—"and get people I *do* care about out of the Creation, then we're golden. I just want to know a smidgen more about this place."

As confrontational as this was, my words seemed to relax Nora who sauntered back to her desk and sat in her chair. Or at least a chair. The office itself seemed too basic to belong to anyone running this place. Would make sense to bring us to a dummy space.

"This is The Chiff, taken from the word chiffonier, which is a dresser or wardrobe. Before this place began, Magics would hide the instruments of their craft in charmed wardrobes with false backs, bottoms, and drawers. Easily accessible, away from the eye of the Blind like a new age magician. When the time came for Magics to protect their businesses and hide from those seeking to destroy them, my family and others took responsibility in creating a cellar of sorts to hide their Chiffoniers since they were no longer safe from the Blind's cruel and unforgiving judgement. When the need grew, so did the cellar, resulting in The Chiff. My responsibility is to ensure our people's safety from those above ground."

"And to make bank."

Nora gave Donovan a withering glare.

I ignored him. "If your family's local, what's with the accent?"

She took in a breath before indulging me. "I'm adopted." Without further explanation, it was what I was getting, which was more than I deserved to know.

She pointed out a bank of windows across from the desk giving her a view of the people of The Chiff. Not all but a helping of passersby. "They pay for the niche and use it as they wish—for sale and trade, to safe-keep their families, or both. Makes no difference to me, as long as they are civil and do not burden others with their short-comings. My mission is to ensure only those who should be here gain entrance."

I was certain she did a lot more than she claimed. "But only certain bloodlines are welcome."

She turned to me. "Evil is not welcome here. If you're as talented as Vincent speaks of, then you can see the result of this."

She was right. I hadn't seen a Tainted soul as we walked through, but I gathered The Chiff was a large place with corners I bet not even Nora could pin eyes to. And if some like in the Sovereignty could hide their souls from me, they could also hide their intentions from Nora and her sidekicks.

"And Rodney and child here are a part of keeping that order, yes?" Donovan didn't look at them as he spoke of them.

"Damn right!" The child in question was as puffed as a rooster.

Donovan raised his hands. "Don't get testy with me, junior. As long as you do your job, I bet Daddy doesn't care if you log extra hours between the boss-lady's legs."

Rodney junior surged forward at Donovan and was stopped by his father who rolled his eyes. He didn't appear to know about his son sleeping with Nora, possibly saving his opinions for a more private moment.

"You know nothing." Rodney junior shook off his father yet stayed put.

"My Psychometry tells me enough. Ask your boss-lady about that later." Whatever Donovan saw during the altercation with Rodney was plenty to let him in on the tidbit, though I suspected Rodney junior's current seething was a reaction to Donovan bringing out the fact he, too, had touched Nora before. Though, this made me wonder how much since he didn't see The Chiff in his visions. Could the place be so protected it could stay hidden from him?

"You will respect me and my people within The Chiff or you can tango with the Sovereignty lowlifes up top. Your choice, Sorrel."

A cocky, dimpled smirk was all Donovan gave Nora in response.

The Sovereignty and local cops would take hours to clear out or test the mall's air quality and question witnesses. Which made me think about something else.

"What about the mall's security cameras? Won't they see Gualichu energy-sucking the masses and what you and your friends or mega-badass warrior Magics did to them?"

"We own the mall." Nora sounded bored with having to explain what she probably thought was obvious. "We came first. The land above was lucrative, and folks itched to build, so we did instead."

Donovan made a throaty noise. "Why would you build a place that caters to the Blind when you hate them?"

"Not all of us hate them. Less than you if I remember." She obviously shared a few conversations with Donovan above the sheets. "We are not imbeciles. The Blind rule the civilized world and all its freedoms. This is our reality. The shopping center above is no different than what it is down here, except we cater to a specific clientele, and our merchandise is less frivolous. The cameras as well as the surrounding security, most believe are laughable, but all belong to us as well. This ensures a comprehensive eye on our investments and comes in handy in times of danger."

"No way the Sovereignty doesn't know about this place."

I had to agree with Donovan.

Nora shrugged. "You will soon learn Magics walking through our doors are not as easily admissible as you were today. The process takes time. When you leave, you will find yourselves unable to speak of The Chiff. An enchantment added long ago to keep the secret of its location, thus the reason why most Sovereignty members would have no clue of our existence. Though it is possible one may have infiltrated our screening process, it is doubtful. Extensive checks into clients' backgrounds ensure the safety of the whole. When the chance is given, your history will be sifted through regardless of if you choose to return."

"Yeah, you're not gonna like it." Nora probably thought my background would be laughable, not like I cared, but if she looked far back enough, finding my relation to Evaristus would likely leave me ineligible for The Chiff's services.

"What of the boy's name?" Nora chinned towards Andy.

"I don't know if he has his father's last name or his mother's. I don't know his father's."

"And the mother's?"

I hesitated. "Berisford."

Rodney threw up his hands. "A Sorrel and a Berisford? Nice company you keep, Llewellyn."

Vincent addressed Rodney with tense annoyance. "He is but a child. Nora is aware of Caine and Jet's circumstance within Diluculo, as you should remember yourself, Rodney."

"What I remember is my people dying for a cause you want to reverse, to save who? A couple of Berisfords? Their fate lies in their name."

"And what about the others also trapped in there?" I intervened. "Let them rot, right?"

"They knew the risks."

"As did you. You made it then. Why not now?"

Rodney shook his head. "Did you bother to look behind you at the bloody fight while you were up at the front fighting your own battle? Do you know how many died? See the carnage? Know the names of the sacrificed?"

"You have no clue the battle we fought either or how many we stayed behind to help bury." Mentioning my genetic relation to Evar or seeing Aunt Lacey when my spirit was pushed out of my body was far more personal than I was willing to get. "You don't need to join this fight. I wouldn't blame you if you wanted nothing to do with it, but you can bet a pack of your greasy-haired scrunchies it'll happen with or without you. Step up and finish the job started outside Diluculo. If your efforts are better used against us, like this stupid argument you insist on dragging me into, then I'd rather you keep your cowardly ass hidden down here."

"I'm sure you would."

Vincent cleared his throat to end the resulting staredown. "Aside from our need of refuge, we have other requirements The Chiff's niches can resolve."

Rodney argued until his whole face went red, but Nora let us go. We weren't an immediate threat, and Vincent vouched for us. Leaving as soon as we could was still on the menu, and I was certain Nora would kick our asses out if we overstayed our welcome. What she didn't ensure was our safety. Vincent had our backs, but this wasn't his domain. I assumed it was an understated part of the temporary visitor's package without betting my lady-berries on it. Three against the hundreds or thousands in this place meant never getting topside in time to ignore Christmas carolers.

Andy remained barnacle close as we left the office and walked along the rows headed wherever Vincent led us.

"Call your aunts." Vincent stopped and stood to the side of passing Chiff residents. Some ignored us. Others stared.

"Why? I doubt they're your type. And if they are, shame on you." He stared down at me.

"Okay fine. But you can only have one." I covered Andy's ears. "No dick is worth splitting sisters up. Not even an immortal one."

He raised his brows high above his glasses. "While your deflective humour is in good repair, I doubt those locked in Diluculo are so sharpened."

"Ouch. Right to the bone with that one, huh?" I appreciated he didn't mention Caine or Jet by name since I wasn't covering Andy's ears anymore.

"Why do you need them?" Donovan didn't share my humour either, too busy scanning our surroundings like a vigilant security camera. Tugs of tension nagged the connection as his eyes darted from passersby to the low cement barrier keeping us from falling to our death.

"The Nexus Transference spell is complex and requires an extensive array of ingredients. With most anything at our fingertips, procuring missing pieces of said list is in our best interests." Vincent left an unstated "in case we can't return" hanging.

Without the ability to explain where I was or how I was in the position to find almost anything, it made convincing the aunts' crabby butts to give me any information they knew about the spell a tad difficult. Telling them Vincent would deliver what was needed in only a bowler hat and his glasses caused minor hesitation, the offer declined on the basis of a bowler hat being the least sexy of vintage head wear.

Vincent was done with my shit and disengaged to save himself the quippy retort which would keep the gag running.

Olive became the voice of reason, taking the phone, and stating we needed a Pompeii Worm. Somewhat rare and twice as hard to get your hands on in this part of the world. I made no promises and relayed to Vincent what it was we needed.

We were off again, Vincent leading the way through a crowd

Donovan was desperate not to let touch him and set off his Psychometry.

The cement beneath our feet was layered in shifting dust and dirt as we shuffled past niche after niche with characters as odd as their wares. The ones living within The Chiff wore the place in the heaviness of their clothing hanging off their shoulders. Being underground seemed to alter them like they were always aware of the high roof, as if it were merely inches from their heads instead of the freedom of the sky.

Keeping them held inside, repressed and away from the reality of the world, seemed like Nora was banking more on their fear of the Blind instead of encouraging assimilation so The Chiff could work as it was intended to. It's supposed to be a place to hide magic objects, not Magics themselves.

"You heard her in there." Donovan's voice in my head surprised me since I didn't realize I left myself open. *"They pay for the niche, and she doesn't give a shit what they do with it. Though, I bet it's her or assholes like Rodney that keep them from doing anything more than squatting."*

"All have good reasons to fear the Blind." Vincent's interjection meant he was keeping tabs on our thoughts. Could others in The Chiff hear us, too? Would explain all the glaring. *"Keep in mind the person we are about to speak with is one who prefers this place to one governed by the oppression of the Blind. The Pompeii Worm needed for the Nexus Transference spell will come from him and him alone. Insulting him when your knowledge of his home could fill a cockroach ear is ill-advised."*

"Fantastic. Now I'm picturing a cockroach's ear. Do they even have ears?"

Vincent's internal sigh was loud before he ducked out of the conversation.

A Google search for another time.

Constant tenseness in my neck and shoulders—or more likely Donovan's—was fueling a headache. He probably knew of potential exits and choke points. Or maybe he didn't, and that's why all the tension. He didn't pipe up into my thoughts this time, and I hoped his hypervigilance was overkill.

Through a door and out the other side brought us deeper into The Chiff by some kind of magic. Quicker than riding an elevator yet confusing since I didn't know where we were going, and the doors didn't tell us where either. Maybe Vincent was the one directing the path since he was the one leading us? I didn't know, and he didn't explain.

We went through many such doors which took us lower and lower into The Chiff until Vincent was satisfied and took a left. The sense of being closed in came with a chill in the air, telling me we were far underground. How deep? I had no clue.

The niches here looked the same. This underground suburbia had me turned around and starting to siphon some of the paranoia Donovan was emitting. Praying Vincent knew what to do in case things slipped nipples north was all I had for a backup plan. And I didn't like relying on someone else to get us to safety.

The niche we stopped at was filled to the brim except a narrow gulch of a walkway for the reed thin merchant to slink through. The mousey brown hair of the young man Vincent called Neilan was mostly covered with an old, oversized baseball cap that settled awkwardly on his skull as he moved with jutting actions like a skittish rat.

Though bright, the man's soul colour was not expected. Red. Not red like Joelly's red, more of a deep blood-red, which swathed Neilan within it while I tried to figure out if the Ballard Tome outlined this soul colour. Pretty sure it didn't. I realized, again, the tome's list was incomplete. Variations of soul colours on other Chiff residents rein-forced this as I had seen plum instead of an Elemental's purple, a dark hunter green instead of a lighter Seers green, and so much more.

Neilan didn't attempt to shake our hands when Vincent intro-duced us. He picked his dirty nails sticking out of ratty fingerless gloves with cautious anxiety. Vincent leaned in at Neilan's ear to whisper something. When Vincent re-established distance between them, Neilan's eyes were larger than natural as he turned to us before looking back at Vincent.

"Who's it for?" Neilan's gaze bounced from us to Vincent a few more times.

Vincent stared down at Neilan without answering. With hesitation and a final sigh, Neilan bowed slightly in what I assumed was an apology and scurried away into one of the walkways of his niche.

While we waited, I lowered my voice to ask Vincent about Neilan's abilities.

"He is a Phoenix."

"Missing a bunch of feathers, no?"

Vincent adjusted his glasses. "No feathers on a true Phoenix and not many left in existence. Neilan lives his life as any other Magic, growing in strength dependant on practice and ages as any other being. Then when he dies, he begins again as a newborn child from the chest of the previous being he lived as. Rebirth of the unborn, knowledge and memory a clean slate, much like the two of you, however, quicker and with precise certainty."

"Damn. The visual is as grotesque as it is fascinating. I would pay to see that." Donovan made no effort to hide what we both were thinking.

"Why doesn't he use his power to the point of agelessness, so he doesn't have to go through that?"

Vincent gave me a contemptuous glare.

"What? No?" I looked at Donovan who was still on the same page as me.

"You speak of immortality in terms of a child's choice. Transitioning away from the decay of life is exceedingly difficult. You will understand soon enough if that happens to be the path you take, though entwining your power with that of Nya's would accelerate the process if you worked harder on doing so."

"*Pfft*. Now who's making things sound easy. How many times

have you melded your essence with the extra one chillin' in your vessel?"

Vincent searched towards where Neilan disappeared, ignoring me.

"Exactly."

"Not to mention how to gift some of it to someone without losing it all."

Vincent spun back to glare at Donovan. "Pardon me?"

Donovan looked at Vincent and then me without apology. I couldn't remember if I told him I wasn't telling Vincent or the other Elders this, but he sure knew now.

Vincent squared his shoulders to me, his intense glare oppressive. "Educate me."

"Relax your 'tude, dude." Before Vincent shifted into full-out interrogation mode, I felt an internal hardening take over at the thought of having to repeat the conversation with Aunt Lacey when Evaristus pushed my spirit out of body like a PEZ dispenser. "If it's possible, we need to do it. It's hard enough for me to remember to protect Donovan when Nya's power flips on. And if it happens too quickly, it could kill us both. On second thought, how am I supposed to combine my power with hers without it screwing with him all the time? Wouldn't I be struggling to protect him every second of every day seeing as how she doesn't exactly give a shit about how he feels when her power is up in my grill?"

Shaking his head, Vincent leaned in closer to me, speaking inches from my face, enough for a spark of Donovan's jealousy. "Nya the woman did not make the journey with her power."

"So I've been told."

He squinted at me, speaking low. "Are you afraid the bond between yours and Nya's power will change you?"

Swallowing the sudden lump in my throat, I found it impossible to answer him. As seconds passed, I stared back at his mesmerizing green eyes.

His brow creased as I squinted back at him. "Can you promise it won't?" My voice was small and with far too much vulnerability for my liking. All the talk about how I needed to mix my power and Nya's together like a supernatural fruit smoothie and Vincent never thought of it? When his expression fell it was clear he had no definite reply.

"Pinky promise?" Andy added for me. I could have high-fived him if I wasn't so worried about Vincent's non-response.

"It could change her?" Donovan took a step forward causing Andy to step aside.

Vincent straightened and took a moment. "With regret, I have no proof of consequences to doing so. The assumption being a greater overall well of power to draw from."

I backhanded him in the arm. "What the fizz, jackhole? You say this now? Why encourage me to do it without knowing what it'll do to me?"

His restrained grimace hid beneath a thin layer of righteousness. "Everything about this life cannot be known. Risks are necessary."

"No shit, Sherlock!" I gained the attention of a few Magics passing by. "You know what I've been through, more than I do when accounting for other lives. I think I've taken enough risk to expect a pinch of guarantee now and then."

Neilan returning had me stewing in a vat of inner "what the fucks." He handed a wicker basket to Vincent, who gave Neilan a leather pouch like he was paying a fifteenth century blacksmith. Neilan peered inside the pouch and smiled with delight, exposing decaying teeth and encroaching swollen gums. Whatever the trade, he was satisfied, and Vincent gave him a strong pat to his shoulder before wishing him a hearty "Good day, friend," and leading us deeper into The Chiff.

We walked by more Magics with odd soul colours while our surroundings appeared unchanged. Every wall and inch of ground were covered in layers of dirt. As with my beloved, yet redecorated, rundown apartment, no matter the condition, home was home to those who made it where they could. Made me miss the simplicity.

Vincent walked right into a niche and put down the basket to began conversing with the rounded fair-haired woman running the niche, asking about sales and of her grandchildren's welfare. Nothing out of the ordinary, by the looks of it, until Vincent invited us into the niche to sit and wait out the Sovereignty.

We hesitated.

The woman thumbed at Vincent. "Up to the boss."

Vincent grinned with warmth our last exchange lacked and grabbed a book from a shelf. He bent in front of Andy and opened it. A gnarly dragon roared and spit fire that lit up Andy's face with orange and red. He jumped back into my legs. Vincent changed the page. What looked like a fairy flew a foot above the pages and giggled while flapping tiny wings like a hummingbird before diving back into the book as Vincent closed it.

I thought it was too much for Andy until he said, "Cool!" and took the book from Vincent who directed him to the back of the niche to read the rest.

"Kids of the Blind would read more if their picture books were so animated." The woman looked up at us. "No offence."

"None taken." Donovan was quick to comment though I thought it was close-minded. He had little to no experience with Blind children. I didn't know about the woman, but it was a generalization at best. Many kids read. It's less of a priority for adults when things like paying bills took over. Plus, books aren't cheap.

Vincent stepped in and asked if we were hungry. I was thirsty more than anything, though figured Andy was due for a snack and a bathroom trip. Assuring Andy the book and others would still be there, Donovan and Andy were showed the bathroom while Vincent retrieved food. Neither were available within the niche, so they were off while I waited around staring at everything and everyone around me in awe of how this operation could have remained a secret for so long.

"Moira." The woman tapped her chest and than squinted at me.

"Vincent talks a lot of you. Soul Seer, right? Never were in your past lives that he knows of. Strong. Not quite this strong."

I nodded. "He talks to you about stuff like that?"

Her laugh came out a cackle. "That Vincent gets talkin' and before he knows it has nothing left." She shook her head with a twist to her thin lips in sullen reflection. "Without much family around, at his age and without one of his own since Cora-Lynn, who does he have to vent to?"

"Who's Cora-Lynn?"

Moira stared at me. "Hmm. I thought he would have confided in you about her. Not that it's a happy tale to re-tell." She leaned in a bit. "Cora-Lynn's Vincent's wife. Sorry, *was* Vincent's wife. Killed when his family came for him. Left Vincent eternally scarred and his love dead and gone. Centuries don't seem to make it easier, not that I blame him. Even you've had trouble convincing him it wasn't his fault and laid strictly on the shoulders of his corrupt family. Kept his grief from drowning him, though. Not that you'd remember, I suppose." She looked away and scratched her arm. I got the hint it was for my comfort and not her own, both of us saved when a customer approached the store.

Vincent could have had hundreds of wives in his immortal lifetime, but Moira made it sound like this Cora-Lynn was the beginning and the end for Vincent.

You would think if I were powerful enough to connect my soul to Donovan's for eternity, I would have had the foresight to be sure I retained my memories in each lifetime to make the process less of a pain in the nips. I knew of Cora-Lynn once. Maybe even knew her. Vincent said he didn't always befriend Donovan and me when he found us. I can't imagine how difficult it was for him to re-tell his life story, and bits of ours, each time we hit the restart button.

A swift transaction brought Moira back to her wobbly stool, bringing me out of my faraway thoughts.

"I've lived here in The Chiff for some time." She didn't need my input to make conversation. "Work is hard to come by unless you're topside, and, at my age, I'd rather not since they treat you like a senior citizen who will keel over at the slightest bump." She gave a resentful chuckle at this. "Vincent's heart overflows with such kindness. I was lucky to be in his path. He hired me to oversee his shop, paying me more than he ought to, knowing my children and grandchildren benefit as much as I do, but he won't listen to any complaints about it. Claiming my expertise is cause enough for the raise." Her huff at the notion ruffled her wispy bangs.

"What's your expertise?"

Heavy creases deepened in Moira's forehead. "Shouldn't you be able to tell?"

"I'm new at this. Your somewhat purple soul colour says you're some kind of Elemental but not what kind or how you'd be useful here in a super deep basement run by a sassy Russian woman."

"Ukrainian. And an Elemental? I'd study harder, for I assure you I'm in no way attuned to the testiness of nature. I'm an Alchemist."

"Hmm. I guess alchemy would be handy down here. Or anywhere, really."

She smirked. "You have no clue what an Alchemist does, do you?"

"Not a clue."

Moira laughed and saw to another customer while I took out my phone to make some notes of the soul colours I encountered in The Chiff. Moira's soul was more a deep plum than a violet. Such a small difference changed everything. I added the Phoenix's deep red and Fox's dark blue Druid colours so I could add them to the Ballard Family Tome's lacking list.

Something in Moira's tone gained my attention. A beast of a man with an orange soul glow was leaning over her little counter with an implied threat of physical oppression. Since his soul glow meant increased strength, I didn't doubt he was capable. And while Moira was throwing around her sass like dick-shaped confetti, he was step-ping to the side of the counter as if to come into the niche after her.

"Whoa, beefcake!" I managed an impressed, yet meager whistle. "How much can you bench?"

The man stopped and shifted his heavy brow in my direction.

"Seriously." I got off my stool and headed towards the man of average height with shoulders wide enough to set my coffee table on. "I bet it's a lot." I continued playing into his blatant ego with a flirtatious tone of an avid fan.

Slipping his tongue along his teeth made me cringe, but I kept up what I assumed was a flirtatious smile, suppressing an eyeroll when he flexed his biceps. While rather chilly underground, he had his guns out as if walking on a sun-beaten boardwalk.

"Could certainly hold your weight, sweetheart."

My laugh sounded fake in my ears, but he didn't notice as I sauntered closer and extended a hand, introducing myself as "Kimmie."

"Conrad." He took my hand, which I made delicate and lingered.

"Ooh, forearms, too." I ran my fingers along his fake tanned and hairless forearm and held it. He went on about regiments and eating habits—including ingredients bought from Moira. I nodded as if he was the most interesting person I had ever met, while I stealthily rose my power and directed it where I wanted.

He looked down at my hand, ignoring an ache I knew he felt, until he shifted his weight and quieted.

I glanced down to see his tanned paler drained to a stone grey. "What's the matter, Beefcake?" He grabbed onto his arm, pulling away from me. "I just wanted to see how much you could lift."

Conrad struggled to hold his limb as it turned to stone, crawling up his arm. He hinged over, his hand hitting the ground with a resounding clunk of stone on cement. He grunted, stuck on one knee as he attempted to right himself, going nowhere.

"Not too impressive, Conrad. A tad disappointing, actually."

"Bitch!"

"Ouch. Never been called that before." I knelt beside him. "You see, Moira here is a good friend, and my other good friend who owns this operation isn't as nice as me and has many more years of creative thinking when it comes to assholes who shake down his people."

He collapsed onto his side and grabbed his shoulder, it too losing its colour as the veins in his neck and forehead bulged.

Moira shifted without interfering, looking out into the walkway where passing Magics were taking notice. Donovan's presence drew closer. He wasn't close enough to see us, but I noticed his worry floating beneath my attention as I made sure to remain out of Conrad's reach.

"And since every soul around here seems to think you're right where you should be, since they keep walkin' on by, they won't think twice about letting us in on who's hassling Moira here if you do it again. Or if harm comes to her while she's away from the store, that kinda thing."

There he was. Vincent and Donovan were wading through the crowd with Andy running to keep up, clutched to Donovan's sleeve as they approached. I stood as Vincent's expression crimped and looked down at Conrad.

"Self-defence. Conrad here,"—I nudged his stone arm with my boot—"thought he could mess with Moira, so I was informing him he can't." I peered down at Andy. "In self-defence."

He didn't respond, looking back at the man on the ground.

"Are you all right?" Vincent directed at Moira. She nodded, fighting a smile. "I think you effectively made your point, Sophie. You should restore him before whatever you did infiltrates his brain."

"Hmm. I don't know." I knelt again. "Think you got the point, Beefcake?"

"Change it back, you bitch." He clawed at his neck, his nails scraping against his stone skin.

"You really need to learn a new insult, buddy."

"Sophie."

I looked up at Vincent. "Yes, Dad."

I gripped Conrad's arm, roused some power, and watched his skin soften and erase the stone pallor. Without his fake tan.

Conrad sprung to his feet.

I jumped up as well. "Anything you wanted to buy? Besides fake tanner." I turned to Moira. "I'm assuming you don't sell that here."

She lifted her shoulders. "Sorry."

I turned back to the weight-pumping douche-bag. "Guess you'll have to make a trip topside. Have fun explaining that."

Conrad flexed his fingers and looked straight at Vincent. "I could have your admittance pulled for that."

"Umm, hello." I waved to gain their attention. "Are you giving him credit? Believe me, it was fun, so if you want anyone banned, it's me. And since I don't give a shit if I am, go ahead. I'm sure Nora will gladly take the opportunity. Though, we could easily have yours pulled for strong-arming Moira, no? I have a feeling that story will be more believable than whatever fairy tale you take to the boss-lady."

"You don't belong down here, bitch. Don't think—"

"That Nora will take threatening anyone within her establishment lightly? I'm sure she's in her office if you want to direct whatever you were going to say to her instead of me. Might streamline this whole bullshitting process."

Fed up with my sarcasm, Conrad left with a lingering staredown before becoming lost within the Magics of The Chiff. His hands in fists had everyone moving out his way real quick.

Moira cackled as Conrad stalked off. "This firecracker is worth keeping around, Vincent."

I shrugged at Donovan as Andy scampered back to his book. "What? No, threat of exposure here."

13

FANTASTICAL THINGS

"Where did you learn that trick?" Vincent handed me a can of orange pop.

After taking a sip of semi-cold and flat liquid, I explained Serena's first accidental display of power. "I figured I'd give it a try and, if that didn't work, I'd use my decaying thing as a fallback." I didn't actually consider it a fallback at the time, but it sounded good.

Donovan stood in front of me as he chomped, wrist deep in a bag of Sun Chips. "While we were in that cesspool of a bathroom, I could've sworn I felt you flirting with someone."

I made a one-shoulder shrug. "Had to get my hands on the meathead somehow. Not his actual meathead. We were in public, after all."

"Mhmm." He chewed another moment. "Does that mean I can do it, too?"

"You're asking permission?"

He crooked an eyebrow. "You say you won't leave, but it doesn't mean you wouldn't be with someone else when the mood strikes."

"So, what you're angling for is a side project with tits? You know, for when the mood strikes."

Donovan dropped his hands, along with the chip bag away from my reach as I tried to snag one. "You know that's not what I want. Is that what you want?"

"I'm not into boobs. Though, I don't have much experience to pull from other than my own set, so maybe."

"Sophie."

"Correction, only since high school. I was a late-bloomer."

"Sophie." The edge of his voice was hard.

"What? You started this."

"No, you did with Steroid Conrad and your, 'I had to get my hands on the meathead somehow'."

I laughed. The eddies of his jealous sarcasm were not easily overlooked.

"So, if I—"

"Relax your hypotheticals, dude." I telekinetically snatched the chip bag from him. He groaned. "It's not like I groped him like a superhero's codpiece." I popped a chip into my mouth and crunched while Donovan stewed. "You know me well enough to know I don't want you following me around like a helpless duckling, but I won't keep a side dish while you and I are still, you know, you and me. Whatever that is."

A hitch in power and the chip bag was back in his hand, he smirking at my yelp, dimples caved in delight of my surprise. He dropped the subject and stuffed his mouth with more chips before handing over an empty bag and taking a look at Vincent's stock.

Since I had no clue what anything was, let alone their use, I opted to rejoin Moira who was eating a sundae treat Vincent had brought her.

She slopped a spoonful down the front of her shirt, swore in a different language, and plunked the sundae cup and tiny, wooden spoon down. She rushed to remove her red, knitted cardigan, then tried to finger-scoop it off, smearing it, making it worse. Vincent pulled a handkerchief from his pocket, but the spot of vanilla, chocolate, and cherry syrup now looked like a roadkill skid mark.

"Would you like me—"

"You've done enough!" Moira threw Vincent's handkerchief at him and stormed out of the niche.

He looked down at the soiled handkerchief, his expression drawn.

"It's ice cream. What's with the dramatics?"

Vincent loosely folded the handkerchief and slipped it into his pocket. "The Chiff is missing the comforts of home."

"No kidding. Unless you grew up under a bridge."

His gaze narrowed. "Have you seen laundry facilities as you traveled down here?"

"Can't say I was searching for them since I don't plan on putting in a rental application."

"Attempt a thorough search if you wish, you will find no such convenience." The stool scuffed on the dirty cement floor as he sat. "Moira is off to the washroom in an attempt to avoid a stain. Unless she wants a washing machine in her niche and to pay for the plumbing, washing must be done in Blind facilities or by hand. Moira does not take travelling above lightly, so you can imagine how such a simple thing can become quite a chore both physically and psychologically."

"We could bring some of her things back to the house."

Vincent was shaking his head before I finished. "If she would allow it, I would have had her set up years ago. I have learned not to insist where charity is taken with much offense."

"And there's no special spell to remove a stain? There has to be."

He shrugged. "For some. Many are more of an illusion spell and not a long-term solution."

What he said about his charity becoming offensive made sense. While a sugar daddy sounded like a dream for some, for others, feeling as if you owe somebody or are owned by someone is a fate worse than walking around with a stain on your shirt. Poverty looked much the same below ground as it did above, even with the extra gifts Magics bring to the equation.

Understanding didn't mean I was beyond trying a different tactic, so when Moira headed back through the crowd, I met her part-way, said my piece, and headed back to Vincent with a smile.

I sat on the stool and spun around feeling far too smug. "She's getting her things."

"What did you say to her?" I didn't need a connection with him to feel his overprotective nature kick in.

"Don't you worry your pretty fake glasses about it. Moira is a woman of a certain age, living in less-than-optimal sanitary conditions. And although your offer was reasonable and with good intentions without ulterior motives, you happen to be a very old, very powerful immortal. And her boss. And a considerably attractive man."

"Why is my gender a factor?"

"She's old school. If you were in her shoes, would you want your younger looking, handsome boss washing your granny panties?"

He nodded slowly as if it was sinking in.

"Not personal, but at the same time, completely personal. I'm no one to her. Not her boss, not her daughter—who I imagine she doesn't want to burden or feel shamed for needing the help from—and not someone who will be in her face all the time to remind her of this little favour. However, I'm someone you trust, so she can trust me with something like washing her clothes and returning them. Being a woman is a bonus because she's traditional enough to feel it makes a difference."

He crossed his arms. "Not personal, yet completely personal."

"Yup."

He inhaled and straightened his already straight glasses. "Thank you for helping her. I assumed her stubbornness was one of shallow pride."

"Pride plays a part, but it's not shallow. No one likes to feel like less of a person because they don't have the things in life others do.

With this type of operation, the fact people down here live in such conditions blows my balls." He smirked at the comparison. "And, I get I know less about this place than I do the breeding habits of sperm whales—saw a documentary in the middle of the night—but, come on. Magics have a tool belt full of tricks. If that doesn't gain them money, then it's because no one is paying them for what they do, or they are literally too terrified to go topside. They probably have their reasons, but someone is cashing in on their terror, and it sure as peach pits isn't someone like Moira. My grandmother is a God-fearing, Magic-hating nightmare, and I still wouldn't stick her down here."

His lips pursed, adding a small nod as if he didn't want to agree with me but did.

Thinking of Moira brought another topic to mind. "She, ah, told me about Cora-Lynn."

His jaw dropped, yet he managed to keep his lips closed.

"Apparently, we've talked about her before. Either way, I'm sorry." His too-focused green eyes had me nervous. "She didn't say exactly what happened but was quick to blame your family."

"Moira knows very little."

"Hmm. The snap in your tone should have me bailing, but I'm dangerously curious as well as, I don't know, urgently compassionate?" His stare didn't waver. "Without knowing everything, I can connect the dots in assuming her death plays a role in the split within your family."

His slacked jaw now ground his teeth. "Their savagery poisoned others long before."

"Sure. She wasn't their first experiment. But after her was the first time you swore to take them down, wasn't it?"

Nodding with a cheerless laugh buried within his chest. He gave no other response.

"Did I meet her?"

"How could you not?" He looked at the floor.

"'Kay." Guess it was inevitable in his mind. "Was she a Magic?"

"Quite. Fantastical things would occur without her understanding. No familial support to help her gain understanding of her power, she was too frightened to practice her gifts." He paused. "I could not ignore the air of power around her and revealed myself. She saw hers, and mine, as a curse and did her best to deny them and try to convince me of the same."

A glint of sadness in the moss of his stare retreated when Moira returned with her dirty clothing. Her presence guillotined the conversation as if Vincent materialized Moira for the exact purpose.

She grumbled and plunked down her sack of laundry, attending to a customer who must have saw us deep in conversation and decided not to interrupt. Taking the out Moira's return awarded, Vincent headed to a shelving unit running the length of the niche, busying himself. I couldn't look away from him. The sadness he carried for Cora-Lynn refused to let him go. What a torture to have to repeat every story with me like a bad case of *Groundhog Day*. Why he bothered at all was the true question.

Feeling he needed it, and willing to risk rejection, I reached out telepathically, at first hitting a wall. Nudging pressure proved his wall was more like cheese cloth. I jumped through with an all-consuming embrace I wished I could have given with actual arms. Envisioning it brought the action to life, and I felt the tension drop from his shoulders as he sunk into it, letting go of a couple of renegade tears as the echoed voices of The Chiff around us dissipated like fog.

With a shuttering breath meant to steady himself, I withdrew from Vincent's head space and opened my eyes with a flutter as the vibration of power within me eased back into disuse. Risking a look, I saw Vincent clutching a shelf, leaning his weight into it, head bowed. He risked a glance as well with a twitch of a smile.

I caught a figure rising from a crouch and saw it was Donovan. I didn't realize I siphoned a hint of Nya's power to comfort Vincent. Maybe his mental fortitudes weren't the cheese cloth I thought it was. By the time I got to Donovan, he was upright and gripping his knees.

"Sorry. I tapped into Nya's power by accident." Weird considering how difficult it was to connect to her power not long ago.

He straightened and rolled his shoulders. "To do what exactly?"

The accusation in his tone drained my sympathy. "If someone I care about needs a metaphysical hug, then I'm going to give them one."

"A metaphysical hug?"

"Yes."

"Because he's contagious and you haven't had your cooties shot?"

"Yes, Donovan. Since, unfortunately, Vincent's germs are the gift that keeps on giving, my precautions were purely selfish."

"Sure. Can't be too careful these days."

I squared my shoulders and relayed what I learned of Cora-Lynn, not because he was calling me out but to shove his jealousy back where it belonged, along with a childish air of "Fuck you" for good measure. Understanding eased his sour features as he absorbed what it would be like to be Vincent. Living an immortal existence without the person you love. Waging a crusade against the Sovereignty and the family that ruined his life was worth the expended lives to find retribution. I was certain Donovan could envision doing the same. I died over and over, but so did he. We didn't have to live without each other in the way Vincent was forced to do without Cora-Lynn. And if I knew Cora-Lynn in my past, chances were Donovan did as well.

While the sense of guarded understanding crossed the connection, a note of stubbornness prevailed. I didn't ask why. I didn't have to. Caring about Vincent didn't mean Donovan wanted to pay for my sympathies when they came with the gut-wrenching consequences of Nya's power.

I huffed. "I'd really like to end all this jazz and get the hell out of here. Why can't we portal out, bring the Pompeii Worm to my aunts, and get this spell over with? We're wasting time."

"Agreed." He headed towards Vincent.

I was happy to see Vincent had regained composure since Donovan went to him before I could check.

Unfortunately, we couldn't portal out. Portals were against some sort of rule that didn't make sense to me. Even when we mentioned the Apporter it was useless since Olson was Tainted and couldn't venture into The Chiff. Vincent did have an idea and went to Nora to discuss it, leaving us in the niche.

Too antsy to stand and do nothing, I checked on Andy, slipping down next to him on the ground where he sat with another book with swordsmen duelling in the air above the pages in shining armour that clanged with every grunting hit. Watching his fascination was comforting, especially knowing his family may never return to the people he knew. Seeing him in this child-like moment, I didn't regret taking him from them one bit.

Vincent returned and waved me over. I left Andy, who I doubted noticed I was there, to meet them near the front of the niche.

"Olson cannot join us within The Chiff, yet we can join him outside the door. Since the Sovereignty may still be patrolling the mall grounds under the guise of regular police officials, we will utilize an alternative exit."

"What about the 'Cuda?"

Vincent looked at me.

"My car."

"I can return for it another time."

"Mhmm. If anyone here fucks with it—"

"I'm responsible, yes, of course."

"Damn right of course."

"Andy can stay while you three traipse off to do whatever it is you're about to do." Moira was looking at Andy still sitting on the ground as a bullfrog jumped out at him, making him flinch and giggle.

Leaving behind my car made me itch. Leaving Andy behind? Not a chance.

My hesitation must have tipped him off as Vincent said Andy could bring the books with us.

Moira thanked me—for Conrad, her laundry, or both I didn't know—hugged me, and wished us well, ruffling Andy's hair before we followed Vincent through The Chiff. Even in his fancy loafers,

Vincent was too fast, especially for Andy who couldn't coordinate reading and walking, so Donovan hoisted him onto his back.

My version of Andy's book distraction was the soul colours we bypassed on the way to wherever Vincent led us. I didn't see the Magic, their niche, or what they were doing, too enamoured by a rainbow of colours everywhere I looked.

Vincent brought us to a set of stairs. He climbed them two steps at a time, his pounding leather loafers shaking the narrow metal. The stairs brought us to a catwalk, giving us an overlook of The Chiff. Shock made me stutter-step and grab for the railing before my vertigo pitched me over. Donovan's complaint was quiet in my ears as I closed my eyes and fought to right myself. When I opened them, I was balanced, but no less overwhelmed.

The level of The Chiff we were on was a top rung. Through the middle of The Chiff was a giant hole, the niches hugging the outskirts level-by-level, winding downwards, delving so deep I lost sight of how far down The Chiff went. It appeared bottomless, though Magics and spelled objects soared across the wide expanse to reach their destinations quicker than the doors Vincent had us go through to reach Neilan and Moira.

If Nora spent the bulk of her time in her office, there was no telling what was happening down in the depths or what the lower Magics had going on with their souls. I doubted the savviest of bosses had eyes on everyone.

We followed the metal-slated catwalk for about fifty feet until the walkway gave way to cement flooring in a slim, darkly lit hallway soaked in the stench of urine. At the back of the pack, I kept a steady pace, noting I was holding up better than I would have before any of this magic stuff came into the picture.

A light buzz of power tingled in my lungs as we speed-walked down the never-ending hallway. With healing power, my ability to breathe better than a seventy-year-old would regenerate when I was gassed. Unfortunately, this didn't stop sweat from running down between my shoulder blades. Though maybe it was Donovan. This was true for the ache in my arms as he ran like a papa koala with Andy's strangling little hands around his throat.

A good half-hour at a constant clip through the tunnel meant both Donovan and I were a sweaty mess, and Andy was complaining about the jolting ride. Vincent waited for us to catch up to him, he standing in front of a heavy metal door more akin to a vault than an exit. He looked far too unaffected with not a glisten of sweat on him.

When we got close, he spoke an incantation. By the time we got to it, the metal door was squealing, and three slated locking mechanisms slid away from the frame. He spoke another incantation, and the heavy door swung open.

The smell of wet, decaying leaves hit me before we stepped out onto a snow-covered forest floor. Skeletal branches slashed across a partial moon casting ominous shadows, leaving dark corners everywhere I looked. Donovan let Andy down slowly, our tension an ache as we scanned the forest, anticipating the Sovereignty to rise from the ground like patient Navy Seals.

The door behind us closed at will and disappeared. Not a seamless blending in with the forest floor of snow and decayed leaves but vanishing all together. No wonder the Sovereignty wasn't waiting for us. No one could know about the exit unless they had used it themselves.

"Where are we?" Andy's small voice punched through the silence, making me flinch.

"Burgoyne Woods." Vincent's warm breath clouded the air in front of him.

"Wonderful. The place of childhood scavenger hunts and picnics has an entrance to the biggest underground playpen for Magics." Digging up salamanders and catching grasshoppers in the summer sun was unimaginable while in the cold dark forest now teeming with secrets.

A figure appeared five feet away. Power rushed to my skin. My heart catapulted to the back of my throat with an acidic taste of bile

Donovan helped fight down as the Apporter and Vincent exchanged identical nods in greeting.

"Jesus fuck a donkey." I folded forward, hands to knees, as my power drained from me.

Andy gasped at my profanity.

"Seriously, dude. How do you stay in shape when you don't walk anywhere? Your version of pumping iron include scaring the shit out of people? If so, it explains the muscles." I smoothed my hair as my heart hammered inside my ribcage.

Moonlight shone off his bald head making his husky blue eyes go near invisible. If this was our first meeting, and not when he appeared and disappeared in the back of Donovan's Z24, I would think he was part animal as the moonlight was a flash of sliver in his steady gaze.

I cringed back when he took a step forward. A blink and we landed in front of Olive's.

Olson cried out and fell to his knees as a surge of red power encased him and burned my eyes. Another shout and the red behind my eyelids lessened and extinguished. I blinked away the tears in time to see Olson land like a rag doll half a football field down the tree-lined driveway. Vincent had given him a telekinetic shove out of the range of the estate's wards.

I didn't know how far from the house the wards reached. Maybe Olive re-enforced them after the break-in? Seems unlikely of Olson to have miscalculated since he had been here before. If he's been alone, he would have been fried. I expected something like this at Donovan's but was happy not to see it too many times. Olive's neighbours were down the road, but if one was outside their house, they may have seen the human fireball shooting through the air.

Donovan and Vincent sprinted to Olson as I stood with what I thought was a horrified Andy, but he was fascinated, eyes wide, a big smile on his face. He probably didn't understand what the lightshow was about or so I hoped. I waited and watched, hoping for some movement. I didn't know Olson well, and was mostly freaked out by him, but I didn't want him dead.

I felt the sensation of Donovan arousing his healing ability as he crouched next to the Apporter. Olson pulled his knees up while still on the ground, taking a moment before he allowed Vincent to help him up. They stood talking before Vincent turned in our direction.

"Olive needs to allow Olson admittance inside."

I thought my mental defences were up. Apparently not.

Olson didn't need to be inside at all, though arguing didn't seem like my best move after my family almost cooked him alive.

I used my key to open the door and cut off a gasp when I saw Olive, Gloria, Iris, Serena, Adam, and my mom sitting casually amongst the antique furniture in the formal front sitting room.

"Hi, Dolly." Mom sat with a large mug in her hands as the fireplace spilled a flickering warm light into the room.

"Talk much, dickbreath?" Adam sat on the arm of a high-back wing chair while Serena sat within it, my mom scolding him.

I hadn't realized how long had passed since I got in the door, but he was right, I didn't respond to our mom.

"Firefly?" Olive turned in the matching wing chair, then placed her teacup on a coaster on the table before standing and coming to me.

I leaned closer. "Why are they here?"

Olive's dark brows pinched. "For the Nexus Transference spell, of course."

This didn't exactly help, and I needed her to let Olson in before I tried to figure out why my mom was here to do a spell when she wasn't a part of the coven.

"Olson?" Olive frowned, not remembering.

"The Apporter."

"I see." She patted my arm. "Let's move everyone to the attic. Did you bring the Pompeii Worm?"

"The wh—? Oh, yeah. It's outside." I pictured the basket still sitting on the ground where Vincent left it before taking off to help Olson.

She lightly gasped. "You'll freeze the poor thing. Tell them to hurry before the worm dies, and we'll let Olson in as soon as possible."

I asked Olive to set Andy up with his books and guarded exposure to the spell as I ran back for the worm, not realizing it was so sensitive.

Olive nodded, her smile humouring what must have looked like me being overprotective. Understandable since she didn't know about our day. Though maybe she did. My brother might have told her the mall part. I was happy to see he got out of the Gualichu situation unscathed and would have to ask him about my dad and Ben.

I ran out to where the men stood, skidding to a stop when I noticed a woman with them. Passing the basket without giving it a second thought, I realized who the woman was when she flicked her long, red hair over her shoulder.

"Kim!"

She turned to see me walking up on them.

I gave her a quick hug. "How'd you get here?"

Donovan put his hands in his pockets. "Olson picked her up since we were just standing around. Figured this was something she'd stick her nose into."

Kim's sweater may have been a beautiful white wool with long sleeves, swaggy neckline, with wooden toggles down the front, but it was clear she was freezing.

"Stick my nose in this? I was supposed to be meeting Frog." She shivered against the cool breeze. "He's pissed, but I told him I had a work emergency and would call as soon as it was done."

"We don't care how you waste your time. You wanna go back?"

She glared at Donovan. "Suck it, dill-hole."

"Stop. We gotta get the worm thing inside before it freezes."

Vincent started racing back to the basket. "I thought you would have already done so."

"And I thought the worm could use a winter siesta. Guess we were both presumptuous."

He grabbed the basket, peered inside, and then headed towards the house.

Olson didn't need a babysitter, but it felt odd leaving him standing alone out in the middle of the dark road.

We went up into the attic, the access to the hidden sewing room and attic hatch door left open. We closed it behind us. I wasn't sure we were expecting anyone else, but if so, they could call Olive.

When I hit the top stairs, I, again, was frozen by who I saw. Not my mom, who was now expected though still for an unknown reason, but because the whole Ballard Coven, Donovan and Kim's Sect, plus the remaining Elders were present. They milled about in my family's attic as if meandering through an interactive museum.

"Did you know about this?" I didn't look at Donovan, but he knew I was talking to him.

"No." He turned to Kim.

She made an incredulous sound. "I didn't know."

Ranlyn's smile dropped as soon as we approached him.

"Why weren't we informed about our Sect being here?"

Ranlyn rose one eyebrow at Donovan before looking to Kim and me. "I didn't have to. Or do you forget I'm their Coven Elder as well as yours?"

Donovan refrained from answering, yet the spirit for a challenge ran through the connection.

"Besides, with you fleeing the Sovereignty, your entrapment, and hearing of the Nexus Transference spell, I portalled in your Sect to support you as you attempt to contact those in Diluculo."

Kim tapped my arm. "Where were you trapped?"

I opened my mouth to answer her and it shut involuntarily, stopping me from talking. I tried telepathically, and the thought was blocked. Holy shit. No wonder The Chiff was kept a secret.

Ranlyn didn't seem annoyed or intrigued as he stepped in and asked about the Pompeii Worm. I let him know Vincent had it, happy I could talk again.

Preparations were made before we arrived, and everyone was

mingling and checking out the place, waiting for the spell to begin. Denise and Adam were cozy again. He was wearing a pair of dark sunglasses as the glowing souls around him were too much, wiping a tear from the strain away here and there. My head was aching at the memory of when my power was still so fresh and headaches were my everyday experience. Considering that wasn't long ago, it seemed I was getting used to this Soul Seeing thing after all.

Olson was let inside as part of the group, and before I could approach my mom and see why the hell she was there, they were calling for Donovan.

Donovan hid his nerves from the attic of onlookers well, outwardly self-assured and composed as usual.

Two footstools were placed near the middle. A large, foot-deep, wooden bowl sat on a wooden tripod thatched together with leather strapping.

Olive motioned for Donovan and me to sit on the stools. We did.

"What's with the bird bath?"

Olive smiled at me and sat on the floor in front of us with her legs crossed beneath her skirt, reminding me far too much of Aunt Lacey. "It's a Tuareg bowl from a nomadic tribe of people in Northern Africa. Some say they're called Kel Tagelmust or People of the Veil. Most likely attributes to the veils their men wear, but in some cases, it speaks of much more." She didn't need to explain that in this case the veil was the one in our way of getting into the Creation.

Jared brought water from the small attic bathroom and poured it into the Tuareg bowl. Iris called for Endellion. I'm not sure how Iris knew Deidra's coven name, since it was never used, and it took Deidra a second to react to it as well.

"Just a little heat, darlin'. No need to steam bath the room." Gloria held out two black rocks for the meek Deidra.

Without further instruction, Deidra took the rocks and raised her power, guiding it to her hand now glowing a smouldering red in rippled heat, reflecting off her dark, almond-shaped eyes. It dawned on me that the rocks were actually coal much later than it should have, as they, too, glowed with an intimidating amount of danger. Deidra then placed the coals inside the Tuareg bowl. Steam rose as she extinguished her power. She lost the red in her hand and gained it in her cheeks.

Iris reached under the basket lid and took out a mason jar full of liquid and the worm. "Poor thing must be freezing."

I nor Donovan investigated the basket to see what a Pompeii Worm was and had no clue what we were carting around. As long as my hand and just as plump, this was no fishing worm. Making its pinkish body look even bigger was inch-long white hair along its back and red feathery plumes sticking out of its head.

"Are they going to kill it so we can do this?"

"Oh, no, Firefly. Too special for sacrifice and not worth much dead unless you're a researcher for biochemical, textile, or pharmaceutical companies."

"I'll have to believe you about that one."

She laughed. "The hair is actually sprouts of bacteria. Their backs secrete a type of mucus that feeds on the bacteria."

"They sure do." Gloria dropped herbs into the Tuareg bowl—for the spell or to feed the thing I didn't know—then spoke loud enough others listened in. "This little worm secretes the mucus we need to activate part of Donovan's brain, to open him up and usher a breakthrough to the ancestor within Caine. Since it can withstand high temperatures, it can survive within the human brain comfortably."

"The brain!" Donovan's booming voice made me jump.

Gloria nodded without looking to him as her sister removed the Mason jar lid and slipped the Pompeii Worm into the bowl, smiling like she had an exotic new addition to her fish tank.

Donovan narrowed his dark eyes my way, but I didn't know what to say to him.

"So, ah, how does it get into his brain, exactly?"

"Well,"—Iris started adding a palm full of leaves Gloria had broken up for her—"once it has a bit of a meal it will be inserted manually via the nasal canal or ocular cavity, left to find the rest of the way on its own."

"Plus, the utterings of the spell, of course." Gloria handed over the next batch of herbs to her sister.

"Yes, of course." Iris waved her hand as if obvious and motioned for Gloria to continue with more worm food.

Donovan had his elbows on his knees and rubbed his hands together so tightly my knuckles ached. "All this just to talk to Caine, huh?"

I shrugged and struggled not to laugh.

Lewis sat forward in a straight-backed wooden chair behind us. "Finding out if Caine is alive, what condition the others are in, and possibly mobilize a collective attack when the Creation is breached makes your sacrifice worthy."

"Easy to say when it's not your nose being raped by a hairy worm."

The edges of Lewis's mouth turned down. "Or your eye."

The look Donovan gave my uncle had Lewis holding his hands up in surrender, who then winked at me when Donovan turned to glare at the Tuareg bowl some more.

14

UNINHABITABLE ENVIRONMENT

"Why haven't we started already?" I couldn't blame Donovan for his impatience. I'd want to get it over with as well.

"Let's stretch and walk around a bit." Since the aunts were taking their time with pampering the worm first, everyone had gone back to their conversations. We would have to take our places again soon, but he needed to gear down before we did.

We joined Kim, Blake, Jared, Serena, Adam, and Denise. As soon as we reached them conversation stopped.

"Say something." I figured Kim could handle the pressure and was happy to find her guard down.

"Where were you guys trapped?"

I stared at her with pursed lips, unable to answer.

"'Kay. Thanks, chatty."

The spell The Chiff used left no wiggle room for minor details, but something did happen I could talk about. Gualichu. Adam had been there, and the others heard about people passing out at the mall as it was all over social media. Speculations were being thrown around, and authorities had no answers.

"Good for us if it only feeds on the Blind." Jared was right, though this was still uncertain.

"We're not sure that's what it was doing, but it's likely." Donovan went on describing the Tactical Team Vincent worked with to try and stop the demon.

"Hmm." Denise drew out. "I don't like that Vincent knows so much he's not telling us." Most of the others' expressions agreed, but they didn't verbalize siding with her, especially Donovan. "You know it's true!" She added then looked directly at my brother. "Because he's immortal, everyone treats him like a god. Why am I the only one with balls to say so?"

"You're not, but he is a Coven Elder." Donovan's voice was cold. He didn't say more. Knowing his hang-ups on Vincent, it took him a lot to stop there. As a Sect Leader, it did him good to keep his trap shut regarding his opinions of the Elders, something Denise didn't understand since she never developed a filter for anything that came out of her mouth.

"I can't believe you're doing the slug-in-the-brain thing." Blake shook his head. "I'd rather eat it then have its slug goo spooning my skull."

"I can't believe you're related to Caine." Adam laughed and hit me in the shoulder. "How'd you work that out?"

I shot him the finger.

"Technically, he's related to Aunt Lacey, right?" Gwen surprised us by joining the conversation.

"Technically." Donovan pushed his hands into his pockets.

"How, exactly?"

"You don't have to answer her." Not that he needed me to remind him. I would be lying if I wasn't also curious.

His dark eyes flicked my way. "It follows my father's bloodline. Dates back to Aunt Lacey's daughter Ima."

They looked as surprised as I was to get a straight answer.

"Is Ima still alive?" Serena's interest added to my surprise.

"If she is, she doesn't send postcards."

Serena raised an eyebrow at Donovan, then turned to yell over her shoulder. "Can't we get on with this already?"

"Eager to see a worm shoved in my brain?"

"Little bit, yeah." Everyone around my cousin tensed. "Though I feel for the worm. Your brain is an uninhabitable environment for the poor thing. Borders on animal cruelty."

Denise snickered.

"Relax yourself there, Serena, or it'll be your brain we let it ooze all over next." Mom approached and put her in place with a smile before looking to Donovan. "They're ready when you are." She rejoined those closer to the Tuareg bowl as Serena grumbled, Jared following as Blake made a whipping noise and headed off with them.

I grabbed Adam's sleeve to stop him. "Why's Mom here?"

He shrugged. "I called and gave her a choice when Olive called me. She said sure."

"Okay, but why?"

He grunted. "Who cares? Let's go."

Obviously, I cared. She knew she wasn't allowed in the attic or to participate in coven activities unless she was joining the coven. Did this mean she was joining? She left us so quickly, like she knew I would ask questions if she didn't scoot off. I had a feeling I would be chasing after her at the end of the meeting.

Seated on the footstools, facing each other, in the midst of everyone, the Tuareg bowl still steamy off to my left, Donovan looked at the crowd like they were leeches on the bleachers of a gladiatorial bout gunning for blood and gore. I wasn't about to point out his displaced anxiety manifesting as anger. I, too, was nervous. Whatever he felt, I felt, and it wouldn't feel nice.

Iris smiled at the large group. "As it may be stressful for Donovan to gather all the information possible while his body is enduring the presence of the Pompeii Worm and the disassociation of his true form, we have decided to add another measure of assurance by allowing all willing to participate in Remote Viewing."

Donovan didn't look happy to have everyone looking over his

shoulder, though the group was excited to be included. Iris made it known that no one else but Donovan could interact with anyone inside the Creation. Since the group, as a whole, would be affected by the Remote Viewing spell, anyone who did not want to participate had the option to join Andy, who sat happily with his book at Olive's desk.

"Can we also add a Recollection Plant?"

Gloria glared at Ranlyn. "Why would we need one?"

"You won't need one, but to have a momentous event stored in the leaves can be useful when recruiting other covens to join in reopening the Creation."

Iris crossed her arms. "Political gain."

"Strategic manoeuvring." Ranlyn stood firm, his expression tight yet friendly.

"How could a plant do that? Can it talk?" My cousin Ronny swept his long bangs out of his face, though they fell back immediately.

Kevin laughed at him.

"In its own way, yes." Ranlyn answering was a shock to Ronny. "Put the leaves in a tea, and the drinker will see whatever we're about to."

This was approved of, but since it wasn't pre-planned, Olive had to sacrifice one of her own plants. Refusing to let go of any that were loved inside the walls of the institution she spent the majority of her life, Ranlyn found a Green Singonium that had been sitting in a corner and not particularly a favourite, though Olive still looked sick to give it up.

Gloria fished out the Pompeii Worm from its new habitat with a metal egg strainer, most seeing it for the first time. Not-so-quiet murmuring washed over the group, all of them, including myself, happy it wasn't going in their body, though I knew I would feel it as if it was.

Donovan fussed with his hoody and pant legs. "I don't see how that's gonna fit."

A few mutterings of "That's what she said," came from the group. I didn't have to recognize their voices to guess from whom.

Gloria let the water flow through the strainer a moment. "Don't you worry, boy, it will fit just fine. Dealer's choice. Nose or eye? I recommend the nose if you're worried about size."

The roiling in my gut was Donovan's as he agreed with my great-aunt.

I tugged on his sweater-covered arm. "Turn to me, I'll distract you."

"Taking off your shirt won't make me forget this, babe."

I scoffed at his comment, especially since Gloria was close enough to hear him. I made my plan clearer as Gloria began murmuring a spell while Veata worked the incantation for the Remote Viewing to include all of us and the Recollection Plant.

Twisting my body to his on the short footstool, Donovan did the same until our knees touched. He side-eyed Gloria who reached between us to access Donovan's right nostril. I didn't touch his skin, not wanting him in our past. Instead, I projected a choice memory I thought he might enjoy, keeping his mind off the big hairy worm wriggling his way.

I chose the memory of us hanging out in the fogging effect of Fox's tattoo, skin to skin, curled up on the couch beneath a blanket, watching a movie like a normal couple without his vision's interference. Something more meaningful than sex and sweat. Something he could find comfort in.

For it to work, I needed laser-guided focus. Donovan may not have been able to see the Pompeii Worm creeping closer as the distraction blinded him in the revelry of our moment, but I could, and the thought of the worm touching me, even second-hand through Donovan, evoked the repulsive need to scurry away. In general, I didn't mind bugs, but the white hairs on the worm's back looked far too similar to the feathery legs of a centipede. Whenever I crossed paths with a centipede, I used my size advantage and anything I wouldn't feel the crunch of the insect's body through and laid waste to the ugly creepy-crawler.

Instead of holding Donovan's dark stare to mine, since his eyes were half-hooded and focused on the memory of my skin beneath his roaming fingers, I closed mine tight and tried not to listen to the shuttered breaths of the onlookers. Losing myself in the distraction I created worked as the spoken spells and incantations fell silent to the sound of the explosions in the movie we had watched that night. That was until Gloria's voice reached a crescendo, and the worm was injected into Donovan's nose, obliterating the revelry.

The action movie explosions from the distraction and Gloria's voice gave way to screams. A gag-worthy drilling into Donovan's sinuses echoed in my own as the clawing worm dug deeper into the nasal passage and into his skull. Pain shot into our brains and made my eyeballs feel like they might burst, liquid draining from my eyes and nose. Tears, blood, or snot, assuming all the above leaked from my face. I wailed, grabbed my skull, and pushed on my eyes. It did shitfuckall to ease the building pressure as the worm did circles until it found a comfortable spot.

Pain peaked, edging us close to unconsciousness, then disappeared in a relieving flush, all pain subsiding, leaving us with a heady, ghostly ache. It reminded me of passing through the veil but much longer, and all the pain concentrated in my skull. I didn't see teeth or claws on the worm, but I would be hard-pressed to believe the little fucker wasn't riddled with them.

15

SEE FOR YOURSELF

Donovan

Damn. A cough punched out from between my lips, my lungs crowded with a thick humidity. I rolled my neck as the pitch black of agonizing blindness took over until the pain subsided enough for me to open my eyes. Okay. Now I was outside. Right. Diluculo. Nighttime like outside the Ballard Family Estate, but it was far too hot for snow.

This was hotter than Aunt Lacey and the other Elders had it. This was still Evaristus's Creation, he kicking it up a notch closer to the sandy wasteland of The Thoth.

Did the heat mean Evar was still alive? How? We tore his body to shreds and buried him in a watery grave.

Great. Nothing but trees. Unhealthy looking ones. I plucked a leaf off a bark-peeled branch, and it disintegrated in my fingers. Everything was dying in this heat. How could anyone else handle it?

Now to find Caine. You'd think the spell would have dropped me off at the guy's feet. No, of course, I've got to find the fucker. As if anything could be easy for a change.

Pushing through the bush as leaves fell, crunched, and dusted beneath my shoes, I didn't know which part of Diluculo I was in, which way I was headed, or if I was travelling closer or farther away from Caine. After fifteen minutes of trying and failing to be stealthy while sweating through my hoodie, I said fuck it and stomped through the trees and overgrowth hoping someone, anyone, would find me. With any luck I'd stumble on Loring. Come get me, asshole.

Another five minutes passed of picturing what I would do to Loring when everything around me started to look the same. I stopped and ran my hand over a tree with bark peeled back like a banana, a knot a few inches above it. I kept walking and a few minutes later found a tree with barked peeled back like a banana and a knot a few inches above it. Exactly the same.

Goddammit.

A shove into my chest stole my breath. My spine cracked as I hit something hard, rocking my slime-covered brain. I tried to stand to defend myself and realized I wasn't on them. My whole body hung like art above the ground in a telekinetic grip. I fought the spins and failing night vision to try and see who tricked me.

As the haze of forest cleared, I couldn't see anyone. Was the tree attacking me? Leave it to Evaristus to turn nature against a Magic. Squirming did nothing, and no branches were holding onto me, so not the trees.

"Come out and let's get on with it." Maybe Loring had found me.

Bodies popped into view as if standing there the whole time. Strangers.

"Is he a Puppet?" The voice of a guy no older than seventeen with tanned skin was strong but nervous.

A tall man more Caine's age huffed with a gloating grin as his hawk-eyes narrowed. "His intuition is less honed than a fruit fly if Ness's illusion had him chasing his tail this whole time. He can't be."

I had no idea what the guy meant but judging by the only chick in the group, she was Ness. She hadn't said a word, but in her mussed plaid shirt rolled to her elbows, worked-in jeans, and muddy

Converse, she, like the others, had gone through too much in the time that passed since the Creation was locked. I didn't care about them. I needed Caine so we could figure out a plan.

Another body popped up in front of me. Caine. His dirty clothing hung off his body, a hardness in his eyes a tad extreme, even for him.

"What plan?" Caine had heard my thoughts.

He sounded foreign. I wasn't sure if it was because I hadn't heard the guy speak in a while or because his voice was different, but something was wrong about him, besides the fact his hair was growing out again.

"Letting me go gets you answers, Caine. Sophie's watching. Wouldn't want to upset her, now."

A zing of pain hit my knees before I realized they let me go. I hit the ground and fell forward, getting my hands out quick enough not to face plant. I got to my feet slowly in case one of his pals got jumpy and still thought I was a Puppet.

Caine said Ness's name like some kind of command.

"No." Ness crossed her arms and sneered at me. "I don't know this kid."

"I do." He didn't look away from me, though his tone was softer than I expected.

The hawk-eyed one stepped forward. "Then where's he been? He could be a charm to trick us."

"He's not here at all."

I smiled. Impressed.

"You see him, could touch him, maybe end his life,"—Caine turned back to me—"but you're at the estate with her." Not a question. Hello confidence. I wondered how he knew.

"I am."

"How did you slip through the veil?"

A silent beat passed while Caine and I remained quiet, not that it stopped his friends from asking about the estate and who we were talking about. Caine showed no ambition to answer them, more interested in staring at me as if searching for something in my expression. Since he talked of the estate, it meant he was reading my mind and was probably doing so now.

"Why are you different?" I bet Sophie was asking herself the same thing. I doubted she could see his soul glow through Remote Viewing since she saw as I did and nothing more, but I wasn't positive.

"Everything's different."

His apathy was the issue. Caine would usually be complaining or asking a million questions and trying to intimidate me.

Ness sighed with more attitude than I thought a sigh could hold. "Do we get let in the know, or you bros gonna stay all mysterious?" Caine didn't answer her, and I had no reason to care if her feelings were hurt. "Fine. I'm over it." She walked off, and a scene around us blinked into view. A camp.

The hawk-eyed one mentioned her illusion. They must have seen me before I saw them, and she acted fast to cover their surroundings. Sweet talent.

No nylon tents and marshmallow sticks here. Wooden lean-tos were low to the ground and did little more than keep the sun away. Hasty fire pits cooked small animals, all for practicality's sake. Not that camping was ever fun. Survival skills saved their lives, but they were losing the battle if this was all they had in way of a camp after all this time.

"Felix." Caine's tone was softer yet no less a command.

"Yeah, yeah." Felix and hawk-eyed guy wandered off deeper into the camp leaving Caine and me to ourselves.

Caine remained stoic. "How did you get here?"

"Is Evaristus alive?"

"How did you get here?"

"A worm with a pelt is spooning my brain." I adopted his detached tone. "Is Evaristus alive?"

"Yes."

Great. "Is Loring?"

"Mostly."

"What's that mean?"

"If he breathes, he is dangerous, and he does."

Right. Okay. "What the hell's up with you? You sure you're not a Puppet? Maybe you're really Evar, and you're fucking with all the survivors."

Expecting a normal Caine-like response was more than I could hope for, but I was confused when he put his hand out in front of me. Wait, he wanted me to use my Psychometry to see it all for myself?

"No." My Psychometry removed the need for blind trust, but I didn't want the headache right now.

Caine kept his hand extended. "Shake my hand."

Simple direction, spoken with the same detached tone he insisted on. Wait, why am I moving? Fuck. No!

My hand gripped Caine's without my permission.

Caine dove back into the water to find his cousin Jet in Diluculo, his frantic search for her, unable to, yet finding others—the hawk-eye guy, Derek, and siblings, Vanessa and Felix Pleitez.

Racing memories spun by me like a movie reel on fast-forward, impacting me, running through me with their accompanied emotions, yet keeping me an observer on the sidelines in a way I was unused to.

So much hiding from devotees, Puppets, and anyone they didn't recognized until Caine took their free will and interrogated them.

No one knew if Evaristus and Loring were alive. The forest made for the best cover in case they were, but Ness and Felix had something better. They called themselves Illusionists, holding the ability to make others see whatever the person desired, or make others see what they wanted. A persuasion of sorts to make the enemy look right past them.

Caine's memories zipped forward to him seeing Jet fly overhead, causing Caine to break Ness's illusion, and instead found himself being attacked. Jet brought other enemies with her, and many of their group were killed. Caine carried a heavy guilt for this and for his family being used as a Puppet by the enemy. Even for leaving Sophie, knowing she would tear herself a part over his entrapment.

Bodies lay in heaps as he and Sophie travelled to find Evaristus before the battle. Those piles grew. Others were created. A body or two was left to rot in the hot sun Evaristus preferred. A sun that charred the trees and grass crispy enough to mar their beauty and threatened every place they hid.

As time melted from perception, many of their group died in battle, some taken over as Puppets, some taking their own lives. Day after day the same dose of blood and destruction wore at their sanity, trapped in a fishbowl of a world where it changed at another's will. A Master with many at their disposal knowing his enemy had no clue how to defeat him.

Then things changed.

They sought out the enemy instead of waiting to be taken down. Caine found a survivor-turned-Puppet, knocked them out, and attempted to excise Evaristus's will over them. It wasn't easy, but with his ability of Persuasion, he found the invading influence and broke Evar's hold.

This became their mission with every Puppet instead of killing them. It took a lot out of Caine, and most refused to go along with his "suicide missions", but Caine would rather do something instead of sitting around in camp waiting to die. Besides, he had been trapped before. This time he wasn't alone and knew Jet was alive.

Caine thought of Sophie a lot and forced himself to do menial tasks to keep his mind off her, pouring his energies into severing Evaristus's ties anywhere he could. As he did, Caine's power grew stronger.

In the beginning, he strayed from using Gareth's power, but they picked a fight with a Puppet, and other Puppets rushed them from the trees. An extra dose of power saved his and Ness's asses, and every day since, Ness encouraged him to use Gareth's power. With her insistence, and the ease with which his vessel's extra essence made saving people from being Puppets, he found himself using Gareth's power with resentment but allowed it to take the wheel when needed.

One day, something changed. His magic fused with Gareth's. This was why he seemed so different. Down to Caine's core, he was different.

Not everyone enjoyed the divergence. Ness felt the chill Gareth's power injected into Caine's soul. An attachment between them she believed the time spent within Diluculo had created, now seemed elusive.

The vision skipped to a day Caine set his eyes on Loring. They assumed he was a goner and only Evar had survived. Inside a cabin Evar's devotees fixed up enough for Loring to be lavished like the king he thought he was, they found the man who attempted to end Caine's life, killed his brother Cole, and took away one of the most precious Magics he ever encountered.

Aunt Lacey's gruesome death scurried in front of Caine's eyes as he watched Loring stand from a chair and hobble to an adjacent room. Moving from window to window like a peeping Tom, Caine saw Loring speak to another devotee, directing them to do something for him.

Loring was a shadow of the glib Magic Caine knew. Parts of him remained crushed from when I threw him in the watery crevice Caine closed in on him and Evar. One arm was shorter than the other. The dress shirt he wore obscured the damage, but Caine suspected this was the case with many parts of his body. Loring was no longer the man he was, which meant he was weak.

Caine jumped through the glassless window to attack. Ness and Derek tried to stop him. He knew the body didn't dictate the power within and took Loring's condition for granted.

Retreat filled him with rage. Exposing himself while attacking Loring meant exposing the others who now dodged attacks from above by Puppet Jet and earned them days of earthquakes, blizzards, lightning storms, hailstorms, fire storms, and attacks from animals and insects alike. Anything Evaristus or Loring drummed up to torture and take them out was thrown their way.

Caine was more careful after that.

The insufficient camp was a by-product of fleeing for their lives.

Ness and Felix could shroud their existence with illusions, but devotees and Puppets wondered into their territory, forcing them to fight or move again. Hiding underground was discussed. They vetoed the idea, too scared of being buried alive, leaving the option for the most desperate of times.

Images of the survivors passed through my head in a blur. I absorbed their exhaustive routines as if they were my own. Patrols, scouting, searches for Jet, severing Evaristus's bonds from his Puppets, slaughtering devotees and leaving them to rot in the sun, and always Ness, Felix, and Derek at his wings. Lots of Ness.

A blinding pulse of light shot a crippling ache through my temples. I stumbled back. Caine broke his hold on my hand and took his memories with him. Sweat dripped off my forehead as I struggled to steady myself on weak knees.

"Prick," I managed between breaths.

"A quicker method than explaining."

"Yeah?" I swallowed and fought against my vision-drunk equilibrium. "Next time keep your hands to yourself. Clearly, your Persuasion is top notch now. Doesn't mean you're allowed to dose anyone you want."

"Quite. Ness has warned me of this as well."

"Ness, eh?"

Caine looked at me as if waiting for me to finish my sentence. I decided against pointing out the obvious, too tired to lay it out for the idiot.

"Sophie better not get all freaky when she fuses her powers."

Caine tilted his head. "She is attempting to?"

"Trying. And trying to pass some of it to me. Know how to pull that off?"

Caine's head shake was slow, distracted.

"Whatever. My point in being here is to learn what I can to get everyone out."

He blinked at me, awareness back in his gaze. "Have you found the discus?"

"Discus?"

"It's required to reopen the Creation. We heard Evar and Loring talking about needing a discus to get out. No specifics or description. Neither of them brought one here and Evar is locked from access to his other Creations."

"We'll find one. Hopefully before our competitors. Civil war is the price for reopening the Creation, everyone with an opinion is making it known, so don't assume your homecoming will be a happy one."

"If you open the Creation before Evaristus is killed, he will escape, and Loring with him."

"Yup. Heard it all. Sophie won't have it any other way, and I'm willing to bet my left nut the rest of your buddies in here don't care as long as they breathe free air. Put Evar and Loring down ASAP. A premonition calls for it, and so far, it's played out like it said it would. You know how premonitions go."

I took Caine's silence as agreement.

"Whatever, man. I'm here to confirm if there's survivors and to let you know we're coming in whenever we can. Oh, and an FYI, your uncle and his wife took you and their daughter getting trapped in here pretty badly. Got in deep with some dark-souled old friends as well as some new ones, opened a portal, and let out a demon now running havoc on the Blind."

"Eli?"

Dismissing the part about a demon on the loose shouldn't have surprised me. "You got another uncle?"

He didn't comment.

"We took the kid off of their hands, figuring he'd be better at my place than magically bound to his room." Caine's eyes were in an unfocused confusion. I didn't enjoy saying it, but he had to know about his aunt's Tainted soul.

"Tainted?" Caine looked most like himself for the first time.

"I don't know how much longer I can be—"

"You and Sophie are watching Andy?"

I swiped sweat off my forehead with my sleeve. "Yeah. As soon as Sophie heard about what they were up to, we scooped Andy outta there."

"Are you two formally together?"

"Umm, depends on the day." *If you can hear me, Sophie, sorry. Had to be said.*

"Meaning?"

I let out a heavy breath and imagined the scowl on Sophie's face. "You can ask her yourself when we get you out."

Caine nodded, giving no follow-up response.

Kill me now.

Ness approached without giving a damn for our obvious private conversation, she asking what was going on. Caine gave her a quick run-down, avoiding details regarding his family and anything Sophie-related.

"Then we make our move." Her moxie included a hand on her round hip, her strength in overall attitude. Even without her illusion spells, I was willing to bet she could kick some ass.

"Not without Jet."

She rolled her eyes at Caine. "No kidding. I wouldn't leave Felix, either, but if it comes down to the wire,"—she looked up into his eyes like she could persuade him from her small stature—"dying in here with her won't make Jet feel any better, even if Evar lets her go."

His head bowed. "I know."

Ness turned to me. "What are you doing to get us out? We've been stuck for what feels like an eternity. Think it could've taken you longer?"

"*Pfft.* It's not like we've been vacationing on the outside, sippin' margaritas in the sun before and after our deep tissue massages. Our lives are in danger every single day. Yours have been, too, but you don't have new enemies popping up everywhere you go." I stepped closer to her, the Creation's heat fueling my temper. I pointed at my head. "A wholly mammoth of a worm was injected into my brain, through my nose, so I could be here, sunshine. Not my brand of fun!"

Ness took on a bored expression. "Then go home to your girl-friend. I'm sure she'll nurse your undescended testicles back to health."

"Ness!" Caine's raised voice shocked the both of us.

I chuckled. "Just 'cuz he and Sophie aren't exchanging saliva anymore, doesn't mean you can shit-talk his ex."

The look Caine received was crystalized. Ness was familiar with Sophie's name yet not with how familiar Caine was with Sophie. Stalking off the way she came, it was clear Ness had heard enough.

"Guess you're not invited into her sleeping bag tonight."

"It's not like that."

"Might wanna tell her."

Caine looked back at Ness as she disappeared into one of the wooden lean-tos, his glance lingering.

"Look. This heat sucks, and I'm not sure how long it's healthy to have this thing in my head. I'm connected to Gareth since we're tech-nically related or Sophie would have come herself. We need to figure out where this discus is, and I don't want to stick around for the domestic when you try and talk your way out of the doghouse."

"I told you—"

"Yeah, yeah. Whatever. Anything else I should know before they rip me out of here?"

Caine gave a half-shrug, very Caine-like. "Tell Sophie I'm sorry, but I had to go back in. And thank you. I knew you would be around to take care of her. I guess that's what you're doing now, plus taking on Andy. I appreciate you bearing the responsibility."

The seriousness of his tone was unsettling. "Sophie takes care of herself, and the kid's actually cool. No biggie."

"He is cool. And Sophie takes care of most everyone. Make sure she does as much for herself."

I tried to smile. Doubt I managed it.

"Find the discus but return and check on how alive Evaristus and Loring are before you use it. We can't let them escape."

"I will. And cut her some slack." It took Caine a moment to realize I was talking about Ness. "She's cute as well as fierce."

His expression hardened. The bastard wouldn't take my advice, but he damn well should.

I looked up as if I were talking to those back at the estate. "'Kay, rip this insect out of my fucking head."

Pressure and a frantic scurrying at the spot where the worm nestled drilled into my brain. I doubled over and bit down to try and cut off my scream. No such luck.

Pain drained from my head and speared me in the gut. If I wasn't already on the ground, it would have put me there. My shoulder joint hit with a jarring jolt onto something harder than the grass I was on. This wasn't right. I know this pain. She's not...She can't be. The grip on my intestines told me she was. Why?

I got a knee beneath me and opened my eyes against the throbbing in my temples. Sophie was screaming at Ranlyn. He stood with his hands up, trying to placate her, but she wasn't having it. Nya's power was behind the wheel. Vincent was keeping others at bay, but some weren't trying to get to her. Judging by the horror on her mother's face, she had no idea who she was looking at.

"Sophie." I coughed, my chest too tight to speak.

No one paid attention as I crawled the few feet to her. Was this Sophie's fear for Caine out of control? Or Nya inside her fearing for its power's equal in Caine? I couldn't see her eyes, but I bet they changed. Too much like Nya's.

I called her name again. Nothing. I fought against the ripping pain in my abs and lunged forward, missing her ankle.

She looked down. Her glare was full of Nya's power. Cruel inconvenience was a slap I didn't expect. I should have.

She dropped the knee of the leg I tried for, it landing on my throat with a crushing blow that left her unaffected. "Disintegration tactics will not stop me from this fight. The Creation will be opened."

A gasped gurgle blocked my airway, her strength too much to

overpower like this while the connection was a brick of fire searing my insides.

Vincent's arms went out in front of him. Sophie anticipated his attack and put him down in a crash I couldn't see. Ranlyn tried reasoning with her again, she looking at him, forgetting about crushing me beneath her boney knee and not giving a shit about all the Coveners and family around her trying to calm her.

"Sophie?" Andy questioned her in a meek, heartbreaking voice. Distracting her.

I gripped her ankle, making skin contact. A shock of vision hit me straight between the eyes and rained over me like ice water.

Loud voices. Muffled, clearing. A guttural moan. Mine.

"Donovan? Open your eyes, asshat. Let me see some dimples. Call me a bitch or something."

Wooden beams overhead came into view, the attic roof, then red hair. Definitely Kim.

"Bitch." Sounded more like "bish" but had her smiling.

I flexed to sit up and she tried to stop me.

"Sophie...."

"They got her back. Good job, by the way. Oh shit."

She took off, leaving me to wobble and hold myself up. Dammit. Andy was crying. Kim knelt in front of him, trying to block his view and lead him away.

What did she mean by "Good job?" Where's Sophie?

People were crowding around what I thought was Olive's desk, but the desk was farther away, my sense of the room all fucked up. I saw Sophie's shoes on the ground beneath them. Others were crowding her. Was she okay? She had to be if I was, right? Please be okay.

I stood, too fast, checking the connection instead of my balance. Tell me she's there. A raw thrum of emotion came at me. Overwhelmed. Pissed off. Embarrassed.

People moved and she, taller than most the others, had her own eyes again instead of reflecting Nya's.

Her mother threw her arms around her, saying things I couldn't hear over her sobs. Parenting done right, though Sophie wasn't listening, her gaze over her mother's shoulder on mine. Unspoken apologies for losing herself, casting everyone aside to complete her mission.

Maybe Nya's power hitchhiked Sophie's emotions, maybe she let it take over, or maybe she couldn't stop it, but it happened as easily as Caine was losing himself to Gareth's power. Being a casualty wasn't my concern. She wasn't in the Creation, but Caine was, so she may as well be. A long time before cracking open Diluculo meant a long time for the separation between Sophie and Nya's power to be at odds. This will get worse.

We needed to get in there.

16

WORDY BULLSHIT

"I'm okay, Mom."

She let go of me. "I'm sorry, Dolly. I—I don't know what's happening."

Neither did I. She knew I was lying. I knew I was lying, but I said I was fine anyway because I was a dick daughter too often these days, and I didn't want her walking away thinking so again.

No, that's not true. I don't care if she did think I was out of bounds, but I acted like I did out of habit. Someone asks if you're okay, you say "Yeah" and keep walking because a larger conversation was exhausting and pointless. I didn't have patience for damage control right now, so a half-hearted hug and a curt placation was all Mom was getting.

Ugh. I was a dick daughter.

Nya's power was gone, resentment a snake of nausea wriggling through my stomach. I looked up and saw Donovan taking off his hoodie and releasing us from the heat of the Creation. The body didn't know the difference inside or outside the Nexus Transference spell, which led to thoughts of how dangerous the experiment was.

He caught me staring and knew I held no anger for him putting me in my place and chasing Nya's power back into hiding. He didn't need words to confirm it, and I was happy not to have to say them. The resentment was something else all together, though I wasn't sure from where.

Ranlyn stepped into my line of sight, and my bitterness roared back, understanding it now, when thinking back through the haze of my attack fueled by Nya's power.

He tensed as I approached him. "I'm on your side."

"Why did it take this, Ranlyn? Why did you have to see Caine and the others back-stroking through hellfire to get your ass in gear? You know what Evaristus and Loring are capable of. And even if they were dead, you know what to expect of devotees, especially ones under Masters like them."

His gaze narrowed. "I'm an Elder. I don't have the privilege of action without facts."

"Please. You've led a crew before. You know how to make decisions with others' lives at stake."

"Exactly. And I've shadowed your ass all over the region and back, keeping it alive even when you didn't know it. A little trust would be nice." He stepped closer. "I don't lead the whole damn Coven. The Elders are a council. Try to remind yourself who the enemy is here and cage your power until you learn to control it."

A wave of that power splashed my throat as if I could have let it loose on a hissing breath if I wanted to. His raised brow called me out, feeling the surge in the air around us, as if I made his point for him.

"Others will see this truth now, too, Firefly. The Recollection Plant will make them see."

I didn't need Olive's intervention on this one, but like whatever Donovan did to me to force Nya's power out of me, it diverted my attention.

I headed to Olive's desk, to the catalogue of attic items. "Where's the discus? Those devotees were here looking for it. It needs to be here." I turned pages of one giant list.

Olive was on the other side of the desk with Ranlyn and others looking at me like I was about to lose it again. "I assure you it's not here." She was talking to Ranlyn, not me, which pissed me off more.

Before I could open my mouth, pressure in my chest bloomed and tingled through my rib cage like a skittering of tiny feet all over me before melting into a comforting warmth, surrounding me like a full-bodied hug. I inhaled and pressed my hand into the spot where it began, an inch below the hollow of my throat. It wasn't whatever force existed within the estate that greeted me when I arrived and kept me in check when I needed it. I knew the estate's sensation too well to mistake it as that.

When I opened my eyes, Donovan stood alone in the midst of the room, touching the same spot below his throat, feeling as I did, his brow cinched in confusion.

Neither of us knew what it was, and it disappeared with the same amount of explanation.

Coveners and Donovan's Sect members were all around us, talking to each other. The combination of this new sensation and how unaware everyone else was had me looking down at the open attic catalogue on the desk in wonder of what I was doing.

No matter how much I needed them to be, the answers weren't here.

I leaned into my hands on the desktop with a sense of hopelessness. If not in the attic, then where?

Iris and Gloria were in full mothering mode, gaining my attention with their cooing and dropping herbs and some kind of powder into the bubbling water a few feet away from us. That damn worm. We managed to stick a worm in a human's head and have a chat with someone on the other side of a locked veil, but it did nothing to free Caine. What good was a phone when the person on the other end was being slowly murdered?

"Sophie." Ranlyn waited until I looked up at him. "I want what's best for everyone, and sometimes that means you're going to be pissed at me. You get to voice your anger, unlike other Coven members. Sect

Leaders do, and the only reason why I'm entertaining all this, and in this forum, is because I know your opinion aligns with your Sect Leaders. Both of them, if not the Ballard Coven's as well."

My hollow chuckle dripped with exhaustion. "Nothing a good ol' fashioned time-out won't fix?"

His light eyes softened. "Whatever works."

"I get it. My bitching is grandfathered in since before you were Elder. I'm still gonna bring flaming bags of dog shit to your doorstep from time to time. Just an FYI."

He smiled. "I can handle that. A little less of Nya's power is appreciated. Even from Vincent who has been taking your shit for centuries."

"Right." A flash of Vincent flying into an antique shelf hit me.

"I'm off to bring the Recollection Plant to as many as I can. Give me a target, and I'll take it out. This political shit isn't so black and white."

I nodded and watched him head towards The Apporter and Veata. If nothing else, expectations were clear. More allies were always a plus, but I would open the Creation alone if it meant getting my hands on the discus Caine mentioned.

"Is my mom a coven member?"

Olive's hesitation was suspect. "She's here."

"Point made since you told her she wasn't allowed here unless she joined."

"I let actions speak where words are lacking."

"Actions? She signed the book?"

"Not yet."

"Then her actions were out of curiosity, and you let her cure it by not holding her accountable. Do what you want, but she'll keep showing up and testing herself until it's too much and she walks away. You made the others promise to join or keep the secret."

"I did. And something tells me it's important she be here." She touched her chest where the sensation of the estate makes itself known.

Whatever made the estate feel this way, I had no argument for something I couldn't see and still had no clue who or what it was.

Movement caught my eye, Donovan waving me over. He stood with a wide-eyed Gwen.

I left Olive to see what hot potato they had to toss me.

"I'm so sorry, Sophie." Gwen tried to smooth her unruly orange curls. "I didn't know. Really. I thought it was bullshit they would write down and file in some filing cabinet until it meant something to someone long after I was dead."

I looked at Donovan. "Can I get the CliffsNotes? Brain is switched to fried pickle mode."

"Gwen wrote the premonition."

I gasped. "Such a better lead."

"How could I know it was about you guys, and in this time, considering your recycling souls thing? When Caine mentioned the discus, I knew it was predicting current events."

"Wonderful. You're like a super confusing news anchor."

She braced her hands on her hips. "Yeah. Pretty much feels that way."

"Excuse us." Kim had Andy in front of her. He clutched his book and looked up at me with a dollop too much fear. "Someone's getting tired."

He scowled up at Kim. "No, I'm not. I said Bosco probably is."

Kim made a face.

I knelt in front of him. "Agreed, buddy. Bet he's missing you, too."

"Really?"

I made a throaty noise. "A thousand times really. Who else chases him outside and then lets him cuddle them with all his snoring?"

He laughed in a way it seemed only children did. Freely and without self-consciousness. "He snores so loud."

"That's okay." Donovan motioned to me. "So does she."

Cue that child-like laugh again. Smack dab in the middle of a crisis, it was nice to smile, even if the joke was at my expense.

"At least Caine looked good." Denise stood close by with my

brother, Serena, Jared, and Blake, talking loud enough for me to overhear.

I stood to better glare at her. "Sure. If you consider battle-worn looking good." The surprised glare from everyone told me they had no clue I was nearby.

Denise scoffed. "I'd call it battle-buff. Did you see his arms?"

"Can't say I was focused on his biceps." Adam didn't seem as put off about her comment as he would have been with past girlfriends.

"*Pfft*, I was. Battle-worn, body snatched, whatever, it's done wonders for his physique."

I sighed. "Can I go back to ignoring you, now?"

She raised a sculpted brow. "Could you ever?"

"Mhmm."

The only thing saving Denise was Andy's close proximity. He had endured enough chaos for one day. We needed to get him back to Donovan's to bed and at least pretend things were normal and not building to the ultimate clusterfuck.

The others were invited back to Donovan's as well, as long as they didn't keep Andy up. Even Adam and Serena were welcome since the Ballards weren't going to be sticking around the attic too much longer. Everyone was buzzing at seeing the Creation in the state it was, some for the first time ever, so they had no comparison, but anyone could see how dark and twisted the place was and how dire Caine and the survivors' situation was. Covens were a support system, and it fell on the Sect Leaders to ensure everyone retained a sense of safety amongst the danger our everyday now presented.

The next day was the Coven meeting. We assumed some would stay the night and right up until the meeting. Unless Donovan curbed them, they would find ways to hang-out and remain involved.

Once the Apporter returned from dropping off Ranlyn and Veata with the Recollection Plant to their first victims in hopes of selling them on reopening the Creation, he got the rest of us back to Dono-van's. Bosco was a wiggling ball of fur at the sudden activity as everyone popped into the living room. Andy chased him through the house, both burning off some energy as my pug baby zoomed down the hallway with his tongue hanging out.

Passing out wasn't an option. Exhaustion was the real deal, but my brain was a whirlwind of what we saw in Diluculo. Caine was alive. Him, but not himself at all. Having the ability to watch Donovan's interactions was an unexpected bonus. Being unable to reach out and touch Caine left me handcuffed on the sidelines in a way I couldn't have described to someone if they asked.

"Read her soul."

I turned from the opened fridge, a water bottle in hand I didn't remember reaching for, to find Gwen standing with an awkward glance at Vincent next to her. She looked as suspicious as I was at his demand.

I closed the fridge door. "No offence, Gwen, but your past isn't high on my binge list."

"None taken. Having my soul invaded isn't on my bucket list."

"For the premonition, you mean?" Donovan had a drink of his own, definitely not water.

Vincent nodded at him. "Not often is the opportunity to view a premonition from the source possible."

Donovan's whisky warmed my belly. I took a seat at the kitchen island and let it do its thing as Kim joined us.

I opened my bottle, playing with the lid. "You see it like a vision?"

Gwen shrugged. "Sort of. Sometimes I just hear words."

"We have the words. Lots of them." Donovan picked up the pages from the kitchen table and held them up as evidence. He had put each line on a page and was listing potential interpretations under each. Kim extended her hand, and he slid them across the island to her. "Unless you have the meaning behind the words, reading your soul is a wasted trip."

"Maybe. I saw who has or had the discus. A little girl I didn't recognize."

I made a throaty noise. "A little girl? If the discus ends up being a Frisbee, I'm getting out of the whole game."

Kim laughed. "Truly. Though any object could be spelled for a particular use. A vibrator could've been our ticket back in if the Creation was more recent."

"Don't discount it being an old-timey eighteen-hundreds version. Or an ancient gourd full of bees. Apparently, Cleopatra was a self-love trendsetter."

Kim laughed louder this time. "Of course you'd know the origins of the vibrator." She shook her head and looked to Gwen. "Are your thoughts protected?"

Gwen nodded. "Not against ancient syphilis imbedded in old, wooden vibrators, but herbally blocked from mind reading, yes. No way I'm leaving them open when I don't have your power to spot the Tainted."

Smart but inconvenient.

I exhaled and looked at Donovan.

He downed the rest of his glass. "Do what you gotta, babe. I'm just happy it doesn't involve bees. Or syphilis."

Nya's power was in charge and shielding the connection to protect Donovan before I was done smirking at his comment.

Gwen stepped back in a gasp at whatever change she saw in me.

"Think of the girl in the premonition." My voice was strong, mine but not mine.

"Ahh...." Frantic thoughts raced through the Prophetess's chaotic thoughts until she closed her eyes and battled for stillness.

Darkness. Not the absence of surroundings but the absence of light. A young girl of no older than ten years knelt in the dark, face lit by a floating, dim spark of power. She focused on a hexagonal slab of rock in her hands, it too large for her little body to wield with such ease. She tilted it in the hazy light and watched stripes of glinting flash like diamonds along the rough, ash-coloured surface. Her treasure reflected in her eyes. Stolen by someone else, yet all hers now, tucked into her secret spot, behind a small wooden door.

With the knowledge of who once had the discus, why not discover the premonition in full?

I sought more, reaching further, diving from the Prophetess's thoughts into her soul for the premonition in its entirety. The Prophetess was right. The premonition was a mix of words and visuals, its interpretation the true power.

With the whole premonition now in my mind, should I enlighten the others? They awaited my response, impatience for answers alive and salivating within the kitchen.

Yes, they needed to know. They will help me reclaim what was mine.

I sent the premonition telepathically to them to witness for themselves. The Kitchen Witch and immortal grabbed their heads and cried out at the onslaught of the vision. The dimpled one closed his eyes and tilted his head, he accustomed to the invasion and practiced in the swift capture and interpretation of information.

"Sophie, come back to us now." The immortal was squinting through residual ache, hoping the use of my name was enough to pull me back.

Sophie? My name. Right.

Nya's power drained from me. The room and the other's judgmental expressions made me feel tiny and exposed. "Shitcakes. Sorry. Easiest way to show everyone, I guess."

Vincent cleared his throat. "Yes. The most efficient avenue is often best."

"Says you, four eyes." Kim pressed her hands into her forehead. "Damn, girl. That sucked. Nya's power has zero chill. We said the visual of the discus, not the whole flippin' thing. I can't even remember all that."

Kim was spot on. Nya's power left little room for niceties. Sometimes it was freeing not to dance around a subject and drive straight to the point. Not that I got any relief out of how I handled things with Nya's power in charge. It was strong enough to bypass the herbal solution blocking Gwen's thoughts, and the others needed to see as I did. Plain and simple. Maybe that was the point—all power, no personality.

Donovan leaned into his forearms on the kitchen island. The blunt edges in my gut were his regret. We now knew a few more things writing down the premonition missed.

"Do we tell him?" My question was met by confused stares from Vincent, Kim, and Gwen. They didn't know whom I was talking about. Maybe they didn't understand the premonition any better.

"No." Donovan straightened. "Let Ranlyn see the Recollection Plant plan fail for himself. He won't endorse working with Rosemary any other way."

"Who's Rosemary? I don't remember hearing that name." Gwen wouldn't have as Rosemary's name wasn't from the premonition itself, but her truce was.

"Hold on." Kim raised her hands. "I think we need to better—"

"Take a look for yourself." Donovan reached across the island and snatched the premonition pages. Sifting through to find the parts he wanted, he then thrust them forward for the others to read.

They looked over the pages, Kim sighing as she skimmed aloud. "'Preserved beneath humanity, they will protect on saturated grass,' whatever that means."

Vincent's gaze shifted to mine. We couldn't mention The Chiff aloud, but it would seem those within it may join the cause. Those being the people "preserved beneath humanity." Though Nora may become another obstacle.

Kim pointed at a page. "'Nature's survivalist' is the Pompeii Worm, right?"

Gwen nodded. "I looked them up. They hang out in volcanos. Where'd you find one?"

Good question, but we couldn't answer Gwen. Vincent stepped in with a curt "From a contact." She wasn't content with the answer but didn't push.

"Shit." Kim stood and flicked her hair out of her way. "Is this the part you're talking about? 'Planted memories swallowed to bring strength among allies, grows roots in opposition, severing forces enough to seek the unsought. Laughing darkness never refuses that which they know to already possess.' Has to be, right? Like we need more people against us."

Vincent pointed at the paper. "Another unsought may be referred to."

"I agree with the immortal, here." Vincent turned to Kim with the barest of surprise she missed. "Just because some stupid premonition says we're going to join up with the toxic uterus that spawned asshat here doesn't mean we have to follow it like our how-to bible to corrupting our asses." Kim tossed the pages back at Donovan and looked to Gwen. "No offense."

"None taken. I don't make the premonitions. I just receive them. Apparently."

Kim braced her hands on the island. "Yeah, how's that, exactly? You're a Tarot Reader."

Gwen's cheeks reddened. "My coven name, Cassara, means Prophetess. Obviously, Aunt Lacey knew something I didn't, which is why she gave me the name. I've been practicing a lot. Trying to let the cards show me what they want but also mimicking the process without cards to see the whole story instead of being held back by the limitations of a tarot read." She and I had talked about it before, and I was happy to see she figured it out. "I went to Ranlyn after flipping my lid. I thought it was mostly wordy bullshit—"

"Because it is."

She widened her eyes at Donovan in agreeance. "But there was more in there. Ranlyn was afraid I might be pressured for my gift or for explanation of what it all meant, so he kept quiet. Which I guess could still be true, but hiding is only helping our enemies and not anyone who might be able to do something about it."

"Your sacrifice is noted. Nevertheless, the rest of your covenmates need not know until you find it prudent to inform them."

The rest of us agreed with Vincent.

Donovan poured another couple fingers of whisky. "Let's get back to the toxic uterus that spawned me."

"Hmm, let's." Kim mock tapped her lips. "Because Rosemary is a seriously deranged woman who will turn on us like a beaten dog the moment the Creation is opened."

"She might not, but the rest of her crew will." Rosemary glossed over this, but she knew it was true or she wouldn't have come to us with the truce. "Your mother slash toxic uterus's gorgeous good looks can't stop her people from capitalizing on a once-in-a-lifetime opportunity." No one could make me believe she would kill her son, or me since it's also killing her son, but the rest were up for grabs. "As far as allies go, she's a nasty facial tumor screening our view of the ultimate goal, and one we can't trust. But, if a truce temporarily muzzles her and limits the death toll outside the Creation, isn't that, like, the responsible thing to do?"

"Responsible? Yes." Gwen drummed her nails on the countertop. "However, you guys do remember this isn't your Coven, right? It's your Sect, but you don't have final say, and the only Elder in the room is being suspiciously quiet." She thumbed towards Vincent next to her who didn't respond. "If the Elders won't buy in, it doesn't count for anything."

"True. Rosemary spawning me won't make for a good argument to team up with a Tainted coven. When Ranlyn comes to you, and he will,"—again, Vincent didn't respond—"remind him Rosemary came to us first. And although Ranlyn previously said he would never entertain a truce with her, he'll be desperate when this plant plan of his not only fails but backfires."

"While I comprehend your meaning, an Elder's broken confidence is never a positive turn for the Magics beneath them who seek guidance. Be it a Sect or the Mother Coven as a whole."

Donovan gave a one-shouldered shrug at this. "If he's the Elder he thinks he is, he'll know it's better to agree to the truce and try to save our asses. Rosemary's people will show up anyway. And with our own Coveners switching sides against us, making an effort to live peacefully with some Tainted for the sake of keeping Evaristus out of this world is as good a reason as any."

Kim made a noise close to impressed. "Aren't you mature."

"Not as much as you. Which is convenient since I'm going to bed."

She gasped. "You are not leaving me to babysit the whole Sect. It's not even my house."

"Maybe not, but the more we talk about Ranlyn while he's not here, the more it feels like gossip instead of strategic planning." Donovan downed the rest of his drink. "We've had a long day full of shopping, demons, places we're magically bound not to talk about, and premonitions. Not to mention the hairy worm up my nose and subsequent trip across the veil. I'm done. And I'm taking your life raft with me."

She looked at me. "Seriously? You're ditching me?"

"Sorry, my fierce Sect Leader." I tugged on a lock of her hair as I passed. "I'm pooched."

She shrugged me off. "Deserter."

"Yup. Don't talk to strangers. Make good choices. And remember who you are."

Vincent gave me a gentlemanly nod as I followed Donovan upstairs. I was grateful for the out. I didn't have it in me to party all night. And while I had no doubt Kim was flipping me off and cursing me for leaving her with the whole Sect plus my brother and cousin, they would be fine. They were adults, and they were safe within the walls, or they were as safe as we could be considering Ranlyn was about to make a boatload more enemies who knew where Donovan lived and had clean souls the wards would usher in like a VIP celebrity.

I sucked in a breath, sitting up in bed, ready for a fight. A mechanical duck quacking sounded on the bedside table. Someone was calling me. Unknown caller.

Donovan collapsed back onto his pillows. "Hate your ringtone."

I slid the answer bar. "Hello?"

"Is it true?"

"I'm sorry?"

"Did you talk to Caine?"

With more words, I recognized the voice. "Yes, Bernie." I hit Donovan on the shoulder. His exhaustion was tugging at my eyelids. He sat up against the headboard, hand on my thigh over the duvet, fighting his bleariness. "We got what was needed for Donovan to talk to Caine directly. Through Remote Viewing, we all saw him. Plus, we have proof if you need it."

"He's alive?" The hardness of her voice made me ache for him all over again.

"Yes."

Shifting on the receiver sounded like Bernie was trying to hide her heavy exhale. Even slightly Tainted, she was a good person.

"Jet is also alive."

Bernie's silence on the other end told me this was what she really wanted to know. She fought to process the new information, a mucusy sniff the broken-hearted relief of a grieved mother.

"I hate to ruin good news, but they aren't together. We didn't see Jet, but Caine assured us she's alive, too."

"What does that mean?"

Being over the phone had its advantages. Like telling someone who currently hates you that their daughter was a Puppet in the hands of evil. Knowing it was how it would be and wishing to never know what it would feel like to be on the other end of the line, I choked up as Bernie's sobs seemed to reach through the phone and squeeze my insides.

Head bowed and ignoring Donovan's silent plea for me to hang up, tears fell as Bernie's tone morphed from the ache of a parent to the savageness of an enemy, painting me a monster who took her vulnerable nephew and turned him into a broken man who showed up on their doorstep. Her words didn't matter. I expected a barrage of blame and projectiles of pain she had nowhere else to direct. I was that place, and I let her have at it without clapping back because a part of me blamed myself as well.

It didn't mean her words passed through me without making a mark. My chest grew tighter, from my sadness or Donovan's anger at someone causing my tears. It didn't matter. I was a mess.

The line was dead with a scathing wish of how I should be in the Creation instead of Jet. What Bernie didn't know was that I agreed with her. I was supposed to be in there with Caine. We faced Evaristus together, and we were supposed to get out together. The fact we did, and he went back in for Jet, was beyond the point. Especially when he was paying so much for caring about his family.

"A sob story of parental guilt doesn't mean she's right."

Donovan meant well. Bernie couldn't stop her daughter from fighting anymore than Caine could, but I couldn't express that to Donovan right now.

"I need a shower."

A flutter of rejection hit as I closed the door and locked it. Donovan could get in if he wanted to, but I knew he wouldn't try. The nudge of him reaching out to me mentally hit a wall I was unwilling to drop. I wasn't snubbing him, even though I got why it would feel like it. I was claiming the space I needed since we could never stray far from the bleak depths of each others' souls, no matter the distance. He would hurt alongside me, cry with me, even understand my pain with a cherished intimacy, but it didn't mean I wanted him to see it happen.

I got into the shower and slid onto the floor, unable to stop the tears from spilling out. Seeing Caine in that place, seeing him taken over by Gareth's power and struggling to keep others safe was unfair. He didn't deserve this. He was alive, on the cusp of survival, but at what price? We could communicate now, but we couldn't rip him out of there. He could be dead now for all I knew. Taken down by devotees or whatever else Evaristus and Loring threw at them. Or by Jet. And for Eli and Bernie to lose their daughter at the hands of the nephew they recently reunited with was the greatest injustice.

The pounding in my head reminded me of Donovan somewhere allowing me to feel as I needed to. Not once did he fight this or try and soothe me. He let me be, even though I knew he didn't like knowing I felt this way. I didn't need the connection for that. He's said so enough times.

My eyes ached. Exhaustion hit me, keeping me under the water for longer than I needed before I could muster the energy to do anything as laborious as washing my hair.

Donovan's control made itself known now, waiting until I was over the crying parts, focusing me enough to keep me from dipping back into the quicksand.

The steamed mirror reflected swollen eyes makeup wouldn't hide, so I wrapped my hair in a towel and surrounded myself in a plush robe before leaving the room.

Donovan was doing up a zip-up sweater over a band tee and looked up as the door opened. I almost broke down again at the sight of his bloodshot eyes.

He shook his head. "Don't apologize."

"I was actually going to thank you. So, thank you."

He smiled enough to cave the dimple in his left cheek. "You're welcome."

Love and gratitude passed through the connection, a balm to my ragged emotions.

I pressed my finger onto my aching right eyelid again and tried to get my thoughts together. "At the risk of dragging you through a repeat episode, Caine isn't right. Gareth's power—"

"I know."

"What if Nya's power changes me? Or changes you if I find a way to give you more power and it's somehow pieces of her power and not mine?"

He came to me still standing in the bathroom door threshold and ran his hands over my robe-covered arms. "Caine and Jet are alive. The experiment successful. Caine was still in there, under Gareth's power's influence. I know you saw him."

I nodded.

"We don't know the side effects of Gareth's power being in charge for so long. Maybe nothing will change. But now we have answers and a lead on getting him out. Right now, Gareth's power is keeping Caine alive. Better alive and full of ancient power than dead, no?"

"For now, sure. But when he gets out? No."

Donovan tilted his head at this.

I wet my lips. "Taken over and lost by an ancient power is the same as being dead. When Nya's power takes over, really pushes its influence, I'm not me. If it were permanent, I would be a husk. Caine would be a body for Gareth's power to cart around in a new world. Caine wouldn't want that. Kept alive by machines in a coma or a hollowed-out vessel, Caine would choose death. I know him enough to know that."

He nodded.

"So would I."

His stare tensed.

"I can't say what would happen to you if her power took me over instead of hints of influencing me. If you're alive, then my heart breaks because she won't give a fuck about you." I clenched my teeth to stop the quiver in my chin. "If you're dead, or close to it, tell someone to take me out before it's too late. I can't have my family seeing me walk around and it not be me. Jet might be taken over, but Eli and Bernie aren't forced to watch it happen."

He shook his head a moment and looked down. "We just have to find the discus."

"Donovan—"

"I know. If it comes down to it, I've heard your wishes and will most likely ignore them. Don't look at me like that. You know it's true. I'm not pushing the reset button until I'm one hundred percent sure you're gone, and if I was still alive, I doubt that would be the case. For now, let's concentrate on finding the discus, okay?" He kissed the top of my head. "Get dressed, babe. I'll meet you downstairs."

What ifs didn't help the situation. He was right to shut me down, but I was certain he knew what I wanted. How to deal with Caine if Gareth's power took over completely was another story. If I had to find another Persuader to pull out Caine's essence, I would.

After brushing my hair out and adding waterproof makeup in case I lost it again, I took a moment to heal my swollen eyes, forgetting I could until my eyeliner didn't look quite right.

I had put on some underwear and was in the process of getting my bra when the door flew open. Kim came in, but Matt was in the hallway about to go into the bathroom and got himself an eye full.

"Kim!"

"They're tits, Soph. They're great, but I dress people for a living, and I've got a set of my own. Seen it all."

"Matt hasn't."

She turned around, but Matt had ducked into the bathroom. She closed the bedroom door, far too late.

"What's up with you and Donovan? Crying during morning sex a new kink?"

"Morning sex is not as much Donovan's thing as it was Caine's. Good ol' fashioned tears this time and nothing more."

"Good to know, I guess. Did you have a fight?"

"Can I hide my nips before you begin, or is humiliation part of the interrogation tactic?"

She flicked her hand at me. "Multi-task."

I huffed and went on to tell her about my call with Bernie and then the talk with Donovan, all the while Kim was vetoing my clothing choices and chucking her approved designs at me, edging me to continue. Her annoyance with my fashion kept the tears at bay while I gave her the short version of my emotional morning.

"I'm not letting either of you 'Hit the reset button.' What the hell is that? We find ways out of everything. That would just be another one like getting Caine and Jet out of the Creation. It'll happen."

"Nope. You don't get to cop out like that."

"Cop out?"

"Yeah. If I'm taken over and Donovan is paying for it, you know what I expect. You can even work on your immortality and explain it to me all over again when I come back as whomever I come back as."

"I'm regretting forcing this conversation."

I held open the bedroom door for her. "Good. That's what you get for barging in on me in my underwear."

Matt was in the kitchen with a stretching grin on his face, standing with a few others, when I came in on my way to the fridge.

"Don't make me erase your memory."

His smile dropped. It may not be enough to keep his mouth shut for more than an hour, but I tried.

17

———

UNINVITED

Caine

"I f we leave, we may as well kill them ourselves." My sweat-soaked and grimy shirt stuck to my back.

"They perish more by the day with or without our intervention."

Not my opinion but not untrue.

Sophie and I were told Nya and Gareth didn't piggyback the ride into our vessels with their power. Not even Aunt Lacey could have guessed how bullshit that was. You'd think Gareth would get tired of voicing his opinions on every little thought I had, but he didn't. Always ready and willing to jump in when not invited.

Every time a survivor died, someone got hurt, or the devotees or Puppets found us, Gareth forced me through a chat on why we should abandon the remaining survivors to fend for ourselves. Was easier to head into the lean-to with the bare minimum of privacy, sit cross-legged, and pretend I was meditating as way to process the incident. At least that's what I told Ness was happening. Best I could think up when she caught me talking to myself.

Close quarters meant tight lies. Made me an asshole, but no one benefitted from the truth.

Fighting and killing every devotee in sight was fine with me. Doing it at the expense of the others was not cool. Gareth insisted he didn't want the other survivors dead yet put his survival above theirs. Not Ness. Gareth loved Ness because she goaded me into using his power as often as I could, she not realizing what Gareth was doing to me. Hell, I didn't even know.

This came with a boundary as well. Kicking ass next to Ness was A-okay in Gareth's mind. Kissing her was not. He shoved images of Sophie into my brain before it could happen. Gareth wanted to see his wife, which meant seeing Sophie. I didn't tell Ness why I was a tease, instead making up an excuse for it not being good for us to start something while stuck in here. She wasn't looking for long-term, an outlet would do. An outlet I sure as hell needed but couldn't manage with Sophie on the brain.

Gareth was unimpressed by Donovan. Had to love the guy for that.

"Knock, knock." Ness came in with a charred hunk of something on a stick. "It's not a hot dog, but it's meat."

I did my best to keep Gareth from interacting with her. By now, it was more like him allowing me to since we both knew he didn't listen to me much anymore. She wagged the meat stick in front of me before I could focus on taking it from her hand. I didn't ask what it was since knowing might mean going hungry.

"Thanks."

She sat a comfortable distance away and ate her own meat on a stick, ripping off pieces with bright white teeth. Everyone lost weight here, and she was no exception, though she managed to keep her curves.

Making comparisons to Sophie was impossible to avoid. They were opposites yet somehow similar. Maybe their inner strength but not how they dealt with it. Even her attitude was fiercer than

Sophie's on her grumpiest of days. Made me wonder what she was like on the outside.

These differences were comforting. Nice to know something stirred for someone else other than Sophie when I didn't think it was possible. Maybe fate threw me a bone for fucking with me in the first place.

"Sorry about the Sophie thing."

She didn't stop eating. "You said that already. Lose your memory on that last outing?"

Being chased by a herd of Puppets was always a wild experience.

Ness was uncomfortable with anything regarding emotions like some chicks were with spiders. If they didn't bother her, she didn't bother with them, and any time a hint of feelings entered the conversation, she got awkward and changed the subject or got snarky. What started out as a game to see if I could get to her became something else and her awkwardness became endearing. She remained at arm's length. Available but not. Something she and Sophie shared.

If only I had the courage to tell Ness about Gareth's reserved parking space in my head. If I didn't think she would assume I was making it up as a reason to stay away from her, I would.

18

GRAVE-SIDE QUIET

Since the Coveners used the Apporter to travel to Donovan's, no one had vehicles. Donovan cabbed them wherever they wanted to go. Some stuck around since it was Coven meeting night anyway. Remnants of a big breakfast we missed was evident in frying pans caked with scrambles eggs, plates with leftover syrup from pancakes and French toast, and empty orange juice containers left on the counter. No way I was cleaning up. Once their stomachs relaxed, someone else was scrubbing the dishes.

Kim walked in as I was picking at a plate of fruit. "Where's Andy and Bosco?"

"Oops." Kim slid to a stop and took off upstairs.

Serena came into the kitchen chomping on a handful of grapes and motioned to where Kim disappeared. "She's playing hide and seek with Andy and Boss, training her power to find them."

Using her guiding light for kid games was much safer than finding us in the Creation, hoping we weren't dead already, as Kim explained happened while fighting Evaristus and Loring.

Andy dragged his feet, beating Kim to the kitchen, Bosco on their heels. "How did you find me? Bosco didn't snort that time?"

I swooped Bosco into my arms and got some morning kisses.

"Told you, kid. I'm the world's hide-and-seek champ." Kim fished a juice box out of the fridge and handed it to him.

Bosco was let loose for his own drink. He lapped up water, most of it pouring out of his mouth onto the floor.

I dropped my voice as I grabbed a dish towel to clean up after him. "Cheating a six-year-old?"

"Oh, come on. I get some practice, and he gets to play. Win-win."

I chuckled. "Mhmm."

A duck quacked.

"You really need to change that ring tone."

"Next in queue is the grunting sounds of turtle sex. Be grateful for quacks." I swiped to answer Vincent. "Hello?"

"We're coming by the Coven meeting tonight."

"Who's we?"

"The Elders, Olson, and potentially another once discussed with Ranlyn."

"Thanks for the warning. I'll make sure we're out."

"Excuse me?"

"Sorry. Crappy morning equals bad jokes. I'll let Donovan and Kim know. Half the Coveners are already here."

"Is the Sect aware of my connection to the Sovereignty?"

"Umm, the Ballards are, so it depends on if Adam and Serena told any of them."

Vincent exhaled far too loudly into the receiver. "This information must be a part of the Coven proceedings tonight. Their involvement is unnecessary, yet they need to be apprised of what most others are."

"If you say so. Not my Coven. Whatever an Elder says would override any objection anyway."

"Yes, I suppose it would."

Vincent was also going to return my car to me and pick up Moira's clothing which I still hadn't washed. I let Kim in on the news of visitors tonight and put in the laundry, being sure to spot clean anything that needed it and use Kim's special Kitchen Witch detergent.

With the number of Coveners at the house, practicing their gifts was a given. Everyone had progressed so much in the last few months, including Matt who earned the slap he got from Caitlyn for using his Chameleon powers to disguise himself as Blake and hit on her. Caitlyn could produce magic and wield it with confidence, even without an innate specialty, but sometimes a slap made for better impact.

Blake had shown his power on multiple occasions but was now more refined, as was Jared since they worked together frequently. Their elemental powers weren't messed with as they created excessive damage and attracted too much attention without it being life or death excusable. Other ones were with mixed results of seriousness.

Adam was on a basement couch watching others practice. I snatched the sunglasses from his face and plopped down next to him.

"Come on!"

"Nope. Been through this, bro. It's the perfect time to practice your gifts, including Soul Seeing."

He groaned and squeezed his fingers over his eyes. "Go away. Looking at you is too much."

"Please. One of the first souls I saw was Aunt Lacey's, and she was an immortal of the immortals. Talk about searing pain."

"Name dropping won't get you in the cool kids' club."

"Says the guy covering his face while sitting in the midst of the cool kids' club I was in first. Have you really felt the power yet? Working on that might help your body catch up with your abilities. Your soul glow needs work."

"I thought this was supposed to be all natural. You're hella pushy."

"Hey, it's your life, but this isn't a hippie commune. No share circles here, so get over it and deal."

"You don't know I can do the same stuff as you can."

"Your bloodshot eyes would argue that fact."

He huffed, sat forward, and leaned on his elbows covering his eyes.

"Y'know, I didn't think you'd be such crusty ballsack about this."

His forehead scrunched as he looked at me, swore, and then looked away. "For a shrink-in-training you're not very supportive."

"Please. You don't need Counselling. You need the Wizard of Oz to grant you some courage."

"Wow. Bruised me with that one."

I pushed his shoulder. "Look where you are. Could you imagine people around you actually have souls? Something others talk about, write about, beg to redeem, or kill for, and we can see them and everything they stand for. What do you see when you look at my soul?"

"If the burning would stop, I could actually answer at you."

"Fine. Here." I handed him his glasses back.

"You're really fucking bright."

"Not what it does to you, what does it mean?"

"Bright means strong."

I nodded. "Now, what about the colour?"

"Which one?"

"Well, that in itself is something."

"'Cuz there's two powers."

"Two essences with different powers because I'm a vessel. What colours are they? What do they mean?"

"Green and pink-ish, purple-ish. It's weird. Green is a Seer thing. I don't know about the other one."

"Yeah, the other isn't classified in the family tome. Most aren't, actually. How about someone else?"

We went through the Coveners, Adam telling me which had soul glows, who was bright, and what their colours meant if they had any. Easy lesson, but it got him to stop complaining about his eyeballs for two seconds. If he did this wherever he was, without his sunglasses as much as possible, he would get used to it. I still get headaches but not nearly as much as I did a couple of months ago.

His limited attention span meant short lessons were best. I left him on a good note, annoyed but schooled.

Coveners streamed in at different times, filling the spaces of the house with laughter and conversation. Since quite a few were already here, Blake and Jared took it upon themselves to call most others in early, eager to have everyone present and share in the exploration of their abilities for longer than normal. This happened to be lucky, since Ranlyn showed up two hours sooner than expected. Being cautious of traditional courtesy, I went to let him know my brother and cousin were still present from the previous night but was stunned at who followed him inside.

Vincent, Veata, and Olson were expected. Rosemary was not.

Donovan called my name before entering the front room, feeling my distress. "How'd you get in my house?"

I stepped towards Donovan as Rosemary stood comfortably with her hands in the pockets of her cranberry-coloured wool coat, focused on her son.

Ranlyn held his hands in front of him looking like the security guard I was used to before he became an Elder. "I temporarily deactivated your wards to allow Olson and Rosemary in."

"You left us unprotected?"

A flash of Donovan's anger curled my fingers into fists.

Vincent took off his coat, draping it over his arm. "A perimeter was erected. Your wards will be re-established upon our leave."

His assurances had no impact on Donovan.

"Sophie." Kim stood with many Coveners behind her in the kitchen. I erected a black-out shield behind her so she was included, keeping the Coveners out of it until Donovan decided what he was doing with his mother.

Rosemary smiled, the dimples she gifted to her son deepening. "I taught you that."

She was looking at her son, somehow knowing he was my teacher.

Whatever she expected from Donovan, her disappointment was

evident in the loss of her dimples when she didn't get it.

"Why are you here?" The silence was too much for me with Donovan's anger clouding my head. Something was going to snap, and I didn't want it to be him.

She looked at our Elders. "Last resort, I expect."

"We knew they would seek you out. The premonition called for it." This surprised the Elders who looked to me in silent question. "This is Donovan's house, not the Coven's, which means you being here should have been passed by him." If I were in Donovan's place, Rosemary would have been knee deep in the curb-side snowdrift before the word "hello" passed her pouty lips. Something I noticed Donovan also inherited.

"Elsa—"

"Is dead." Donovan shutting down Vincent was a sting almost as bad as whatever he would have said. "She gave me this house, and I continue to let the Sect use it. It doesn't belong to the Coven." He turned to Rosemary. "You're allowed here because you weaseled your way in and because this truce is necessary. After tonight, you can pick up a phone. You're not welcome here."

Vincent and Ranlyn nodded. Veata stood as if she wasn't a part of the ploy. Rosemary smiled again. Whatever she thought of her son, she was proud to hear him put the Elders in their place. Probably not the best thing in front of the enemy, but boundaries wouldn't be crossed again without consequences.

I dropped the shield.

The Elders and Rosemary started moving towards the kitchen to the basement where our meeting usually took place.

I stood in their way. "Hold up." Erecting another wall would have worked but was rude, so I switched on Nya's power, protecting Donovan, and reached into his head. I knew his mind would be secure and dropping it would let the heavy-hitters in on what I wanted to say. Nya's power was made for this.

"You're letting Rosemary into your home. You don't have to let her into the space we train and convene as a Sect. She doesn't belong there.

And what about Andy? I don't want to leave him upstairs, unpro-tected, while we're all in the basement. And I'm not locking him in."

He took a moment and then nodded.

I let Nya's power go.

"The meeting will happen in the living room. Standing in my house is one thing. It doesn't mean you deserve a tour."

She dipped her head. "Fine by me."

Besides their morbid curiosity, most of the Coveners didn't want to be there. They came into the room, looking at the players, and unsure where to sit or how to act. I went to settle Andy and Bosco in Andy's room. He had toys and his books from The Chiff he couldn't put down, so he should be okay as long as Rosemary wasn't around long.

When I came back, the Coveners were seated around the living room, grave-side quiet. The couch was spun to face the expanse of the room where the Elders sat on or around while everyone had a chair or the comforts of the thick carpet.

Ranlyn remained standing. "The face most of you don't know is Rosemary." She inclined her head, most smiled in return. "Rosemary is not of this Coven, but her flock is of our cause and is willing to join in the pursuit of rescuing the trapped within Diluculo."

Donovan spoke up quickly. "And since I'm not about to stand around shovelling you spoonfuls of bullshit and allow you to make your own assumptions, Rosemary is my mother."

Rosemary smiled enough to showcase a hint of her dimples. She didn't need them for the others to see the resemblance, but it was unmistakable when she did. Not that they could compare in the moment as Donovan was not smiling.

Serena gave me a look. I returned one she understood, and she kept her mouth shut. I would give her more details when we were alone.

"Why's this such a big deal?" Blake looked at the Elders and then Donovan. "You're clearly not happy she's here. Is this family drama or something more we should be worried about?"

I left it up to Donovan. His non-answer was my answer and, again, I flipped Nya's power on, protected Donovan, and projected a visual of Rosemary sitting next to the Elders. Her dark soul gleamed in contrast to everyone around her.

It was overkill with Adam since he knew before the others anyway, but now he knew what it was like to see without his inexperienced strain.

Proof of evil was different then telling them she was Tainted. Whether this coloured their opinion of their Sect Leader, it confused the hell out of them as to why the Elders were working with Tainted.

"Relax, everyone." Donovan was loud, but it took a moment for them to settle. "We're not turning this Coven into a pack of Tainted souls, so shut up and listen. Ranlyn didn't want this. But Rosemary came to us, and a premonition calls for a truce to open the Creation and save the others inside. Due to this temporary truce,"—far too much emphasis on "temporary"—"and because we're insisting on opening the Creation, Mother Coven members will fight against us, they assuming we've turned to a darker path. We've all seen the survivors inside. Caine's one of us. This truce means Rosemary can keep her flock from attacking the Mother Coven members and focus on fighting Evaristus or Loring or any devotees who try to escape."

"We're trusting a Tainted Magic to keep their word? For real?" Denise's attitude was right on cue.

"Loyalty is a strong motivator." Rosemary stood comfortably amongst her enemy. "When harnessed, it takes on a more literal sense."

"You speak of an Allegiance spell?" Veata spoke for the first time.

Rosemary smiled. "I do. Not one of my flock can do anything against my command. They can want, they can seethe with hatred, but their actions will go no further than my words allow."

"Your sanction dies with you. You know this. Our protection is why you're truly here. Making enemies in your own ranks?" I loved Veata's mind. Leave it to her to reveal important information Rosemary should have told us.

Rosemary didn't balk at presumption. "I said I would do everything in my power to keep your people safe from mine. Enemies are unavoidable, and in wild packs, someone always strives to usurp the leader. This truce, albeit temporary, benefits us all including the Blind."

Donovan made a hollow laugh. "Makes sense it took death breathing down your neck to come to us."

"Actually, my concern was for you. With any coven, there're leaks in intel. The Mother Coven is no different, whether you like to believe it possible or not. We cracked your premonition before you did. I knew what was coming. I knew who would be involved. And before you ask, no, I won't reveal my source. If you can't sniff out the mole, I'm not about to do it for you. Plus, they may be funneling useful information from our side as well depending on their personal agenda."

The Elders didn't argue or display the barest flicker of surprise. They all knew of the moles. This begged the question of if they thought one was within our Sect. We already knew Veata was used by Evaristus as a Puppet, but that's not a mole. She didn't willingly turncoat.

I had to lockdown my facial expression so I didn't let my shock show.

Nice distraction from the "I told you so" I could have sent Donovan. Not on the mole but on Rosemary's focus being his safety. She was evil, but he was her Achilles' heel. The sad part about it was that it didn't matter. He needed a mother to protect him when his father and his coven tortured him, and she was busy protecting herself as she was now.

Vincent clearing his throat was a punch to the lingering silence. "Our objective this evening is to educate everyone present on our true enemy and expectations moving forward. If you volunteer to be one among the soldiers, know you will face those you consider comrades, convenmates, and friends. A battle which will involve the Sovereignty is not a battle I encourage you to take on. They are an ancient, complex system of law our kind is accountable to if our actions move outside of reason. They decide what is reasonable depending on how it fits into their shifting political or personal priorities."

Vincent paced a step and adjusted his glasses. "As with Donovan, I come from a family of Tainted individuals who wield power over others for profit or sadistic entertainment. My family murdered my wife. My quest to rid them of their power began before her death, however, stands on principal and not vengeance. Also, I am the heir to the Sovereignty throne." This caused another round of shocked faces. "My brother is the current throne bearer of what is essentially a kingdom. My father, alive and thriving off the backs of Magics and the Blind alike, still holds great influence over those within the fold. So, again, this is not a battle I encourage any of you to join."

Rosemary crossed her legs. "Then you're not planning on releasing Cora-Lynn's soul?"

Vincent and Rosemary exchanged hard glances as the rest of us, including the other Elders, found something to be surprised about.

Vincent's gaze cast downward, but a tireless sadness shone in his eyes. My heart broke for whatever this meant to him.

He turned to me, and I had the sensation of standing on the edge of a tall building as I waited for him to speak.

"The deal is still on the table."

Judging by his delivery, he expected this to mean something to me. I remembered his brother Chase saying it but had no clue what it meant then or now. Was this a past life thing? Shit. I should know this.

When Vincent turned back to those in the room, I felt like I let him down. "Sophie has had the unfortunate privilege of meeting my brother and current head of the Sovereignty. During this introduction he made a point to deliver a message: 'The deal is still on the table'. Among the many depravities my family has committed, that deal was amongst the worst.

"Years passed since my wife Cora-Lynn's death without seeing her again. Souls recycle. I won't pretend to understand why, yet hers I did not cross as I hoped. My brother informed me that they had not only tortured and killed Cora-Lynn, but for no true reason other than to punish me for abhorring them, they intercepted her soul at the time of her passing, capturing it, so she could never find me again. This would continue onto forever, unless I conceded my rebellion and joined the company, an irreversible decision and blatant disrespect to the legacy of the woman I love.

"Would I destroy every Magic standing in my way of releasing Cora-Lynn's soul? No. Not every Magic." He glanced my way. "However, I would hope they understood and allowed me to do as needed."

I was willing to bet not a single Magic present would stick an ill-kept toenail in Vincent's way of freeing his wife's soul. A hundred questions begged to be asked, but no one did.

"Rosemary exposed a weakness by mentioning my wife." Vincent's tone was lighter than I thought she deserved. "Regardless of her motives, my belief in a temporary truce with Rosemary's coven is ironclad. My worries extend beyond the battlefield, after reopening the Creation when they no longer are held by a loyalty spell, though is unworthy of such energy at this time."

Rosemary inclined her head as if she was leaving the choice up to him.

"As a new Elder, I find it prudent to make you aware of all of this. With the stakes as high as they are, for all of us, to save Caine and the other survivors and to stop Evaristus and Loring from escaping into the world, we need to operate in transparency. I promise to make attempts at this whenever possible."

Vincent looked back at Ranlyn in a silent indication. Ranlyn stepped forward and reiterated his faith in the cause, the truce, and in the leadership of the Coven, asking any with questions to come forward at any time.

I was lost in what Vincent said. I pressured him to be an Elder. For reasons like this, I knew he would be a good one. When it came down to it, he spread-eagled it on the sacrificial alter and spilled his guts for the good of the Coven.

"So, you guys are fine with fighting your own people, possibly some of us, but are bunking up with Mrs. Goth-Mother-of-the-Year here?" Leave it to Blake to make his questions colourful.

Rosemary turned to Blake. "Goth?"

I was surprised that was the part she called him out on. Not that he responded to her.

"Will we be booted from the Mother Coven if we don't fight?" Caitlyn's question brought tension to the faces of many others.

"No." Ranlyn raised his hands. "No one is expected to fight."

Matt lifted two fingers, his expression sour. "But if we fight against you because we don't believe saving a few people is worth letting an ancient evil out, you're saying you're not gonna oust us from the Coven? No way I buy that."

"I hear that," Denise added, though I didn't see her fighting against the Mother Coven. She just liked getting her two cents in.

"Nothing needs to be decided this evening, though our hope is—" Vincent tried but was drowned out by a torrent of the Coveners questions, vocalized over each other before any answers could be made, other Coveners answering them instead. Or more like judging each other for asking them in the first place.

This didn't end well and caused some to storm out of the meeting. Donovan didn't make any effort to stop them. Kim did, but she couldn't force them to listen and, ultimately, we watched them leave, taking a mental note of who left to try and contact them later to talk when tempers cooled. Would some fight against us? The premonition said they would, but I assumed, or at least hoped, it was Magics from other sects and not our own.

It took a good ten minutes for things to cool out, and even then, people were shaking their heads and on edge. Some internalized their thoughts, unable to sit still, while others, like Blake, shared his opinions to anyone close enough to hear him.

Those who remained and kept their cool enough for conversation and not simple outrage, waited for Ranlyn to finish speaking with Rosemary, no one willing to interrupt with more questions. Whatever they talked about had Ranlyn with his arms crossed, his blond brows furrowed in a way I had seen before. He wasn't happy, but he was attempting to be.

Vincent took a couple of steps away, closer to the foyer, wearing an expression I had also seen before.

I followed him. "I don't know what's nibbling at your undercarriage, but it's going to break the skin if you don't spill it."

Donovan was behind me, either tipped off at my dread or, more likely, using whatever excuse he could to dodge yet another Covener's question he couldn't answer.

Vincent adjusted his glasses, again. "In the interest of the transparency I spoke of, I must also confess that my brother made his threat to you with purpose."

I crossed my arms. "Threat?"

"The claim of the deal being on the table, that is." He looked at Donovan, shifted his footing, and focused on me. "I shared a love with Cora-Lynn in one lifetime. I've known *you* for centuries. After you told me Chase visited The Lush, I confronted him, and he made another threat I believed he would not follow through on. He made no effort to harm you as he did Cora-Lynn. Instead, he provided tokens of his excursions within your apartment and within this house as proof he could cause harm if he so desired."

Donovan blurred in an eruption of rage, charging at Vincent. A crack of bone and metal sent Vincent's glasses flying off his face. Vincent landed on his back as I stood frozen, locked in Donovan's fury with clenched fists and burning hatred. A gasping shriek had me down on one knee. Vincent's feet jerked as Donovan rained down power-fueled punches so consuming I stopped myself from joining in by driving my fists into the ceramic flooring.

Cartilage and bone cracked beneath Donovan's knuckles, the dull sounds of a beating alive beneath the outcry of the Coveners and my scream of hate-bound frustration.

Ranlyn rushed forward.

I drove my impotent rage into a snap of movement to stand back up and zapped the power from everyone in front of me. It now resonated in my hands as I had snatched it from them and held it between my fingers.

Ranlyn looked to his outstretched hands in confusion as to where his power went, the others equally awed.

A flurry of movement shocked this power out of me, Ranlyn regaining his own, but he didn't need it. Vincent had pinned Donovan by the collar against the wall. I braced for a hit that didn't come.

Donovan smiled as he looked over the damage he did to Vincent's face. "You think it's okay for your brother to skulk around my house, threaten Sophie, and walk away like it's some game? Your lies put her in danger."

"I told you!" Blood flew from Vincent lips, pouring from his nose and beneath his eye. "The threat was for me. To prove he could strip me of another woman in my life and break me of my obsession of crushing his throne. I would sooner trap my own soul than have Sophie suffer as Cora-Lynn's has." He let go of Donovan, who stood tall without striking back. "My ancient history is at the will of my family. Due to that history and the fact Sophie is the longest running example of my past since I have known her longer than any other, longer than even you, their mode of using her against me is predictably heinous. Rosemary discovered Cora-Lynn. Chase discovered Sophie. My enemies know my weaknesses. Now, you have had a shot at me and have taken it. Do not suppose I will stand another."

"Being an Elder won't stop me from killing you the next time I find out you held something like this from her. You do, and it'll be *your* soul stuffed into a mason jar and placed on my mantel until I decide when it's convenient to let you go." Bluffing was not Donovan's game. He swiped blood off his chin and pointed at Ranlyn. "You done with share time?"

"You know we are."

"Good. You," he pointed at his mother, "out of my house so he can fix the wards to keep you out."

My mother would have wilted at this. Rosemary beamed as she left her son's house without a single rushed step, her misplaced pride confusing.

Donovan retreated to the basement with the Coveners. There was a bathroom down there to clean up if he needed, but it was Vincent who was covered in blood. The Coveners and Kim followed Donovan. I couldn't tell what they thought of how their co-Sect Leader acted but figured if I waited long enough, Denise would tell me.

Moira's laundry needed to be folded. When Vincent cleaned himself up and healed the damage to his face, he found me in the laundry room. His button-down shirt was draped over one arm, leaving him in a simple white t-shirt looking the least immortal I can remember ever seeing him.

I closed Moira's laundry bag and leaned against the small counter. "You know, the premonition refers to the people in The Chiff. Nora probably won't, but do you think the people of The Chiff will fight with us?"

Ringing the shirt in his hands, he hesitated. "Your death in this fight would be tantamount to losing Cora-Lynn all over again. Though, I have lost you many times."

"Okay." Not what I was expecting. I waited for more as he walked around me and leaned against the counter between the machines next to me.

"I remember the first time I met your acquaintance. You were merely a teen, but so was I."

I nodded, then processed what he said. "Wait a tick. I knew you before you were immortal?"

A smile tugged at his lips. "My mother assisted a Healer in the small town where I was born, and since my father was absent much of the time those early years seeking employment elsewhere, I spent my hours as a boy at the small healing house performing tedious cleaning of spilt blood and other bodily fluids, offering patients food and drink, changing basic bandages, and completing odd jobs to support her in what she considered admirable work. And it was.

"You had been injured in an accident and suffered a few broken bones and lots of superficial abrasions. While my mother attended a more grievous patient from the same incident, I attended to you." He shifted his weight. "You accused me of flirtatious advancement. Strong-willed and blunt even then."

"Vincent—"

"We enjoyed each other's company without my misguided hormones getting in the way. A few weeks later, Donovan's family moved to town from a neighbouring village seeking land to cultivate, and your futures were set. Looking back, I do not believe it was your first encounter, yet I cannot be certain."

Wow. I couldn't imagine being a part of the memory Vincent spoke of and wondered what things had been like. "You said I was injured. Was I not a Magic?"

"You had unfostered abilities with no knowledge of your family's power in a time before everyday superstition landed in persecution if kept relatively out of sight. Your family preferred you to arrive at your gifts naturally. When your wounds healed as the Blinds would without your power's intervention, they assumed the traits of your ancestors skipped you as sometimes occurred. They had no reason to heal you themselves and asked the Healer to treat you as any other patient."

"And I didn't know you were a Magic? Or Donovan's family?"

"Donovan was the one who introduced you to the power. You were astonished by the possibility, and he opened your world. Eventually, my power came to light, and your family power revealed. We became friends in that lifetime and have been since in many others."

I nodded. "Ain't that a bitch of an origin story."

"Indeed." He laughed. "Gaining your sympathies is not my motive here. No tale of unrequited love is behind a word I tell you. Nothing close. You are my oldest friend. Someone who lives, creates beautiful and profound magic, and dies at the side of your lover far too often. However, you keep coming back, and the magic you cast on yourself and Donovan will always bring yourselves together. I am eternally envious my family's brutality will not allow me the same fate with Cora-Lynn."

"And you didn't think telling me that would've helped? Especially with Donovan?"

He shrugged and inhaled. "Sometimes it has. Sometimes it makes it worse. Wisdom does not always come with age, neither does my ability to deal with my past any better than the common man. Most times I am willing to forget about both of you, and then you cross my path again, and it starts over. Donovan has punched me before."

A laugh burst from my lips. "He'd probably be as happy as a shit-flinging monkey to hear that."

"I pray tell he would."

A comfort eased between us. I didn't know if it would help Donovan to hear any of this, but I was happy to know it.

I wanted to get Cora-Lynn back for Vincent, so he could see her thrive again with or without him. If this soul capture thing was possible, Cora-Lynn was overdue to live another life.

"So, The Chiff?"

His lips twisted. "The people of The Chiff will take convincing. They hide with good reason. Add the fact the fight is not theirs, it would be an arduous sell. We can begin with Nora then work through the ranks of her guards and the like. With a substantial following, others may unite."

Sounded good to me, especially in regards to my history with Vincent. I knew there was a reason behind my belief in him. This was why.

We met up with Ranlyn, Veata, and Olson. Before they could speak, Vincent demanded no consequence follow Donovan's insubordination and left to be dealt with as a personal attack and not one against an Elder.

No one argued.

Ranlyn looked to me. "Joining Rosemary makes us a bigger target."

"Too late, Jeeves." Veata adopting my nickname for Ranlyn was the highlight of my day. The second was his expression at hearing it. "It was a cogent decision. Justify it how you want—we lessened our enemy pool. Now get me home. I still have enough time to salvage my evening." Guessing what Veata did with her nights was laughable. As an immortal she had all the time in the world and resources to do as she pleased, but somehow, I pictured her cozying up on a La-Z-Boy and listening to rock music.

Before they left, Olson popped outside to my trunk and returned with the gifts I bought. I didn't ask him to. Maybe Ranlyn or Vincent did. Either way, they were out in the open, and I had to shove them into the front closet under a cover spell I hoped would hold until I could find a proper hiding spot.

Vincent said his goodbyes as well, not forgetting Moira's laundry. I didn't want Donovan and Vincent to leave things as they were, but Vincent insisted Donovan needed his space, and he had a meeting with someone from the demon-tracking team. With Gualichu not giving a nut hair of concern if the Blind saw him, the damage control became high priority for the Elders among the issues they were juggling, while finding the demon was as easy as following social media reports of a disappearing teenybopper.

Magics blend into everyday society and can redirect the Blind, but eventually Gualichu would do something the mafia's best cleaner couldn't cover up.

I gave Vincent a hug, a real embrace. It wasn't filled with as much sorrow as the mental one within The Chiff but was bloated with an understanding I knew my old friend would value before Veata ruined it by calling us Chatty Cathies and the Elders zipped off with the Apporter.

19

WAKEUP CALL

Donovan

The sect meeting ended early for a change. After some of the Coveners stormed out, and then the remaining watched me pound Vincent's entitled face in, I didn't blame them for having their fill with the bullshit. Returning to their boring existence was easier than looking war in the face. Same with anything close to Tainted families and past life conflict. How nice of them to be able to retreat into their happy homes while we continued to deal with the nitty-gritty. They didn't sign up for this, but they knew things wouldn't return to how Aunt Lacey had them. They should be prepared at all times to shovel shit and ask how else they can help. Few of them did. Now, even less if the ones who left didn't return.

Fine by me. Like Veata, I wanted to salvage my night, if Sophie wasn't too pissed at me. Kim had Frog on the phone before she could tear her boots on. Sophie let Kim borrow her car and stipulated she drove home as many of the Coveners as seat belts could fit, including Serena and Adam. The rest were cabbed home.

An empty house and a busy couple of days meant Andy was

snoring louder than Bosco, and Sophie and I got to lay around with a few drinks and *River Monsters* re-runs. We changed venues to gain a little elbow room and ended up laying in bed with our drinks, snacks, and more *River Monsters* in a more comfortable setting. Damn near close to living the dream. Never my dream, but somehow it became one.

I drained my glass and headed into the en-suite to brush my teeth as Sophie already had, figuring she didn't want to wake up next to stale whisky breath. I scraped my gums when her concentration on the TV set me to automatic, the pressure on the spot probably her finger or maybe her tongue.

The excited description of the host having finally caught some giant beasty the world thought was extinct turned into the beginning sequence of *CSI: Miami* screaming into the background as I stood at the en-suite door, toothbrush still in my mouth.

"You like punching people too much."

Where'd that come from? She loved hitting me with surprise comments. Guaranteed she had been thinking about my fight with Vincent all night, managing to hide it until now.

I spit out toothpaste and rinsed my mouth before re-entering the bedroom. "I like punching people who deserve to be punched. Especially khaki-wearing immortals who think they surpass consequences to their selfish decisions."

The TV glowed on her face as most of her disappeared in the middle of my dark sheets. "You don't know what it's like to be him."

Ugh. Come on.

The scent of her shampoo wafted from my sheets as I got into bed next to her. "I never said his situation wasn't fucked up, just highlighting how jacked it is for you to pay for it considering it all happened before you were born."

"In this life."

"Yes. In this life."

She straightened and flattened the blankets over her lap as if preparing herself. Wonderful. She knew something I didn't, and I was about to be schooled.

She went on to tell me how she and Vincent met. I tried to drown my sarcasm under a layer of intrigue, knowing I did a shit job of it when she bent her knees and shifted her body my way.

"He doesn't gain anything by lying to me."

"Hmm, let's see. If he wants us to take down his psycho family who murdered his wife, then a story like how you two met as pre-pubescent seedlings in some old-timey hospital is nothing but pure gain. Boner rage for the soft-hearted."

She smirked at me. "You think I'm soft-hearted?"

"You care about damaged people. Proof's in the fact you're in my bed."

"Mhmm. Right. Well, not everything he said would give him brownie points. Telling me you've punched him in past lives would do the opposite." Her dark eyes scanned over my face. "Full dimple treatment, eh? You're far too happy about that."

"Not denying it. He deserved it today, probably deserved it then. Proves he hasn't changed much."

"You, too, since you forget when you punch things my knuckles are wrecked along with yours."

Fuck. She got me there. I was used to looking out for myself. Change wasn't my oldest friend anymore than it was Vincent's.

I settled on my elbow and looked up at her.

She backed up a few inches. "What do you think you're doing, now?"

"Your suspicion is adorable. Not that a part of me doesn't want to jump your bones." Flannel pyjama pants and a *Supernatural* t-shirt was never my preferred brand of lingerie and yet, somehow, it did it for me on her.

Before she could say anything, I slid my fingertips along her hand. The chill of a vision hit me. More power meant I was still blinded, but I felt her soft skin instead of the metal handle of the cutting shears from a past life.

I pressed my lips to her skin and ignored the images my Psychometry cooked up and almost pulled me into as the vision of her with a different name, laughing at something I couldn't hear. My detached reality fought for my attention when all I wanted was to see Sophie's true reactions in this moment. The stronger she became, the more difficult it was to pull off.

"Sometimes I forget." Sophie and my conversation in the past was a low echo in my ears. I kissed her knuckles again, fighting the pressure of my grasp as much as the volume of my response. "Curbing my rage doesn't always work. Sometimes I lose it. There're few people I give a shit enough about to fight for."

Her inner turmoil wasn't my goal. Shaving off my hard edges by bringing up my faults didn't get her off. Many others have enjoyed my pain, but never her. Sometimes I needed Sophie to see my cold strength. Right now, as I pressed my lips to her wrist, I needed her to see equal tenderness. I wasn't completely broken or incapable of putting her first. I understood what it meant to her when I did and when I forgot.

"It's what you know." Her voice was soft, careful. "In this life or the past, at least it's honest."

I paused, my lips hovering above her wrist. This was what it was for her. After her relationship history, honesty was sacred. I never had that with anyone, never knew trust at someone's word. She wasn't always open with me, but when she was, it was sincere. For us, I wanted more, and I wanted to accomplish it without a trail of wreckage behind us.

She pressed her hand into my shoulder, making me lie back as she straddled me. She wasn't in my thoughts, but she knew what I wanted and rolled her hips, causing a moan to rattle in my chest.

"I'd prefer you not punch Vincent again."

I ran my hands up her plaid-covered thighs and sat up, letting the promise of a kiss linger a couple of inches from her lips. "How 'bout we don't mention Vincent anymore tonight?"

Her warm breath washed over me as she giggled before leaning back a bit and pulling her shirt up and over her head. I had to stop myself from reaching for her skin so I could enjoy the sight of her.

She rolled her hips and giggled again, causing me to groan louder. "You should know better than to be jealous of him."

"Oh yeah?" I spun us around, she now under me, her arms above her head and spelled in place without the need for love-cuffs. I trailed my finger between her breasts down to her belly, teasing the pit of her hip and along the hem of her pyjama bottoms before slipping them off. "You like it when I get jealous."

Languid anticipation drifted along the connection. "I do if it means this kind of attention."

I couldn't help but laugh. I didn't have to ask how much she wanted me. Torqued up desire through the connection was a hair trigger away from throwing us into chaos. Hot and heavy wasn't a bad thing, but pausing to ensure she was pleasured did as much for her as it did for me, and showed her I cared for more than myself.

A rush of heat soared through us as I removed her lace underwear, her expression a challenge and a question of what I meant to do next.

When I backed up and spread her thighs, my intentions were clear. When expectancy overruled patience—hers or mine or both—we lost ourselves to everything but the feeling of pleasure until we were twin husks of sweat-slicked exhaustion.

———

I know this room. No, wait, do I?

People stood in two rows out in front of me, the rows facing each other in a sparse dark room. Familiar. The vibe or the faces, maybe.

"I look forward to our reunion, Son." My father stepped into the forefront, walking through the gauntlet of men towards me.

Another man nodded at him. Brandon. Shoulders straight, hands clasped behind his back. I could have been a piece of shit like my brother had I drank the Kool-Aid a while longer. Did he set this up?

My father looked at him with something close to gratitude or as if acknowledging a job done by a servant. Done at his command without a hint of outward pride.

My father lifted his chin, staring down at me. "Your aversion to my reign has been absolved with the confirmation of a truce."

I couldn't move. My arms and legs were pinned with invisible dead weight. He meant the truce with Rosemary. What the fuck did he have to do with it?

My father laughed in a low, smug celebration. "Rosemary is no longer one within my flock, but she and her substandard coven still wade within dark waters. Now that you have led your desperate Sect and deplorable Elders to our willing ends, no righteous coven will consider you sided with that of the idealistic Magics you defected to. You will be branded traitors. And when we show alongside the ungrateful womb who bore you, this will be indisputable. We will slaughter you and all others to ensure the Master's ascension."

Again, I tried to move, tried to speak. Struggling did nothing. However he did it, Tobias had a tight hold. I struggled more. My ribcage burned. I tried to grab at it and couldn't move my hands. Couldn't even look around.

Shit, Sophie. She was beside me before I passed out. Could Tobias hurt her? I couldn't turn to the side to find her. A cowardly part of me was too scared to if he let me.

Tobias moved, and I saw a symbol on the wall, jagged and damning. A sigil of judgment.

I did know this room.

Flashes of shocking pain tightened in my gut as if my father's blade sliced me open again. The sensation of blood dripping down my bare thighs was real enough to make me nauseated. The witnesses standing and doing nothing were like those who watched my father tear up his heir as if he were carving the holiday ham. They didn't care. They had a role here, but it wasn't to save me. They wouldn't help me. They were the same faces I saw while I died and the first ones I saw when I was brought back, when I wished my father had ended it all.

"My presence in your dream state comes with purpose. I care not of your fantasies of the woman at your side who can hear my words and knows my face but to make it known that I myself will end your life with great pleasure." The sentence rolled off his tongue as if stating the fact was delight enough. "Too many times have my attempts to quell your conscience failed. I consider you an adversary worth extinguishing since you carry my blood with such dishonour. Fight as you might, you will die."

"Where is he?!"

A high-pitched scream echoed off my ringing skull. Power set me on fire, breaking what kept me helpless. I rushed forward with blurring speed, landing a bone-crunching blow as my brother cradled his blood-gushing face on the ground.

A redhead threw her body over him, screaming for me to stop.

Kim?

She moved Brandon's hands. Blood dripped across his chin and nose onto my carpet. Shit. Not my brother. Kim's Blind boyfriend, Frog.

"What the fuck are you doing in my house?"

Kim got in my face, her hatred-fuelled screaming driving my blood pressure higher.

Everything went black.

Voices. Bright light. Insides burning.

I rolled onto my side and heaved. Pressing into my stinging sinuses, I gagged at the stench of last nights' whisky dessert.

Kim's voice hovered around the room. Sophie responded to her complaints un-Sophie-like. Too calm. Too much like Nya.

Grabbing anything I could for leverage got me to my knees. Kim paced as Sophie sat on the side of the bed staring down at me. She took a deep breath, and my gut pain drained away so fast the room swayed. The dresser shook when I fell against it.

I looked for Frog. His chest moved, but he was out.

"I thought it was your brother, too." Sophie was herself again. "Nya's power stopped you from being stupid. Not sorry, though I didn't plan it."

"You could have killed him!" Kim checked Frog's throat for a heartbeat.

I pulled on sweatpants since I was buck-ass naked. "He's lucky we're not burying him in an unmarked grave in my backyard. Perfect timing for my father's torture scene to end with your boyfriend, who happens to look like my brother, deciding to bitch slap me in my sleep. Real fucking winner by the way."

Kim glared at Sophie.

Sophie tightened her robe. "Don't look at me like that. You're lucky Donovan's not the gun-toting type. Why didn't you spell Frog before waiting until he got his ass beat? And what's with the midnight visit? Booty calls shouldn't end in blood."

Kim ran her hands through her hair. "I slipped up."

"Jesus Christ, Kim. How much does your boytoy know?"

"Nothing!"

Sophie gave me that look, a silent nudge to calm my shit. "Out with it, girl. You know I love you, but we're in damage control mode."

Turns out Kim mentioned something about Caine's hair growing back, forgetting her audience was a Blind idiot and she wasn't supposed to know anything about Caine, though she thought I was the asshole for reminding her of this.

"Okay, you two." Sophie kept us in line. "Get to the climax, Kim. I'm over the foreplay."

Kim huffed and explained the last time Frog spoke to Caine, Caine mentioned meeting Sophie. Frog joked about staying clear of Donovan or giving him a call so Frog could watch Caine take him down. I laughed at this. Kim gave me a death glare then went on with her fuckup of mentioning Caine's growing hair. Frog knew Kim had seen Caine when everyone thought he was missing, and she was too inept at backpedalling and too panicked to stop him from rushing over to confront me, he assuming I had done something to Caine.

"So, he figured, what? That I had Caine chained up in my basement because I'm a jealous psychopath?"

"People do worse for less." Point Kim.

I doubted Frog intended to kill me. Not that this would have mattered if I hadn't stopped.

I wrapped the bastard up in a binding spell, healed him, and woke him up so we could see how far he was going to take this.

When he shot awake and realized he couldn't move, he glared at Sophie.

"Bitch! Let me go."

Sophie laughed. "This bitch could have let him kill you. You should thank me."

"Thank you? What the fuck d'you do to Caine?" His angry glares were for Kim as well, though she wilted beneath them.

The cool wall on my naked back helped douse my inner flames a bit. "Caine fucked himself over, Froggy-boy. Question is, how much should you know?"

"We can erase his mind."

Frog stared up at Kim. "Who the fuck are you?"

She didn't respond. Leave it to her to flake and make us out as the bad guys.

"Well, bestie. Here's your chance. Tell all, see if he can take it. If not, you got a foolproof backup plan."

"Or we can scrub you from his mind all together." I swiped at my nose, a drop of blood staining my hand. "Might leave some holes, but I bet you won't be able to tell a difference."

Sophie hit me with another silent nudge to relax. I gave Kim options. Not my fault she if didn't like them.

Sophie insisted on giving them space to talk, which meant me leaving my own damn room since we left Frog bound. Frog yelled a few times before he went silent. I didn't think Kim had the stones to shut the wanker up. Did she use her power on him to get a word in?

I slid down the hall wall to sit next to Sophie. "She should've ended this a long time ago."

"She loves him. Couldn't stand the thought of him not loving her."

"Then she shouldn't've went for a Blind guy."

"Can't always help who you love."

"No, but you can help who you hurt by not dragging them into a shit-pile of drama they can't fathom."

She agreed though didn't comment.

Silence dragged out as we waited. It felt like a long time, and all I wanted to do was go back to bed. If it didn't mean potentially putting us back in my father's hands, I would have found another room. He knew about the truce, and he planned on being at the Creation opening to help our enemies out and to take me down as a bonus. Father of the year right there.

The click of my bedroom door handle was loud in the quiet house. Kim left the door open in invitation.

Frog was still magically tied down. The look on his face was one of heavy knowledge and incredulous reality. I never went through this, but I saw it on Sophie and other enlightened Blind before her.

"Let him go." Kim's eyes were bloodshot.

"No. How was your talk?" I was happy Sophie didn't argue with me on this.

"Informative." Frog didn't lift his gaze to us, his tone set to growl.

Both Kim and Frog claimed he could handle the secret. The particulars of their relationship weren't divulged, but I didn't give a shit.

I looked away from Kim to her not-so-Blind boytoy. "Too bad I don't believe you."

Boytoy peered up at me. "Fuck you, asshole."

"Your thoughts, moron. I can hear them. As soon as you scurry away from us, you're going straight to your and Caine's friend Dom to tell him all about it. You're pretty sure he hooked up with that chick from the club you guys hit up last weekend. Apparently, you didn't care for her friend because she smelled like stale Sugar Crisp cereal."

Frog's eyes narrowed as Kim looked to boytoy with betrayal.

Sophie knelt in front of the guy. Sick pride hit me when he flinched. She placed her palm on his chest. He cringed in a whole-body flinch as power rolled through the connection. Soul Readings were helpful, but I wasn't sure why she did it in this case.

When done, she stood and crossed her arms. "You love her. I see that in your soul. You thought Kim was someone you could trust. What she lied about was to protect an entire race of people. We're in constant danger, and she's gone to great lengths to keep you from that danger. Makes her more amazing than you thought she was, not less."

Sophie sat on the edge of the bed. "Caine lied to you, too." His face an array of emotions as she explained how Caine was in a sleeping curse, how he was freed, and then moved to his current entrapment.

Frog was quiet, but his brain was wide open and whirling with thoughts. He came to gain information about Caine, but he learned a lot more than he bargained for.

"If you can keep your trap shut, Kim'll stand by you. Doesn't mean you can break into my house and fuck with me again without ending up as ritual ingredients."

"Don't be a dick." Kim huffed. "Don't listen to him. We don't use human parts. Well, we do, but not like in the movies. It's voluntary."

"Unless they're Tainted, evil fuckers. They'll use anything." My correction was necessary. Kim could coddle Frog all she wanted, but I wasn't about to sand down the ragged edges of the truth.

Kim clucked her tongue. "Really, asshole? Not helping."

"Not trying to." Fear could be a good motivator, and in this case, it could save his life. "You realize if you lie, I'll kill you and the buddies you squeal to, right?"

Frog shook his head as if unimpressed.

"He means it." Something about how Sophie said this made the biggest impact. Whether he believed it or not, he knew we were serious and dropped the macho man bravado enough for Sophie to cut the binding spell.

Frog scrambled to his feet, back straight. His tough guy act not the least bit intimidating, but I understood his need to save face. Everyone in the room, including his girlfriend, was more dangerous than him.

"This is the second time you've attacked me unprovoked."

His jaw flexed. "Sorry. I guess."

"Nah, he deserved the first one." Sophie's slight smile eased Frog's discomfort a fraction.

"Get Caine out of—"

"Diluculo." Kim was trying to be helpful but slunk back as if speaking out of turn.

He turned back to Sophie. "Get Caine out of there, and I'll forget about it all. I don't know what the fuck I stepped in, but this isn't...I don't know how Caine deals with this."

"Well, once you know, you can't un-know it. Unless we make you." Sophie raised her hands. "Not a threat. If you want to forget all you learned, we can arrange that and make you think Caine will come up for air when he's had enough tits and tequila on whatever island he disappeared to."

Exhaustion darkened the guy's features. "I really wish Caine was off getting tail on a beach somewhere."

Sophie's smile was sad. "Me, too."

A selfish sprig of happiness hit me in the feels at this. Sophie wanted Caine safe but was okay with him catching a workout with someone else if it meant he was.

I clapped my hands together. "Great. How 'bout we take this party somewhere other than my bedroom?"

I grabbed a shirt while Sophie quickly dressed before we met Kim and Frog in the kitchen. Frog didn't move with his normal overconfidence. Guarded was closer to any description I could drum up, which meant the ape was smart enough to know he was not the top of the food chain. I was surprised he wasn't racing out the door. Maybe too afraid it would look suspicious, like he was going to race off and find Dom anyway. Kim could leave, too, though she had to be apprised of Tobias's threat and connection to

Rosemary outside the obviousness of them contributing to my DNA.

I refused to bleed out my tragic history right now. Kim's imagination could fill in the blanks if Sophie hadn't already told her. As could Frog since I had no intention of share-time with the guy.

Revenge, in any fashion, was unsurprising. My father never gave up on his mission to take me down or turn me into the heir he bred, and I was never deluded enough to believe he had. Living everyday as if it was my last outside the confines of a Tainted coven worked until Sophie entered the picture. Now I had every reason to stay far away from anything my father touched.

What I did tell them was facts about my father's coven as well as what I knew about Rosemary's and how this pertained to the invasion into our dream world. Kim was surprised Tobias could manage it to not only myself but Sophie as well. Frog didn't say a word. The guy probably didn't believe any of it but gave a slow nod after I explained why he dodged a bullet by attacking me at that precise moment and how badly it could have ended.

Andy came out, sleepy, having heard voices, ending our conversation. Sophie told him to get dressed for the day, and she would fix him cereal. He yawned and went back to his room, bringing Bosco with him. It was early, but not too early for morning cartoons.

Sophie clued Frog in on who Andy was and why he was with us. Her hands shook a bit as she did. She hid it the best she could while pouring orange juice into a small glass for Andy's breakfast.

The sound of the front door opening had me rushing out of the kitchen to confront whoever came in. Vincent stood shaking snow off his shoulders. We didn't feel the sensation of him crossing the barrier into the house. Not with Frog either, unless the dream state my father trapped us in blocked us from the warning.

"I thought you were going to fix the wards? Forget something when you tucked-tail last night?"

Vincent's stare followed over my shoulder to see a six-foot-five stranger in my kitchen.

I sighed. "Kim's plaything, Frog. Recently awakened Blind. As in, baby fresh."

Vincent approached Frog without saying a word, presumably listening in on the guy's thoughts.

Frog saw something in Vincent he didn't see in me—the immediate knowledge of looking at someone who would bury him. Frog was right. Vincent could kill him cleanly, but it proved the guy was an idiot if he thought I couldn't.

Vincent turned down a drink Sophie offered and sanded his hands together. "We are ready to proceed with the alternative as soon as the Sovereignty is removed from power."

No one said anything for a moment.

"Umm, wow. I feel like we should clap." Sophie wasn't joking. "Do we get to know what it is?"

Vincent's gaze wavered on Frog. "A Creation."

Perfect. People joked about sending criminals to an island to keep them from harming others. Another Australia full of those a tad harder to curtail then the thieves and murderers in the sun-baked sand. This was better. A jail system hidden within a Creation could not be stumbled upon by the Blind.

Vincent pressed the extensive vetting of lawyers, judges, guards, administrators, psychiatrists, and those devoted to assessments and re-education conducive to eventual release where possible. Revolutionary when considering current incarceration methods, even for the Blind. All personnel involved were voted upon and found worthy of their posts as to better avoid corruption issues like with the Sovereignty. Families of the accused will also play a role and be kept apprised of their loved one's status while within the system.

All well and dandy, but first we needed to take down the current regime and survive the reopening of Diluculo. Vincent was still adamant his family should be killed before the reopening, that others were suffering every moment they lived.

I grabbed the premonition pages from the kitchen table and tossed them in Vincent's direction. "It doesn't matter. The premonition dictates us reopening the Creation before the 'Son of Law' gets his crew together."

He didn't look down at them. "It is not uncommon for premonitions of this sort to be out of sync."

"I'd believe it except it states in the same verse that an 'evil brings the Son of Law to his blood enemies while the crowned enlightens the Blind'."

Kim plunked into an island stool. "My head hurts. Spell it out for me."

"Evar gets loose."

"Oh. Wonderful." She looked at Frog. "Extremely uncool."

"No matter how you read it, Evar gets out. Then your blood enemies,"—I pointed at Vincent—"clearly your fucked-up family, who make mine look like the *Brady Bunch*, are dealt with by your band of rebellious misfits. I've been staring at those pages since the Creation was closed. That's how it's going down."

Sophie popped up to sit on the counter, looking far too childlike. "Can't we change it since we know it's going to happen?"

"While I love you for your optimism, babe, I don't have an answer. Either way, we know Magics from the Sovereignty will be outside Diluculo. Why risk exposure by bringing the fight to their doorstep?"

"Because my brother will not be at Diluculo, which means my family and the Sovereignty survives."

I scratched my two-day stubble. "Maybe, but at Diluculo we have a chance to strike down some of the Sovereignty's heavy hitters before meeting them in their offices. Having Evar on the loose will be an issue for them as much as it is for us. Even if they want to use Evaristus, he won't play ball, and will expose Magics to the world. The Sovereignty might be pricks, but they're all for keeping our power a secret so they can exploit it. They may help with Evar. When it comes down to it, we'll need them."

Silence meant I made a point he had to live with whether he wanted to or not.

"We will need to speak with Caine again."

"What? Why?" Dread stuck in my chest.

Kim's self-indulgent smile grated me. "As if you don't know why. You just don't want a worm in your head again."

I shot her the finger. "Then you do it."

Vincent fixed his glasses. "It would be done without your involvement if possible."

"Thanks for making me feel extra special."

Vincent ignored me and looked to Sophie. "Can you contact Olive to do so tonight?"

Sophie opened her mouth to respond.

I raised my hand. "Wait a sec. Tonight? I just talked to the guy!"

"Much can happen in the span of hours let alone a night. Caine may have made his move on Evaristus. If they can defeat him or even Loring while inside, much will be taken care of for us."

"Or he could've gotten his ass killed!" I paced the floor. "He's not Caine anymore. He's a Caine version of Gareth. Balls of steel get people killed, and once he heard we'd be moving on the Creation, he'd take the opportunity to move on Jet."

"You have only solidified my point."

I thought back to what he said. "Fuck me."

20

FLASHES OF HELL

Caine

Telling myself it was a reconnaissance mission was a lie not even I could swallow. Since Ness and Derek knew me best, they were on board, detecting the guise of an assignment the moment I mentioned it, though John and Tate were complacent enough to have faith. They were in this mess because of me. I knew it, and I hated it. The understanding in the eyes of Ness and Derek helped, but I still felt like a schmuck.

Suiting up for battle doesn't take long when you have nothing to put on. Armour would have been nice, but it did little against magic. Gareth was handy backup and took care of most of the enemy simultaneously when the mood struck him. Even now, the vibrations of power coursed through my blood, strengthening me, but unless I fought for the others' safety, Gareth wouldn't.

Last thing I wanted was to watch Ness die bloody and to burn her bones in fire like she wanted. Burying her there or leaving her to rot was something she could never handle, and, unfortunately, when your everyday consisted of death, it was a conversation we all had.

I sent Gareth's senses out like an umbrella, covering the woods with invisible feelers, detecting minute movements of the Creation's creatures, looking for anything that might kill us. An elusive buck not far off to the northeast warned his dwindling herd and moved as far from us as the Creation would allow without running into the devotees' stomachs. These weren't the creatures we were worried about, but having them gone made for fewer distractions when feeling like you could eat a hippo. Squirrels and rats were tastier than I ever imagined, but they didn't stop the hunger pains.

Fanned out like a search party, I was dead center, Ness on my left flank, Derek on my right, while John and Tate took up the ends of our party. Quick and steady, we moved towards the area they kept Jet. Always close enough to Evar and Loring to be used whenever they needed, so of course, we were walking into the dragon's lair.

Tension was piano-wire tight. Communication never crossed our lips, hand signals being the safest option when our thoughts could be rifled through if left open.

Getting closer to our target meant ramping up our intuition and seeing passed Evar and Loring's wards. Even Masters had their back-up plans. Guess they had to sleep at some point.

Pain hit a nerve in my back. Not true pain, but a signal we were close and set off the wards, ones we expected. As I pushed forward, an image coupled the pain. One of Evar ending his victim with a strike through their back as they ran in fear, the emotion with the vision meant to overwhelm me and get my ass running away. The first time this happened, I backpedalled a step, but we knew what to expect and fought through the bloody flashes.

The closer to Evar and Loring we pushed, the more our bodies quivered as we saw bursts of limbs torn off, heads rolled with broken necks, and escalating blood and gore as well as the smells. Encased in fire without the scorching flesh had Derek growling in pain. Mind over matter was easier for me when I had two minds to deal with it, but Ness was twitching all over as she refused to let whatever horrors were in her head overwhelm her.

When we saw the cabins Evar had his Puppets slaved over rebuilding, we were covered in a layer of sweat, muscles shaking, exhaustion levels tested. We survived the worst while devotees paced their perimeter and talked in twos about thirty yards away. Trapping devotees was easier on the conscience, knowing they deserved it.

Ness kept an illusion up around us so the devotees would see the trees they were already looking at. They didn't tend to be detail focused, so it was easy, or so she said. This allowed us to gather inside the wards to work out a plan. They didn't argue with me even though I knew some wanted to.

Ness crawled to the closest devotee. Still shielding herself, she added the illusion of the devotee standing directly next to the man himself. The man gasped at his clone, and Ness pulled him inside the curtain we all hid behind. His eyes widened a moment before I snapped his neck so he couldn't warn others.

We inch-wormed our way closer to our target, snatching and incapacitating devotees as we went. Ness updated her illusion to include the devotees we took down, so anyone looking wouldn't see their comrades were missing. Over the time trapped in here, we had a lot of practice at this slow assault. We were golden, and we knew it.

With her illusion in place, it gave us access to the entire left side of the cabin we creeped up on. It didn't seem like much, but Ness could stay where she was, keep Felix at her side to deal with curious devotees, and give the rest of us free rein.

Peering through windows and gaping wall boards, we found someone tying his thick black hair back and scratching at his bushy beard before turning around.

Evaristus.

Evar had no soul, and to look into the man's shadow-darkened black eyes and grey pallor, it was an easy guess without Sophie's Soul Seeing insight.

The psychopath may have found a way to bring his body parts back together after we tore him apart and shut him up tight in the earth, but it left him riddled with scars, his soulless body an array of dark lines. Nothing deformed like Loring, yet every discoloured pucker made me smile for the fight still fresh in my mind as it proved Evaristus wasn't untouchable no matter his age.

If the Puppeteer knew we skulked around, he didn't care. He picked at a plate of food as devotees moved around him like worker bees. Every tabletop was covered in piles of paper, scrolls, and tomes. He was searching for something, maybe a way out, like we were. I didn't care, I needed to find Jet.

I pulled myself away from the enemy, keeping an image of Jet in my mind. She was the goal here.

We rounded the cabin, taking out a couple more devotees. A whimper from inside a large bush stopped our advancement. Someone was hiding. Why didn't they attack? Hiding out in a mess of tangled vine and branches was a quick way to piss off the Master and become a Puppet.

"Caine?" The weak voice came from inside the bush.

Rolling thunder answered it.

21

SUCH LENGTHS

Donovan

"I can't believe I'm doing this again. Sober! Why doesn't your aunt have a bar up here? Prime place to get trashed." I wiped sweaty palms on my jeans craving a drink enough to make Sophie wet her lips and twist her long hair around her hand.

She shifted on her footstool across from mine, using what she called "grounding skills". Whatever it was, it helped a bit but didn't change my attitude when I saw Kim's blond beefcake's face screwed up looking at things on the Ballard shelves as if he would rather stick his hands in a music festival porta-potty than touch them. Asshat was too closed-minded to comprehend what he was looking at. His kind was the reason we needed secret attics in the first place.

"Does he really need to be here?"

"It's the only way he'll know all this is real and the only way to prove Caine's alive so he'll shut up about it. Caine's his normal."

"Yeah, well, he won't be thinking Caine's so normal once he sees him."

"No, he won't."

Shit. Caine was special to Sophie, too, and he wasn't her normal Caine either. I couldn't win. And now I was getting ready to let a worm burrow into my head to give her the chance to see him and verify he was still alive. Chivalry was alive and fucked up.

The whole Coven didn't need to be there. Not my Sect, the Ballards, or the Mother Coven, but as far as I was concerned, having the Elders, Sophie's aunts including Olive, and the Apporter was more than enough to witness the drama firsthand and be sure it was caught by another Recollection Plant.

Sophie's weird aunts were busy fussing over the worm like a newborn baby as the Elders and Olson stood off to the side talking lowly to each other. The way Vincent kept looking at Sophie made me want to punch him again. Not like he wanted to jump her bones, but still. He was hovering too much.

The Pompeii Worm was taken out of its new home, a dark aquarium with simulated temperature of deep-sea hydrothermal vents. It was added to the Tuareg bowl, but not before I caught a glimpse of the furry bastard. Hot damn. It was a plump little heifer of a thing, now. As if it wasn't healthy enough before it doubled in size.

Even Frog looked sorry for me. As if I needed the jock's sympathy.

A tap on my leg drew my attention back to Sophie. "I could use last night as our distraction, though it was more my treat."

"Between your thighs in any form is fine by me."

Her smile at this was distraction enough.

The vision came from Sophie's perspective, the sensation both ours as experienced in the moment. Bowing my head was not within my control, and her excellent memory made it difficult not to vocalize the effects. I didn't care who heard but knew Sophie would.

Iris began the incantation for the Nexus Transference spell as Veata began the one for Remote Viewing, their voices below the intoxicating sound of Sophie's moans.

I tilted my head back, knowing what was to come. Pain shot

through my nose into my brain. I screamed and grabbed at my head, falling forward, and feeling wet grass beneath my hands.

Wet grass? The pain vanished. I looked around, seeing the camp the survivors constructed. Not the same as the last camp. They moved again.

Panicked voices came from a group of people. I stumbled when someone ran into me, they looked back a moment before racing off to join the others in the huddle. Someone was hurt.

Don't be Caine. Please, don't be Caine.

"Do not move him." Caine's voice. Too stiff, not so Caine-like.

I ran up on the group and grabbed Caine's shoulder. "What happened?"

He spun and grabbed my shirt, face inches from mine, and pulled me down next to him. "Heal him!"

"Him" was the one with hawk-eyes, Derek. Blood poured out of the guy from his neck and chest. The rags of his clothes so saturated I couldn't tell from where.

"Why can't you?" Gareth had to have healing abilities even if Caine didn't.

"Do it!"

Jesus fuck. Fine.

I sparked the charge of my power, feeling healing run through me and into Hawk-Eyes.

Hawk-Eyes awoke in a rage as if in mid-attack. I caught a right hook to the jaw before the others jumped in to stop him.

Caine kept me from a reactive retaliation as everyone talked over each other in a flurry of chaos.

Hawk-Eyes righted his twisted shirt. "You?"

"Who's he?" The man who ran into me, and the stares of others, wanted to know.

"This is Donovan, my Sect Leader." Many looked astonished Caine even had a leader. "Your eyes fool you as he is not on this side of the veil. A great spell brings him to us as those on the outside ready to release the hold on this Creation. If you see him again, trust his instruction."

Nothing about the speech was from Caine. Far too Gareth to be comfortable. Caine may not be my bestie, but to see the guy talk and know it wasn't him gave me the jeebies.

Many looked at me with a glint of paranoia. Understandable considering how many Puppets they had faced, though Caine's word held weight. They retained their guarded stance and allowed Caine and me to walk away together without chasing after us or insisting Caine answer questions about the plan to bust them out of the Creation. They looked to Ness instead. She threw her hands up, unwilling to get into it with them.

Following Caine to a pile of logs, he surprised me by lifting two tied pieces and having it all fall into place like a pop-up tent from Canadian Tire. Practical considering how much they must move, but more inventive than I thought he was capable of.

Caine sparked an instant fire.

I took a seat on a sodden log as Caine added tinder to the small fire for some life beyond his magic. "You could've healed him yourself. Why have me do it?"

"Now, when the time comes, they will trust you with their lives."

The delivery was so indifferent. Our history didn't nurture any brand of friendship, but Caine had to be in there somewhere.

"We've made a truce that will turn most of our Mother Coven against us." Caine remained quiet as I explained Rosemary and the conditions of our pact, explaining what players to expect on the outside.

"The Covens will reunite in our success."

"Right. Guess we'll see."

Caine sat back onto the grass and pulled something from his pocket. Looked like a tangle of fabric, but I couldn't tell. I had to get him talking, or I was wasting time with a worm in my head.

"Sophie's not sure about fusing her powers anymore."

As soon as I said her name, something in Caine's eyes cleared, and I knew I was looking at him and not Gareth for the first time. Minute twitches pulled at the muscles in his face as if struggling to keep himself with me, his grasp tenuous.

"She needs to." Caine pressed on a spot under his eye. "She'll die if she doesn't."

"How do you know that?"

"Gareth knows."

"Will she lose herself?"

"No." A very Caine-like smile answered, somewhat forced so I was confused on who spoke. "Gareth's and my union was necessary for many reasons. I'm told once our freedom is guaranteed our roles will change."

"Hmm. If Gareth has the ability to change roles, then how do you know he won't take it back whenever he wants a joyride in a new century? This is almost as bad as being a Puppet."

He shook his head. "Gareth has purpose. He's not there all the time. Only when the occasion calls."

He didn't specify if Gareth gave him a choice when the occasion came knocking.

"I've heard what Gareth thinks of the truce. What do you think?"

Caine's lips twisted in thought. "By the sounds of it, you were desperate, so instead of gaining another enemy, you're bound for a short time in a common cause. Makes reckless sense. Having part of the Coven against you doesn't sound good. Politics are...annoying."

I laughed, happy to get what I expected from the guy. I didn't care if he agreed with us as long as it was him answering.

"How was Derek injured?"

He rubbed his hands together. "Jet."

When he didn't speak anything more, I reached out my hand. "Show me. No offence, but with you and Gareth switching places so seamlessly, I can't tell what's true, and I'd rather not have to try and see through a filter."

Caine nodded and extended his hand to grab mine.

My hands—Caine's hands—tore at branches or vines as thunder rumbled above. Hawk-Eyes and another male had an ear cocked at a bush, it making mewling noises. They were confused at what they were hearing and kept checking over their shoulders as if expecting an ambush. Caine didn't care who was coming or who heard him. Jet was in there. Stinging slices into my hands, Caine's hands, didn't slow me down, I needed to get to her.

The vines started moving on their own. Caine stepped back as the knotted vines moved like snakes uncoiling themselves, revealing a hollow center. On the dirt floor of the brush was a body.

Jet.

Curled into the fetal position, Jet was dirty and half-starved. He knelt next to her, calling her name.

Her eyes fluttered open.

"Come on, Jet. Let's get out of here."

She started screaming, pushing him out of the dome of leaves and vines. "The dead can't die! Leave! You can't kill the soulless! The dead can't die!"

Caine grabbed her arms, stopping her from hitting him. The screaming went silent. She straightened and stared at him in an odd way, so unlike herself.

Caine scrambled back, tripping over himself to escape the cocoon of vines.

Jet followed, stepping out of her little prison, and stood with controlled grace her thin body couldn't have done on its own. Evar's magic bloomed within her, untangling her unruly long blonde hair, the natural pallor of her skin returned, filling out her cheeks and sunken rings around her eyes. In a sick way, Evar taking her over was keeping her alive.

"Your record for failure is impressive." Evar's strength filled Jet's voice, a strength she lacked with a foreign cadence that made me grit my teeth.

Thunder increased as the voices of Puppets and devotees grew, Evar bringing them out of hiding to protect their Master as the sky opened up with rain.

Jet struck out at a man with them. He died before he hit the ground.

Wind whipped up as Puppets and devotees came at them from all sides. Jet hovered above them with a goading grin as the blood of the survivor she killed clung to her soiled clothing.

Caine came back in view instead of Jet. He had pulled his hand away from me, cutting me off from whatever happened next. I didn't need to see the destruction Jet brought down on them or the damage Evar's people created. The survivors were dwindling, and they weren't freeing enough Puppets to re-stock their ranks.

"We tried to get her back, but Evar's holding on tight." Caine stared at the small fire. "He can read her memories and knows I'm important to her. Every time we try, more of us die. Derek was close. It could have been worse. It has been worse. Some of them were Blind before they were Puppets. All they can do is run, and most have died trying. Both Evar and Loring are alive, and we're around long enough to be pawns. I don't know how much longer we can keep this up."

"I see that." And I did. The others were in survival mode, but they were no match for an offensive attack against some of the oldest Magics of our time. "We haven't found the discus. We know what it looks like now as we saw it through a visual repeat of the premonition, but it's not where we hoped it would be."

Caine gave a small nod as if expecting I would disappoint him.

Felix ran up on us. "Incoming!"

Caine sprung to his feet. "Where?"

"West treeline." Felix pointed. "I tried to keep up the illusion, but I'm sorry. I was too tired."

"Where's Ness?"

"Sleeping."

"I'll get her. Round everyone up."

Caine was moving before spouting orders at Felix. I followed Caine to a lean-to with ratty fabric for the facade of privacy. Caine whipped it aside and bent over who I assumed was Ness before pulling her out, she halfway to her feet before waking.

"Why didn't he wake me up?" She collapsed her lean-to and shoved it with a few things into a bag she slung over her shoulders like a backpack, ready in seconds.

"Doesn't matter. Incoming. West treeline. Help with the others."

The enemy were shadows in the trees, closing the distance. I didn't know if I could die in here or kill others, but I could heal, which meant my power was accessible.

"How's this work?" We backpedalled, shuffling the slower moving survivors into a run in the opposite direction.

Caine turned with a deadlocked stare on his enemies. "Run or fight."

Power poured out of the guy and slammed me in the chest. Far more powerful than anything I had felt from him before as I wasn't so close to the action last time.

Light flashed in the forest. Caine shot his arms up over his head. A sparking cage of magic popped up like a wool blanket in front of us, stinging my eyes, before it was shot into the trees. Puppets and devotees caught in his cage-like web were electrified, fizzled out, and turned to ash. Caine shoved my face into the dirt half-a-second before the evading Magics who dodged Caine's hit almost decapitated my ass.

We scrambled up and took off to find the others who made good of the head start Caine gave them.

"This way!" Caine grabbed my shirt and pulled me towards the trees on our right.

Fallen logs and forest debris of denser brush slowed us down, but trees took the hit our bodies could do without.

A man with a brush cut kept pace with us, his asshole grin telling me he wasn't one of the survivors. His power of celerity helped him catch up as his buddies were struggling yards behind us.

I tossed some magic his way, trying to trip him up. The man evaded the hit and telekinetically lifted a fallen branch at my feet, sending me flying into open air, careening into the dirt, the skin of my hands, arms, and face thrashed.

I spun onto my back, anticipating another attack. A steel-toe smashed into my jaw, the crunch of cartilage in my face and nose laying me out.

Power surged from somewhere instinctual within me and cut through my blinding rage. An oppressive shadow curled over me gripping a power-infused blade. Buzz Cut was hit by a stream of power from my hands and sent him flying into a tree with a fleshy crack, falling in a heap of smoking flesh.

"Hurry!"

I sat in time to see Caine take off.

Up on my feet, I grabbed the blade from the dead guy's steak-scorched hand. A pitchfork of agony shot through my ear. The blade? I dropped it. The pain increased to skull-gripping intensity. Not the blade.

"No! Don't pull me out yet!"

The point of steeping my brain in worm goo was to see what the survivors were working with. No way I was coming back in in a few hours to check if they survived.

The pain ceased. They were backing off. I panted and pushed to my feet, my neck aching as I grabbed the knife and took off to catch up to Caine, refusing to look back at how close the enemy was. The energy from the cloud of power building behind me was enough to know if I didn't hurry the fuck up, I would be a burnt-out husk on this plane and the one in the attic. Sophie's aunts would rip my skull open with their bare hands and scoop out their precious worm.

And people call me a psycho.

A melodic whistle stopped me. I ignored a pinching digging in my rib under my arm and looked around, gripping the knife's handle, scanning the trees, and coming up with nothing. The sound came again. I followed it through thick brush and downed trees, it increasing in frequency as if confirming my direction as I fought the nagging paranoia of the enemy waiting to pounce on my nutsack the moment I got within striking distance.

A cabin popped up in front of my face. I skidded to a stop and slipped through a mud puddle.

"Shhh." Caine knelt next to the cabin, the other survivors behind him, Ness and Felix standing narrow-eyed in concentration.

We were in one of their illusions, hidden from the enemy.

Whatever the illusions they chose, the enemy kept pushing forward, running or walking, focused on a target they thought they had in their crosshairs. Each was as filthy and blood-caked as the survivors. The Puppets were different from the devotees. With their faculties intact, they complained to each other and strolled behind the Puppets, letting Evar's playthings take the frontlines as further protection. Morons. As soon as the Puppets were cut down or worn out, Evar would use his precious devotees next. They had to have known this.

They disappeared in the trees before the survivors allowed themselves a moment of relaxation.

I got up and felt the tug of discomfort under my arm again. Maybe a broken rib? I sent some healing power over my body, but the ache worsened with every inhale. Guess I needed to get out of here before I could do any true healing.

Caine placed a hand on the small of Ness's back. She blinked with a small smile. She said something to her brother, who nodded, and looked to take on her load of the illusion to cover the group and the cabin for them to take a break in.

I leaned onto the cabin wall and flinched, putting my arm down as a spark of pain flashed through my ribs.

Ness approached, looking in my eyes. "They watchin' again?"

I nodded. "So is Frog."

Caine glared at me in confusion.

"Good." Ness either didn't care or didn't know who Frog was. "Now maybe they'll hurry their lazy asses up and crack this egg open already."

"Lazy?"

Caine cut off her reply. "You have to find the discus."

I pulled my glare away from Ness. "No kidding." Licks of pain spider-veined through my chest. I pressed my finger into my breastbone, finding my shirt shredded from the fall. "My father's coven will also be outside Diluculo. Someone else to dodge when you break out since he's not included in the truce. Same with assholes from the Sovereignty."

"The Sovereignty?" It surprised me Ness knew who they were, but she was smart enough to know what this meant.

"Will Eli and Bernie be there?"

"They're stupid enough, so I'd bet on it."

"Wanting their kid back is stupid?" Ness cocked her head with so much attitude I would have laughed if I wasn't annoyed at her existence.

"Don't worry, princess. I'm sure your boyfriend's family will welcome you with open arms."

A sparkle of black danced in front of my eyes. Dizziness weakened my knees. Something hard hit my shoulder and then my ass, jarring up my spine. When my sight cleared, I was on the ground, having slid down the cabin wall. My lungs screamed in zapping pain and had me cramped over fighting for my next breath.

Ness stood behind Caine, she sneering down at me. "What's wrong with him? Besides the obvious."

I sneered back at her, breathing through the pain. "Your sexual tension's making me nauseous."

Ness made a throaty noise and stalked off.

Caine looked after her but didn't follow. "What *is* wrong with you?"

"Broken rib, I think, but I'm not healing. My cue to go." I handed him the knife I got from the Magic who attacked me. No ordinary knife, and some of the Blind survivors could use it.

"Don't return until you're outside the gates or leaving us in here for good. Even if Evar and Loring are dead, we'll survive in here."

"Mhmm." I squirmed, fighting the pain as well as the urge to tell him he was an idiot. If Evar was dead, who would control the Creation? Was Gareth strong enough?

Whatever. I needed the fuck out of here.

Blinding skull pain trumped my spasming. Mouth open in the ghost of a scream, I opened my eyes seconds later to the dim light of the attic, arguing ringing with the loud thumps of my blood pumping in my temples.

I braced a hand on the footstool I had fallen off during the ritual. Pointless fucking thing. I gripped my other hand under my right arm and hugged my chest, the pain climbing and peaking any time I tried to move.

Sophie sat, restless, head bowed with her left arm wrapped around her chest, cradling her right side as I was. "I can't—" A wheeze cut her off, a cough shooting an extra dose of pain through us.

She rolled onto her back, the pain worse instead of better. Nothing eased it.

Our healing power was enacted, it trying and failing to fix this.

"Firefly?"

The barking arguing of the others continued as Olive leaned over Sophie, holding her shoulders as Sophie rocked in place, her cheeks blotchy with the fight against suffocation, yet refusing to breathe and igniting the pain further.

My shirt was still thrashed, the damage from inside the Creation following me here. I struggled to peel my shirt over my head.

Shirt gone, I probed a spot under my arm, it wet with blood. In a space big enough for my fingertip, something hard was below the skin.

"This is why!" Ranlyn was using me as evidence against something he argued over with Vincent. If he would stop bitching and help me, I could figure out if he had good reason to be pissed off or not.

People really looked at me now. Small gasps of disgust had me cursing them for their weak stomachs.

Not Ranlyn's. He was still busy arguing. "He could die before we have a chance to move on Diluculo."

"Thanks, blondie." He didn't appreciate my gritted appreciation, he glaring down at me, hearing my disdain.

I shoved my fingers further into the hole and stretched the small entry site, trying to grip whatever was stabbing me in the lung. Slick with blood, my hold slipping reminded me of trying to pull out the remnants of a broken porcelain black cat in Sophie's arm. Shit had gotten real complicated since then, but here we were, still getting beat down by nonsense obstacles as our leaders stood around and watched.

My nails snagged the hard edge of the anomaly fucking my lung up. I gave Sophie a look she understood, we both biting down as I yanked whatever it was out of me. A gush of blood spirted as we collapsed in relief, our healing power taking over and sealing the damage with one last grip of stabbing pain.

A four-inch-long twig was covered in blood and stuck the landing where I tossed it to the floor. A goddamned stick.

The tattered mess of my shirt was a slop rag for the excess blood before I pulled my hoodie back on.

Deep breaths without pain made listening to Ranlyn and Vincent's argument easier. Blondie pointed out I was an integral part of the truce with Rosemary, that risking my life came with a price too high for a chat with the survivors in the Creation. Especially with the division they had already created in the Mother Coven.

Wouldn't want to be an embarrassment.

"One more time is required. Before the opening of the Creation to warn them of oncoming battle should suffice." Vincent was used to being right as evident in his smug insistence. "Our focus is best utilized on finding the discus or our efforts will be for naught."

Olive helped Sophie to her feet, not that she needed it now. "I suppose it could be anywhere."

"At least we know what it looks like." Sophie took my bloodied shirt and used it as I did, she having to wear the same clothing. "Not that it helps since the flash Gwen got was so quick." This attracted a look from Ranlyn he still had from being pissed at Vincent. "We didn't tell anyone else."

Olive touched Sophie's arm. "Can you show me? Maybe if I can get a look at it, I'll know for sure if it's here."

A flare of power sparked as Sophie showed her aunt the piece of the premonition Gwen showed us.

"Oh." Olive touched her lips, looking around her.

"Does the estate possess it?" Vincent wasn't the only hopeful one.

"I—I've never laid eyes on it. The young girl, however, I am well acquainted with." She looked over at Sophie who stared back in anticipation. "Elizabeth."

"Elizabeth? Wh—Grandma? No."

Olive was nodding as Sophie's incredulous anger burned in the tips of my ears. She must not have seen many photos of her grandmother as a child to remember what she looked like. Having only met her once, no way I could have placed her as the woman who institutionalized Olive and hid her family's power from them, let alone her being the child in the dark vision hiding the discus. Why would she have it? And why would she hide it? She couldn't have known what it was or how important it was for the future of our people.

Sophie and Olive headed towards the stairs leaving the rest of us standing around looking at each other. Everything in me wanted to follow her, but she didn't ask me to. I knew where she was headed and, as far as I knew, her grandmother wasn't much of a threat. Or so I hoped.

22

HANDS-ON APPROACH

Was it my nervousness making my stomach tilt or Donovan's? He was back in the attic waiting to see what I was doing. I left so quickly, figuring he would know the likelihood of where I was headed or race after me. Staying put was difficult for him. Giving me this space was even harder judging by the waves of worry hitting me from all sides.

Standing in my grandmother's kitchen staring at her dampened soul painted with layers of savage neglect and hate-filled enamel was heartbreaking, but her expression had me pissed.

Olive stayed in the car, thinking my grandmother would dig in like an ostrich if we came at her in force. Not like I was on her good side these days, evident in her raised chin and matching scowl as I sat at her kitchen table without being officially invited in.

My grandmother crossed her arms, refusing to sit. "What do you want?"

"If you didn't want visitors, why don't you lock the door? And if you didn't want Magics in your home, why not add wards, since we both know you can?" Yeah, I was being a dick pimple. She wasn't going to answer me anymore than I expected her to. "Now that basic human courtesy is out the window, how about straight answers? We need the discus. I know you wouldn't knit a potholder to save a Magic, but good people are trapped in the Creation, non-Magics, people who knew nothing about anything before Evaristus made them his Puppets. Where did you hide the discus?"

The creases of her face deepened, hard eyes behind her glasses narrowing. "I haven't a clue of what you're talking about, why or where people are trapped. Sounds like a bunch of chaos brought on by the evil you traipse about."

I resisted the urge to roll my eyes. "As a little girl, you hid a flat rock looking thing somewhere dark. We saw you."

She straightened. "You saw no such thing." She was a grade-A liar, but her reaction was genuine. "Now, I don't know what this is all about, but I want you out of my house this moment."

Hunter's car was gone, so I assumed he and my aunt Karen were out. If not, they may have heard my grandmother as she continued to rant about my newfound disrespect and who was to blame for it. No movement upstairs was a good sign.

A pulse of power gave me all I needed to stream the vision of my grandmother as a girl in the premonition right into her thick skull. She gasped, eyes wide, stumbling a step back. She blinked as the vision ended and braced a hand on the back of a chair, the other on her chest, before sliding into the seat.

I rushed forward thinking I gave her a heart attack.

She slunk back and batted me away. "How dare you force your wicked abilities on me? You may think you have the right to impose the tricks they taught you, little girl, but you're gravely mistaken." She pushed up out of her chair and came at me. "Leave this house. And do not step foot back here again."

"You'll have to look at my soul glow a tad longer, 'cus I'm not leaving without knowing where you hid the discus."

She huffed and turned her back on me as if wanting to prove she wasn't scared of me, but when she grabbed the kettle to fill it with water, the metal rattled.

"I will not tolerate this irreverence."

"Tell me where the discus is, and you won't have to tolerate me again."

She put the kettle on the stove and squared her shoulders to me. "No."

This was her last stand? Thinking she could say no and I would walk away? Saving innocent lives wasn't enough for her stubborn prejudices.

I sighed. "Fine."

Reverent superiority levelled her chin before her jaw dropped, her back straightened.

Power rolled off me as I took her in a telekinetic hold, keeping her still as I approached. Her eyes widened as I got closer and placed my hand on her chest. A cocoon of misery wrapped itself around me. The acidic consequence of her shunned gifts left its imprint on her soul, it now pecking at the light I brought with me, simultaneously trying to break me down and feed its desperate hunger.

The war within my grandmother was hers to fight, and I wasn't willing to let it devour me to bring her understanding. I focused on my search, fighting to protect myself while ignoring the nibbles like pesky mosquitoes. Proof of the discus was here. I needed to find it. Saving my grandmother's soul would have to come another day.

I pressed back until I saw my grandmother's face in her reflected memories change, even seeing Olive as a girl to ensure the right timeframe.

There. Darkness all around, the hexagonal rock discus in her hand as she reached forward and tucked into another dark place and closed it behind a little door. She then ran through the darkness, up and up cement stairs, until she pushed through a door and slammed it shut with both hands. A couple heart beats passed as she turned to run through a large open space. The attic.

I backed out of the sorrow-coloured soul reading with answers and a newfound despair for the Grandma Lizzie I loved. She stood in the way of what I needed, so I stole it from her, but I didn't feel good about it.

Tears strewn down my grandmother's cheeks as she closed her cardigan over her chest, building a thin barrier against my invasion.

If only she could see what I saw.

Before the idea fully formed, I projected the image of my grandmother's sickly soul glow back into her mind for her to see as I did. Again, her eyes widened, mouth agape. Judging by her reaction, I assumed it was the first time she saw her soul glow in years, if not the first time she ever saw the consequences of her hate.

The time for long-winded speeches was over. I turned and left my grandmother with her thoughts. This was more than anything I could have shouted at her or beat down with logic. If this didn't alter her belief system, then she could be happy in her darkness as long as she didn't hurt others.

Olive was pacing next to my car. "Did she tell you?"

"Not exactly."

Olive and I drove back to her home and stopped in the kitchen for something to drink. Olive was opening and closing drawers and cupboards as I was lost in thought.

I leaned against the counter. "Do I look different?"

Olive paused pouring what I noticed was a cream liqueur into her tea. "Different? In what way?"

She finished her heavy pour and capped the bottle, listening as I explained how I got the information I needed.

"I thought maybe it might Taint me. It happened so quickly with Caine's Aunt Bernie."

She tilted her head with sympathy. "Oh, Firefly. I can't say what you did showcased your brightest side, but knowing my sister, I can certainly vouch for you believing you did everything possible before resorting to a hands-on approach. Elizabeth can test the best of patience."

The tired note in Olive's voice made me a believer, even if only to satisfy my need to agree.

"Can you show me my soul through your eyes?"

Olive smiled. "I'm surprised you haven't asked before."

I dropped my mental walls and braced myself. I blinked as my eyes adjusted to what Olive showed me, hearing her small laugh in the background.

"Yes, you're a bit difficult to take."

The Seer green so vibrant and earthy, radiated into the empty space around me, pulling it in and caressing it with more colours. Magenta. As with Caine, the magenta was so vibrant it threatened to upstage my Seer green with erratic movements, as if it was more around me than inside me, sparking with flashes of uncontained energy.

One thing for sure, I wasn't Tainted.

Olive dropped the show and tell and took her mug of tea in one hand, my arm in the other, walking us towards the stairs. "Bernadine Tainted because her base ideals changed into something which altered her path. You may have acted against your natural instincts, but you took on someone who was too busy holding onto a grudge without a second thought of the lives they put in jeopardy to retain it. Elizabeth isn't evil—she's selfish and small-minded. Above all, my sister's a bitch."

I burst into shocked laughter while Olive led the way, sipping her spiked tea as if she didn't regret saying so.

Donovan stopped me when I got back into the attic. He grabbed my head and planted a loud kiss on my forehead, waves of relief racing through the connection, before asking what happened. I skimmed the conversation resulting in knowing where my grandmother hid the discus and praying to some chaos gods to take a step back and let it still be there.

We set up Andy with Frog and Kim. Kim hated to miss out on the adventure, but she had to watch Frog in case he decided on some rogue take-down-the-house type bullshit.

I led everyone else to the door I saw in my grandmother's memories, the one which Ranlyn said went to the cellar and some type of interrogation dungeon.

Fine white sand in the large hourglass threw Ranlyn and Donovan's balance off as they shifted it enough to allow the pressure lever beneath it to pop up. A metal sound in the wall was muffled beneath draped tapestry. I pushed it aside to reveal the door I saw in my grandmother's mind.

A flutter of nervousness at what I may or may not find curled in my gut. We saw Evaristus as a dark cloud on the family he created and tried to destroy, but the basement had a reputation if Ranlyn knew about it. My imagination cooked up a dozen movie scenes of revenge-driven ghosts and underground serial killer lairs.

The open door proved to be exactly as I feared. Stale air hit my nostrils while a few cement steps of a staircase spiralled down into a dark hole. Muscles tight, anticipating something heinous about to jump out at me, I took a breath, held it, and descended one slow step at a time.

A flash shot out in front of me. I squealed and ducked.

"Just light, babe." Donovan batted the ball of light hovering in the air like a bored cat. It kept itself afloat and was easily directed by a shove in the right direction.

As I shook off the feeling of being a dumbass, I exhaled, batting the ball of light out in front a few feet to see the steps before I got to them, leading the way down the cement steps which grew danker the deeper we got. No little insets for torches or candles were built into the wall of the thin, windowless, stairwell, a clear sign they expected Magics to make their way down here with some form of power and unconventional sources of light.

After what seemed like forever, the stairs opened up. The feeling of claustrophobia remained as the floating light didn't chase away the darkness as much as I would have liked.

This worsened once we got to the bottom of the stairs. Not because the basement was small, the opposite being the issue. I got the sense I was a tiny speck of nothing in the center of an abyss. The walls and ceiling too far away to glimpse, the corners too dark. As large as the basement was, the air was suffocating. Shut up too long, dust-clogged, and windowless.

A wash of calm went through me from the connection as a comforting presence of the estate tingled in my chest, both a silent promise of support. Whatever happened down here was in the past. I focused on my grandmother's memory of running through here as a child and retraced her steps to the right-hand side a ways in from the entrance to the basement.

The others followed as I led the way around a couple of aging barber chairs laid out like loungers, their side tables ones of convenience for dull metal instruments instead of coasters and ashtrays.

I batted the ball of light forward hoping to leave my imagination of what the barber chairs were used for behind. It illuminated a gurney against a wall with some type of symbols on it. Maybe I would ask Donovan what they meant, but for now, I didn't want to know. Not about them or the ones on the stained floors we scuttled across. They added to the aura of the place, it full of enough dense memories to threaten Donovan with imposing visions I, again, would ask him about later if we could find the discus and get the fuck out of here.

I batted the light ball forward and saw what I was looking for, stopping in front of a wooden desk as tall as me.

"A chiffonier." Vincent's tone was awed as he knelt to inspect the carved piece without touching it.

I moved around him, reaching for two small mirrors below a larger one the way I watched my grandmother do, hesitating when my fingertips grazed thick spider webs. I pulled back, and with a pinch of power, blew at the sticky webs, clearing them from the section I needed to access.

Donovan's quiet amusement was a bonus.

I reached for the smaller mirrors now without the spider webs, tilting the left one up and towards me until I could see my reflection in it as well as in the main mirror at the same time. The smaller right one took some extra elbow grease to shift it into position, the owner of the webs I destroyed coming out, the black, little thing sitting and staring as if to confront me.

My face was now reflected in all three mirrors from where I stood.

A short incantation from my grandmother's memory was more of a password. Something in Gaelic, maybe, sounding clumsy from my lips. A wooden panel shot out between the small mirrors, the small piece of flower-carved wood a hidden drawer.

I pulled out the carved rock with hexagon edges, dusty yet dark with finger-like paths of white sparkling granules from the hovering ball of light. The discus. Smaller than in my grandmother's memory, yet lighter, too. The slab of rock should have been a beast for my under-developed muscles but weighed not much more than turkey bones, the burden an easy pass off to Olive behind me.

She took it with a hint of shock, she too seemingly surprised by the ease of lifting it.

I pushed the door shut, hesitated, and pulled it back out when I noticed a few more items inside: a locket, folded paper, some weird coin, and a small old key.

"One sec."

Everyone had turned to leave, but why would a small key be here if not to be used? I looked the chiffonier over and saw a small metal trimmed keyhole in the bottom left.

The key opened a panel like a new age filing cabinet. Instead of a drawer, it had small shelves, and on one of them was a book, the rest of the drawer empty. I grabbed the book and shut the drawer before we headed back past the tools my ancestors used for a hell of a lot more than dental care and back up the stairs to the attic floor.

By the time we got back upstairs, my thighs burned as much as my curiosity about the items I found and didn't touch my excitement for finding a way to get Caine out of the Creation.

23

NOWHERE IS SAFE

The discus was the ticket item, one the Elders insisted on seeing, though Olive hovered. Her house, her possessions. And like the Anatolian Idols she used to close the Creations, she wasn't letting the discus out of her sight.

They debated the sedentary origins of the stone, undecided on if it was from the Mesozoic or Paleozoic era and settling on it being radiolarite with quartz lending to the veins of shimmer from the Paleozoic. Something Vincent insisted was over two-hundred and fifty million years old and astonished at how the Ballards would have stumbled upon it, questioning if it came to them in raw form or if they were the ones to carve it into the hexagonal shape. Olive had no answers, and I was too annoyed we weren't headed right for the Creation. I didn't care about its history. It had a future purpose to fulfill, and we were wasting time talking about it.

I could throw a fit and stamp my feet, but they wouldn't listen. They should have, but taking a minute to plan how and who would be involved was important when there would be a host of Mother Coven members and enemies alike willing to cut us down to stop it from happening. Guaranteed they had scouts outside the Creation for that purpose, waiting for us to show up so they could warn the others. Or maybe they warded it in some way to notify them of our arrival. Either way, I had a little time to check out what else I found in my grandmother's hiding place, and it helped my insides from quivering with the impulse to hold the Apporter hostage until he zapped us to the field outside the Creation.

Seated in a plethora of comfy pillows in the meditation area with Donovan pressed at my side, Kim and Frog were close by asking questions. I half-answered them as Donovan fully ignored their presence, both of us too focused on the leather-bound book I found under lock and key.

My grandmother's personal tome.

At first, it read like a journal. The awkward writing portrayed a young girl new to her craft. As the pages went on, it was filled with spells, incantations, notes, and ideas.

"Is this Olive and your grandma?"

I looked up at Kim. She held out the antique gold locket, now opened to show tiny pictures inside. The chain was seized in place and broken. The pictures in each side of the locket were black and white, spotted with age. The girls in each picture with short curly hair and bright smiles could have been Olive and my grandmother, but I wasn't sure.

Kim got up to show Olive, Frog following without the same excitement.

I went back to the small tome, flipping the fragile pages, finding an evolution in my grandmother's focus as if they grew with her age. The writing changed like the journal was forgotten for some time. Instead of love spells and warding off bullies, her spells became complex—spell armament, knowledge seeking through objects, and centered on spells to discover and strengthen her power.

"These are originals." Donovan took the book and turned pages. "Who would've thought your grandmother was so inventive."

"What do you mean?"

"See. Most of the spells were created on spot. Lines crossed out and rewritten, squished within the margins. She knew the result she wanted but struggled to find the building blocks to get there, so she writes and rewrites, looking for perfection but convoluting the message. Essentially busting the spell."

He turned pages beyond where I had, revealing spells for detecting lies and notes of scrying into the future.

I took the tome back. "Bet this was when Olive was named heir instead of her. She must have been angry and looking for answers."

Evidence of the downfall was sad. The pages were never dated, but the style of writing, irritation within the pen as it dug into the paper, said enough to make assumptions. My grandmother was once a precocious young Soul Seer and a title turned her into what she was now. I wanted to pity her. Most of me did, and I would have more if she could have found a way to reconnect with the little girl who was worried about bullies instead of becoming one herself. Some useable spells were in there, somewhere, though the tome was more so a lesson in what happens when ego overshadows humility.

Disappointment had me closing the book of a woman who loathed me because of what I was and not who I was. A fact not softening the reality of my grandmother hating me.

"It was them." Kim's eyes were a bit red as if she was crying or trying not to. "The locket? It was Olive and your grandmother."

I nodded and looked in-between Kim and Frog to see Olive near her desk looking down at the locket in her hand. The sheen of restrained tears in Kim's eyes mirrored Olive's before she put the locket in the desk drawer.

I stood to go to her and stopped myself as Ranlyn approached her, probably to ask her something about the discus. She smiled at him before concentrating on whatever he said, content to leave the locket and its memories in the drawer she closed it in.

"So, Frog, happy you got to see Caine?"

The sprig of surprise at my left hook in conversation crossed the connection, as did pride. Donovan thought I was being an ass on purpose when my goal was to divert attention.

Frog responded to my rhetorical question with arched blond brows.

"At least you know I didn't kill him."

Kim's and Frog's glares slid over to Donovan and narrowed.

I sighed. "Though, you can tell Caine's not the same."

I waited until Frog nodded.

"And you see why you can't tell anyone what you saw."

Frog nodded again.

"And why Kim couldn't tell you before."

Again, Frog nodded at me but with only a small head movement.

"You might be Blind and pissy you found out your best friend and girlfriend pulled a 'Wizard of Oz' on you, and you don't like what you found behind the curtain, but whether you and Kim see 'happily-ever-after' or not, you can't tell anyone about anything regarding tonight or nights like it, since chances are you'll see more." He looked around as if second-guessing rolling his eyes, though it felt the same. "You don't know how important some aspects of tonight were and explaining it won't clarify anything. If you spill our secrets out of ignorance or revenge, even to someone you would never guess knew anything about our world, you could get Kim killed, you could get Caine killed, plus people they both care about."

"I get it." His words didn't match the resistance I met in his stare.

I stepped closer to him, ignoring the rise in Kim's power. "Feel lucky Kim loves you or you'd have a lot of questions and missing hours of your memory."

"I said I get it."

Backing off made Kim more comfortable and did the opposite for Donovan. He wanted more than my less than intimidating threats. Sure, a failsafe was something Olive or someone could cook up, but anyone Frog told would think he was insane. His mind was open to other Magics, unless Kim was dosing him. Didn't sound like such a bad idea if he refused to take it on his own, though not so great for an honest and healthy relationship.

Ranlyn approaching us stopped me from pointing this out in front of them both.

He looked at all of us, registering Frog's discomfort as he straightened and backed up a step, then ignoring him. "We have the discus. Please—"

"I know, Jeeves, but don't expect me to wait forever. Stall too long and I'll show up at the Creation myself and fuck the whole thing up."

He smirked. "I know you will."

"And you'll have guards following me twenty-four-seven to ensure I don't."

He tilted his head, taking his smirk with him as he wandered off back to the Elders and Apporter, leaving me to wonder if there were invisible guards creeping around every corner.

———

Heavy lids made it difficult to fight for focus through the haze. Vertigo tossed Donovan's bedroom sideways, softness catching me before being pulled up again. Crumpled clothing on the floor was Donovan's. The abstract of black, red, and grey colour on the wall his, too. Not the dresser. Not his style. The black bookcase was all him.

Bright light blurred my vision. My head was heavy, my neck sore, the shadows of the stuccoed ceiling deepening and reaching out to me as I fought to focus. Voices muffled in the distance, though someone was here with me, their closeness suffocating. Stale coffee and vinegar of pickles or maybe olives washed over me with their breath.

A shove knocked me, hard, into something. My eyes lolled, and I looked up to see I was leaned against Donovan on the side of the bed, his dark eyes shifting around the room without focusing on a target, neck slick with sweat.

Pain gripped my shoulder, pulling on me, throwing me aside. A crash was muffled in my ears. Pain in my arm dull. The table lamp split to pieces against the wall.

I tried to move to fix it. A hand kept me down, their nails buried in my skin. I followed the tattooed skin of the arm to a woman's face. Her deep eyes narrowed, her lips pulled back and moving, talking to me, but I couldn't hear her.

Hinapouri.

I couldn't fight back and didn't understand why the ousted ex-Elder who tried to kill Caine and me was in Donovan's room.

She yelled. Her voice breaking through in a warble I still couldn't understand, then looked to the side. I followed her gaze in a whirl of dizziness that had me squeezing my eyes shut.

A meaty mitt had hold of Donovan's shoulder. Miklos, the Hungarian ex-Elder, shook Donovan's shoulder and yelled at Hinapouri, his words lost. They waved their hands in a failed game of charades.

A shock of pain hit me all over, space rushing at me, a jarring pain rocking me. I rolled over, my arm caught in sheets, trapping it. Another blow to the head and tugging on my tank top had me rocked and then looking up into the eyes of the Maori warrior again. Her lips moved as they had before, no words hitting my ears, my gaze affixed on hers as she grabbed my face.

I said something, the words lost as a dull sledgehammer inside my skull. Hinapouri squinted, her lips fluttering again, more hammer hits in my head.

Hinapouri stood up and stepped back, holding out her hand. I moved in the air, crashing down onto the bed and back into Donovan again.

A chill of his vision activating drilled through me until I pushed myself off him, my body weight doubled, ripe with pain yet oddly numb.

Two others stood at the other side of the room. I knew their faces. A blond man with a scruffy beard and a dark-haired man with a ponytail. Easy on the eyes. I tried to remember how I knew them, coming up blank.

I blinked into blackness.

———

I shifted in the comforting swath of Donovan's blankets, smelling his intoxicating scent before opening my eyes to see I was snuggled into his side. The light of the day slipped through the cracks of the blinds, slicing across his relaxed expression, the tingle of my vision-inducing closeness no doubt colouring his dreams.

Creating distance between us had him sucking in a breath and stretching out his long limbs right down to his toes. Felt great for me, and I didn't have to move a muscle.

"I hope your dreams were better than mine." The side table lamp was in its right place and unbroken. Made sense I would dream of two of my Elders who tried to kill me since we were potentially facing the same fate again, and soon.

Donovan gave a lethargic growl, swept his feet to the floor, and headed into the bathroom.

I may as well do the same.

Donovan's clothing was still crumpled on the floor where I remembered seeing it, it finding a way into my dreams as well.

I itched a tickle on my left bicep, looked down, and saw my tank top strap hanging loose, broken.

"No."

Details of the dream flooded back. Could I have ripped it myself tossing and turning? Would be a first, even after the dreams with Caine in the park before I knew magic existed.

I leapt out of bed and barged into the bathroom.

Donovan was standing in front of the toilet, a hand on the wall in front of him, bracing his weight. "Didn't think we were at the watching you pee stage yet, but alright. Enjoy the view."

"My shirt is ripped!"

"Hmm." He shook, tucked himself back in his underwear, and flushed. "I don't remember having sex last night." He ran his hands under some water then reached for his toothbrush.

"Do you not remember anything from last night?"

"At Olive's?" He leaned back against the counter, vigorous with his brushing, enough for me to feel it against my gums.

"After that. After going to bed." His cinched brows told me he didn't. "Did Miklos throw you around in your dreams last night?" He stopped brushing. "Was everything all euphoric and hard to hear, and Hinapouri and Miklos kept asking us stuff?"

He looked around as if searching his memory, then spit in the sink. "Two other guys, too. I think one was the Will kid from Eli's."

"Ponytail guy! I knew he looked familiar. They must have put us back to bed like nothing happened and missed my ripped shirt. But why would Hinapouri and Miklos be with Will? And how could they get by the wards? Also, why the hell didn't they kill us when they had the chance?"

Anger simmered through the connection. "Do you remember what they asked us?"

I threw up my hands in defeat, shaking my head.

Bosco's bark from downstairs had me running. How could I forget about him and Andy?

I ran through the living room to the corner into the hallway to Andy's room.

"Sophie."

I skidded to a stop when Donovan called my name. He was looking in the kitchen.

Andy was pouring cereal into a bowl, Bosco at his feet, his bark most likely a demand for his friend to share.

"Andy!"

He jolted and dropped the box, spilling cereal all over the ceramic. Bosco scrambled to gobble every piece as I raced to apologize and reassure Andy he didn't do anything wrong.

Once his bowl was filled and he was chomping on his breakfast, I looked him over. Other than his sweater being on backwards, he seemed fine.

Donovan filled a small cup with orange juice for Andy then looked at me as if waiting for me to do something.

Kids are resilient but also so fragile. Eating cereal as he would normally do could be his way of creating normalcy after something bad happens. Pretending like nothing happened wasn't good, but I also didn't want to scare him.

I used a pinch of magic to fix my tank top and then sat down at the kitchen island next to Andy, stealing a flake from his bowl.

"Hey!"

I chomped loudly, making him laugh, and then knew I had to push through.

"How'd you sleep? Did you dream about anything last night?"

He shrugged, a drop of milk running down his chin as he shoved another mouthful of cereal into his mouth.

It would have been nice to think Hinapouri and Miklos had left him alone, but there were two other men whom I only saw at the end. They could have been with Andy.

I motioned for Donovan to drop his mental walls.

He nodded.

"Can you touch him? Maybe your Psychometry will pick something up."

"It won't be accurate. Soul Reading would be better."

"Better at freaking him out. Or hurting him."

More soundless bickering didn't get us anywhere, and Andy looked at us as if we were being weird. Telepathy worked better than Pig-Latin, like my mom and Aunt Karen used to use, but even as a kid you picked up the 'some-shit-is-going-down' tone.

We needed to know what happened to him, so I explained to Andy what I was going to do and went into a Soul Reading slowly and with gripping control, focusing on Vincent's lessons to ensure I didn't get overzealous and hurt the kid. If Donovan and I were thrown into a seizure or worse, Andy would only have Bosco. He didn't need the trauma.

Delving into the memories of a child should be all grasshoppers and mud puddles. Pockets of happiness surrounded me, but most wore a backpack of sadness. Memories of his father, alive, then with spots Andy's power showed as an indication of his father's impending death, then actually dead in a satin-lined casket. Jet alive, then gone, and him crying alone over missing her. Eli and Bernie, baking cookies and doing "man stuff" with Grandpa and then seeing them change and me taking him away because people were mean. In a lot of ways, Andy saw things exactly as they were. A child's eyes didn't attempt to change their circumstances into what they wanted to see. No rose-coloured glasses or wishful thinking. Cold reality and not much more.

I should have already encountered what happened last night, so I pulled back and searched closer to the present, unable to find it.

Could he have buried the memory already? Maybe nothing happened.

"*He's getting squirmy.*" Donovan's telepathic interference reminded me I was dealing with a child and not a patient teacher like Vincent.

"*Tell him he's doing good and I'm almost done.*"

Donovan backed off, and I kept searching until I found the blond man with the scruffy beard I knew but couldn't remember from where. Again, I couldn't hear what they said to him, like I couldn't hear Hinapouri or Miklos when they talked. The room in Andy's memory swayed, darkness blanking out the room as if he couldn't keep his eyes open. A jolt of the room and Andy's cry proceeded with the man in Andy's face got my blood boiling. The fucker hit a kid. One now trying to put his hands out in front to protect himself only to have them batted aside and to be shaken in the man's frustration.

Andy saw Bosco shoved off the bed, a small, distorted yelp coming out of him as the man refocused on Andy, now crying.

I didn't need to see more. Since the audio was useless, I had nothing but the fact the guy was a familiar-looking abusive prick who hurt kids and animals for his own ends.

Will wasn't in the room or interrogating Andy. Maybe he was a lookout.

"Thanks, bud." I cleared my throat of the anger stuck there and ruffled his hair.

He cringed. Not in an annoyed way, but in a "that hurt" kind of way. He didn't complain any further and tilted his bowl in clumsy hands to drink the leftover milk.

I moved behind him and put my hands on his shoulders, talking to Donovan about needing to get ready for the day as a cover. Standing behind Andy, I saw the small cut behind his ear, as if the man grabbed it and scratched him. I released some healing power over Andy, watching the cut close and disappear.

He itched the area but paid no extra attention.

I let him know his sweater was on backwards, and he struggled to pull his arms back inside of it and twisted it around without taking it off.

I picked up Bosco and kissed his nose, sending a flash of healing through him as well. I didn't know if he was hurt, and he couldn't tell me, so it seemed the best way.

He sneezed in my face and smiled, wiggling in my grasp before I set him down.

I motioned for Donovan to follow me back upstairs. We left Andy and Bosco in the kitchen, both healed and occupied with each other.

Angry tears fought to bubble out while I reined in my power from whipping out into nothingness for the sake of doing something more than nothing.

I told Donovan what I saw. He didn't read it from my mind in the moment as he was distracting Andy. His anger was as strong yet held no surprise a Tainted Magic would hit a kid or toss aside an unintimidating pug like a stuffed animal. Given his past, he seethed in a way too personal for me to understand without suffering as he had. His outward appearance kept his trauma his secret as he sat in thought on the side of the bed.

"We have to stay somewhere else."

His attention snapped up. "You want to leave?"

"And take you with us."

His spry panic dissipated.

"Miklos and Hinapouri brought two others into the house, took advantage of us in a way we don't even know yet, and hurt the most vulnerable things I can imagine. Safety is compromised."

"I hear you, babe, but leaving isn't the answer. Any Magic could get to us depending on their strength. Miklos and Hinapouri are immortals, plus, have inside knowledge of the way the Coven wards their properties. It had to be how they got in."

"You make my point. We can't pull sleep shifts with our connection making us sleep at the same time and can't have the Sect here twenty-four seven. Or Vincent or Ranlyn. We're supposed to be protecting Andy. Yes, Eli and Bernie locked him in his room and Magics were mean to him, but he wasn't hurt, as far as we know. We're not the only ones to worry about. I can't risk him. I'm taking him and Bosco to Olive's. Yes, they broke in there too, but the attic is a virtual panic room."

Donovan didn't argue. Either he knew he had a better chance at convincing me to shave my head, or he didn't care as long as I wasn't leaving him behind, which seemed to be his initial worry.

Keeping focus while driving was difficult. I kept seeing Andy's abuse through his eyes, his hands being batted away while he tried to stop the stranger from hurting him. He thought it was a dream and didn't understand why we were going to Dunnville, but still. In the back of the Barracuda with Bosco and a couple of books from The Chiff, with nothing to worry about but others in their cars spotting the dragon jumping from the pages, you would think he was fine. He was old enough to remember this time in his life, and I hated this was part of it.

Thoughts came at me like a swarm of wasps. Donovan helped me fight through the fog until we got to the estate.

I called Vincent once in the safety of the attic. Andy and Bosco got comfortable in the meditation pillow pit while I explained to Vincent what happened.

"Sounds like a distortion spell. A basic interrogation tactic, one which impedes the senses, including the memory, to give the gatherer of the information time to act on what they discovered without the target knowing of the deception. You can read your soul over and over yet will not break the distortion as it is how you experienced the event. Your soul knows no other truth. Whatever you were coerced into revealing to them is not your fault and will eventually come to light."

"I know, but I still need to figure out who the one guy is. It's bugging the shit out of me."

He talked about re-warding Donovan's with a spell he knew, something the ex-Elders potentially were unaware of. I agreed it needed to be done, but I wasn't ready to return to his place yet. With the attack on the Creation happening any time now, chances were this was the best place to be, even if other devotees knew where it was.

Those who broke into the estate had their memories wiped but were sent by someone. "Holy toe-fungus, I can't believe it!" I threw my hands up into a happy dance.

"Hello? Sophie?" Vincent's voice was faint as he called for me through the receiver.

"The blond." I looked around for Donovan, he and Olive busy searching something. "The devotees who were sent to the estate to search for the discus. We didn't know what they were looking for at the time, but I read the one guy's mind and saw who sent them. A blond dude. The same blond dude who was the baby and pug beater last night. I don't know his name, but it's the same piece of bacon dick. Hot damn! It was needling me like an ingrown ass hair."

"Congratulations are in order, I am sure, though adds another to the fold of those attempting to procure the discus. With the other you knew, Will, involved, it is wise to assume Caine's aunt and Eli are also implicated."

"Well, I don't think they would agree to letting their grandson be beat up to find an object to save his mother. Even if Bernie is now Tainted, she's not that Tainted."

"Time has passed since you have glimpsed her soul glow."

"I know, but come on, man."

He hesitated, then sighed into the receiver. "As with the consequences of the demon being released, it is also plausible they knew nothing of the methods of the previous Elders and of this man. Will was absent from any physical role, unlike the others."

He was right. Eli and Bernie were desperate and probably didn't ask how they planned to procure information from us if they were a part of it at all.

Donovan approached me. "The discus is gone."

Vincent swore in another language on the other side of the line, having overheard Donovan.

Olive's shoes slapped against the metal stairs as she raced down it.

Donovan chinned in the direction where Olive disappeared. "Resetting the access code to the attic."

Olive would never lose the discus. Someone took it and it was my fault. Donovan didn't know the code. Who else did? The Elders accessed the attic once without us allowing them in.

"I'll call you back."

I hung up on Vincent and dialled Ranlyn. He didn't pick up, so I dialled him again and again until he did.

"Hel—"

"How did you get into the attic?"

"Excuse me?"

"The day you walked in here during the restoration celebration. How did you and the Elders access the attic?"

"We didn't. We used a spell to enter the small access room, and the attic door was already opened."

"Do you or any of the Elders know the code for the attic door?"

"Not that I know of. Why?"

I groaned. "Fuckin' shit-weasels."

"Sophie, what's going on?"

It took until he called my name again for me to answer. "The discus is gone. It's my fault."

"Of course it's gone. What the fuck happened?"

I filled him in on how Hinapouri got the information out of me with a distortion spell.

Olive came back into the room, cheeks puffed with exertion and anger-hardened focus as she moved papers around on her desk before sitting down and writing something.

I let go of Ranlyn and went to Olive, spilling with apologies. I wasn't even heir yet, and I was already fucking up.

"It's not your fault, Firefly. You can't keep out those willing to do everything to accomplish evil ends. Even without the code, the exiled Elders are misled, not Tainted. Since the estate was neglected, it may not have been keen enough to tell the difference."

Donovan's brows popped up as if not believing her, then his attention shifted to me when the flare of sensation in my chest was echoed in his own. The estate's regret was undeniable, its presence unignorable.

A quiet moment past before the sensation dissipated.

"I'll never get used to that." Donovan cleared his throat. "Okay, so if the other side has the discus now, it still benefits us. Whether it's Caine's family, Rosemary, or devotees, they all want the Creation opened for their own reasons. We make sure to be there when it is so we can get out the survivors, take down as many others as possible, and we're golden."

"Your exiled Elders don't want the Creation opened." Olive had a point, though Donovan didn't agree.

"We don't know what they want. All we know is they don't want us to take down the Sovereignty for fear of splitting the Mother Coven. The Mother Coven is already split. They may have the discus and are sitting on it, hiding it from everyone."

I sat on the arm of the chair. "Nah. Not if they're working with Will and whoever blond dude is."

"They can dissolve ties at any point, Firefly."

This is true. Since they had what they wanted, who knows what they were doing.

Lookouts in the clearing from all sides were probably outside of the Creation. No one could move without others close behind. We all knew this, but no one wanted to be the side who got the last-minute heads-up and were scrambling to get their shoes on while Magics and survivors were spilling out into the field hoping they were running towards freedom.

No matter what the exiled Elders planned to do with the discus, we knew they had it. Best-case scenario, they still did. All we hoped for was that they had a plan not involving giving it to a Tainted coven. They were working with Magics from one, we knew this, so some type of deal had to have been brokered. No telling what a deal like that looked like.

———

It shouldn't have, but it surprised me when my cell rang a few hours later showcasing Eli's number on my Caller ID. I was going to let it go to voicemail, let him sweat it out, but created some distance from Donovan and the other Coveners in the attic before answering, too curious at why he would call me. Maybe he knew something about the ex-Elders and the discus.

A deep inhale did nothing to cramp my nervousness. "Sophie's Bait and Tackle. Providing southern Ontario with the tools for the big catch. How can I help you?"

A hollow laugh filtered through the receiver, then silence. If he wasn't going to break it, I wasn't either. I waited, knowing he warred with whatever he wanted to say.

"I think I've lost her." Thick desperation in his voice broke my sarcastic humour.

"We'll get Jet out of the Creation. There's no do—"

"I meant Bernie."

I didn't say anything.

"She's obsessed, crazed with revenge, tapping any resource possible. With Andy gone, nothing's stopped her from turning the house into her personal war room. If she wasn't my wife, I would've ended her myself."

"Ohff, shhhiitt. I—I didn't expect you to say that."

When Bernie Tainted before my eyes, I assumed Eli would follow. Guess he didn't. If he was playing me, I couldn't tell. Everything in his voice was heavy with hopelessness and a truth he didn't want to admit to.

"It's too much to land on your plate, I know. I would leave her to her obsessions, but I can't bring myself to. If it's possible, I'll stop them and untangle my wife from this path."

"Who's them?"

"Richard and his miscreants."

I bit my tongue, letting his venting session go on in hopes of learning everything I could, pacing the attic floors, trying to absorb all the things we would never have found out otherwise. The Elders were now in the attic as well waiting for some type of move from those who stole the discus, hoping they would contact Olive or make another move they could circumvent.

When we took Andy and walked in on the releasing of the demon, the others in the barn were members of a regional sect of devotees. Richard was the name of the man in the passenger's seat of Donovan's vision before they entered the farmhouse. He was a high-ranking sect member and Eli's contact. They had met in earlier days when Eli's conduct followed a much darker path, making it easy to re-establish the Tainted acquaintance. Above Richard in rank was Michael. When asked, Eli confirmed Michael was the elusive blond man who interrogated Andy and was a part of stealing the discus. I made sure Eli knew who he was bedding with.

As for the wayward Elders' involvement, Hinapouri and Miklos surprised Eli by showing up during a meeting. They acted mannerly compared to the others, but their agenda was the same, and the devotees allowed them to believe they ruled the roost when the Coven Leader called the shots when they turned their backs.

"Who's the Coven Leader?"

"She goes by Rosemary."

Donovan turned and looked at me, gaze squinting at whatever he felt crossing the connection. My mental walls were down. He may not have been listening in the whole time, but my shock tipped him off, and he heard enough to know what caused it. Fury hit me in response. He was a seething mess of flared nostrils and gritted teeth.

Unlike Donovan, the others were listening in the whole time. By the unsurprised looks on them, they knew of Rosemary's coven and her connections, and they hadn't told Donovan.

Blood pounded like a shotgun in my temples. I fought hard to focus on Eli, pressing my fingers against my skull. Donovan was stuck in his head, eyes clouded and vengeful while I fought to regulate my own distaste at the Elders testing our trust.

Eli went on about finding out they let out the demon Gualichu on purpose, hoping while the Covens battled, their energy and chaos would rouse the demon's curiosity and draw him close enough to use him against their enemies to ensure their Master's release.

I wanted to let Eli in on the truce details with Rosemary.

Vincent started coming towards me, shaking his head, warning me not to.

I started to tell Eli anyway. My lips clapped shut and wouldn't open.

Eli called my name on the other end of the line as I struggled to do more than muffle and stare daggers of hate at Vincent, refusing to reach out to him wordlessly since I shouldn't have to explain myself. Instead, I used my power to trump his, disintegrating the invisible tape keeping me quiet. A crook in Vincent's brow exposed his acute astonishment at my spell reversal, as I went on to tell Eli what I knew.

Small inane rebellion? Maybe, but Vincent's attempt to shut me up fuelled the need to tell Eli every single little thing about what Rosemary had claimed to be doing to keep us alive.

Making no further attempt to stop me, Vincent stood stone-faced as I spoke, while I looked directly at him as I did.

Once I was finished, I thought about bringing up Jet and Caine, but there was nothing new to tell him. He wanted them out of the Creation regardless of how they survived within Diluculo. Anything I said would be used as fuel to Bernie's Tainted soul.

He surprised me by asking to speak with Andy.

I didn't like the idea of it. The only reason I relented was because I hoped the voice of his grandson would give Eli strength to pretend he was one with his wife's plan, to get him through all of this. To him, Bernie was saveable, and thinking Andy wasn't afraid of him would give Eli hope for his family's reunion.

Andy agreed with little resistance, more annoyed he had to leave his book.

I put my cell on speakerphone, not trusting the interaction otherwise.

When Eli said hello, his voice was off, his fear spilling out into the phone. I smiled and nodded at Andy when he hesitated, then he was okay.

The call was what Eli promised. He wanted to speak to his grandson, to know how he was, and to ensure he was safe. Andy answered as a distracted six-year-old does, Eli not holding back with exchanges of love and promises of a speedy reunion. Although his voice was shaky, the white lie was more a hope as he didn't have faith he could reunite all of their family and live as they had before.

After Andy said goodbye, Eli and I both promised to keep each other in the loop. I may have been naïve but nothing about the exchange led me to believe he was manipulating me. He wanted to save his family, all of them, and felt a responsibility for their downfall.

I felt bad for him. Soon, we would see each other outside Diluculo. If he turned on us, my sympathy would vanish.

24

———

BRUTALITY FOR SPORT

ndy was alight with joy and skipped across the attic to make sure everyone knew he spoke with his grandfather and how he would see him soon.

With him out of ear shot, my smile fell and matched Vincent's as I stood looking up at him.

"May I remind you I am your Coven Elder."

"May I remind you and your judgey smug face who convinced you take up the position since you were too much of a pinky-squatter to do it yourself?" Vincent's gaze turned sour and narrowed as I stepped closer. "I don't give a shit about your stature or your strength or even your immortality, 'kay? I have no delusions you could end me. But don't you dare think you can pull your strong-handed bullshit with me like I'm your cowering wifey. Free will was meant for all humans, Magic or otherwise. Next time, I won't hesitate to fight back, using Nya's power you so helpfully taught me to control. Consider that the next time you try shutting me up."

"You should not have put me in the position to quiet you."

I scoffed. "Take the phone away. Wave your hands like a deranged mime. Speak the fuck up! You had plenty of options, and instead you turned to magic because you rely on it for everything. Eli wouldn't have told me all he did if he wasn't telling the truth. There was no need."

"He knew it would open you up to share equally."

"Really? I didn't see Ranlyn making a move to stop me. Or Veata." Not as if Veata would care enough to intervene.

I moved to walk away. He grabbed my arm to stop me.

"I stepped in where I believed you could have taken the fate of the Coven in your hands for the need of a learning moment."

Vincent prattled on about his duty to the Coven, taking him too long to notice I wasn't listening and had raised my power.

He pulled back, sucking in a breath in a startled gasp, and looking down at his hand, which had turned black. Being pissed off made driving my disintegration power to my skin easy, no need for direct contact with my hands.

I crossed my arms. "I warned you."

Donovan called my name. He sounded farther away than I knew he was.

"You wouldn't dare try shutting them up like that if I was Ranlyn or even Donovan." I grabbed Vincent's hand. He held it like a claw as my power still ran through him, blackening his wrist. I shot him up with a dose of healing power, he gasping as it fought against the disintegration. "Next time pretend I'm one of them and remind yourself our history doesn't mean you can use it against me."

I let him pull away. He looked at his healed hand and flexed his fingers.

"Or I'll be tempted to turn your past on you and see how you like it."

Maybe a tad dramatic, as I had never used my deadliest gift against him, but I was right. He overstepped. If he was smart, he wouldn't do so again.

A long time passed before we met each other's gaze. Staying clear was best for the both of us. Whatever he thought of me now, he knew I was willing to bite back if needed. I didn't want to have to, and he may not have realized the boundary he stepped over, so I hoped we didn't have to test our friendship again.

When Donovan and I finished talking about my putting Vincent in his place and the new information about Rosemary and her coven's involvement, he was calm enough to think of something else. I updated him further on the conversation with Eli.

"Michael, the blond man, is Rodney's brother." Vincent stood at a shelf to our left, looking at vials of items I didn't know, holding them up to the light and moving the contents around before putting them back.

"Rodney?" Did I know a Rodney? "Rodney, Nora's right-hand asshole from The Chiff?"

Vincent nodded.

Donovan made a smug noise. "So, that was the threat Nora gave her dog. When she said she would strip Rodney's mind and give him over to Michael, she meant his brother. Interesting."

I had forgotten about the threat until now. "As long as we can trust Rodney isn't in on it with his brother as a mole working from inside The Chiff, we should start with him and Nora since we wanted to recruit The Chiff's people to fight to reopen the Creation anyway."

"Agreed." Veata approached us, cloudy-eyed yet staring at Vincent. "Nothing's more promising in our enemies than to pit blood-kin against blood-kin. If we can excite half the fire the two of you create,"—she flitted a hand between Vincent and me—"then we've got a grasp on their undercarriage where it truly counts. Get the enemy in hand. Keep them close. We'll be able to steer them anywhere we desire with a mere tightening of our fist." The slender and knobbed fingers of the blind Elder was in a clawed grasp in front of her as if she cupped the testicles of her enemy. I would have laughed if I didn't think Veata was anything but serious. "I bet my good hip as Rosemary crumbled at the thought of her son's blood spilt at her Coven's feet, The Chiff's bottom dwellers will battle for what drove them underground, and evil will cower at their fierce revenge."

Call me entertained.

"We already talked about this possibility. Did you ask Nora?" I found it hard to hold Vincent's gaze.

"The opportunity has yet to arise."

"Create one." Veata leaned more into her cane. "If time is needed to convince them, we have little of it. With the family names we have with us, our struggle for their acceptance will be great."

Berisfords and Sorrels I knew, but along with our new allies, it wouldn't go well. Guarantee some of those hiding in The Chiff were there because of Magics like Donovan and Caine's families.

"You may want to mention if they refuse, Evaristus, our wonderful Puppeteer, spent time stretching his legs inside my head. If he manages to slip our fenders on the field, slaughter them bloody, or turn them into more of his drones, he has the knowledge to show up at The Chiff's doorstep wearing the shells of their friends." She turned to walk back to Ranlyn. "They've hidden for far too long."

I couldn't picture Vincent repeating Veata's threat. Maybe if he was desperate enough, but I doubted it. He would rephrase in a button-down Vincent-like manner. A flash of the intensity with which he sold it to us reminded me that he found some things worth breaking his collected façade for.

I suggested he mention Michael being outside the Creation. If Rodney knew to expect his brother there, he might wear down Nora to serve his own purposes.

Vincent's pursed lips questioned the tactic but didn't outright dismiss it. I was willing to bet it was a more attractive plan than begging. And someone like Nora wouldn't respect him or his cause if he did.

Losing the discus, the only key to accomplishing the Creation reopening, didn't mean we were without an invitation to the party. I was positive when it came down to it, Eli would let me know when everything was going down. We wouldn't need to rely on guesswork or spells, only trust in the word of a man who may or may not be lying to us. A lot to bank on, yes, but he may corroborate information if the

Elders had their own insiders. I enjoyed having my own and sensed Eli's authenticity.

Vincent claimed to still have clean contacts inside the Sovereignty who promised to tip him off if they caught wind of others reopening the Creation. They planned to be there themselves, so it benefited them for Vincent to bring in the cavalry. Though he was certain those in his direct family wouldn't show up.

All well and dandy, however, none of it was within our control anymore.

Vincent headed to The Chiff and then for an update on Gualichu while Ranlyn and Veata worked on the Sects of the Mother Coven who still straddled the fence on where they stood in the fight. Veata was not as hopeful as Ranlyn, though resolved to call out every one of them who refused for their "spineless decision." No one wanted war, but it was happening, and a Witch War between friends and fellow Coveners was worse.

Though I had barged into the estate expecting Olive to accommodate not only myself but Donovan, Andy, and Bosco, my great aunt didn't mind having company in the house. She agreed with Donovan in assuming the wayward Elders got what they needed and wouldn't return, but equally understood my caution, especially considering Andy. Thankfully, he thought being at the estate was a fun sleepover with cool magical toys.

Donovan took Andy into Dunnville to a local fry truck to pick up orders for dinner. It was always my favourite, so I was salivating the moment they walked out the door. Olive wanted to cook, but I insisted it was my treat, so instead, she promised dessert in way of homemade cookies.

I wasn't going to fight her on it.

First, I called my mother, craving normalcy. I was disappointed when she asked about progress regarding the "whole Witch thing" though I understood it came from worry. I skimmed the surface of latest issues and barrelled through my mother's gasping reactions. Getting it out with such detachment alarmed her. I didn't have to ask her this as it was obvious, but I didn't want to delve too deep into it. I needed to talk to her about stupid things even though I knew it wasn't fair to expect of her when she needed details of what life and death situations her daughter was facing.

I surrendered and delved into grittier details. Repeating them was closer to a story plot than reality, reminding me I missed my books when they were all fantasy and not akin to real life.

Promising to see Mom at the next Ballard Coven night, as she decided she could at least handle the meetings, I decided to leave the whys about this decision for another time and called Kim.

No normalcy there, but curiosity about Frog won out. He was still freaked, yet his enlightenment took away his doubt in Kim and spared the future lies she would have inevitably had to tell. Frog's concern transformed from Kim having a side piece to Kim being murdered. Somehow this was better. Risking her life was Kim's choice. By now Frog knew it was her decision to bring him into something much bigger than himself.

Telling Kim the lovely new event updates, she was appalled at losing the discus and swore to let the rest of the Coveners know, including the venomous actions towards Andy, though adamant I shouldn't blame myself for being taken advantage of by the ex-Elders. While I got her point since we couldn't have stopped them from getting into Donovan's, a place they had been countless times, I still felt responsible.

Once Donovan returned with food and with a belly full of burger and home fries with the potato skins attached and doused with vinegar, plus Olive's spiced shortbread cookies, Andy fell asleep in the meditation pillow pit and was moved to an old cot in freshly laundered sheets surrounding him in soft lavender on the far side of the attic. Both Andy and Bosco were snoring within minutes, safe, cast in quiet beneath a bubble of silence from the rest of the attic's activity yet visible.

Donovan and I went to bed early as well. The night before was full of non-dreams, and we needed a couple of hours' rest before we had no chance for it. We slipped under easily, dragging each other to sleep faster than I thought possible.

A sinister face appeared, surrounded by the darkness of night. Tobias.

I couldn't look around to get a handle on my surroundings. As before, Tobias let me see exactly what he wanted me to see and nothing more. And judging from the match-hot fury coursing through me, Donovan saw what I did and was equally incapable of doing anything about it.

Numbness kept us as observers while Tobias moved through dark rooms too shrouded in shadow to recognize. Panic had me thinking it was the estate and he was coming for us or coming for everyone but us. For Olive, Andy, and Bosco and to leave Donovan and me as witnesses of their deaths. A familiar design on a wall in a thin hallway wasn't in the estate, but I couldn't recall from where.

Another figure stood in shadow. As Tobias got closer, Donovan's brother Brandon's features crested in a slit of light from a cracked doorway. His light-brown brows drew down, below a hood, surveying whatever he saw within the room behind the door with the menacing focus of a stalking panther.

Tobias turned and faced us again. "The ease with which we kill is our strength, son. You never accepted this."

While the doting father stood in watchful appreciation of the favourite son, Brandon widened the door. The wood swung open on soundless hinges, revealing a heap of blankets and the quiet drone of a television.

Brandon shot to the bed with whispered footfalls, taking up the heap of a body closest to him in a chokehold with the blanket still over their face, spinning them so Brandon sat on the bed with the person's upper body against his chest, his legs pinning theirs down.

Tobias charged in behind him and took on the second body now shocked awake. His telekinetic hold dragged them out of bed by a slender foot before the owner could see what was happening, grabbing them by the hair and forcing their head back.

"What's going on?" Fuck. It was Bernie, she now grabbing at her hair in Tobias's hold, trying to look around.

A choked cry was further cut off as Brandon removed the blanket from Eli's face and squeezed his throat tight enough to make Eli's tongue protrude from his mouth.

Eli's light eyes widened when he saw Tobias and his wife on her knees on the floor.

Tobias twisted his hand, evoking a screech from Bernie, as he pulled her to her feet by her hair. He didn't let go, instead used the other hand to hold her to his body, facing her husband.

"Now, now. Quiet."

Bernie sucked in a sob and quieted as much as she could.

Tobias nodded at his son, who adopted a snake of a smile. Something metal glinted in Brandon's hand as he shifted. I saw what it was but couldn't scream or protect Eli before Brandon hugged Eli tight and dragged a blade across Eli's throat with agonizing slowness. Eli struggled, unable to get his hands out from beneath the blankets to defend himself.

Bernadine wailed as her husband choked on his own blood and tried to buck Brandon off him. Blood spewed out of Eli's gaping wound, eyes bulged.

Brandon smiled from ear to ear, looking from Eli to Bernie, seeing what his work did to the victim and the onlooker.

It took far too long for Eli's body to go limp. In the movies, it's a quick slip of the knife and down they go with an overdramatic kick of their feet and twice the blood in a human body. This was worse than watching Aunt Lacey die. Even in her binding of barbed wire, she went peacefully. This was heinous brutality for sport. Eli never saw it coming, and the shock and helpless fear on his face would forever be etched in my mind.

Brandon tossed Eli's body aside and wiped his blade on Eli's plaid pyjama pants, standing proudly next to his kill.

Tobias still had a weeping Bernie in his grasp, craning her head back into his shoulder, hindering her breathing as snot and tears ran down her face.

"Now, Bernadine, you walk the line between light and dark. Make your choice."

He shoved her down onto the ground in front of Eli's lifeless body. Tobias didn't need to elaborate on his ultimatum. If she didn't choose to become one of his flock, she would end up a bloody heap next to her husband.

She didn't ask for clarification. She didn't barter or beg for her life. Bernie turned her back on her dead husband and bowed before her new Master.

"Good. Now repeat after me. I swear my allegiance to my Master and abhor all that was, to embrace all that shall forever be."

Bernie swallowed and repeated his words.

Soul glows were a wishful thought in this form, and I wondered if I could see Bernie's soul glow Taint further, if she truly believed in her new Master's cause or if she was saving her ass.

Something in her eyes wasn't right. I wasn't looking at the woman Caine was so excited for me to meet, the woman who took him in as family in her home regardless of Caine's likeness to his evil father, so much like the person she was now closer to than Caine ever was.

Tobias grabbed another fistful of her hair at the hairline. Bernadine cried out but bit down on her lip to muffle the sound, refraining from grabbing onto his hand though her fists clenched. "Speaking to the indolent pigs hidden amongst the Blind makes you a traitor." Tobias shook his hand entangled in her hair making Bernadine squirm in pain. "Traitors to pigs are slaughtered like pigs. Understood?"

"Yes!"

Tobias let her fall then turned to us. "I beg you to reach out to your allies hidden within our ranks." He retreated, leaving Bernie with her dead husband, Brandon following. "Though it dwindles my flock, it will be my pleasure to escort them to their deserving deaths, especially now that you lack the discus." He clucked his tongue in contempt, as if Eli's death was fashioned as an arrogant lesson. "I may not possess the discus, nevertheless, it makes no difference. It will be mine. Remember, my faction is not bound to Rosemary's word nor her traitorous associations. Many others have waited lifetimes for the return of the Puppeteer. Others who care nothing for alliances or treaties."

Tobias's sly grin flashed before he and his obedient offspring turned their backs on the crime scene and left the farmhouse.

Bernie's shrill scream chased away the remnants of Tobias's link, dropping us back in the attic in a puddle of helplessness. Tears streamed down my face as hiccupped breaths caught in my chest, the pain gripping and tearing my insides as Bernie's scream was still alive in my head, along with Eli's face as he struggled for life.

A fierce cry in my head came alive outside my body. Donovan. He was up and pacing, releasing the tension trapped within us before kneeling and hanging his head in his hands when his voice gave out.

I turned to see Andy still safe in his bubble of quiet with Bosco lying on his back, no doubt snoring. Andy didn't know he would never see his grandfather again like he was promised, or if he was reunited with his grandmother, she would be a changed woman and a danger to him. Everyone was taken away from this little boy, and he didn't even know it yet.

Anger swirled under my skin, Donovan's, along with my own. A hurricane of useless emotions, none of which would bring Eli back or repair Andy's family. Faint memories of how things were before his mom went missing would be rooted in Andy's core memories, but so would the devastating aftermath of her choice to join the war against Evaristus.

Eli was murdered for reaching out to me, for hoping for a future where he would recognize his wife again. I didn't have the power to create this much destruction, but it didn't stop the guilt.

How would Caine take this? And Jet? If she survived, she would still have her son, but she wouldn't be the same either.

The Tainted takes and takes. Now I understood why Donovan

never believed I could stroll the same path as someone like Loring. The pain his father created would ripple through anyone who knew Eli and Bernie Berisford, and I could never picture myself justifying forcing others to live with such agony.

"I'm so sorry." The ache in Donovan's voice was filled with a quiet vengeance. I didn't have to ask him to know he would find a way to make his father and brother pay for this.

I wanted to speak, but words were second to fighting back dry heaves of terror and desolation. More tears spilled, more sobs I fought to hold back as the living nightmare replayed over and over in my head. So much blood, so much unjust retaliation, so much disregard for life. I couldn't wrap my head around it.

Donovan's muscular grasp pulled me in, his nerves frayed. All I could do was hold onto him as he held onto me. This fight took a nasty turn, and right now, there was nothing to be done but grieve.

We couldn't call the police. How would we explain knowing about the murder and the murderer? Eli was gone. Showing up at the barn to help Bernie bury him when she could have her new allies there by the time we showed up was asking to be buried along with Eli. Bernie might be lost to her Tainted path, but I didn't want to be forced to take her out or watch someone else do it.

Sleep wasn't an option, but when Donovan shifted us to lie back on the bed we dragged upstairs from another room, I didn't fight him. We stayed in the cage of numbness and raw nerves until Bosco jumped onto the bed, and I noticed the light of day coming from the high rounded windows. The attic was alight with a sunrise Eli would never see, and I was out of tears to give the thought the amount of despair it deserved.

Donovan waited for me to come back from the bathroom to bring Bosco outside. He didn't need to ask to know I didn't want to leave Andy as he still slept. I cleaned up my face and healed my pounding headache and swollen eyes. I sat on the side of the bed and watched Andy sleep, wondering what he was dreaming about, hoping it was something happy yet too exhausted with magic and all that came with it to check for myself.

Donovan came back upstairs with Olive. I don't know how long he was gone. Long enough to have told Olive what happened as she came right for me with her arms opened wide for a hug as Bosco ran to wake up Andy, lying on his chest and licking his face.

"My heart breaks for all of you." She let go and looked around me at Andy. "Poor child."

Right now, that poor child was laughing and trying to push Bosco off him as my pug companion did everything to be sure he didn't fall back to sleep. How could we tell him about Eli? This was too much for him to understand.

Andy went to the bathroom with Bosco on his heels, refusing to let him do anything alone. Maybe Bosco knew more than he let on about the needs of those around him.

"It's not above something my father would do, but forcing us to watch was his biggest mistake." Donovan's unstated threat was clear.

Olive sighed. "It amazes me you faired so normally with Tainted genes in both parents."

Donovan smiled, a one-dimple reflex without any emotion in his eyes. The thread of doubt within the connection was for himself. He didn't think he faired well at all. He wasn't either of his calculating and power-hungry parents and sure as hell nothing like his blood-lusting brother, but this didn't stop his first reaction being one of lacking self-worth, which made my heart hurt.

"Fox is on his way." His deflection telling me so was further evidence he found no weight in Olive's comment.

"Peachy, but it's not my house."

"I know. I already talked to Olive when I came in with Bosco. Figured you've had enough surprises."

I nodded. "He headed over for a self-care day or revenge strategizing?"

His smirk carried a little more of his personality. "Since the sigil Fox tattooed worked, I figured I'd get more and ramp up my power."

"Wait. It worked?"

"Yeah. It threw the Tainted Photographer into his greatest nightmare—hence all the screaming and fainting—and then shielded you from the cold so you could go balls-out with Nya's power and consequently kept me warm. More should've happened, but I think I was too taken over by the cold to direct its power anywhere, so it just gave you what you needed to save yourself. You don't remember the pain in your shoulder?"

Right. His tattooed sigil was on his shoulder.

I had to think back. "I guess I did. And I didn't miss the Tainted Photographer screaming like a banshee. I just didn't realize it was from the sigil."

"Fox does good work. Remember, its purpose was to protect those I love from my enemies, specifically stating 'Evil will fear all I protect.' Sometimes the one who needs protection is me. Sometimes it's others. You should get another one, too."

"Another? Oh, right." I touched the area behind my left ear where a Triquetra symbol nestled, forgetting all about it. "If he can make them disappear and keep the protection, I'd consider it. I'm cool with ink, but I don't want magic sigils all over me."

"He can hide them in whatever design you want. Which gives me an idea."

"Is this where the revenge plot comes in?"

"Revenge on you? Nah, babe. Though you'll have to wait to see what it is."

He went to Olive's desk and asked for paper and a pencil. She handed them over, and he found a place away from me. Whatever he was doing, it made his blood pressure rise a few notches in determined excitement.

After what happened last night, I wasn't about to spit in his Corn Flakes.

———

"What are you talking about?"

Fox smiled at my confusion as Donovan lugged up Fox's equipment like he was still his employee. "An invisible tattoo. Frankly, only chicks and ravers come into the shop for them, but you are a chick, even if you're not scared your parents will see it or think tattoos makes them ugly. They fluoresce under black light. It will glint a bit in normal light, so I don't recommend marking your face. Causes a small discolouration of the skin, so placement is buyer's choice." He turned to Donovan. "Ask for one, and I'll cuff ya."

Donovan looked at Fox as if he was insulted he would think otherwise.

"I wouldn't even know what to get."

Giddiness rose in Donovan as he reached into his back pocket and handed me folded paper. I unfolded it, in awe at the careful shading, confident lines, and shocking creativity.

Fox peered at the paper, standing back and looking at Donovan with raised unkempt brows. "Of all the shit you hide, talent like that shouldn't be one of them, kid."

Fox was right. Donovan had talent. I was thoroughly impressed. Donovan was careful to make sure others knew only what he wanted them to know, making them assume his you-get-what-you-see persona was all there was to him. The layers were fine and frayed, but they were fog clouds ready to be raised when he saw fit.

Picturing the art in front of me on my body forever was easy. Not generally the prettiest creature I ever saw, the firefly Donovan illustrated didn't care to live up to the butterfly hype. It enjoyed the uniqueness of its black, red, orange, and yellow colours. Its double set of wings fluttering in flight adopted a power instead of fragility of its little body in real life. The shaded background displayed its strength to thrive in darkness. Donovan's inspiration was clear, though the execution was impressive.

"Let me see." Andy reached up at the paper.

I knelt to show him.

"Cooool."

"Totally cool."

Andy looked up at Donovan. "Can you draw me one?"

Donovan smiled. "I can draw one, but you're not getting inked for a long time, kiddo."

A warmth in my chest was akin to the sensation from the estate, but it was all Donovan. He was happy to see me speechless and flattered by Andy's interest.

Andy still didn't know about his grandparents, and I didn't plan on having that conversation with him yet, hoping to get Jet back first. This happiness in them both was a small window of time I refused to scar.

I felt like a poser after having Fox explain the invisible tattoo option. This type of art was meant to be seen.

"We can also add these." Donovan pulled another piece of paper from his pocket. "Invisibly, if needed, or worked into the piece. Most won't see the difference." Smaller sigils scattered the paper while he described them with a glint of subdued enthusiasm in his dark eyes. I missed most of the explanation as was too taken aback to focus but understood they were for varying degrees of protection, strength, and courage. A pick and choose selection.

Set-up and sterilized, I was first in Fox's chair. A pattering nervousness paced around in my gut and chest as I settled in to get Donovan's creation across my back and trailing down my spine. The nerves weren't due to laden regret in getting the tattoo, though I wasn't looking forward to the pain, but due to knowing what would come after. Temporary reprieve from Donovan's Psychometry meant freedom from his invasive visions, allowing me a fraction of privacy even if our emotions were still open to each other. He didn't need a corresponding visual with every turn my thoughts took.

Donovan sat facing me as I straddled the back of Fox's chair clad in only a plaid shirt of his—worn open and backwards to give Fox the free rein of my back. Donovan leaned forward, elbows on his knees as he entwined his fingers with mine until his visions disappeared. Then as Fox's proprietary connection-dampening concoction sunk in deeper, whatever transcended lifetimes to keep Donovan and I together, numbed out as it hadn't the first time around, leaving us single players for the first time in centuries. Either Fox tweaked the recipe or the higher concentration of his special ink in my skin caused a greater impact than it had the first time we met.

Donovan looked down at my hand, running his fingers over the skin, dimples caved, with a minute shake to his head. A slight giggle earned me a scorn from Fox, telling me to hold still or Donovan was going to find something else to do.

Being good was worth it. Sitting in the dry air of the attic with the lingering scent of Fox's leather boots and cigarette smoke in his shirt as Donovan's fingers explored my skin without restriction was my version of priceless. Fuck conquering the earth or enlightening every Blind to Magics existence. This was it for me. His happiness swelled my own, and knowing it wasn't him influencing the kick in my smile was another gift all its own.

Once the piece was charged with Fox's Druid powers and healed using my own, I looked at the finished product through Donovan's thoughts, including the protection sigils I decided to align with my spine and in black instead of the invisible option.

One bonus with being my brand of Magic, if I decided I wanted other sigils or if these ones didn't work for me, I could use my power to remove them and start over.

No matter what, the firefly was staying.

Olive's and Andy's awe matched mine. They took turns looking until Andy went back to chasing Bosco around the attic.

I switched places with Donovan, a little awkward still in Fox's shirt. "I don't suppose you have the stamina to add a bunch of these to every Covener. They could use them."

A resonating laugh grew from Fox's chest. "If only they could afford me."

I looked at Donovan in question.

He could gage the emotion attached with the look he read on me and called Fox's bluff by turning to Olive. "You cover your members, and I'll cover mine?"

"Absolutely. As long as I'm next."

"Yesss." I raised my hand for a high-five Olive countered before she got on the phones to invite the Ballards as I handled contacting Donovan and Kim's Sect.

Fox grumbled something but didn't refuse.

As Donovan was getting a second part of Fox's creation down the length of his left inner forearm, the attic was filling up with eager Coveners. Since they had a solution for the ones needing to hide the sigils, with the addition of spells to hide them completely if needed, all could rest easy with a higher ratio of safety when it came time to fight. None were arrogant enough to believe it would secure their survival, but it was another weapon in their tool belt.

No one enjoyed Fox charging their new safety nets. The pain sucked balls, but it didn't last long, and Coveners like Jared and Blake enjoyed their friends' discomfort, high on adrenaline by the end of it.

Kim and Serena had fun and took pictures as Olive was getting a few sigils in a cluster on the right side of her chest, as did Ronnie and Kevin, they underestimating the pain level since she made it look easy.

Since Jared knew firsthand the potential of one of Fox's tats, he was on everybody there, with Bosco as Coven mascot under his arm, coaxing the members who came to watch their "idiot friends", reminding them Donovan or I could erase them later. By the time Jared made his rounds, Fox was packing a hefty sum of pocket change, even with sticking to quick and easy smaller sigils and not the larger pieces like he did for me and Donovan.

Donovan and I found a corner to enjoy each other's company. Not in the way we would have preferred, but it was intimate all the same and not without a bottle of some good whisky for Fox and another for us.

"Sorry to interrupt."

We looked up to see Ranlyn, Vincent following close behind, Veata off making herself comfortable in Olive's chair.

Donovan held onto me tighter, keeping me in place on his lap. "Whatever you have to say, I guarantee you it's going to piss me off."

The heat of my cheeks was a combination of whisky and embarrassment. Vincent was probably used to this, though I wasn't so sure with Ranlyn as Donovan and I usually kept a fair distance in public.

"It likely will." Ranlyn looked at Vincent as if expecting him to continue in some pre-planned strategy.

"If it's about Eli, we already know." They both looked at me as I clenched my teeth. The whisky may have given me a boost in the emotional department, but it also kept them on an unstable teeter-totter.

Vincent cleared his throat. "How, may I ask?"

"My father ensured we got front row seats while we slept. Complete with fourth-wall breaking commentary and a psychotic sidekick. My brother."

Both Elders shifted their stances and stared at us before requesting the whole story. I chose to sip from the whisky bottle and look around them to ensure Andy was long out of earshot—he was too busy arm wrestling my brother to overhear anything—as Donovan gave a boiled down description of Eli's murder and Bernie's consequential path-choosing.

"Since my father has indirectly cock-blocked another moment with Sophie, are we done here?"

The look Vincent gave me appeared stoic yet knowing, as if he saw the look on my face before and regretted its reason. I didn't care but was happy he didn't call me out for using old tactics to find emotional distance. We ignored Ranlyn and Donovan and were looking to each other. Nothing in mind, though he may have been reading mine and doing so without announcing his presence.

"Yes, you will." I answered as I heard Ranlyn say something in the periphery about keeping quiet on the incident with Andy potentially overhearing one of the Coveners discussing it.

Ranlyn nodded. "Many more will be mourned for later. We'll leave it until we know which of us to grieve over."

"Whatever works for ya, Jeeves."

Donovan squeezed my arm, and this time, I was too blindsided by the recount of Eli's death to interpret his gesture as one of praise or a warning to watch my ass on the fire I was drifting dangerously close to.

I got up and walked away from them, headed towards Olive whose expression was more concerning then rehashing what I already knew.

If I wasn't left standing at the end of this, it wouldn't matter who I grieved for. Aunt Lacey's soul's appearance after death challenged my previous atheist ways, but it didn't mean I would be on the other side mourning all those I was responsible for dying, including Donovan. He may not care as we would go together and start over together, but I couldn't plan on my next life being so informative. I hadn't even looked back into my previous lives to see if I left myself breadcrumbs to follow. An oversight or avoidance was an introspection for another day, a different one than the inevitable atomic bomb of grieving looming in my future.

25

COLD HIT OF REALITY

Word of the truce made its way through the Ballard Coveners. Between Adam and Serena finding out when Rosemary showed up at the sect meeting at Donovan's and the presence of the five members for the second round of Donovan's dance with the Pompeii Worm, most already knew. For one person, it was headlining news.

As I got to Olive, my Uncle Dwayne was making his objections to the deal clear, though I had to set him straight. "The decision had nothing to do with her."

He shifted his cowboy hat like he contemplated throwing it on the floor in anger. "Don't I know it. Do you even comprehend what you're playin' with here? You want us to lay our lives on the line when you have one of those evil things setting up shop in our ranks?"

"You don't have to do anything. If you remember what I said in one of the last meetings, I'd rather no one fight at all...ever."

"And you won't be." Ranlyn came up behind us. "None of the Ballards will be permitted to fight. Especially now with the discus out of Ballard hands."

"Excuse me?" Kevin and others around us overheard the Elder and were quick to defend themselves.

Even Elliot, the young man spat out of the Apish Coffer when the webbing locking the Creation down was stripped away, was looking on in a silent, intense stare. His words were reserved for my cousin Chelsea in private, she still the only one he would speak to.

When Ranlyn argued their perception of their strengths was bloated, he then turned to me, wanting me to show them their soul glows.

I squared my shoulders to him. *"I'm not your minion like Olson. They can make their own decisions. And you can't stop them from showing up."*

"Maybe not, but I can revoke their seat within the Mother Coven."

I laughed aloud. *"Go ahead. You think they care? You've already lost members. Swing your dick around more and see where it gets you."*

"Their death is your responsibility."

"Add them to the fucking list. They've seen battle before even if they did nothing more than dodge bullets."

Dwayne put his hand up between us. "I don't know what you two are talking about, but I'm sick of the disrespect. Talk out loud or leave."

I huffed and looked at him. "Uncle Dwyane, you and I both know you don't have the power to kick anyone out of here, so let's quit with the idle threats, yeah?" I turned back to Ranlyn, keeping the conversation aloud. "Now, no one gets to decide how they are taken out. If it's a bloody death in a field already filled with shallow graves, then that's up to them. Telling people no only makes them want to rebel." I thumbed towards Dwayne. "Keep pushing, and you'll have my uncle here showing up on horseback with spit-shined spurs, a lasso, and a I'm-not-staying-in-the-car attitude."

"Now, hold on a minute." Dwayne was interrupted by anyone else who wanted to jump in, which only gained spectators and more opinions.

As the premonition called for, this discussion brought about a division in the Coven. Of course, we never expected it to mar the meek Ballard Coven, and yet it pit family members against each other. A few would stand and fight with more who wanted to and were persuaded otherwise. Some flat out refused. Dwayne was one of those vehemently against it.

As expected, Olive, Lewis, and the aunts would be there to see Evaristus escape or perish, to look their ancestor in the eyes and stand before him instead of running in fear as most others in the family he slaughtered. Tapi and Leon were in for a fight. Leon might be missing a limb, but as a Transmutator he was more useful as a three-legged panther than in human form, in his opinion.

Adam and Serena were up for it, but neither were ready, and I couldn't bear to see them die. Same with Kevin, though Chelsea was now undecided as Elliot begged for her to think realistically of her powers compared to those she would face. Losing her seemed to be his greatest fear. She was his whole world now.

Ronny, for all his talk, backed out. Shannon would have liked to possess the power to stand and make a go of it but knew she didn't and wasn't as arrogant as some to assume so.

As the crowd began to disperse into smaller groups, Kassie approached me with her chin slightly raised in her usual superiority.

"Do I possess enough power to join up?"

Kassie may not have been my favourite, but I had to agree she had power and could probably put up a good fight if she tried. I told her this and offered to project her soul glow to her mind so she could see for herself. She took my word for it, looking disappointed, and gave a stout nod before walking off.

Of course, Serena argued Kassie couldn't be stronger than her, but her protest was lost as the attic door slammed. Dwayne was pissed and found he couldn't stay under the roof with people who were willing to allow their inexperienced the opportunity to die.

Olive shook her head but made no move to stop him.

With the knowledge of the truce and the discus stolen, demoralized spirits had a greater chance of ending them if they stepped onto the field with lowered confidence. Some things can't be accomplished in "fuck it" mode.

Fox was helpful with raising some spirits. When another Magic would step up to get their tattoo, whether they were fighting or not, he would land a few words in their lap about battle, the realities of the coming struggle, and the tragedies of possible losses. It was good for them to hear all sides.

Taking a break, Fox hit the head. When he came out, Donovan was there at his ear. I didn't hear what he said at first, but as they came closer, Donovan was calling on Fox to join the fight. I was standing with Kim, Serena, and Gwen, they not noticing when my attention was on the men behind us.

"Don't make me slap you around." The growl in the Druid's voice was for Matt, who put Fox's tattoo gun down and scurried away like a frightened mouse who dodged suspicious cheese in a trap.

"So?"

Fox huffed at Donovan's insistence. "I know you want me there, Van, but it's not my place."

"If Evaristus gets away from us, would you fight to put him down after he's slaughtered his fair share?" Silence stretched, an exchange I couldn't see. "You know what I mean. You'd fight if it came to that, so why not now when you can prevent people from dying."

"My years in battle are long gone, kid."

"Yeah sure. You know everyone here is useless. I doubt I can make a good fight myself."

More silence.

I smiled at my cousin in the guise of participating conversationally, but I didn't hear what she said.

"I know you want to save her, kid. My fighting won't guarantee Sophie's left breathing."

"Then do it for me."

Fox gave a small chuckle. "I think I've done quite enough for you."

"You have. I owe you my life. I know the evil I'd be if you'd turned me away. And you know what I was before her."

"Didn't say you weren't worth saving, Van." I heard a click of his case as he packed up. "But I'm not the Magic to do it. Standing up to Tobias was one thing. Ancient history, for one. He didn't give it his all to get you back. Now, he'll have guns blazing, and I ain't built for that shit no more."

"Cop out. Tobias doesn't fight with his muscles any more than you would if you had them."

"I've made my contribution. Besides, we both know you and your mate will make it out of this." Donovan's laugh wasn't easy to interpret. "I'm attuned enough to know when to stand and fight. I'm also aware of my capabilities and when they will not only come in handy but will secure my survival. This one's not in the cards, kid."

"You can't know that."

"You're so sure I can't, huh?"

If serious conversations between the two were rare, you couldn't tell. Donovan trusted Fox more than anyone I knew, besides Aunt Lacey. If the guy was saying he didn't see himself surviving this fight, why not trust his conclusions as well? I didn't know if Fox had the ability of foresight beyond a general Magic's intuition, but if he did, why ask him to die for this, for those in the Creation, after finding out the stakes he was facing? Guaranteed he never thought he would outlive Aunt Lacey. How could Donovan assume the same with Fox? Why risk it?

Fox's heavy boots preceded seeing the man bypass the same group. Apparently, not one for goodbyes, he turned to me without stopping and winked, continuing on his way through the crowd, tattoo kit in hand, out of the attic.

Did he know I heard them? Shit. Probably.

Others followed soon after. As the numbers dwindled, the usual suspects hung around the longest. Donovan read through some ancient text, sifting for anything Sorcerer related in search of mentions of passing along the gift, reminding me of Aunt Lacey's plea to find a way to give Donovan some of my power. She didn't say why, but she said it, meaning it was important.

Was Donovan so worried about us dying he thought we needed this to happen before the fight to reopen the Creation?

A rush of anger drilled through me. Not my anger, an echo of someone else's so great my fist tightened as if I was holding a weapon. The compulsion to thrust it through someone made me grind my teeth in anticipation of hitting a target with squishy bits, one who would beg for me to stop. I wanted them to plead for their life after how they disgraced me.

The righteous vengeance within me washed away like a passing fever.

What the fuck was that?

The heat rising up my throat was of embarrassment as much as it was remnants of the anger I felt. The curl in my gut and cramp in my diaphragm didn't help me figure out where it came from. Fox's tattoo concoction to numb our connection was stripped away like a home-made waxing kit to a hairy ass crack.

Donovan stood, the old book he was reading a splay of pages on the floor, his wide-eyed expression one of fear and confusion. Was what I felt from a vision he had? Did the book cause it?

Regret filtered through Donovan. Why? I didn't see what the vision was, but if it was from an old book, why would he have regrets?

I stepped towards him. Anger rushed back and stopped me mid-step. A splash of red dappled my face. I flinched and touched my cheek, nothing coming off on my fingers. The attic disappeared from around me. Pale skin was swathed in blood, it flying at me again before it disappeared. The glint of light off of a grouping of bottles in the attic was more welcoming than the blood, yet held the same glint of dim light.

"Sophie? What is it?"

Vincent loomed over me, the attic rafters behind his shoulder as he knelt cradling me just off the floor as I must have fallen. I turned.

Chandelier light glinted off of glass bottles on the attic shelves, shining as much as the blood.

What blood? Who was bleeding?

I had been looking at Donovan. I turned from Vincent's green eyes filled with bald concern to find Donovan. The book was still on the ground, Donovan now on his knees next to it, but no blood.

Vincent called my name, asking a question I didn't hear.

The icy thrill of a vision hit me and took over.

Pale skin gleamed with sweat where the blood missed. It poured down a skeletal body, a young boy's, skin and bones. He hung from the wrists, his toes dipped into the stink of his bowels on the stone floor below him. He was no older than twelve. Twelve years of disappointment, of embarrassment. Punishment had not yet fractured his will, but his submission would follow. I knew this. He must or would endure the sting of my blade over and again. He wanted to live amongst the Blind and broken. He could die by their tools and be resurrected over and again as proof only the way of my flock brought salvation.

Disgust permeated the room. Not for the slop of intestines, but for the audacity of this child. This boy of mine had to face his father, his Master. To turn his nose up at the empire built beneath his backside while countless others vie for the attentions of the current throne bearer proved his weak blood.

No matter. He will learn.

A slash of metal across the thin skin of a quivering throat was a banal end to an anticlimactic existence. My son, heir, and my sinful vanity choked on his impish scream and wriggled on the end of the rope like a reeled-in tuna. Efforts to turn his head into the pit of his shoulder to save himself was useless, as was his search for mercy. Pathetic. How dare he look at me as if I betrayed him.

Rage boiled and tightened my grip on the blade before a fast blow to the chest removed all defiance in the boy's eyes. A power-laden drag of the metal down through the sternum and heaving belly left no room for hope, it bleeding away with the rebellious child's meager life force.

The sight of internal organs hanging from the small form reminded me of gutting a wolverine in my boyhood, the splat as they fell out and landed in a large bowl was another hit of welcomed nostalgia from a time I, too, was educated on my birthright, my expectations, and consequences for failing to live up to my station.

I would not allow Donovan to fail and bring shame to my legacy.

I caught his chin between my thumb and forefinger, pulled his ashen face close, refusing to miss the moment the life drained out of his soul. His deep eyes rolled a moment before falling empty, and his body hung lifeless.

A slap of energy tore the boy away from me. I blinked and looked around to see large rafters above me.

The Ballard Family Estate attic.

I was me again.

Vincent clutched me tightly as the vision of the tortured boy and the emotions of his torturer still rushed through me. Not a nameless boy, but Donovan, he as a child who refused to fulfill his father's life plan. This wasn't a vision. It was his father's memory plucked out of his sadistic mind and shoved into Donovan's brain so forcefully I saw it as if I wielded the knife that sliced Donovan's body in half.

I clenched my fist, it now around Vincent's arm instead of a knife handle, my other hand at my chest as if to hold myself together like Donovan struggled to do as an innocent child. Vincent was talking, but I couldn't hear him over the blood pounding in my ears.

Donovan was on the floor, he too grabbing at his chest, the memory of the pain still alive in his bones.

How could Tobias do this to him? Their dynamic wasn't the normal father-son relationship, but the heartbreak was deep in Donovan's boyish eyes. So clear, tears wet my cheeks and choked me as I fought to understand how someone could do something like that to a child. It didn't matter they were Magics and could resurrect Donovan. Healing magic still left psychological scars, ones Donovan's father counted on remaining when the blood stopped flowing.

"He cannot hurt you here." Vincent's voice was low. "Tobias knows this. His tactics are tiresome yet transparent."

"You saw it?" My voice cracked so much I could barely understand myself.

Vincent nodded.

"I wish I hadn't." Ranlyn was off to the side, a tad wide-eyed as he cursed under his breath.

Vincent's pursed expression agreed. "The horror of the scene, or perhaps something else, obliterated your mental defences. Tobias refuses to be ignored."

It made sense Donovan's father would have sent the memory to him, probably hoping to break Donovan down, though I doubted he expected the Elders to see the memory through our broken-open minds. I didn't know who else saw, since those who were still around were now hovering and asking questions.

Donovan hated anyone knowing, let alone seeing, what his father did to him. A cramp of rage pulled at the muscles in my throat, runoff from Donovan fighting to keep it together. I tried to regulate my sympathy—something else he would hate. He didn't want anyone feeling sorry for him. He didn't want anyone feeling anything for him, but if they did, sympathy was unwelcomed.

I swallowed what felt like a chunk of dry roast and tried to stand. Vincent rushed to help, his gentlemanly hand a tad too tight on mine.

A splash of blood deafened me as much as the scream that followed. Was it mine? When I opened my eyes, I was on the floor again. Vincent was frantic to cradle me before dodging my vomit.

Voices around me hit my eardrums like a sledgehammer. I cried out and grabbed onto my skull, my own scream another overwhelming hit to my senses.

Not again. Tobias, the piece of shit, had nothing better to do?

A flash of blood and gore. Donovan's guts spilling out at my feet with the feeling of Tobias's righteous satisfaction railing through me alongside Donovan's present fear and my hatred for being forced to endure the disgusting scene. I couldn't take it, and I couldn't escape.

The onslaught intensified. Piercing. Voices from the forced memory chanted, and voices from the attic pleaded for answers. The suffocating roar of desperation cramped my muscles and made my power bleed into my skin with an unforgiving sting.

A second source of power fought for space in my chest. The entity within the estate? Nya's power? It didn't feel familiar.

Hands grappling to hold me down or hold me close spurred on the violating power until I arched backwards. Cold wood flooring snapped my eyes open long enough to see the helpless faces of my family and covenmates basked in an opalescent light. Whose light was it? Denise's?

Fuck, it was me.

I struggled to extend my taut muscles with a deep growl, forcing my limbs in front of me to grip myself. Curling into the smallest bundle I could, trying to gain a sense of grounding, of safety from whatever this was, gave this unknown power renewed strength.

Power burst from me. Not in an explosion like a popped balloon. This power wasn't lost. It took over, spiralling my body out flat on my back as the opalescent force then rained down over me, blinding me.

Friction burned my face, arms, and the whole right side of my body as I spun. When I skidded to a stop, an icy wind whipped against me, pelting my skin, raking my eardrums.

I curled back into myself. The unknown power was gone. When I opened my eyes, I no longer saw the frightened expressions in the attic. I saw no one and nothing. I was outside in a snowstorm.

Snow and ice pelted me as I managed to move onto my knees. The calf-deep snow bled through my jeans and socked feet. An uncontrollable shiver took over as I tried to wrap my head around where I was. I couldn't see the estate. If I was in the yard, the house, the backyard greenhouse, trees lining the street...something should be recognizable. Blowing snow made it impossible to see more than a foot in front of my nose, which burned with every breath.

When Rosemary manipulated me into getting lost outside Donovan's, I had boots on. Walking around aimlessly without winter gear would get me nothing but frostbitten.

I needed a plan.

I flexed my power. Good, it was still there. Wait...wait. Fuck. I lost it.

Shivering was distracting. I shifted onto my knees and folded forward, bringing my sweater-covered arms around me as my face was buried into my knees.

Relentless shivering took over, taking everything I had to focus. I survived the wind and snow Jared manifested when we fought the devotees who broke into the estate. I could do this.

I held my breath and squeezed every muscle I had, digging deep to find my power. A flush of what I was looking for sent relief down my spine, a shot of healing warmth enough to take care of my injuries and keep me going. I sent out the power I could muster to encapsulate me, cocooning me like a warm hug.

Water soaked through the shins of my jeans. I opened my eyes enough to see that, indeed, it was water and no longer snow. Around me was a small clearing of soggy grass. Snow still battered my eyelashes, blinding me, so I curled back into myself and found power to build a shield. It worked so quickly I thought I went deaf until I heard snow battering against it.

Sitting up, I pushed my dripping wet hair out of my face and stood, stretching out my stiff muscles and giving them a break from the freezing ground. Not that I could see anything beyond the shield, which didn't come with window wipers.

I bought myself some time, but not much. I needed to get somewhere warm.

Anger flooded the connection. Donovan was somewhere, maybe back at the attic. You would think he would be worried and not angry, but I didn't have time to think about him right now. A snowy grave was not my kind of death wish, and if I stood here much longer, the choice would be taken from me.

Think.

If I had Kim's gift, I could direct myself somewhere. Though, her gift only found specific targets she knew or had been to before. I needed a general "get me to safety" spell.

Everything had a pulse, a liveliness to it, as proven when I saw some of the objects in the attic while using Nya's power. I had been hoping to connect to Caine that day and saw the souls or impressions of souls on objects. Maybe I could do it again.

With nothing to lose, I dipped into my power, directing it to my eyes, covering them with sweater-covered hands as the force within me built and settled in.

"Show me the way." My voice was more of a whisper, almost lost beneath the battering snow against my shield. I repeated myself like a chant, focusing on my sight and thinking about how I saw the objects in the attic when I did this before. I needed to see more than my normal soul glows, and it needed to be on something instead of someone.

Warmth spread across my back, shoulder to shoulder and down my spine, with urgent comfort. Colourless light fluttered in the distance, bands of it a football field away in front and behind me. Details were obscured by the snow, but I was certain they were buildings.

"Holy shit. It worked!"

I blinked a couple of times, surprised the light remained and ecstatic I pulled it off without the help of Nya's power. Was this the evolution of my Soul Seeing gift? Or part of my power in general? Could Olive or Lewis see the impressions souls left on objects? I didn't remember it specifying this in the family tome, but I wasn't looking for it.

Maybe it combined with the protection sigils within my new back tattoo? The sensation blooming out across my skin followed the fire-fly's wings, setting off the sigils within the art piece. What did the sigils mean again? So many were hidden in Donovan's design I couldn't remember. No time to figure it out now. Which way do I go?

I decided on the place with the brightest light in front of me. If the light was an imprint left by the Blind or Magics, it meant there was either many people inside or many who frequented the place. Trouble was the light gave no indication of if those people were a safety net or an awaiting trap. If it was a place for Magics, I might be walking into a den of Tainted. Tobias and Brandon could be polishing their ritual knives, ready to slice me open.

Flashbacks of Tobias torturing Donovan as a child came to me as I dredged through the snow. If Tobias was in the building coming closer with every step, I was happy Donovan wasn't with me. Tobias didn't deserve to see his son and what those reminders did to him. I didn't relish seeing him either and prayed to a goddess or two to find some old folks' home full of lovely knitting, storytelling, grandparents, and helpful Personal Care Workers.

If only Jared and Blake were around to use their elemental powers to give me a break from Mother Nature's wrath.

I pushed faster, feeling my power slip and begin to fail, arriving at a long one-story building. The brick wall appeared in front of me so quickly I barely raised my hands in time before running into it. I set off to the right, hoping for a window or door as the building's soul impression went dark, leaving me blind again. Cold seeped through my shield as I lost hold of my power little by little.

I kept my left hand on the rough brick and ran as fast as the deep snow would allow. Weightlessness was a shock when the wall disappeared, the ground a jarring hit to my whole body. A large overhang above me protected two metal exterior doors with small windows. I scrambled for one of the handles, finding it locked.

Two unlocking spells failed before success. A hard pull at the handle and it opened, blasting my face with warm air as I stumbled inside onto cement floors. An alarm blared. The old kind with a hammer beating a bell at high speed. I rushed to the one closest to me and threw a shot of magic at it, shattering the bell into pieces and causing them all to silence. An echo in my ears remained as I peered down the long hall in front of me, it lit with dim security lights.

Long hallways with opened doors branched off every twenty

feet or so. Colourful signs were taped to the walls. The lockers were a dead giveaway for me being in a school. By the size of the desks in the classroom to the left of the entrance, an elementary school.

Chattering like a Halloween skeleton, I fought to control my muscles as a glint of something on the floor caught my eye. Wet boot prints. I froze and stared, examining them with adrenalized eyesight in the dim light. They were fresh, and they weren't Donovan's. Last time I saw him he was wearing black Converse.

I waited for dull footfalls or wet squeaks on the hard floors. No one rushed me, but a delayed reaction didn't mean they weren't waiting for me to walk deeper into the gauntlet of the hallway, farther from the only exit I had seen.

Paranoid tension bound my shoulders, not all my own. Wherever Donovan was, he was either feeding off of my uneasiness or was encountering a reason for his own. The tingle along my collarbones told me his power was at the ready at a scaled down dose as not to attract unwanted attention from nearby Magics. Or it was possibly an emotional reaction beyond his control.

Soggy socks wouldn't hide me from the boot-wearer, so I pulled them off, tossed them into a dark corner, and tiptoed to peer into darkened classrooms. I wouldn't stand around and wait to be attacked in my bare feet. I needed to get moving and figure out where I was and why. They would reveal themselves soon enough if I didn't find them first.

The first few classrooms were empty, the small desks sitting in waiting. A bulletin board between rooms had a copy of their monthly newsletter stapled to it, the heading reading "Parnall Public School".

I resisted the urge to scream "No flippin' way!" I used to go to this elementary school. Which meant I was in the north end of St. Catharines, a residential area an hour away from the estate where I was before getting pounded with the memory of Donovan's childhood consequences for his rebellion and being zipped away into a snowstorm. From grades two to six, I was a Parnall Pirate in a black and white jersey on every sports team it offered, soccer being my favourite.

The soccer field was where the protection sigils landed me, it searching deep and finding a place of carefree safety in my formative years. It was a reminder of how my and Donovan's childhoods were polar opposites. He would never be subjected to invasive memories of my parents murdering and resurrecting me. They never even spanked me.

And while knowing where I was removed a layer of questioning, it didn't answer the why of the situation nor the how. If someone triggered the sigils on purpose to lure me out of the attic and away from those who could protect me, then they understood the power behind the sigils better than I did and had a plan still working its way out.

Too bad I couldn't reverse the sigils' process like a TV remote switching to the previous channel. Or if I could, how could I tell the sigil where I wanted to go? I should have asked Fox more questions before getting under his needle.

I had to find a phone. Mine wasn't in my pocket, it either back in the attic or getting a snow bath outside. I couldn't remember where the administration office was, though assumed a few phones were there. Squinting into shadowed corners and second-guessing every direction I took slowed me down.

Fearing my power might tip off another Magic, I refrained from using a cover spell. I didn't feel another's power, or I thought I didn't, assuming the low hum of energy was still filtering my way from Donovan. It wavered a bit but less than the runoff of his emotions, both easily ignored.

I found the office, grabbed the reception phone, and knelt behind the desk. No way I remembered phone numbers, but calling Information had to lead me to someone.

The line was dead. I hung up and tried again, hit number nine, and chose a line or two thinking it was a fancy administration phone I was using incorrectly. I wasn't. I wanted to believe it was from the snowstorm, but my intuition told me it was something more and that the low thrumming energy I sensed the whole time was from someone keeping me trapped and ensuring I wasn't calling out for help. It fit Tobias's flare for torture as well as Brandon's.

I wasn't sure who I feared more, Donovan's father or his brother, both equipped with an unpredictable psychopathic streak. Vincent's brother, Chase, was another possibility. The Sovereignty was no friend of mine. All of them outweighed me in terms of power. Though, maybe not if I gambled with Nya's additions.

What was clear was that I would be better off braving the elements wrapped in continuous power to survive the snow than sticking around this rat trap.

I pushed my hair behind my ears and headed for a window rather than bet on strolling out of the front door.

Something hit my feet. I broke my fall on a desk, catching the metal corner with my hip. Paperclips, pens, and extra staples were scattered on the floor. Had I knocked them over? Not a chance. No uptake in power clouded the office. Could it have been a ghost? Right. What were the chances my childhood school had spirits wandering around it?

I rubbed the spot on my hip, eyed the debris, and took another step towards the window.

Binders from the top of a filing cabinet flew at me. I couldn't duck in time and caught one to the left ribs and thigh.

"What the tits?" Energy around me was a notch higher, crowding me. "Okay, now. Whoever you are, I'm not up for game night. Play face-to-face or back the fuck off."

A beat passed and nothing happened, though the heightened level of power remained.

I rushed to unlock the window and pushed out the bottom half. The glass snapped shut on me, smashing into pieces and showering me in shards. I scrambled to escape the office. Whatever smashed the window made chase as I ran down the dark hallway.

The slaps of my bare feet on the floor punctuated my cowardice and had me berating myself for fleeing. I needed to run, but I needed to get somewhere with purpose.

A plan came to mind, and I headed for the gym. I remembered it contained multiple doors to the hallways as well as outside, including behind the stage.

I took a right down the hallway praying I remembered the route and hoped to get there before the force behind me got to me first. Paper was torn off of the walls and thrown at me as I ran, flying in front of my face as something metal bounced on cement floors, took out my legs, and clanged into lockers. My healing ability sprung into action as I rolled in pain, saw the fire extinguisher that took me down, and crabbed walked in the direction I needed, still unable to see my attacker.

I amped up my Soul Seeing. It vibrated my eyes to the point of nausea, earning me the outline of my stalker erupting from the nothingness.

Light in a dark soul, partially Tainted. A cur.

Whomever it was, they weren't the darkest enemy I had faced, but a soul glow and outline didn't tell me who it was or what they were capable of.

A glimpse was enough to get me back on my feet, dodging a rush of power that heated me from thighs to crown but missing as I rounded the corner hoping I was headed in the right direction. When I passed the vending machines, I knew I was.

I slammed against the first gym door I saw. It jarred my whole body. Locked. I ran to the next one down the hall. A whoosh and crash next to me was a vending machine flying into the cement wall. I shoved the door shut behind me and did a quick locking spell, seeing the chain links of power across the door before they disappeared and fortified the door against whomever was coming after me.

Adrenaline pulsed in my temples as I sprinted towards the door across the gym that led outside. My escape was a few strides away.

I ran into the push bar of the exit door. An explosion of power hit every nerve. I flew off of my feet, landing on my back. I blinked, looking up at the ceiling as cramping energy lurched through me.

Light in the room pulsated. I looked around, unsure what I was seeing. Iridescent blue shapes and symbols. Sigils? They covered every inch of the walls including the ceiling, the entire room alive with an unseen force. The symbols weren't spray-painted graffiti, but casted, like a magical brand, thrown around like confetti. Whatever they meant, whomever made them, threw them up while I wandered around trying to find a phone. They planned to bait me into this rat trap, and I made it easy for them by rushing right for the poisoned cheese.

I thought I was saving myself. Now what?

The door I entered whipped open and flew off its hinges. Energy zapped around the room and threw me. I writhed, the floor falling away from me. Energy pulled me up by the strings of power within my soul. An uncontrollable scream thrashed my vocal cords. I strained to right myself, to curl in and soothe the driving pain.

Tears blurred the room it a barrage of light and energy. Panic tightened already strained muscles as I realized this could be it. No saviour to swoop in; no one knew where I was. The dead can talk. Maybe a Summoner could tell someone like they did with Aunt Lacey. The mere thought of her flooded me with heartbreak. So much would be left behind. How could it end like this?

If I was going to die, I needed to see who was doing this to me. My soul would remember this. It could tell the others, or I could find it myself in the future. Some Magics had long lives, and my essence had a long memory.

The symbols and sigils all over the walls pulsed with Tainted energy as the one who trapped me remained shrouded, watching, content for me to suffer.

Fuck them!

I tucked in, holding onto myself, and searched for my power. A bolt of zinging pain went through my whole body. The room blotched in black as I fought to hold onto consciousness. The symbols on the walls did more than trap me. They disabled my power by over-whelming me with pain. Or so they wanted.

Tingles across my back reminded me of my wings, my tattooed wings and sigils. I had my own arsenal. I let the tingle build in small increments, testing my enemy's boundaries. A zap of energy hit and put me in my place when I pushed too far.

Time moved fast and yet too slow as I still writhed in the air, struggling to gather my shit together enough to make a move. I had to ditch the gradual climb.

I opened myself up like a broken dam. Every sliver of power, be it my own, Nya's, or from Fox's tats, unleashed in an assault to my surroundings. Weightlessness overtook me, dropping me in darkness as the walls of sigils died, landing me on the gym floor.

Disoriented and shaking, I heard the heavy breathing of my voyeuristic attacker, coming from close by the door where I entered.

I needed to see who I was up against.

They must have been conscious and saw better in the dark than I did, as the walls started flickering like failing fluorescents, showcasing the heavy cracking in the cement and downed basketball net but leaving my attacker a mystery.

Before the walls of sigils regained full power, I found my own. Desperation became a reflex and flushed away lingering shock enough to find my power to see the outline of the soul glow of my attacker getting themselves up off of the floor. How they managed to retain their cover spell I didn't know, but it was another testament to their strength.

My prying energy met resistance as the weight of the sigils wall-papering the walls became blinding. Not only to my eyes but bled out my Soul Seeing. I pushed harder, feeling like I was losing an arm-wrestling contest inch by inch.

An extra dose of power fortified my Soul Seeing gift. The growing oppressive light and energy from the walls of sigils threatened to overwhelm and take away my opportunity to put a face to this trap-layer. I shook with effort as the gym burned with energy.

My attacker moaned. The sound deep, male, and familiar. I couldn't place it, but I knew who this was.

Everything hurt as I pressed my hands out at my sides as if I could physically push away the force that crowded me. It drove me back a few steps until I fell to my knees, bones pressing into cement.

My attacker growled as if they were expending great effort to keep this up. Again, I knew the voice but couldn't remember whose it was.

Their outline sharpened, as did their cur soul glow. I saw their height, how fit they were, even how bald they were a second before the figure became clear.

The Apporter.

We knew Olson was Tainted, but Ranlyn trusted him enough to rub elbows with the guy during battleplans and secret meetings. Ranlyn said he was on our side, that his soul was only Tainted because of the stuff he had to do in the name of fighting on both sides for the good of the Mother Coven.

The Elders needed to know about Olson's betrayal. I couldn't die and leave him to continue his two-faced reign at the Mother Coven's expense.

Olson's expression soured with pissed off determination as if he read my mind. His game of hide and seek was over, and he knew it.

A pitch in energy and a dip in his chin sent me running moments before he rushed me. I slid on the floor, grabbed the bench along the wall, and held on as tightly as I could as Olson snatched my leg. The world spun. This happened before in the Creation when Olson tried to apport me out and I grappled onto Kim so he couldn't leave her behind. I was too grounded for him to disappear and take me with him. I was banking on the bench being bolted down as it had been when I was kid. It was.

He growled, grabbed the bench, and tore the bolts from the cement floor.

When I opened my eyes, my scream echoed off of the walls but not the gym walls. These were drywall. Carpet was under my back instead of the cracked cement, and I was alone.

Clicking came from across the room. A woman in a pencil skirt entered and yipped, dropping the manila folder in her hands when she saw me on the ground.

I scrambled to my feet. She was surprised to see me, but how could I know if she was in on this?

"Who are—?" She put her hands on the back of her desk chair as if ready to shove it at me if I attacked.

A warble of light appeared beside me. A soul glow. Olson's was the only soul glow I would see before the person themselves. The area of his presence there before he apported through.

I sprung at a door behind me. It was locked.

Olson popped into the office, his hand on Donovan's shoulder. Donovan looked around, his dark eyes narrowed in confusion as he saw the woman in heels who screeched a second time.

I must have made a noise as I gained Donovan's attention, then he searched behind him as if expecting an explanation from Olson.

Shit. He didn't know Olson was behind this.

"Dono—"

Olson disappeared and reappeared in front of me with Donovan in tow to the sound of the woman continued screech and my interrupted "Fuck!" before everything went black.

———

Sleep held me tight. I didn't want to wake up. Needed another few hours. Too cold to be comfortable, I curled up and tried to pull my duvet over me as my limbs and eyelids were in league with each other, craving comfort and nothing else. The foreign scratch of thin material against me had me opening my eyes.

A white cotton blanket was in my hand, my fingers going through the loose knit as I held it up, wondering where it came from.

The floor beyond the blanket was cement. I sat upright, blood rushing to my head with such strength I cradled my skull as vertigo spun me in circles, making me clutch my roiling gut.

Nothing was right. Not Donovan's blankets. Not his floor.

I saw concrete windowless walls, a small desk bolted to the wall, and a clothing rack with a white robe hanging from it. A bathroom without a door and an uninviting shower was clean but clinical. Not hospital clinical, more like a prison. Everything was within view. The main door didn't have a sliding communication hole like I've seen in documentaries but left me with the same sense of captivity.

I knew before I tried the door that it was locked.

The last faces I saw were Olson's detached, evil mug and Donovan's, who couldn't be more confused if I told him we were headed for high tea.

I stood in the middle of the room and searched for Donovan along our connection. There. He was contemplating something, furious but trying to keep his cool and soothe me. Curious since we were locked in separate rooms. Olson kidnapped us, but Donovan didn't want me to worry? Not in a "don't worry, it'll be okay" sort of way, I noted. More of a "don't freak out, but this is bad" way. Which meant whatever was happening was far worse than he was letting on, and managing not to freak out was impossible. Sweat hit the back of my neck, the heat climbing and burning in the tips of my ears.

What I did know was that Olson didn't try to kill me. He wanted me captured alive. For himself? I doubted it. He was a henchman no matter what side he played for. So, which side was he playing for now? And how fucked were we?

26

———

DUPED

Kim

After fifteen minutes of Olson not returning with Sophie and Donovan, Vincent and Ranlyn started giving each other looks, clearly having a private telepathic conversation.

I approached them, looking to both as they looked to me and dared to smile. "You two suck at subterfuge. You want to share what you're freaking out about?"

They stared at each other again.

"Really? Come out with it already. If it's pillow talk, you two can keep it to yourself. But you might want to sit down before we all get a glimpse at the result."

They straightened, shaking their heads, and shifting their weight.

"No? Okay, then it's something else. Something important and most likely about Sophie and Donovan. Out with it."

Vincent checked his watch.

"I know." Ranlyn exhaled and glanced across the room.

I followed his line of sight seeing the leftover Coveners and the attic itself, but nothing—oh shit, that's where Olson had left from a created portal on the floor.

I stepped closer and lowered my voice. Not to whisper but to intimidate. "The Apporter should be back by now."

"Yes. Yes, he should be." Vincent righted his cuff over his luxury watch. An understated BVLGARI, I noticed. And not a knock-off, which meant it cost more than my car.

I pulled my attention away from Vincent's expensive taste in accessories and focused on why they weren't raising the alarm. "Can't you do your Apporter calling thing?"

"Already did."

"What did he say?"

Ranlyn's expression was tight. "Couldn't get through."

Vincent's scowl transformed his face. "He thwarted your attempts, and you fail to mention this until now?"

"There must be a reasonable explanation."

Vincent fixed his glasses and glared at Ranlyn. "Must there be? A clear reason has already presented itself, I would think."

I clapped my hands. "Okay, fellas, what's reasonable? What's presented itself? Spell it out for me."

They didn't answer me and kept staring at each other.

I scoffed and took out my phone, calling Sophie. Her phone was off. I dialled Donovan's. It rang and rang until I heard familiar metal music behind me.

"It's loud." Andy held out Donovan's phone, the ringtone blaring, the display reading "Annoying Redhead".

I thanked Andy and hung up. He ran back to his cot and resumed tug-of-war with Bosco and what I was pretty sure was one of his socks.

"Be straight up with me before I start screaming. They're gone, aren't they?" I searched for a sign from the two of them for the fortieth time. "The bald asshole took them."

"We don't—"

"Yes, he did." Vincent interrupted Ranlyn without apology.

"Of course, he did." Veata was standing next to us, leaning on her cane. "The summoning pathways have been broken, yes? Answers are answers whether you like them or not, Ranlyn. Slough off the ego and know when you've been duped."

"It doesn't make sense. All this time—"

Veata rolled her opaque eyes. "Yes, all this time. It makes perfect sense, and you know it."

No. What they implied was disastrous. "But he has access to the attic, to Donovan's...to everywhere."

Veata dipped her head in agreement, her thin lips pursed.

I raced towards the symbol on the floor which permitted the Apporter to bypass the estate's wards and return.

"Don't!" Ranlyn sprinted after me, his hand out to stop me.

I pulled away before he could grab me. "He has them and has access to here. We can't leave it open."

Olive approached. "What's going on here?"

I guided her closer to the symbol, pushing passed Ranlyn. "Olson kidnapped Sophie and Donovan. We need to remove the symbol now."

This got people's attention. A conversational lull hung over the attic, all attention on us.

Ranlyn straightened his shoulders. "We don't know for sure, Kim."

"Don't use your nice-guy tone with me because everyone's listening. If the Apporter isn't a mole and brings them back and can't get through, he can drop them off outside the wards and we'll redo the symbol. Better than him showing up here and taking someone else."

He couldn't argue with me then, especially since Olive agreed and went ahead and erased the symbol. It was her home.

At the thirty-minute mark with still no sign of them, Vincent was a rash of small movements, like his skin irritated him. He didn't like this waiting around anymore than anyone else, but I couldn't think of who else to contact. The pool of people Donovan knew was small, same with Sophie. Plus, they wouldn't be chillin' at a friend's place.

The people we needed to reach out to were not in my contact list or were already in the attic. They didn't skip out to take a break. They were in trouble, and I was done with Ranlyn's refusal to accept Olson's betrayal.

"Who would'a taken 'em?" Adam was drumming on the side of a shelf with his fingers like he was playing the actual drums. Nerves. "She's got herself into some shit but kidnapping? Really?"

I slapped his hands, stopping him from annoying me to death. "Wouldn't be the first kidnapping attempt. Not even the third."

He didn't have a response to that.

"What about Donovan's mother?" Priscilla was locked in thought, eyes narrowed.

"Or her people?" Lewis sat in Olive's desk chair, leaning back. "The woman went through great lengths so her flock wouldn't attack on the field. Maybe this is their loophole. Since they weren't in battle maybe the Allegiance spell didn't cover a pre-emptive strike."

"Not Rosemary herself." Ranlyn's nail grazed his lip as he crossed his arms and paced. "Whatever latent maternal instinct sparked for Donovan, it was enough to protect him. Though, yes, her people would stop at nothing to bypass the Allegiance spell. If you thought of it, so have they."

I huffed. "Since the Magic world knows our plans, it could be anyone. Evaristus or Loring's devotees, your brother,"—I motioned to Vincent—"or any other Sovereignty member. Donovan's psycho father, even Caine's Aunt Bernie." I looked towards where Andy was in his bubble of silence, playing with Bosco. "Bernie's down a husband, a daughter, and a grandson. She has nothing to lose. And the others have everything to lose and know Sophie and Donovan were among those trying to take it."

"Don't forget Hinapouri and Miklos." Veata was right. They had their own bone to pick with them, though they could have kidnapped or killed Sophie and Donovan when they got the information about the discus and didn't.

Reaching for any possibility, even Gualichu came to mind, yet lacked motive. The demon had no use for them, unlike the vigilante Eradicators who hated all Magics and tried to kidnap them before. Unless someone was using the demon. Or if the Eradicators fabricated another of their devices to screw with our powers.

I stopped Vincent when he paced by me for the thousandth time. "You're old as dirt. You have to know people on all sides. Someone who can reach someone in a Tainted fold. Kidnapping Sophie and Donovan isn't something they would be quiet about. All their little minions would be gossiping about the big catch, especially if any of them had a part in it."

He nodded, quiet in thought a moment. "I may know someone."

27

SHARP AWARENESS

Donovan

Step after step in circles got me nowhere. I was familiar with the box I was in. I'd been in it before, yet never thrown in here by Olson, the traitorous piece of shit.

How could the Elders not know? All this time. He knew everything to bring us down. Enough to bring me here. If he had been flying under the radar for countless years, then something big was in the works for him to break protocol now.

Shit. This was bad.

I was confused to go from the attic to back home until I realized Sophie's sigils were activated and sent me somewhere I deemed safe. That was always Aunt Lacey's for me and remained so when I took over the place. Dropping into the creamy-walled office with Olson was the opposite of safe and more confusing until I woke up here. Pretension and self-righteous entitlement was embedded in childhood memories of the then receptionist, Agnes, who stared over her bifocals at me after I was dragged into the office to wait for my father to later be tortured and publicly humiliated.

Until I refused to go to the office at all and insisted on skipping to the torture and seclusion. Talking never helped. Neither did screaming, so why bother?

Shoving me into one of his cells must have been my father's way of telling me he was in charge again, the head asshole who would always put me in my place wherever he saw fit for me to be. Again, stuck in this room where the ghost of my past paced along with me.

Escape was always possible. I managed it before. Though, back then, I was alone. Death or escape, dealer's choice, but I wasn't sticking around the compound for more torture and had no clue about the connection or how death meant killing Sophie, too. I would stay if it meant getting her to safety, but while I was here, neither of us were truly safe.

I tried to cool my shit. Sophie was worried, but I didn't need her panicking. The Elders had to have sent Olson to get us when we disappeared from the attic. They would know to look for us, though not where.

This was my fault. I dodged my father's insistence to make me heir or make me pay for refusing it too long, and now he was throwing a tantrum. If he did his homework, he would know torturing Sophie was the same as torturing me. If causing pain was all he was after, he would break us down into human-flavoured cubes, but then what? Killing me took me out of this life, but it didn't take Sophie from me, and he had to know this as well.

What was he planning?

Sophie couldn't be far. There were other cells like this one. With the Apporter whispering traitorous words into Tobias's ear, Father knew keeping us too far apart would only put us in a stupor. No way he would let us die without sharp awareness of him ending us.

The ghost of a cold blade's edge burned my chest until I pressed my knuckles into the spot. How I survived all those times was a fucking miracle or a curse. I never wanted them to bring me back. I couldn't stand the thought of Sophie going through the same thing I did. She may survive, but I wasn't strong enough to fix what the healers couldn't.

Of all things I could be responsible for, anything that happened to her within my father's walls was all my fault.

With the cell's warding system dowsing my power, magic was useless, and Sophie had no clue. The flexing stir within me told me she was struggling. Maybe to use her magic, maybe to understand where we were. At least I could feel her. No matter how strong the wards, they couldn't counteract our connection.

Standing stock-still in bare feet on the cement floor, I focused on the thread within me tethered to Sophie and attempted to ease her. Strength she had in abundance, but never a captive in the way I've experienced, her endurance for it was questionable. I hoped what I was doing, plus the emotional numbing I would fight through when it came time to find some happy place while Tobias had his fun, would be enough to keep her sane.

A tug in response made me smile as her warmth reached back.

I retracted from Sophie when the door lock sprung and began to open before the next emotion hit, not wanting to freak her out. Before Tobias stepped into the doorway, I steeled myself, ready for a new version of a decade's old conversation.

———

Sign-up and stay current on book cover reveals, sales, giveaways, and more with S.J.'s newsletter! http://www,sjcairns.com/newsletter-sign-up/

———

Read on for a teaser of the never before released DEVOTED, SOUL SEER CHRONICLES, BOOK 6 coming July 2023.

DEVOTED TEASER

Devoted, Soul Seer Chronicles, Book 6

Some prisons are physical, others psychological. What if you're trapped in both?

Locked in a cement box, Donovan's sadistic father held the key, but Donovan inflicted far worse damage. I knew better than to trust him but fought my instincts, riding on the fantasy of our connection and how deeply our Soul Magic ran. Why was loyalty too much to expect? I didn't deserve this and can't fathom how to live with it.

All factions had grand plans, derailing my own as I rot in this cell. Some vowed to lock the Creation up tight forever with Caine and the survivors inside, others wanted to blast it wide open to save all they could, and a diabolical few planned to capitalize on the chaos releasing my evil ancestor would inflict on Magics and the Blind. No matter the outcome, a civil war is imminent.

After everything I went through in the Sorrel Compound cells, Fate had more in store, and conspired to take away all my sense of control. Could I get it back? Was I strong enough?

Will my life ever be mine again?

ABOUT THE AUTHOR

S.J. Cairns creates paranormal fantasy romance from her hometown in Southern Ontario, Canada. When S.J is not plugging away at her laptop on her comfy couch, you can find her chasing around her three-year-old daughter alongside her husband of over twenty years or working in true chaos at the local women and family's homeless shelters and anti-human trafficking safe house.

Website: www.sjcairns.com
Facebook: www.facebook.com/SJCairnsauthor
Twitter: www.twitter.com/SamiJoCairns
Email: samijocairns@gmail.com

www.ingramcontent.com/pod-product-compliance
Lightning Source LLC
Chambersburg PA
CBHW051454030726

47592CB00006B/1921